Beethoven's TENTH

a novel

RICHARD KLUGER

Rare Bird
LOS ANGELES

This is a Genuine Vireo Book

A Vireo Book | Rare Bird Books
453 South Spring Street, Suite 302
Los Angeles, CA 90013
rarebirdbooks.com

Beethoven's Tenth

Set in Dante
Design by Steve Larsson

HARDCOVER ISBN: 9781945572982
PAPERBACK ISBN: 9781947856776

Printed in the United States

10 9 8 7 6 5 4 3 2 1

Publisher's Cataloging-in-Publication data
Names: Kluger, Richard, author.
Title: Beethoven's Tenth a Novel / Richard Kluger.
Description: A Genuine Vireo Book | New York, NY;
Los Angeles, CA: Rare Bird Books, 2018.
Identifiers: ISBN 9781945572982
Subjects: LCSH Beethoven, Ludwig van, 1770–1827—Fiction. | Zurich
(Switzerland)—Fiction. | Composers—Switzerland—Zurich—Fiction. | Zurich
(Switzerland)—History—Fiction. | Historical fiction. | Mystery and detective
stories. | BISAC FICTION / Historical | FICTION / Mystery
Classification: LCC PS3561.L78 B44 2018 | DDC 813.54—dc23

For my witty, irrepressible nephew Bruce,
gifted wordsmith and faithful supporter.

"Heard melodies are sweet, but those unheard
Are sweeter; therefore, ye soft pipes, play on…"
—*John Keats, "Ode on a Grecian Urn"*

"He left thirty-two piano sonatas and nine symphonies,
yet the more intimately they are known, the less can one even
hazard a guess as to what the thirty-third sonata or the tenth
symphony would be like. They would be Beethoven, and that is but
the statement of a formal enigma. How many movements they would
have…whether the theme would be slight and the handling sublime,
whether there would be an orgy of rhythm or a feast of melody or
both, whether they would follow an old form or invent a new one:
all these are matters of which nothing intelligible can be said…"
—*George Dyson, The New Music*

"…His emotions at their highest flight were almost godlike;
he gave music a sort of Alpine grandeur."
—*H. L. Mencken on Beethoven*

Overture

Vienna, 22 April 1814

Dearest father, dearest mother,

There is such excitement here as I have not felt before, you see it everywhere on the people's faces & hear it in their voices, all due to the news that has just reached the capital that Paris has fallen to the allied armies & Bonaparte is at last a captive. The very skies exult! Every bar of music in the air sounds a glorious anthem. And to crown my exhilaration, whom do you think I should encounter last night when a few friends and I went to celebrate at the Zum Schwan, our favorite haunt but much too dear for threadbare music students like us to frequent except on rare occasions? None other than the maestro himself! And at the very next table!

I had arrived at the tavern early & took a table in the back to sip a beer & await my friends when I spied him, in his great coat and wide-brim felt hat, taking choppy little steps & claiming the large table next to mine. He threw off his hat and coat, revealing a none too tidy blouse with a hole at the right elbow. Shaking off the server & saying he would wait for the arrival of his companion, the maestro spread open his copy of the *Wiener Zeitung* to catch up on the momentous news— which gave me a fine chance to study him without seeming rude.

Sad to say, but the supreme genius of the music world does not cut a striking figure. He is short, wide, bow-legged, and almost homely by the usual standards of male beauty. His face is dark and pocked, the eyes deep-set fiery coals, the nose broad & flat as an African's, the front teeth jutting so as to cause his lips to thrust. Yet his brow is magnificent, very full and round, a titan's head made larger still by the superb hair, so wonderfully abundant & admirably unruly, like some male Medusa's, and when he runs his hand through it, the coarse & bristly locks go comically in all directions. His hairiness extends even to the backs of his hands, & his fingers, I saw, are wide, almost splayed at the tips—not a shape at all suitable for sublime mastery of the piano, such as he once commanded.

I was struck most of all by his uncongenial, indeed nearly repellent expression. Not quite a scowl, but very little hint of merriment within. And no wonder, considering the pathetic spectacle his hardness of hearing has reduced him to of late. My friend Berthold attended a concert at the Augarten a short time ago at which the maestro was to conduct his own compositions. Uncertain of the orchestra's sound & tempo, he tried to compensate by sheer physicality, sinking on his knees during the soft passages & almost disappearing behind the conductor's platform like a dwarf, then leaping up like a giant by way of signaling the forte passages, his hands & arms beating with a frenzy. This gymnastic exhibition did not entirely distract the musicians at first, but soon the maestro began to run ahead of the orchestra & reverse his pattern, which totally unhinged the musicians & left the kapellmeister no choice but to relieve the maestro of his wand & force him from the stage. The scene was equally sorrowful when I myself attended a concert at which his keyboard play lacked all clarity & precision. They say he will perform no longer.

How gravely his deepening deafness is troubling the maestro I learned with the arrival shortly of his dinner partner, a man perhaps a dozen years his senior & rather better attired. His friend sat close by him and spoke into his left ear. They were not exactly shouting at each other, but I could overhear their every word. His companion asked if he had read all the war news, & the maestro said he guessed the emperor would sleep better that night, adding, "not that I care much—"

"So they've treed your hero—glory be," said his friend.

"No hero of mine since the day he crowned himself," said the maestro. "Anyway, I'm off politics for good."

"Then why are they doing your 'Battle' Symphony five times next week, Ludwig?"

"It's not politics, Nikolaus," said the maestro, "it's money. That's what they want to hear when their armies win—and I didn't arrange it." As a pleasantry, Nikolaus asked whether the watch he had sent him as a gift was keeping good time, & the maestro replied, "How should I know? I can tell tempo, but the time of day eludes me." Nikolaus smiled and then asked the outcome of the maestro's appointment with a certain physician. "Ah, Dr. Weissenbach, you mean." The maestro shook his head. "Do I dare trust a surgeon from Salzburg?"

Nikolaus looked reproachful. "I know, maestro—you're sure they're all quacks with their charlatan cures of almond oil and herbs and ear drops and cold baths—"

The maestro shrugged. "At least this Dr. Weissenbach isn't prescribing miracle pills. He says the deafness has nothing to do with my belly and bowel problems—and all those halfwits who told me so have no understanding of anatomy." His affliction, the Salzburg doctor told him, is likely the result of nerve damage from an infection—the ringing & buzzing that he hears prove it. Nikolaus wondered what sort of infection could be the cause, and the maestro cast his fierce gaze heavenward. He had once contracted a bad case of typhus, & Weissenbach suspects that's what planted the evil seed that has eaten away at his auditory nerve for years now. His friend asked if the Salzburg healer held out even faint hope that the process could be reversed.

"He fears it's degenerative and unstoppable. In a few years I'll hear no music whatsoever—or anything else."

Nikolaus grasped his friend on the upper arm. "Weissenbach is not the last word, you know. There are other healers—and Salzburg, as you say, is not the medical capital of the world."

"Quite so. Weissenbach himself said as much. He wrote out the names of some healers of the deaf he knows of, if I'm willing to travel. I told him of my possible trip to England, and he said there was someone of high repute in Edinburgh—another in Amsterdam and a third in Zurich."

That mention of dear old Züri nearly made me jump. How I wished to turn openly to them and say, "Zurich is my home city—and the maestro's music is greatly beloved there. I am here to study the violin and would be immensely honored to be of help, maestro, to cure your terrible malady. Please tell me the name of the Zurich physician you were given, and I shall write my parents at once to inquire discreetly in your behalf. Pray, let me!" But of course I dared not be so forward.

Soon my own friends came, gay revelers like the rest of Vienna just now, and I could eavesdrop no longer. When I thought again to look over at the next table, it was empty. Only then did I recount to the fellows with me what I had overheard, & Berthold said he thought the maestro's woes could be solved if he would just get his hair cut instead of letting it overgrow his ears. I think it was a cruel joke. It is a great misfortune for anyone to become deaf, but how should a superb musician endure it without giving way to despair?

I hope the both of you are well and cherishing the spring. How I shall miss the sight of the chestnut trees in bloom at the lakeside and along our lovely Limmat. There is nothing half so delightful in this beautiful city, not even the pastries that the locals adore. Please give dear Katherine a hug for me.

Your loving & devoted son, Kurt

{1}

T he blinking light on Mitchell Emery's office phone signaled that he had a voice-mail message—two of them, as it turned out. The first was from his wife Clara.

"Oh, hello, mister—sorry I missed you." The tone was pleasingly low with a barely perceptible edge of wryness. "Forgot to mention before you left that I'm on for lunch with Lolly today—my treat, no less. She's had me out three times, so I owe her—and she *is* your lord and master's wife, so I'll have to put on my best imitation of good behavior." Clara's good breeding and continental education indelibly shaped her speech, even the most casual remark. "Anyway, I won't have room left for our usual gourmet dinner, so if you don't mind, I'll pick up some cold cuts, and we can have a sandwich or something else light. Feel free to pig out at lunch, though I know you're heroically abstemious on workdays. Anyway, hope all's well at your shop and—um—still love you like crazy, big guy. Bye."

Mitch smiled inside. Her calling him "big guy" had become a long-standing gag between them because in her flats she was a half inch taller than he was—and she was careful not to wear heels except when they had a dress-up occasion. Not that he minded her height; on the contrary. He had thought her statuesque from the first moment he saw her, and it only added to her appeal. Of course, if he had been on the shrimpy side himself instead of six feet even, it might have been a different story. Physically and emotionally, they were well matched—two highly independent people who had elected to blend their contrasting backgrounds and temperaments.

13

Mitch's other voice-mail message was more urgent. "Something a bit out of the ordinary has come up," said his caller. "Drop by whenever the mood suits you. Sooner would be better."

The voice was reedy, its cadence deliberate yet fluid, with every syllable equally uninflected, and the speaker's message typically terse and cryptic. Its imperative tone was nonetheless unmistakable. Since he owned the place, Harry never bothered to identify himself when phoning subordinates. In fairness, though, his superior air seemed neither put on nor a character flaw; to Mitch it was simply natural that anyone named Harrison Ellsworth Cubbage III would sound, act, and be like that, considering that he owned a Harvard PhD in fine arts and half of Cubbage & Wakeham, the New York- and London-based firm that had been in the connoisseurship business for six generations.

C&W, as the auction gallery was known in art and big-money circles, owed much of its sterling hallmark to the expertise of its Department of Authentication and Appraisal. This crack unit, now under Mitch's supervision, included nine full-time curators: three in the paintings and sculpture office and one each in manuscripts and documents, jewelry, ceramics and other collectibles, relics and artifacts, arms and armaments, and textiles. Every curator, moreover, was authorized, whenever it was deemed necessary, to draw upon a far-flung network of specialists in the academic, museum, and commercial worlds, so that no bidder at a C&W auction ever had to fear purchasing something less than advertised. Only the genuine article reached the house's auction block. True, there had been rare exceptions over C&W's 137 years in business, but in each case the full purchase price was repaid promptly along with interest, abject apologies, and the proprietors' redfaced discomfort. The erring authenticator was dismissed summarily; there could be no margin for mistakes in such a high-stakes game.

"Sorry, just heard your summons," Mitch said, appearing in the open doorway of the co-owner's office at the other end of the second-floor hall. "Something interesting come up?"

"Everything that comes up here is interesting," Harry said in mild rebuke. "I thought you knew that by now, Mitchell." From the first, his boss had insisted on calling him Mitchell, saying he thought nicknames were undignified—except his own. Harry was big on dignity.

Mitch gave a slight nod. "I misspoke—sir."

"I wanted to give you a heads-up on the meeting you're booked to join us for this afternoon at three," Harry said. "Chap from the wilds of New Jersey is coming in with his lawyer—Gordy has spoken with him and recommends that we give them a hearing. They're bringing us a manuscript of something called the *William Tell* Symphony—well, it's in German, as I understand it—the title page, that is."

Mitch shrugged. "Is the title supposed to mean something special to me?"

"Probably not. But according to the lawyer, his client found the manuscript at the bottom of an attic trunk while cleaning out his late grandfather's house in Zurich a few weeks ago."

"I see. Well, yes—that would follow—William Tell—Switzerland. Probably a patriotic pastiche, and pretty dreadful."

"I wouldn't be surprised," said Harry, twiddling an unsharpened pencil of the kind he occasionally chewed on as a pacifier, "but possibly it's a bit more than that. Would you care to hazard a guess at the name of the composer on the title page?"

"Swiss composers are not really my thing, to be honest. In fact, I don't think I can name a single one."

"Me neither, to be equally honest. But the listed composer definitely wasn't Swiss." Harry savored being in charge of any exchange, especially with an underling.

"All right," said Mitch. "I'll play your silly game. How about Duke Ellington?"

Harry snorted. "You might have tried Rossini, since he did the—"

"Rossini didn't write symphonies, so far as I know—only operas."

"The Jersey lawyer told Gordy that *this* symphony has singing parts."

"That," said Mitch, "would probably qualify it as an opera."

"Nevertheless, the composer apparently called it a symphony—and he should know."

"And why is that?"

"Because," said Harry, "the name on the title page is Ludwig fucking van Beethoven."

Harry was allowed to say "fucking" whenever he chose as a kind of *droit de seigneur*, even if everyone understood it wasn't entirely dignified for him to do so.

A small, quick intake of breath betrayed Mitch's momentary loss of nonchalance. "Well, him I've heard of."

"Good man."

"Hold on. Didn't Sotheby's auction another Beethoven manuscript a little while ago—it supposedly just popped up in an old filing cabinet at a Philadelphia seminary or someplace? The story got a lot of print and airtime, as I remember."

"Not to mention a couple of million bucks for the finder," Harry confirmed. "And that wasn't even a new composition—I checked it out online right after the call came in from New Jersey yesterday. The manuscript was Beethoven's attempt to adapt his *Grosse Fuge* for the piano—which is pretty small potatoes compared to a purported whole, spanking-new symphony by the all-time world champion of that musical form."

Mitch wondered if Harry was pulling his leg as a kind of playful test of his gullibility. "What if that recent episode inspired a copycat or two to start digging around the old homestead for an inexplicably abandoned Beethoven manuscript? Or maybe this New Jersey gentleman will also be bringing us—for good measure— Saul of Tarsus's left sandal, found by a passerby after a sandstorm near the northern end of the Sea of Galilee—"

"Possibly." Harry flipped his chewing pencil onto his desktop. "But that would interest me a lot less than a lost Beethoven symphony. Sandals are a dime a dozen."

Mitch struggled to regain his cool, though the enormity of the Beethoven fish story had plainly caught him off guard. "Is there any reason whatever to suppose that this character isn't totally off-the-wall and the little goody he's favoring us with isn't a complete crock?"

"None that I've heard about so far. He's almost surely a loon—or an arrant charlatan."

Mitch was surer now that Harry was toying with him, so he played along. "But it would be an immense sensation if the thing miraculously proved to be authentic—and earn us a very handsome commission and worldwide attention."

"Quite true, which is why we always keep our door—and minds—wide open."

"But why," Mitch asked, "would Beethoven ever have written a symphony to honor William Tell, of all people? Attila the Hun, maybe—but a Swiss folk hero? Seems preposterous."

"Beats me," Harry said in his best blasé manner. "If we don't toss this Jersey fellow out on his ear this afternoon, it occurs to me that you may want to run this whole subject past your better half. Isn't Clara's Columbia dissertation more or less concerned with Beethoven and the German Romantics?"

"Mostly less. It deals primarily with Franz Peter Schubert."

"Well, close enough," said Harry. "All those German biggies must have known one another and their work. Weren't Schubert and Beethoven contemporaries?"

"They were a generation apart, I believe—but both lived in Vienna. I think Clara told me that Schubert was one of Beethoven's pallbearers." The subject suddenly ignited another weird recollection in Mitch's head. "Say, here's a funny thing I just remembered—Clara also told me that the manuscript of Schubert's great symphony, his Ninth, was found among a bunch of his overlooked papers some years after his death."

"Mmmm," said Harry. "So you see, strange things happen and always have. You're right, of course, Mitchell, to be supremely skeptical about miraculous discoveries of this sort—and especially of this magnitude—it's what we pay you for, as I recall. But prejudging any claim, however farfetched, isn't really good for our business. Let's give our New Jersey visitor his day in court."

His boss's tone left Mitch in no doubt he was about to face his sternest test at C&W.

NOTWITHSTANDING CLARA'S THOUGHTFUL SUGGESTION that he put on the feed bag for lunch, as she was doing with Harry's wife, Mitch grabbed a bowl of sludgy pea soup and a cup of fresh fruit salad at the luncheonette around the corner on Madison and then headed for a stroll in the park to the sailboat pond and back.

Beethoven! His brain was clanging with all that titanic sound. All that *Sturm und Drang*. All that big hair. Just to conceive of a brand-new masterwork by *numero uno*, suddenly materializing from beyond the grave, was dizzying, and, to be sure, a huge turn-on for anyone sharing Mitch's occupation. Harry was no doubt right that Clara would be fascinated by the very idea, however absurd on its face, and more than likely laugh herself silly that grown men at Cubbage & Wakeham would entertain such an idea even for a moment. Still, Harry had made his point about their need to suspend disbelief when confronted by even the most implausible claim about any historical document or art object—it was part of the auction house's very reason to exist.

On the other side of the same coin, however, was Harry's impassioned caveat, delivered when the two of them had first connected, that unless his firm's authentication procedures were utterly trustworthy, the whole business might as well shut down. His rigid standards of legitimacy, like his undisguised elitism, were daunting to most newcomers in his employ.

Those who had been at C&W a lot longer than Mitchell Emery, only in his second year there, confided to him that Harry had let his hauteur over-ripen a shade or two after Sotheby's and Christie's came tumbling down from Olympus as a result of price-fixing scandals. This startling reversal of fortune, deftly seized upon by Harry and Sedgwick Wakeham, his partner in London, had allowed their smaller but more discriminating enterprise to elude the long shadows cast by the former twin giants of the high-end auction trade and take command of its center stage. So respectable was Cubbage & Wakeham's style of doing business, so artfully crafted its glossy catalogues, so unimpeachable its imprimatur on the rare and exquisite items offered at its monthly auction in the chaste auditorium of the Frick Museum on Fifth Avenue, that attendance often had to be limited to bidders with the highest credentials and deepest pockets. The pride Harry took in C&W's fine-tooth vetting regimen was understandable, given his family's pedigree and economic prowess dating back to colonial New England and, a bit later, to Ezekial Cubbage, who had founded the mercantile house of V. C. Craig & Sons in Boston in 1817. It was all the more ironic that Ezekial's great-great-great-great-great-nephew Harry should have invited Mitch to join its successor firm, Cubbage & Wakeham, despite the fact that Mitch had quite publicly kicked mud on its escutcheon a few years earlier.

Mitch, as an art history major at Princeton, had briefly flirted with the notion of a career that might one day place him in charge of a world-class museum. Attaining a post of such lofty cultural eminence would no doubt have been a notable achievement for a boy from Red Wing, Minnesota, not exactly the intellectual hub of the American heartland, albeit a pleasant and wholesome place to have grown up. On further reflection, though, the actual administration of a big art museum seemed likely to entail far more tedious and irksome time-serving, not to mention avid bootlicking, than he could stomach. And, after four years at an elite college insulated from life's rough and tumble, Mitch opted for two years in the Peace Corps and a chance to tend the needy in non-elite Tanzania. Sobered by witnessing the natives' desperate struggle for survival, he came home and elected to try his hand at journalism—that way, he might at least stay in touch with reality and perhaps cast light on some dark places—and managed to get hired as an investigative reporter for the *Washington Post*, covering consumer affairs and the culture beat.

It was while thus employed that he first came into contact with C&W. One rainy Saturday, while taking in an exhibition of recent purchases by the Corcoran Gallery, Mitch confronted a canvas attributed to the seventeenth-century Dutch landscapist Jacob van Ruisdael. In the course of preparing his Princeton senior thesis, titled "Painterly Skies in the Works of Tiepolo, van Ruisdael, and Constable," he had devoted long hours at a dozen museums to contemplating every billowy outcropping and fleecy contrail of cloud in the renderings of the three marvelous artists. "Brilliantly observed," wrote his faculty thesis adviser, who gave Mitch a 1+ and added puckishly, "Have you considered a career in meteorology?" Suddenly, at the Corcoran that Saturday, as the clouds outside opened and were deluging the nation's capital, it all came back to him. Something about the museum's newly hung van Ruisdael, recently hailed by the *Post*'s art critic as a superb example of its genre, struck the attentive young journalist as—well—*off*. The glow of the sky, he sensed, had a bit too much pop to it, even for a freshly restored work, yet the execution of the clouds was oddly muddy in spots. Perhaps this was the misattributed work of van Ruisdael's well-regarded uncle, Salomon, or of some apprentice in his studio. Or perhaps—the delicious possibility tantalized the byline-hungry reporter—it was a forgery.

Making a few casual inquiries with the *Post*'s clout behind them, Mitch learned that the painting had been anonymously donated to the Corcoran by a novice collector, who, through a dummy bidder, had paid a bundle for the work at a Cubbage & Wakeham auction some months earlier. Further questioning over the phone of C&W's media relations officer yielded reassurances that the authenticity of the painting had been certified by three ranking art historians, among them the leading Netherlandish authority on van Ruisdael. Alas, he had died recently. "In that case," Mitch prodded, "I'd appreciate seeing the paper work on the provenance of the painting as far back as it goes."

"We don't normally allow outsiders to examine any of our internal documents," the auction house publicist told him, "unless they are considering the purchase of an item being offered."

"If your management has nothing to hide," Mitch replied, "I think its—and the viewing public's—interests would best be served by transparency on your end."

"Well, it would be quite irregular, but I'll pass along your request."

"Please do—I trust I'll hear from you Monday."

"It may take some time, I'm afraid—"

"Not if you tell your superiors that a delay or stonewalling might prove embarrassing."

His persistence, along with the *Post*'s high standing for its art and cultural coverage, earned Mitch an invitation to C&W headquarters, housed in three joined brownstones just down the block from the Metropolitan Museum of Art, and a face-to-face meeting with a detectably miffed Harry Cubbage. "No one," he grandly informed Mitch, "has questioned our integrity for a very long time. Is there some special reason, Mr. Emery, beyond your trade's usual pandering to the yahoos, that brings you here?"

"I'm not questioning your integrity," Mitch answered calmly. "I'm just curious."

"About the provenance of a masterly painting we've vetted backward and forward and inside out, as we do routinely?"

"That's right—if it's not too much trouble."

"No trouble at all," Harry said caustically and thereupon launched into a long recital of forgeries or otherwise fraudulent articles that C&W's staff of vigilant investigators had uncovered in the course of his venerable firm's history and that, accordingly, were not offered for sale. These pretenders ranged from a fragment of papyrus said to have come from the earliest known version of the book of Exodus, a beaten gold Minoan drinking cup reportedly found in the royal apartment in the palace at Knossos, and a rough draft allegedly in Cicero's handwriting of his eloquent harangue against the arch conspirator Cataline, to three impeccably articulated interiors attributed to Vermeer, twelve claimed (and suitably treacly) Renoirs, a memorandum setting forth the peace terms reached at Appomattox Courthouse by Generals Grant and Lee, and a detailed Picassoesque sketch for a huge mural in memory of the Holocaust that Pablo was supposedly planning to render in the manner of his *Guernica*.

"What," Mitch asked at the end, feigning disappointment, "no *pietà* by Andy Warhol?"

Harry gave him a sustained squint through his wire-framed glasses, decided he liked his cheeky visitor, and burst into laughter. In short order, Mitch was allowed to explore who had owned the van Ruisdael in question and when. It was not a line of inquiry that C&W's experts had pursued half so vigorously as their X-ray study of the canvas, chemical analysis of its paint, and intensive appraisal of the composition. Mitch soon learned that the trail of ownership was, to understate the matter, faint. According to the C&W file, the painting had been purchased by a merchant in seventeenth-century Amsterdam and sent by sea to hang in his villa outside Jakarta in the Dutch East Indies. Centuries of equatorial climate must have taken their toll on the work, and in 1937, it was purportedly sent for restoration to an art dealer in Hong Kong, long out of business, who ran a shop in the back renowned for its repair skills, faithful copying, and—as Mitch discovered by a series of phone calls—many forgeries. There was simply no way to tell from the subsequent documentation whether the van Ruisdael hanging in the Corcoran Gallery was an original heavily touched up, a copy, or an imposter altogether.

While not definitive, Mitch's revelations in an exclusive three-column exposé in the *Post* forced the Corcoran to relabel the painting as "Attributed to Jacob van Ruisdael" and stirred its donor to threaten suit against C&W, whose client—the one who had put the work up for auction—naturally professed complete ignorance of any intrigue. In the end, it was C&W that took it on the chin by having to repay the buyer his purchase price of $2,365,000. Mitch's article portrayed the auction house management as mortified by the discovery but, out of kindness, included near the end of the piece a sampling of other bogus items C&W had detected and duly squelched. Harry was impressed but not grateful. The heads of five of his staffers rolled as a result.

By the time Harry invited him to lunch in the Oak Room at the Plaza in New York, where Mitch and Clara had lately moved, seven years had passed, Mitch had embarked on a legal career, and whatever hard feelings Harry had nursed against him appeared to have turned to pudding. He oozed cordiality while avoiding all reference to the unfortunate van Ruisdael episode. It was evident from his questions, moreover, that Harry knew a lot about Mitch's resumé, starting with his splendid record at Yale Law School, where he migrated on leaving the *Post* and served as Notes Editor of the *Law Journal*.

"In my ignorance, I assumed Notes Editor was a lowly staff position," said Harry, "but my sources tell me that it's the second-ranking job on the masthead—and that you graduated close to the top of your law class."

"Somewhere up there."

"May I ask," his host continued, "why you chose not to accept the clerkship that was offered to you at the US Court of Appeals—on the what—Second Circuit? Isn't that quite a plum? I'm told that anyone with your glittering academic record, a federal clerkship at the appellate level, a suitably ingratiating manner, and a modest degree of competence could have landed a lucrative position at any Wall Street law firm. Why opt instead for a job as assistant prosecutor for Montgomery County, Maryland? Seems like grunt work for anyone with your splendid promise."

Why, Mitch asked himself, did Harry Cubbage care what the answer was? Something up his sleeve in the way of payback for what Mitch had cost him? A little late for that. Well, there seemed no harm in the question or being cordial in response.

"Corporate law didn't much interest me, frankly—or not enough, anyway, to take the big money and slave for fat cats."

"Aren't business people entitled to top-flight legal representation?"

He could tell Harry was baiting him, but it hardly mattered.

"There's a lot of talent out there for them to hire—it's just not my idea of a calling. I'd rather work with ordinary people facing real issues—like survival—

with a little dignity, maybe." He paused half a beat, then quickly added, "Not that I'm against money—or people whose mission in life is to stockpile it. But it's not my mission, and they certainly don't need my help."

"You're for the downtrodden."

Mitch thought he detected a sneer in the remark. "Not exclusively—and I'm not a closet Marxist, if that's your next question—I think those guys are fanatics without any understanding of human motivation. I just think working people deserve a fair shake out of life."

"I gather that your stint in the Peace Corps left an indelible impression on you?"

"It certainly opened my eyes after growing up in a peaceful Minnesota town on the Mississippi and attending Princeton."

"And left you a deeply caring person, from the sound of it."

Mitch shrugged. "Excuse me, Mr. Cubbage, but is there a point to any of this?"

Harry raised a hand defensively. "We're getting to it." He took a swallow of his sauvignon blanc. "What happened when you joined the county prosecutor's office?"

"I learned a lot—and helped dispose of a bunch of rotten apples—but also saw how the justice system is screwed up and run by too many burnout cases who cling to their jobs way too long. Fortunately, my boss wasn't one of them, and after almost three years at the repetitive grind in his office, he encouraged me to move on to something more challenging." His sterling record and a Sunday round of sociable golf—Mitch was at best a low-intensity duffer—at Burning Tree with the head of the Department of Justice's criminal division got him recruited on the spot for the federal anti-racketeering unit. "It was demanding work, and I was thriving on it."

"But?"

Near the end of his second year at the DOJ, Mitch said, a new federal administration took power, and its overseers in his department soon proved clueless, aimless, and nastily politicized. "I guess I wasn't terribly discreet about registering my objections when they kept telling me to hold my horses, and before long they pointed me to the door."

"And left you at loose ends—which I believe you are at the moment?"

"Well, it seemed like the right time to catch my breath and regroup. My wife and I decided to travel awhile—thanks to her parents' generosity—so we stayed with them in London—they have a townhouse in Chelsea—before taking a cycling trip up to Scotland and then through France and the Low Countries. I got to see her native Holland."

"And now you've moved to our fair city and taken a prewar apartment on Riverside Drive while you explore your options," Harry said, "and your wife is pursuing her doctorate in musicology at Columbia."

"Sounds as if your spies have been working overtime. What's this all about?"

Harry nodded. "We're almost there. Just one last thing—tell me about your people."

"My *people*? What do you mean, my family tree?"

"Well, a few branches of it, anyway. For example, do you come from a long line of horse thieves? If not, then from whom?"

"Why does that matter? This is America—we specialize in social mobility."

"Humor me a minute or two longer—I like to know something about the people we bring into our organization."

What an insufferably snotty bastard, Mitch thought. "I didn't know I was an applicant."

"We don't have applicants—people who ask don't get hired. We do the asking."

"So I see. What in the world makes you think I'd be interested in working for an auction house, of all things? I mean I'm sure it's a respectable business and so forth—"

"You didn't think so last time we met," Harry reminded him. "Tell me about your dad."

The man was incorrigible. Almost laughably so—yet his attention, perhaps because it was entirely unsolicited, was flattering.

"He's a nice man," Mitch said. "He doesn't say much, but what he says is worth hearing. He's been the deputy administrator at our county hospital for as long as I can remember, but he never got the top job. I think he lost out because he didn't have a college degree—only a business school diploma—but he took evening courses in health services and worked hard to get ahead, as far as he got. He's taking early retirement next year."

"And your mom?"

"She's nice, too—more outgoing than Pop. She was an English and Latin teacher at our local high school for a long time—and made sure I didn't goof off in my studies. Otherwise, I'd never have earned a scholarship to Princeton. She's also an excellent landscape painter—for a hobby. She used to take me and my sister April to the museum in Minneapolis all the time—it was only thirty miles away—and explain what made a great painting and what didn't. I guess that's why I majored in art history at college. But I don't have her artistic talent— I'm just an appreciator."

Harry nodded a few times and lifted his wine glass to Mitch in tribute for having endured his little inquisition.

"Okay," said Mitch as their poached salmon plates arrived, "my turn now. Why specifically have I had my privacy rummaged through by your thugs?"

"Gordon Roth is not a thug," Harry replied evenly. "As our house counsel, he occasionally makes tactful inquiries into the background and character of people we're interested in—usually would-be clients but sometimes potential employees. I've come to the conclusion that you're someone who could be of considerable value to our firm, and that you, in turn, would welcome the unique sort of challenge that Sedge Wakeham and I have in mind for you in the international sphere of art and cultural artifacts. There'd be a certain amount of travel involved, mostly to places you'd enjoy being in. You would not find the work monotonous, I think I can assure you of that."

Harry Cubbage's self-sureness knew no bounds.

"Why all your kind solicitude," Mitch wondered, "considering that I once did my best to spatter your twenty-four-karat reputation?"

"You did us quite a favor, actually—we were growing lax. Besides, spattered gold cleans up quite nicely, in case you've never noticed." Harry's archness had reached its apex. "We've decided to create an entirely new position of chief investigator, coordinating the authentication procedures in all our departments. The operation has been too hit-or-miss until now, very ad hoc. It needs to be systematized under the direction of an enlightened but dogged inquisitor. You would fit the bill, in my judgment—though I could be wrong, of course."

It was not what Mitch had been expecting. "You want me to—do what exactly—play detective for your firm?"

There was a detectable absence of delight at the prospect in Mitch's tone. "In a manner of speaking," Harry answered. "Our merchandise happens to be among the costliest and most fascinating on earth—and, accordingly, it needs to be validated beyond a shadow of a doubt."

"Why not just hire a presentable former FBI guy? They're trained investigators—"

"I've considered it—even brought in a few of them for a chat. The problem is they're neither fine-arts-oriented nor particularly couth—they all seem to wear mid-calf socks, which I find unacceptable on a grown man."

Mitch frowned. "My socks aside, how do I qualify? Any fool can ask lots of questions—"

"*Au contraire,* pal," Harry countered. "To ask the *right* questions, ideally one needs a broad frame of reference, and without puffing up your hat size—if you had a hat—"

"I don't, actually—just a Minnesota Twins baseball cap."

"My point is that you rate high in well-roundedness. You've been educated at superior schools. You have a worldview enriched by a firsthand ordeal in a place where no one in his right mind would ever go. You write at or above professional standards. You know the law and more than a little about criminality. You seem to have a keen appreciation of art and culture. You have an attractive wife with European connections. And, if I'm not mistaken, you savor adventure, which you've enjoyed too rarely in your interesting but checkered career. You *have* jumped about a bit, employment-wise, Mitchell—which is my sole reservation about bringing you in to work closely with me. I'm not much enamored with flighty sorts."

"I see," Mitch said with a betraying smile. He decided about then that there was something elusively likable about Harry Cubbage. "Is there anything else?"

"We pay decently—plus travel and all other expenses, of course, and generous fringes. If things work out, you could make quite a nice living—and enjoy your work. And there's room for advancement, though it's a relatively small shop."

Mitch had the sensation that he'd been hooked and was being reeled in by a masterful angler.

"And what is it exactly that I'd be doing?"

It took Harry only a few moments to sketch C&W's painstaking authentication process, starting with their forensics people, who tested the physical properties of any article offered for auction to see if it conformed with its alleged age, materials, provenance, and the like, and ending with still more intensive scrutiny to determine not only whether the object in question was indisputably authentic but just how high its quality and/or historical value might be.

"Not all Da Vinci sketches or Lincoln letters are equal in importance," Harry noted.

"And you want me to ride herd on your various experts, from the big-picture view?"

"Exactly."

Intrigued by now, Mitch said he appreciated the offer and agreed to think about it. "How long do I have?"

"A week should do," Harry said. "Longer means you're reluctant—which won't do at all." He began attacking his cold salmon. "Oh, in the interest of full disclosure, I should add that we don't provide first-class air travel. But we compensate by billeting you at four-star hotels for up to a week's stay—which usually covers even our most demanding field trips. If you prefer a Best Western, we'd oblige you, but you don't get to pocket the difference, I'm afraid."

Mitch accepted Harry's offer two days later.

A month before the end of his probationary period, Mitch won his permanent spurs in the course of checking out a canvas offered to C&W for auction and said to be the work of the early-twentieth-century American Cubist Charles Demuth. In the same style as the artist's well-known *I Saw the Figure Five in Gold*, the painting had supposedly been withheld from public sale by the artist and given as a gift to a relative, whose descendants now wished to cash it in. But the paint tested badly; its chemical components varied suspiciously from the pigments available in Paris in the early 1920s, the place and the time that the work was said to have been done, and the execution seemed to lack the crispness of Demuth's other museum-hung work. Mitch's further investigation, in tandem with the firm's modern art curator, disclosed that Demuth's signature appeared on the rear of none of his bona fide canvases, as it did on this purported work of his. Apprised of all these discrepancies, the would-be C&W client at first theorized that the signature may have been added later as a certifying device, but then lamely withdrew the painting with a pledge never again to try to palm it off as genuine.

After that, Mitch Emery was Harry Cubbage's new golden boy, given a 20 percent raise and offered a five-year contract, which was promptly declined. "Thanks, but a contract would make me feel like an indentured peon—I've never had one."

"Peons don't generally get contracts," Harry remarked. "They get whipped."

But Mitch insisted on his freedom of mobility, even if it left Harry with misgivings that his valued new hire might sponge up expertise at the house's expense and then jump ship just when he was becoming truly useful. Over the next nine months, though, nothing occurred to make either of them regret their arrangement. But neither had it been tested by a complex challenge that would have given Mitch a true sense of job security; the Demuth episode had been easy pickings. Which was why Harry's droll disclosure of the imminent arrival at C&W's premises of what purported to be the lately exhumed manuscript of the—for God's sake!—*William Tell* Symphony by the Biggest Bopper of Them All left Mitch's brain in a frenzy. He crossed Fifth Avenue, hurried back to his office, and Googled the "Beethoven" file on Wikipedia. This *Tell* symphony, he told himself as he scrolled, had to be pure bullshit; the composer had never had anything to do with Switzerland so far as Mitch could see. Still, he left a message for his wife on their home voice mail saying he had something of interest to share with her.

UPON ARRIVING A FASHIONABLE but annoying eighteen minutes late with not even a hint of apology, Lolly Cubbage wasted no time letting Clara Emery know that, by venturing all the way across town from her apartment on East End Avenue to the Café Luxembourg, a few doors west of raffish Broadway, she was practically slumming. "I'm never over here," Lolly said dismissively, "except for theater or Lincoln Center. What's up in this neighborhood, anyway, except that—that lox store—with all those—those—" She groped for a sufficiently abusive yet still civilly utterable epithet, but none sprang to her tart tongue, so she settled for "people," said with enough edge to register detectable scorn. "I'm here only to make you happy, darling—but your treating me is totally unnecessary."

Clara thought otherwise. She was months overdue with a reciprocal gesture. Welcome or not, Lolly's embrace had served to propel the Emerys onto the New York socialite scene and its outlying dependency in and around the Hamptons. Ever since Mitch had gone to work for Cubbage & Wakeham, Lolly had taken Clara under her warped wing like the younger sister—there were twelve years between them—she never had. This generosity was, alas, accompanied by an urge on Lolly's part to make Clara feel somehow inadequate and thus in need of mentoring that only she could provide. Lolly's handiest target was Clara's clothes. "I see you've got your usual weekday uniform on," she would begin her carping, "not that it isn't fetching on you, sweetpea—but then absolutely everything would look fabulous on you, with your height, coloring, and those good Dutch bones. I'd love to see a more playful outfit on you."

Clara's "weekday uniform" consisted of five virtually identical black suits, cut severely to emphasize her tallness, and invariably worn with one of her dozen vanilla silk blouses. For the merest glint of visual elegance she always added a small gold brooch delicately spiced with tiny gems—she owned fourteen of them in various shapes (including a bow, a butterfly, a spray of lilies, a bunch of grapes, and a tiger with ruby eyes)—worn on her left lapel. Hoping to be taken seriously in the realms of academia (as a Columbia doctoral candidate) and philanthropy (at Lincoln Center, where Lolly had arranged for her to do volunteer fundraising), she did not wish to be *noticed* for her wardrobe. It just had to be low-key and smart. Dolling herself up was reserved for parties or when she and Mitch dined occasionally at a pricey restaurant. "I don't do playful," Clara told Lolly. "And forgive me, please, but you really needn't keep casting me as your Eliza Doolittle."

"Sorry, my dear—but honestly, I'm not trying to turn you into a fashion-plater," Lolly persisted as always. "It's just that a teense of pizazz would go a long way with your raw material." And Clara, as always, gave a demure nod of thanks, and then Lolly, as always, took back half the compliment. "Of course, you could do with more meat on that frame—you are depressingly lanky for a grown woman. But then I suppose it comes naturally—you don't have to live on goat cheese and endive like the rest of us matronly types."

Dream on, Clara yearned to correct her but didn't. In fact, to keep off the dreaded pudge, she followed a punishing schedule, jogging three days a week around Central Park reservoir or in Riverside Park along the Hudson, and slogging away on the treadmill for an hour on three other days, listening to a CD to cushion the numbing ordeal. Sundays she vegged out.

Clara tolerated Lolly and her slashing tongue mostly because Mitch worked for her husband and to spurn the advances of so willful a woman who had taken an obvious shine to her would have been impolitic. Possibly disastrous. That Lolly was a borderline alcoholic, able but unwilling to slake her intake, did not excuse her verbal onslaughts. That they sometimes took the form of gross disparagement of her spouse Harry, who plied her with a surfeit of worldly goods and comforts, made her sometimes savage indiscretion still more objectionable.

Clara decided the woman was consumed by self-hatred. An honors graduate from Wellesley who lacked the moxie to pursue a career and the selflessness to be a devoted wife and mother; she had shipped their only child, a whiny daughter, off to boarding school at an early age and distanced herself from a husband who all too often treated her, according to Lolly, with sadistic callousness—unless, Clara guessed, cause and effect were in truth reversed. Whatever the cause, Lolly's principal daily activity was self-indulgence.

For all Lolly's disagreeableness, Clara recognized her own complicity in fostering their relationship. Its utility went beyond protecting Mitch's professional standing. Lolly had not only conscripted her as a sort of *noblesse oblige* fundraiser for the Lincoln Center culture gulch but also soon began including her and Mitch at some of the dinner parties she gave monthly from October to May, dedicated largely to spreading goodwill for the Cubbage & Wakeham company name among the well heeled. Paying Lolly's dues, though, meant humoring a sometimes abrasively out-of-control lady.

Hardly into her first Dewars with a splash at their Café Luxembourg lunch, Lolly began on an upbeat by exclaiming how happy Harry remained with Mitch's work ethic and sunny disposition. "I told him it's probably because you two are good in bed—he doesn't acknowledge that other people exist below the waist. I think he digs your stud because Mitch is the only one in the place who doesn't kiss his ring three times before noon. Harry says it's because Mitch has enough f-you money, so he can always walk away from his job if it gets him down."

"What's 'eff-you money'?" Clara asked.

Lolly gave her a slit-eyed look. "F-you, f-you. What are you, lady—a vestal virgin?"

"Oh, yes—I see. I just haven't run across the expression." Clara asked the waiter for a glass of cranberry juice in place of anything alcoholic. "But what makes Harry think Mitch is privately wealthy? He comes from a modest background and has never held a high-paying job before now—he was a newspaper reporter and a government employee—"

"Harry means *your* family, sweetheart—he knows you come from Old World money and probably just assumes you and Mitch are sharers."

Lolly's revelation was disturbing. "And just how does Harry know about me and my family's private business?"

Lolly took a large swallow of her scotch.

"Beats me—he hires investigators all over to check up on C&W's clients and the stuff they bring him to auction. Anyway, it's hardly a secret, is it? Harry says your father is a big deal in the corporate world—what is he, again—CEO of Unilever? Isn't that a humongous company?"

"He's CFO, as a matter of fact—and yes, it's a large and powerful company—but he doesn't exactly own it."

"Well, close enough. And Harry's partner, Sedge Wakeham, actually knew your father from the Second World War—Sedge was in British Intelligence and had secret meetings with your father—I gather he was very active in the Dutch Resistance and something of a national hero. I've been wondering if you'd ever get around to mentioning his exploits—"

"I'm very proud of my father, of course, but one doesn't talk about such things casually," Clara said softly. "It's not the way I was brought up. Nor, by the way, do my parents believe in showering Mitch and me with earthly goods—love in abundance, though—"

"Drat," said Lolly. "Well, I won't let on to Harry—I think it's good for him to have someone around the office he thinks he can't bully. Trust me on that—"

The next moment Lolly was careening into one of her boozy monologues that would soon turn into an unstoppable, polluted stream of consciousness and numb her captive audience. Clara had learned months back how to make just enough eye contact and utter a few timely uh-huhs so that her own mental gears could grind away undetected while being subjected to Lolly's venting.

"...We figured that any moron panting to pay us three hundred thou to rent for August in Southampton isn't going to squawk about the hundred-thou deposit Harry insists on for any damage they could do to the place." Lolly shoved the remnants of her pear-and-arugula salad to one side. "To be honest, I hate the idea of anybody else spreading their nasty cheeks over our upholstered furniture—greasy fingers on the draperies—you can just imagine—" She sighed wearily, yearning for a cigarette to finish off her third Dewars. "But as Harry says, everything has its price—and he should know."

"Uh-huh."

"Shit, I can see I'm boring you, angel—"

Caught. "Not in the least. I'm just a little—"

"You mustn't let me rattle on—it's those long Dutch silences of yours that do me in." Lolly instinctively reached for the check on its arrival, but Clara stayed her hand and smiled demurely. "Well, all right for this time," Lolly said. "We need to huddle again soon—I want you to help me plan my dinner lists for the rest of the spring so we can have more people for you to hit on—in your adorable way—for fat gifts to the Center."

Clara's head throbbed. "I don't like to think of it as 'hitting on' anyone—I'm just asking them to support the cultural life of their community. It's a civic duty, the way I see it."

Lolly shook her head, severely plucked eyebrows arching. "You're such a dear bunny."

{2}

I know a thing or two about carpentry—it's kinda my business," Jacob Hassler said as he took his seat at the conference table, "and this paneling in here— what is it, mahogany, right?—is one gorgeous piece of work."

Mitch sensed at once from Jake Hassler's rapid speech and antsy body language that the guy was uneasy, surrounded by the baronial splendor of the Cubbage & Wakeham library, which doubled as the firm's meeting room, and four dudes in black suits. Jake himself was a rougher-hewn sort. Even before he had uttered a word, his clothes suggested as much. A nice-looking fellow with a rosy, round face, snappy blue eyes, neatly trimmed mustache, and a full head of short, graying hair, he had dressed for the warm mid-June day in a seersucker jacket that was two sizes too small on him. And he was understandably quick to shed the garment. Beneath was a short-sleeve, powder-blue dress shirt, worn tieless and open at the collar, and gray trousers in need of pressing. His lawyer, Owen Whittaker, Esq. of the Princeton firm of Gibbons & Lavish, was fiftyish, less fleshy than his client, and professionally attired in summer-weight gabardine.

"Thank you very much," Harry Cubbage said, examining Jake obliquely and trying hard—Mitch could tell—not to reveal dismay at the sight of such an unpromising client. "We try our best to maintain the place." Harry's eyes settled on the large wooden box Jake had placed carefully on top of the conference table. "That's a handsome piece of lumber you've got there as well," he said in his best approximation of bonhomie. "Cedar, I'd guess. Nice dovetailing, beautiful hardware, maybe original—may we assume your exciting discovery is inside it?"

31

"Assume away," Jake said heartily. "It's blowing my mind, to be honest."

"Well, let's try to put you at ease, then," Harry said, warming to the challenge, however bleak its prospect. "Just tell us all about it—take your time, we're not your adversaries. Gordon Roth here is our house counsel and may have a question or two as you go along, but don't let him throw you off track. Likewise, Mitchell Emery, our resident specialist in charge of authenticating all items brought to us for auctioning."

Jake nodded soberly, then turned to his lawyer and asked, "Where do I start?"

"Maybe with Switzerland," Whittaker suggested, unsnapping his attaché case and removing a yellow legal pad and a needle-nosed pencil, "and your grandfather."

"Right." Jake leaned forward, his muscular, curly-haired forearms on display as he clasped his hands in front of him. "The strangest thing," he began, "is that I didn't know my grandpa at all, really—I saw him maybe three, four times in my whole life, his living over there and all. My father took me to Zurich a couple of times when I was a kid—" Jake stopped, sensing he had gotten off on the wrong foot, and paused to regather his thoughts. "The point is, I never had much to do with Switzerland, except that I went once to see Grandpa Otto on my own—that was maybe fifteen years ago—he never wrote or invited me or anything—I just thought maybe I should—he was gettin' real old. Anyhoo, he told me I should be proud of being Swiss and not blame the country for my good-for-nothin' father." Jake turned up his palms and shrugged. "Grandpa didn't like my old man any better than I did—thought he'd gone to America on a goose chase just to get away from the family—"

"What was your father's occupation?" Harry cut in, trying to keep Jake from rambling.

Jake explained that his father had come to America as a master mechanic after the Second World War, because the family-owned Hassler Tannery Works outside of Zurich had been mismanaged into the ground, and opportunities for a fresh start did not abound in his regimented homeland. Lured by the wide-open spaces that did not exist on his native soil, he managed to become a railroad engineer on the long freight hauls across the immense American West, found a bride at a church supper in Altoona, Pennsylvania, and fathered three kids with her. But aside from an occasional reminiscence about the old country, Jake's father was a taciturn, cranky bastard who preferred communing with the prairies to sharing himself with his family. "We all kinda thought he'd up and fly the coop someday," Jake added, "and sure enough—" Thus, he had never been able to whip up much enthusiasm about his Swiss heritage.

"But you liked your grandfather enough," Gordy coaxed Jake, "to attend his funeral?"

"Yeah—I mean, all I'd ever known about Switzerland—besides the knockout scenery, cuckoo clocks, and William Tell—was that it never took sides in all the stupid wars going on in the rest of the world, which I thought was pretty smart but not very brave. Grandpa Otto explained it to me that last time I saw him." Swiss neutrality had everything to do with national self-preservation, the old man said, because the little country was always outmanned and outgunned, so under the guise of stouthearted independence, "they always had to kiss up to the neighbors—and everyone else, too—and never crap on anybody or take sides— that would have been bad for business, and business came first. 'Besides, fighting is hopeless,' he said. So I asked him about the Swiss Guard and why they were off at the Vatican, protecting the pope. 'Protecting is not fighting,' Otto said. 'And we're not stupid, Jacob—what banks do you suppose the pope puts all the Holy Church's money in?'" Jake's features took on a remorseful look. "I should've gone to see him more, but—well, you know—woulda-coulda-shoulda—and, hey, he lived far away, and my family isn't exactly rollin' in bucks—not that I'm complaining—"

Mitch could detect nothing disingenuous about the man's bearing. "So you felt it was your duty to attend his funeral," he asked Jake a bit pointedly, "even though you hadn't seen your grandfather for many years, and it would be a long, expensive trip?"

"Right," said Jake, "besides which there was a legal reason to go." A phone call had come from his grandfather's Zurich attorney, advising him that Otto Hassler had passed on at the overripe age of ninety-eight and designated Jake as his sole heir. He took a week's leave from his job as head of the hardware department at a lumberyard in Lambertville, a riverfront burg on the Delaware, New Jersey's western boundary, to reach closure with his Swiss ancestors.

"And to find out whether you'd come into anything?" Mitch prodded gently.

"Sure, wouldn't you? I mean, there's a lot of money over there they don't fling around—who knew if Otto was worth anything or just scraping by? All I knew was he lived in this big old house—well, it seemed big to me, dark and pretty gloomy—and smelled of cat piss."

Any delusions of windfall wealth Jake had allowed himself to nourish on the trip over were quickly dissipated. There were barely funds, it turned out, to cover his grandfather's burial. The substantial five-story house on Napfplatz, a little cobbled square in the old section of Zurich near the student quarter, where members of the Hassler family had lived for nearly three hundred years, was in hopeless hock. Otto's dwindling income after the family tannery closed and his accumulating debts would have landed him in a state nursing home years before if not for the largess of softhearted creditors and well-wishing neighbors. None had exhibited greater generosity toward him than the family immediately next door, the Erpfs, whose fortune gained in the realty and insurance businesses placed them among Zurich's financial and social elite. The Erpfs held a lien on the Hassler house and everything in it, all of which would become their property as soon as Otto met his Maker. Meanwhile, they sent their staff over once a week to keep the Hassler house habitable and supply the old man with their leftover food. "They were real swell to Grandpa is what I heard," Jake reported, "and I made it my business to thank them."

By the terms of Otto's will and his lien agreement with the Erpfs, Jake was bequeathed only a handful of sentimental but otherwise worthless keepsakes—a few photo albums, a favorite ornamental paperweight, a busted antique clock that Otto had always intended to have repaired—and what his will called "such other personal family papers, records, and memorabilia as my creditors would otherwise discard."

Jake shrugged off the bad news, reasoning that he had never harbored serious expectations of inheriting much of anything from his grandfather, and respectfully buried Otto Hassler. On the evening of the funeral, the Erpfs gave a buffet supper of bereavement, open to all in the immediate neighborhood, at which Jake was the guest of honor. "It was real nice—I heard lots of stories about Grandpa's good nature and popularity," Jake recounted with evident pride. Before he had lost virtually everything and become bedridden, Otto never closed his door on needy passersby, and neighbors were regularly treated to a smile, a joke, and a cup of tea or coffee while sunning themselves nearby in the square. For many years during the December holidays, Otto used to dress up as Father Christmas, park himself in front of the little gated fountain at the lower end of the sloping Napfplatz, near the shops, and amuse the local children by telling stories and leading them and their parents in a nightly round of caroling by candlelight.

"You should get to the nitty-gritty," Jake's lawyer told him. "These folks are busy."

Jake turned up his palms. "I was just tryin' to—they asked about Otto—"

"Take your time," Mitch told him, not bothering to glance at Harry for approval. "It's all part of the picture we need to get."

"I figured." Jake pulled his chair in closer to the table and picked up the tempo of his narrative. He dwelled now on how, during the memorial supper at the Erpfs' house, he renewed his acquaintance with Ansel Erpf, the prodigal son of the wealthy neighbors' household. Ansel told him that he used to go over once a week whenever he was in town to visit with old man Hassler. He would drink and smoke with Otto, read him the paper, or play a CD or a few songs for him on the piano. "He loved my Chevalier impersonation," Ansel told Jake. "Otto was a gorgeous human being."

Jake had a dim but fond memory of Ansel from his two boyhood visits to his grandfather's house. On his first time over, the Erpfs' lad organized a hiking party for Jake's benefit, and during the walk, Ansel tried out his then halting English. He confessed to Jake how much he hated regular school subjects and wanted only to learn to play every instrument in the orchestra. Jake learned from other supper guests after Otto's funeral that Ansel did in fact turn into a musical prodigy and had performed creditably as a cellist for a dozen years with the Philharmonia Helvetica National, better known as the Swiss Philharmonic, until he fell out with the orchestra's director and found work abroad as an itinerant performer. Nowadays, Ansel was back living in his family's imposing home, secluded on the third floor so his music playing would not disturb his parents when they were in town. He divided his time performing pop classics at a piano bar behind the Savoy Hotel across the river, on the tennis court at the elite Platypus Club, where the Erpfs had been longtime members, and drinking far too much, as Jake soon noticed. "Plastered or not, though, Ansel was really nice to me after the funeral. But he's sure pissed at me now."

Gordy Roth perked up at that disclosure. "How come?" the C&W counselor asked.

Jake smiled sweetly, like the proverbial cat that had just gulped the canary, and patted he cedar box in front of him. "He thinks this should be his—just because he helped me find it."

"Well, it's a little more complicated than that," Jake's lawyer inserted. "Just tell them what happened—they don't need to know Ansel Erpf's life story."

His years in pursuit of lawbreakers had taught Mitch that lawyers often erred on the side of overprotecting their clients out of fear they might blurt out something incriminating.

"I'm a former prosecutor, Mr. Whitaker," Mitch told him, trying not to sound as if he were pulling rank, "and used to examining suspects, but no one here is viewing Mr. Hassler as a suspect—we just need to know the full circumstances of his discovery, and there's no way of telling in advance what may or may not be relevant to our judging the merits of his claim. Go ahead, Jake, and relax—there's no meter running in here."

Reassured, Jake sat back, wearing an appreciative look that told Mitch he was savoring all the attention.

"Well, so this Ansel came over as the dinner party was breaking up and offered to help me go through Grandpa's house the next day—ya know, to see if there was anything I wanted—any souvenirs or special things that I might not be exactly entitled to because of the Erpfs' lien but nobody in his family would give a hoot about if I wanted them. 'Except maybe Vampira over there,' he said to me, meaning his sister, Margot. 'Let's go through the place together before she can get her hands on it.' Margot runs their family realty business, he told me, while their folks mostly travel now and enjoy themselves. I don't think Ansel and Margot get along—she probably figures he's the family leech. Anyway, that's my take on them."

Mitch nodded slowly.

"And you didn't think that was a little…pushy, on Ansel's part?"

"Nope," said Jake, "I figured he was just being neighborly—and he knew the house a lot better than I did after all his visits with Grandpa Otto over the years."

So Jake accepted Ansel's offer, and the two of them went through the house from bottom to top the next morning, segregating a few trinkets that caught Jake's attention, among them a silver-framed photograph dated 1896 of what was probably the entire labor force of the Hassler Tannery gathered in front of a large white workhouse. On their way upstairs, while Jake was lingering in the second-floor drawing room, Ansel sat down at the old grand piano at one end of the high-ceilinged chamber "and fooled around with it for a few minutes," Jake related. "He said the room had great acoustics, and even though the piano was pretty rinky-dink by now, it still sounded good because the Erpfs kept it tuned, figuring they'd own it soon enough." Otto told him that for a long time they held recitals in that room—because the Hassler family used to have traveling musicians as lodgers on the fourth and fifth floors, and they'd perform for friends and neighbors in exchange for free rent. They were still doing it when Otto was a boy, but the practice stopped during the First World War and never resumed.

Eventually, Jake and Ansel reached the attic, and a dark, musty coop it was, with only one small window to illuminate it. "Ansel went back to his house to grab a flashlight so we could see this big jumble of whatnot—it just looked like a whole lot of crapola." After a cursory inspection, they were about to abort their mission when Ansel, over in the far corner, "where I could hardly see him—

he says, 'Whoa, baby,' and lifts up a folded-over, moth-eaten old carpet that was hiding a great big wooden trunk with kind of a rounded top—"

For the first time, Jake's folksy rendition set off an alarm bell in Mitch's head. "Excuse me, Mr. Hassler," he asked, "but did Ansel—"

"You could call me Jake, if that's okay—"

"Sure—and I'm Mitch, okay? Tell me, Jake, did Ansel seem to you to have known about that trunk's being there even before the two of you went up to the attic?"

Jake considered the question. "You mean like was he leading me to it or something?"

"Well, something like that."

"Nahhh," Jake said. "I think he was just poking around down at that end—and he was holding the flashlight, so he could—"

"Okay, go ahead—I didn't mean to distract you."

"Hey, not to worry." The trunk latch came undone with a gentle tug, Jake went on, and the two of them lifted the top carefully, its hinges creaking in protest. Greeted by a rank aroma of rot and mildew, which lingered in the hermetic chamber, they proceeded to examine the trunk's contents by flashlight. If any jewelry or other precious heirlooms had ever been in there, they'd been removed long before. What remained were some neatly folded but now shredding garments of white silk and lace along with tied bundles of papers and letters, several photo albums, a metronome, two crocheted afghans, and, finally, at the bottom, a cedar box, about two feet long by a foot and a half wide and a foot high. "This beauty," Jake said, giving it a fond, proprietary pat as it sat in front of him on the table.

The box lid yielded as readily as the trunk top had, its cedar fragrance still detectable, and its contents of books and papers presented no immediate clue of their nature. But something, perhaps the workmanship of the box and the careful arrangement of the material inside, suggested to its discoverers that the container deserved further examination. Ansel offered to carry it, but Jake instinctively recognized it as properly his chore, so he lugged the heavy box down five flights of stairs and deposited it on the dining room table.

"This is exactly what was in it," Jake said, standing in front of his chair and slowly lifting its lid. Reflexively the three C&W men at the table rose in unison and, thoroughly spellbound, gathered behind Jake for a closeup view. Owen Whittaker surrendered his chair to Harry Cubbage, who slid right into it and invited Jake to complete his show-and-tell.

It all came out in a single, odd-shaped armload. The core of the bulky pile was a pair of what resembled old, gray accounting ledgers. Sandwiched between them was a batch of papers of assorted sizes, and on top was a small, leatherbound book with an envelope tied to it by a loosely knotted, faded blue length of ribbon. "Here's what we got here," said Jake, carefully separating the elements and introducing them one by one. Mitch pressed in closer as a surge of excitement began to pulse through him.

The first of what looked like two bookkeeping ledgers proved to be, as Jake began flipping slowly through it, a worn workbook with music staves ruled across the full width of its pages and a blotchy torrent of notes, chords, circles, dots, illegible abbreviations, mysterious signs, and jagged markings flooding each one in inks of different shades and thicknesses of line. Crossouts abounded, along with smudges, ink drips, and blurred mirror images on opposing pages, likely caused when the book was closed before the latest inked entry had dried. Here and there, new notes or a change in tempo had been inserted with a lead pencil. Whoever the composer was, he or she was not neat about it; the work appeared to have been carried out in a sustained paroxysm of creative energy. Just a bit more graphic turmoil, Mitch thought, and the pages would have resembled a Jackson Pollock canvas. The paper, uneven at the upper edges of each page and moldy-looking in spots, was thick yet pliant without showing any sign of crumbling at Jake's touch.

The second ledger-like book, in sharp contrast to the other, densely packed one, presented much cleaner and more carefully written music on both sides of its first twenty or so pages; the rest were empty, save for the ruled staves. After glancing about him to make sure he had their full attention, Jake ceremoniously turned to the beginning of the second book. It was a generously spaced title page, the top two lines of which read, in large Gothic German lettering,

Wilhelm Tell
Eine Dramatische Symphonie

Below, in smaller letters, was the byline, *Ludwig van Beethoven,* and directly below that, in still smaller writing, *In Memoriam J. C. F. v. Schiller.* Running down the left side of the page was a list of musical instruments, presumably the ones to be used in performing the work.

Irresistibly impressive, Mitch thought, for all his unfamiliarity with musical manuscripts. If a counterfeit, this was fastidious workmanship. It all certainly *looked* real. Very.

Jake held the page open for several triumphant moments, letting the impact of the sight sink in. "Something, huh?" he asked when his hovering observers kept noncommittally mum.

"Definitely some thing," Harry allowed, breaking the word in two, "but just what kind of a thing—that's the question."

"Meaning—what, exactly?" asked Jake with a trace of a frown.

Harry did his best to regard Jake charitably and not as a member of some rudimentary species, then gestured to Mitch to field the question.

"Meaning," Mitch said not unkindly, "that what the title page says, Jake, is not necessarily what it is. That has to be determined by experts, no matter how authentic it may look to you—or to us. I, for one, haven't a clue what 'a dramatic symphony' is—I guess that's what this German subtitle means. I can check that with my wife—it's her field of study." He pointed to the other contents of the box now spread on the table. "Now what else have you got here—what's the little book?"

Jake slid off the attached letter and ribbon and handed the book back over his shoulder.

"Ansel thinks old Ludwig probably used this as a kind of guide for what he was composing. It's got lots of scribbles all over its pages and inside the covers—"

The dark brown leather cover, flaking at the top right front corner, bore no markings, but Mitch could figure out the German on the title page: *William Tell: A dramatic play in four acts by Johann Christoph Friedrich von Schiller.* He glanced at the swarm of penciled notations that speckled the front and back endpapers. "Well, *somebody* wrote *something* in here, that's for certain." He handed the book back to Jake. "And what's in the envelope that came with it?"

"Okay, this is the most interesting part," Jake said, warming to his task. "It explains the whole thing—more or less." He pulled out a cream-colored letter from a matching unsealed folder—three sheets filled on both sides with small, precise handwriting—and explained that Ansel had translated it into English for him soon after they found it. "It knocked us both for a loop, so I asked if he'd please write it out for me in English—which he did that night." Jake turned to his lawyer. "Here, we've got photocopies of it for you folks."

Whittaker reached into his attaché case for the copies and handed them around to the C&W team, urging them to digest the translation carefully. "It's a real eye-opener."

Mitch leaned over his copy of the stapled, three-page document and, his astonishment swelling by the line, read:

14 September 1814

To dearest Mama and Papa—and all the world forever,

Should any of you find this packet of papers, I wish to explain what they are and why I put them here, so you will not think I have done a horrid thing.

Maestro Ludwig van Beethoven departed our house here in the Napfplatz today after having occupied the top storey apartment since the latter part of July, during which period he endured treatments almost every day for an ear infection that is said to have greatly reduced his hearing. The conditions for his tenancy included the transfer of the pianoforte from our drawing room up to his quarters and a pledge that his identity and visit here never be revealed. We called him "Herr Schmidt" and said, when inquiries were made, that he was a renowned traveling concert pianist.

Maestro B. was in a sour humour for much of his residence with us, as I can vouch, being the daughter of the house and given charge of tending to our tenant's needs. His daily program was unvarying. Early each morning he went to work at his piano, and judging by the musical books and sheets scattered on and about the instrument and from the way he played—in fits and starts—we all believed he was creating a new composition. At noon, he went to the physician for his ear infusions and afterward would walk beside the lake, where he appeared preoccupied and could be heard humming aloud to himself and seen pausing at times to scribble something down with a pencil in a little notebook he drew from his pocket. Once, I came upon him in his quarters shortly after his return and he was still wearing his hat while scratching away like fury in the large book he kept beside the piano. Evenings he would dine at the modest taverns in the student neighborhood or with acquaintances unknown to us. More than once he declined with gratitude an invitation to sup with our family, wishing to keep his distance and privacy.

I summoned the courage one day to inquire of him the nature of his new work, and in response he asked if I was familiar with William Tell. Every Swiss knows the story of the great bowman and his son and the apple, I told him. And did we all know what foreign nation was oppressing Tell and his people, he asked me, and I confessed I was not sure, not wanting to give him offense, since I knew well it was the country of Austria, where he lived. No matter, he said, "I am writing a symphonic version of your glorious legend, with singing parts as well, but it is proving very difficult work." I then made the error of asking whether he might play me a small part of it. He grew angry, saying he did not give recitals for chambermaids, which caused me to remind him that I was also the daughter of the house and for that reason (and others) ought not to be disrespected.

His temper, I am sorry to say, did not improve much, probably because the medical treatments he was taking were not benefiting his hearing. He used an ear trumpet whenever I addressed him and asked me to please speak louder. Once, however, he admired the dress I was wearing and spoke appreciatively about the sunshine flooding his rooms.

I was much troubled, though, when, preparing to conclude his stay at our house this morning, he pointed to his music composition books and some other papers he had piled into a corner. "Please do me the kindness of destroying this material," he said. When I asked him why he did not wish to take them on the coach ride home, he quite bristled at me. "It is none of your affair," said he. "Will you do as I ask?" But think of all your work, maestro, I said to him, what a great pity to give it up. "No, no!" he shouted. "The pity is that it is so poor a job that I can not put my name to it." I wondered aloud if he might not perfect it at a later time, or perhaps hold a higher opinion of the work when his spirits had lifted—all of which caused him at first to charge me with impertinence. Then he saw I was trying to be kind, so he shook his head, saying that beyond its inferior quality, the work was "far too dangerous" and so had to be destroyed. I said I feared it would be a sin for me to do so and wondered why he did not discard it himself. He looked forlorn and said, "I have not the heart for it."

He took my hand upon leaving and made me nod assent to his request. But almost at once I had regrets and thought it could do no harm for me to store his papers for safekeeping somewhere in our house—in the event he should change his mind. I ran over to the casement and began calling down to him, but then soon realized that of course he could not have heard me. I write this, then, to explain why I have taken it upon myself to defy the wishes of such a great man, who I am sure has not been himself due to his medical infirmities. Perhaps I shall write him some day and confess what I have done. Or perhaps not—and this composition will

remain hidden from mankind until many years from now, when we are
all long gone, along with whatever "danger" the maestro imagines might
result from the creation of this symphony. May the world forgive me then
and understand why I have acted so.

—Nina Hassler

The scale of the thing, the sheer daring of the concoction—if it was one—nearly arrested Mitch's breathing. It was so toweringly, outrageously preposterous a scam: a Moby Dick in a sardine can. And the letter of explanation was too transparently perfect. Yet—yet—confronted with the object itself sitting right *there*, with black-and-white evidence apparently in the composer's own hand and presumably certifiable, Mitch found himself witlessly hoping against hope that somehow, through a confluence of forces he could not even guess at, it was true. Beethoven's Tenth Symphony: the *William Tell*, about to take its place proudly, if more than two centuries belatedly, with the other three symphonies of his that bore a name as well as a number—the Third, the *Eroica*; the Sixth, the *Pastoral*, and the Ninth, the *Choral*. The fantasizing lobes of his brain at once discounted the likelihood that the peerless composer was right, that the work had been properly cast aside because it was, to be direct about it, piss-poor. No, that sadly stricken titan must have been an emotional basket case at the moment he discarded the manuscript and had likely lost his powers of discernment, as Nina Hassler, wise maiden that she was, had dared to suggest to him. It *had* to have merit—assuming it was actually *his* work—and here it *was*, albeit in a still raw, apparently unperfected state, just waiting for destiny to arrive and...

"Terrific," whispered Gordy Roth, the first of the C&W team to break silence. He was shaking his head and reading the letter through a second time. Mitch looked past him to see Harry's perplexed brow undulating in tempo with his eye movements as he absorbed the text.

"See?" Jake Hassler said, a little smile pasted in place. "I told you it was something."

Mitch's tolerance for the supermiraculous fled as fast as it had come over him. Jake's naïveté made him recoil. Was this guy a used car salesman in sheep's clothing? "But anyone could have written this letter," Mitch said with clinical blandness, directing his words to the room at large, "and put it in this box—and put the box in the trunk—and the trunk in the attic—"

Jake spun around to face him.

"You gotta be kiddin' me! Why would anyone do—"

"So we'd all think it's real," Mitch cut him off quietly.

"Why all the rigmarole to hide a fake?"

"That's a very good question, Jake." Mitch placed the Nina letter on the tabletop. "It just might have something to do with money—isn't that why you've come to us?"

Jake's roundish face grew pinched with bafflement.

"Sure, to sell it for a bundle—but I don't get it. How would—how could—anyone else make money off it—if I've got it?"

"Another good question," said Mitch, his mind racing now over the complexity of the sudden challenge he faced. The most exotic document investigation he had overseen since joining C&W involved certifying an early sixteenth-century map of the Spanish Main. Even when fully authenticated, the map sold at auction for just $12,500. But an entirely new Beethoven symphony, if that was what this was, and the accompanying rights to its commercial uses would be a spectacularly different matter. Think of all the performance and recording revenues—they'd gross in the tens of millions. But Jake had a point: How could hypothetical perpetrators of an international, high-stakes forgery scam prosper by allowing their work product to fall into the hands of a hardware salesman living in the New Jersey hinterland?

Harry, Mitch recognized, had gone down roads similar to this one many times in the past, so there was no need for him to voice his skepticism at this stage. Instead, he put two questions to Jake: What was Ansel Erpf's initial reaction to the stunning find, and had there in fact ever been a Nina Hassler on his family tree?

"Oh, Ansel—he nearly had kittens," Jake chuckled. "I mean, he's a musician, a pro—and we're talkin' Beethoven here—so whaddaya think? His eyes bug out of his head, and he says it's got to be a mistake or something—this Nina must've got it wrong—or it was maybe somebody masquerading as Beethoven. Then he started going through these two big composition books here and shaking his head like crazy and begins to change his tune the longer he looks, and next thing I see, he's cryin' his eyes out—and probably pissing in his pants. That's when it started getting to me, too."

Jake took a deep breath. "I asked him what we should do with the stuff, and first he said he wasn't sure, and then he asked if he could have it to himself for a few days—ya know, so he could look it over and try to figure out if it was legit—because that would make it historical and all. He said it would be best if he could take it all back to his house, right next door, to study it and fool around with it a little on the piano, so he could, ya know, hear what it sounds like."

"In other words, he tried to grab it away from you," Harry prompted.

Jake shook his head. "Nah, it didn't seem like that—at least not right away. It seemed natural enough—Grandpa's house was dark—Ansel probably wanted to spread the stuff out, so he could get a real good look at it."

"You weren't a little bit suspicious of him?" Gordy wondered.

"Like I said, not then. The guy's a musician—I thought that was a lucky break—he could probably figure out what the hell it was all about. Also, he'd always seemed like a good guy to me from when we were kids, and his folks had let Grandpa stay there all those years." What did concern him, though, Jake added, was the possibility that Ansel, heavy drinker that he was, might somehow mess up the precious discovery by, say, spilling coffee or liquor all over it or burning it with one of the cigarettes he practically chain-smoked. So he told Ansel as nicely as he could that it would be better if he left it all where it was and used the old piano upstairs in the drawing room if he wanted to try out the music. "But he didn't much like that—gave me a fishy look like maybe I didn't trust him worth a damn, which wasn't true—I mean, I wasn't thinking he'd just take off with the stuff or anything like that. It was only when he began to get pissy about it that I kinda wised up."

All at once it hit Jake that, since Ansel's family had first claim on the house and everything in it except the personal Hassler family things, the excited look in Ansel's eyes maybe meant he was thinking that this could-be-Beethoven discovery legally belonged to the Erpf family now that Grandpa Otto was dead. Jake's attitude turned resolute. "So I told him that was the way it had to be—he could spend the next day at Grandpa's looking over everything, and meanwhile I would get hold of old man Schacht—he's Grandpa's lawyer—Martin Schacht. But Ansel wasn't too tickled by that idea, either. He said maybe we should just keep it all hush-hush for a little till we could sort it all out. That really got my motor racing."

Once he had hauled the box from the dining room back upstairs to the drawing room, Jake called Herr Schacht, and the lawyer and one of his assistants came over as fast as the old boy could totter, and soon they sent a clerk to Zurich's official recording office to try to certify the former existence of Nina Hassler. By the next afternoon, there was an answer. Nina Christine Hassler was born in 1792 to parents residing on the same square as Otto's house, though no numerical address was given. With a little genealogical homework, they conjectured that Nina was probably Jake's great-great-great-great-aunt—"maybe there was another 'great' in there that I lost track of," he said. Further research, however, failed to uncover either a marriage or death certificate for Nina. "Chances are, they said, she went away and got married somewhere else and died. Schacht and I, we figured maybe she never had a chance to tell anyone about the box she'd left in the attic—or maybe she just plain forgot about the whole shebang."

While Ansel devoted the following day to poring over the *Tell* Symphony at Otto's house, Jake and his lawyers tried to unpuzzle the miscellaneous papers that had come in the cedar box with the composition books and the copy of Schiller's play about William Tell. Much of it seemed to be irrelevant junk, invoices and dinner invitations and routine correspondence, all of it addressed to a "Johann Schmidt." Three of the letters, though, appeared likely to have some bearing on the credibility of Nina's written account. Two were from the same man, a Zurich resident named Nägeli, who was apparently acquainted with the maestro in some professional way and a keen admirer of his. A third, much longer letter, also in German, was written in a hand difficult to read—only the signature, the single letter "R," was unmistakable—and bore some sort of crest at the top of the first page, suggesting it might have been sent by one of Beethoven's noble patrons. All three letters, Mitch mentally noted, would now require the most scrupulous examination by his department.

After his labors in the drawing room, accompanied by intermittent and somewhat halting strains from Otto's old warhorse of a piano, Ansel reported back that evening more exhausted than exhilarated but definitely gratified by his findings. He told Jake he believed the composition was very likely genuine Beethoven. The far messier composition book, Ansel thought, was the one in which the maestro had sketched out his work in rough fragments and then refined them as he went along. While the musical handwriting was often difficult to decipher, it looked to him very much as if the composer had begun the work using the operatic form and after a dozen or so pages abruptly abandoned it for a predominantly instrumental approach. But the new version integrated a substantial number of vocal segments unlike anything else that Beethoven had been known to write, other than the last movement of his Ninth Symphony— "which," said Jake, "I just bought a CD of the other day. Fantastic!"

The second composition book, Ansel advised Jake, was the one he used for transcribing the rough draft into more finished shape, with the parts for the various instruments added page by page. This portion of the manuscript, far cleaner and thus easier to follow, was the one Ansel had concentrated on. "He said that, at a guess, Beethoven had finished the whole first—whaddayacallit?—the first movement— and a good part of the second one," Jake related, "which meant he was still fussing with the last half of the whole thing, but it looked as if the raw stuff was mostly all there, back in the first book. So I asked—I mean, I know diddly from classical music, but everybody knows Beethoven was the greatest golden oldie—so I asked Ansel whether he could tell if it was any good, since the Nina letter made a point about the big guy's chucking it all out because he thought it sucked. Ansel was really beat by then—I mean you can just imagine, he's the first one ever to play this thing because it was stuck away in that attic right next to where he'd lived a lot of his life." Jake shook his head sympathetically. "Anyhoo, Ansel said he really couldn't tell for sure, not using that old piano—he said there actually wasn't any part of the music written for the piano 'cause they don't have pianos in orchestras, which I never knew—but Ansel said from what he could make out, some of it was very—um—he said powerful and—well—I forget just what he called it, but it was definitely a winner." Still, much work remained to be done, Ansel told him, to edit the whole composition into shape before a sound critical judgment of it could be ventured.

All of which left Jake and Otto's local lawyer facing a very large dilemma. "What was I supposed to do with this unbefuckinglievable thing?" He glanced around at the C&W trio, all nodding at the enormity of the problem he had to confront. "So I sat down with Schacht and asked him what he thought, starting with whether, under Grandpa's will, the thing now really belonged to me—and if so, then what?" The old lawyer tried gamely to focus and finally counseled that there was no easy answer. The will and the lien that the Erpfs held on the house said Jake was entitled to keep only family papers and personal items of no real value to anyone else. But a symphony by Beethoven, if it really were one, would obviously have considerable commercial value—perhaps amounting to a small fortune or even a large one—so it might not qualify as Jake's to inherit. On the other hand, the entire contents of the trunk could arguably be considered family papers, since that was essentially what they were—papers the family had kept up in that attic for one helluva long time. It was a question that the courts would ultimately have to settle if the Erpfs chose to contest Jake's claim—"and Schacht guessed that they would, which you had to figure, since Ansel knew all about the thing and was working up a real hard-on over it. You could tell how hot and bothered he was, acting like he was the one who had discovered the music all by himself and this was gonna be his great big thing—on account of he'd rescued it from—you know—oblivion."

Jake drummed his fingers on the side of the cedar box. At any rate, he went on, Herr Schacht said that even if the manuscript was judged to be his, Jake might have Otto's creditors and substantial estate taxes to deal with, so maybe he'd be better off voluntarily bringing the whole kit-and-caboodle to the Swiss government and asking them to protect it and figure out what to do with it, maybe even buy it from him—since the symphony was about William Tell, the nation's superhero—as a reward for his coming forward and offering it to the Swiss people.

"In other words, you might want to give it away to avoid big trouble," Gordy suggested, "and hope for a gesture of gratitude from Switzerland."

"Yeah, exactly. Since I didn't have any better idea, I ran that one past Ansel, just to see how he'd react. And right off he says screw that—here this thing falls into our laps—get that, *our* laps!—and maybe it's worth a fortune and maybe it's worth peanuts, but why not find out which? And, anyway, once the government got its claws on it, he said, that would be the end of it so far as we were concerned. They'd turn it over to the bureaucrats, and those jokers would set up umpteen committees to study the thing down to the last G-string, and then probably take it hat in hand to the German and Austrian governments, since Beethoven was German but lived in Austria, and they'd all get into the act, and we'd wind up never getting a blessed thing out of it."

"Not to mention," Gordy put in, "that the Swiss police might charge your family with unlawful possession of the thing for a couple of hundred years, so your claim to ownership might go up in smoke, anyway."

"No way!" Jake shot back. "My dear Auntie Nina didn't steal anything, the way I look at it—she just didn't toss out the stuff like loony ol' Ludwig asked her to. Where's the crime in that? I mean, she was just saving a very valuable thing for—for—all mankind, if ya see what I mean. She should get a medal on her grave, wherever that is."

"Maybe so," Gordy said, "but her stashing the manuscript away in the family attic didn't really establish the Hassler family's ownership rights to it, even if what she did wasn't criminal. Could be that there are some Beethoven relatives kicking around who'd have a lot better claim to the symphony than you do."

"Hoo-boy!" Jake expelled, eyes rolling upward, and turned to his attorney. "I thought you said these people would be on our side?"

Whittaker put a calming hand on Jake's sleeve. "They're just trying to help you be realistic about the problems the manuscript presents. And it would be their problem, too, if you want them to try to auction it."

What had been realistic for Jake was to tell Ansel and Schacht to go home and let him sleep on the situation. Once they had left, he put everything back inside the cedar box, secured it with rope, and headed for the airport and the first flight out of country in the morning. He also left a phone message for Herr Schacht to have the attic trunk air-freighted to his home in New Jersey with the cost charged to his AmEx card. "'Course, I nearly shit a brick at the airport check-in," Jake added, "what with all the souped-up security since Nine Eleven. Naturally I took the box as carry-on—no way was I gonna risk stowing it with the regular baggage. They made me open it and explain what it was, so I said just some old family papers from my late Grandpa—which was pretty much the truth. Listen, I honest-to-God feel this box here rightfully belongs to me, and I didn't want anybody grabbing it away—no neighbors, no creditors, no Mickey Mouse Swiss officials. I didn't do anything wrong, and neither did old Nina—and if you guys can help me figure out whether this thing's for real, maybe we can all make a little something off the deal."

"Assuming," said Gordy, "the Erpfs don't come after you. Didn't you tell us earlier that Ansel—and his sister, probably—is unhappy with you for taking off with the manuscript?"

Jake deferred to his lawyer. Whittaker reported that Schacht had heard from the Erpfs' family counsel, expressing dismay over Jake's actions and urging him to return the box and its contents so that the title question could be properly settled by the parties or, if they couldn't agree, by the Swiss courts. Whittaker asked for a translation of Otto Hassler's will, which he had received and examined—"I'll give a copy to Mr. Roth here"—and left him satisfied that Jake was well within his rights to claim unencumbered ownership of the box and its contents. The Erpfs had their pound of flesh now in the form of the Hassler house and all its furnishings, which was what had been intended by the lien arrangement—nothing more. "This discovery, as Jake says, was among the Hassler family's private papers. I very much doubt that these Swiss folks will pursue Jake in the courts over here."

"Fair enough," said Harry, applying his lean posterior to the nearest corner of the conference table and turning to address his visitors. "I think my colleagues will agree that this item isn't the sort of thing we deal with on a daily basis. If authentic, it could constitute a find of monumental artistic importance." But if C&W were to become publicly associated with the *Tell* symphony as its auctioneer, Harry added not quite sternly, and it proved a fraud, the damage to the firm's reputation could be ruinous.

He dismounted from the table edge and began to circle the room. "So, gentlemen, there are some hard realities here for all of us to consider, starting with what it might cost to determine if this manuscript is marketable." To arrive at that figure, as Harry saw it, would require an affirmative answer to at least four questions, number one being whether Jake really had the right to sell the property, with C&W or anybody else acting as his designated agent. Number two, was the manuscript authentic Beethoven? Number three, was it good Beethoven, not just a historic curio that the august composer correctly wanted destroyed? And number four, if the work proved both authentic and meritorious, could the material be protected and commercially exploited under existing copyright laws?

The sheer rock wall presented by these obstacles sucked all the oxygen out of the room and reduced it to stony silence. Their astute recitation reminded Mitch why Harry was the boss.

"I guess Mr. Hassler wants to know," his attorney finally asked, "whether Cubbage & Wakeham would be willing, based on what you've seen and heard, to undertake whatever investigations need to be made—and, assuming you're satisfied with the results, what price—at a ballpark guess—you think a new Beethoven symphony, along with whatever rights its ownership may convey, could command at an open auction."

"The situation," Harry said acidly, "doesn't exactly lend itself to ballpark guesses." He looked to Gordy Roth. "What do you think, sport?"

"I think," said Gordy, not one to show his cards before they were called, "that it would be absolutely marvelous if the work proves to be (a) the genuine article and (b) a masterpiece in the bargain, despite having been abandoned by its distraught creator. But the odds are that it's neither the real thing nor much good—and it could cost us more than we'd ever earn to find out."

"Mmmm," said Harry. "But suppose, in order to protect ourselves, we consider offering Mr. Hassler a somewhat different commission arrangement from our usual one."

He turned to Jake. Normally, the auction house was entitled to a 10-percent commission from both the buyer and the seller on items that it sold for more than $100,000, he explained—and this property, if saleable at all, might command ten or a hundred times that, maybe even more if deemed a masterpiece. "But in this case," Harry proposed, "given the staggering difficulties and price of the authentication process, we might ask the client to split the cost with us to determine whether the manuscript is genuine. Jake's half of this expense would be deducted from the realized sale price—"which would mean that all the out-of-pocket expenses and the rest of the upfront risk would be ours alone if the project doesn't fly—that is, if the manuscript doesn't check out and never goes to auction."

Whittaker gave a tentative nod. "That sounds like a proposition Jake might consider—provided we had approval rights of your budget for the investigation. Otherwise, Jake could come away with next to nothing if the manuscript sold for a disappointing figure."

"That's a possibility," Harry conceded. "We wouldn't make very much in that event, either, of course. That wouldn't concern Jake, I suspect, but it does me."

"Suppose," Whittaker countered, "Jake got charged with only twenty-five percent of the authentication costs, assuming the manuscript checks out—and provided he winds up netting at least half a million. Otherwise he gets charged just your usual commission."

"We'll consider that," said Harry, turning now to his chief investigator. "And where do you come out on all of this, Mitchell?"

The scope of the challenge had set his competitive juices flowing. Tempted as he might be, though, to align himself with the underdog's cause in this battle—Mitch liked Jake Hassler, who struck him as a salt-of-the-earth guy and not into playing games—he knew he had to resist being swept away by the sentimental current. Even if he were reflexively inclined to take this *Tell* tale at face value, it would not lessen the very real possibility that Jake was being used by highly sophisticated schemers in a manner no one in the room could fathom.

"I think it's possible," Mitch said to Harry, "that a relatively short investigation—of perhaps one or two weeks—might disprove the authenticity of the manuscript on its face, so we wouldn't have to invest heavily in sustained scrutiny of the documents by an army of experts that would otherwise be necessary before we could bring the property before the public in good conscience."

He looked over at Jake and his lawyer. "If it were my call, I'd try to persuade Mr. Hassler to entrust the manuscript and the supporting documents to our care and protection for that preliminary study—it would be in his interest at least as much as ours to nip this thing in the bud if it's a transparent hoax—and we would give him every assurance, of course, that his property would remain on these premises and that one of us three would know at all times exactly where it is in this building and who's examining it. Also, Mr. Hassler's discovery would reside here on a strictly confidential basis until he and we can reach an agreement on how to proceed—or not to."

"What about fire or theft?" Whittaker asked.

"We've got a fireproof vault in the basement, a twenty-four-hour security guard, and multimillion-dollar insurance coverage," Gordy told him. "If it would help, we could guarantee you the payment of a fair price in the event the manuscript were destroyed through our carelessness, but that would have to be the extent of it."

"What kind of fair price?" Whittaker asked.

Gordy deferred to the proprietor. Harry studied the bronze ceiling fixtures for ten whole seconds. "Half a million seems fair to me."

"A million would make Mr. Hassler more comfortable," his counsel said. "And, as Mr. Roth says, you have insurance to recover what you'd pay Jake."

"Seven-fifty, final offer," said Harry, "and we'll be back to you inside thirty days with a preliminary opinion as to whether this alleged symphony may actually have been composed by Beethoven or is, in our studied opinion, a worthless counterfeit. Meanwhile, Mr. Roth here will be looking into the legal issues of ownership and copyright, and Mr. Emery will want to visit Mr. Hassler at home, so we have a little better sense of how solid a citizen he is." He turned to Jake. "It's nothing personal, my friend—the laws and the professional ethics of our business require us to exercise what's called 'due diligence.'"

"I getcha," said Jake. "Bottom line, you guys gotta scope out if I'm a sleazebag."

"Bottom line," said Harry and extended his hand to seal phase one of the deal.

{3}

The eight-block walk back to her apartment allowed Clara to stave off hyperventilation after holding all her internal systems in check throughout the luncheon ordeal. Had Lolly not been such a trial, Clara's ulterior purposes in cultivating their relationship would scarcely have triggered a guilt seizure after every time they met.

By the time she turned onto Riverside Drive, she was nevertheless wondering if Lolly had been right about her and Mitch's joint financial resources immunizing him from any need to toady to Harry Cubbage. Aside from the distastefulness of the charge, it struck her as wrong on the merits. Mitch's easy confidence and self-containment had been there before the two of them had ever met; attributing them to so coarse an influence as a substantial investment portfolio—especially as it was hers, not his, and he had insisted that it remain that way despite her stated wish—was a groundless, indeed vile, suspicion on Lolly's part. Mitch Emery had *character*.

Not that he was perfect, mind you. Was anyone? But unlike Lolly, who needed to tell her all about Harry's shortcomings *ad infinitum*, Clara would never have disclosed Mitch's intermittent outbursts of petulance over life's endless little indignities. He was not good about queuing up for anything, for example. Toward clerks on power trips he was detectably resentful—and practically abusive in dealing with mulish bureaucrats, who survived, he would grumble, only because of a severe shortage of quality people willing to devote themselves to public service. His sporadic pouts paled, though, when measured against his virtues, including his good sense, directness, and appreciation of her playful nature. This last tendency, so vital to the instant chemistry between them, was evident when they met six years earlier at a summer weekend party in Amagansett, held by one of Mitch's old Princeton roommates, while he was still an assistant prosecutor in suburban Washington and she was working in the music recording business in New York.

"Why," he asked Clara on their walk together along the beach an hour after they had been introduced, "are Dutch girls so unnecessarily tall? Not that it's unflattering on you, of course, but I'm just curious. The few times I've been to Holland I couldn't help noticing—"

Her gene pool was of mixed nationality, but she had always thought of herself as more Dutch than English, probably because her father, Piet Hoitsma from Delft, had been a more directive force in her life than the former Gladys Tuttle of East Anglia. "You sound intimidated," she said to Mitch, beside whom she stood nearly eye-to-eye. "I could stoop a bit if you'd like."

"Maybe I'll just stand straighter," he said and comically stiffened his spine. "Seriously, though—what is it with Dutch girls—the drinking water? All that cheese? Droste's cocoa?"

Clara decided he was not just making conversation or a clinical observation; the guy really wanted to know. "Since I've probably had a thousand cups of tea for every one of cocoa in my life, we can eliminate that explanation right off."

"Well, then—what? Something to do with wearing wooden shoes in infancy, maybe?"

"A tiresome cliché," she said with a poker face. "Look, we've just met, but I feel I can trust you with a national security secret—okay?"

He nodded, but with eyes narrowing.

"Well, you know how clever the Dutch have been about reclaiming their land from the sea—more than half the country used to be under water five hundred years ago—"

"I had no idea it was as much as that."

"Oh, absolutely. We keep building these immense dikes, then pump out the water with the energy our windmills generate, and finally we plant lots of reeds of a certain species—which cleverly absorb the sea salt from the soil—and after ten years, the land is arable."

"Amazing. But I don't quite see the connection to—"

"I'm getting to it," she said. "The secret part is that the very month that every Dutch girl experiences her first period, she gets fed about a bushel of these salt-gorged reeds—often sautéed with parsnips and garlic—it tastes better than it sounds—and bing-bang-boom, it does something no one can explain to her hormonal secretions, and soon she's sprouting just like the reeds—"

She paused and waited for his response. He looked blank for a long moment, then caught her sly, sideways glance. His whooping, unconditional laughter recommended him to her at once as a promising soul mate.

The rest of the weekend she tried to satisfy his gentle but endless inquiries about who she was and how she got that way. Her parents were at the root of many of the answers she provided. Her dad Piet Hoitsma, she confided, had been embraced as a national paragon when he was barely out of his teens. A daring operative who repeatedly risked his neck sabotaging Nazi cargo truck convoys for the Dutch resistance during the Second World War, he was considered all the more admirable because he never spoke publicly of his heroics. When peace returned, Piet blazed through his studies at the university in Leiden and, through his connections with former agents in British intelligence, won a tuition-free doctorate from the London School of Economics before entering the business world with the Anglo-Dutch giant, Unilever. Transferred from its Amsterdam office to company headquarters in the Blackfriars neighborhood of London, he rose over time to serve as Unilever's chief financial officer, just half a rung beneath the pinnacle of corporate power. Although as a practical matter Piet had become a de facto Brit, he had never relinquished his close ties to the Netherlands and he became a fixture on the board of overseers of the Concertgebouw, Amsterdam's classical music showcase.

While every sprouting inch a young Englishwoman, Clara was awarded dual citizenship at her father's request and spent many a holiday with her Dutch grandparents, sopping up their national and folk heritage. Out of respect for her Hoitsma lineage, she chose her father's alma mater at Leiden over Cambridge, where many of her London friends spent their university years. Her degree with highest honors in fine arts, supplemented by her father's deft pull, won her a job with the Concertgebouw, writing the performance programs and seeing to the care and feeding of visiting artists. From there, she moved to Philips Electronics' classical music division, writing liner notes and arranging recording sessions as she shuttled between London and Amsterdam. When the Philips album label was bought by PolyGram, she found herself transferred—quite willingly—to New York and a churning new environment that she took to at once. She also began to rethink her career path and signed up for graduate studies leading to a doctoral degree in musicology at Columbia. Midway through her course work, she came upon Mitch Emery, then a hotshot young prosecutor for upscale Montgomery County, Maryland. After a year of passionate courting, they married in London, where Piet Hoitsma gave the bride away and, as a wedding gift, a trust fund amounting to mid-seven figures in Unilever and other stocks. Clara put her doctoral studies at Columbia on hold—it would prove to be a three-year hiatus while she worked as a low-level staffer at the National Endowment for the Arts—and the newlyweds moved into a pleasant but hardly extravagant garden apartment in Chevy Chase, not far from Mitch's office.

The couple's first order of business, in working out a *modus vivendi*, was determining how to deal with Clara's trust fund. Mitch, whose job provided enough for them to live on—Clara's modest salary was strictly for extras—wanted nothing to do with her money. "That's yours," he told her. "Your father worked hard to make it and was proud, I'm sure, to be able to present it to you. I'm not interested in living off it or you, sweetheart."

"That's really dumb for you to say," Clara told him, "and you're not really all that dumb, so what's going on? You're annoyed with me because suddenly we're financially independent?"

"I'm not in the least annoyed," he said. "I'm happy for you."

"And what is it you think I'm going to do with my treasure—buy a stable of race horses? Or jet to my two-hundred-foot yacht moored at Piraeus for a weekend spin around the Aegean?"

"Why not berth it on the Chesapeake? Much more convenient—"

"Stop it, Mitch—I'm serious—"

"I'm serious, too," he said. "It's yours, sweetheart—do whatever you'd like with it."

"What I'd *like* is to share it with you—and make our life together more comfortable and pleasurable—I mean, we share everything else. What am I missing, Mitch?"

Her vehemence sent him backpedaling. "I...it's...I don't know exactly. It feels as if I'd be sponging off you or something. I've always been self-reliant—"

"Spongers are leeches—no one could possibly accuse you of that, buddy—"

"I know, but it might spoil me, turn me lazy, rob me of incentive—to, you know, make the best of myself, become more useful, run something..."

"I don't believe that," Clara said. "I think it may actually be sexist. It bothers you that my parents have made me financially self-sufficient—and guys want their women to be dependencies—to be subservient. Admit it!"

Mitch shook his head.

"That's feminist bullshit," he said. "I *like* your independence—you were that way before they set up the trust fund for you. The truth is, your being such an independent character makes you *trés* sexy—but don't let it go to your head."

"Okay, look," she said, dipping her head onto his shoulder, "instead of fighting me on this, why don't you embrace it—help me run the trust fund and figure out how to invest it?"

"I don't know crap about investments," he said. "You should get expert advisers to help you manage it—it's not a toy."

"Hey, we're not talking rocket science here—we can learn together—and no doubt we'd make mistakes together and learn from them. It could actually be fun. That way, you'd be taking a real part of the responsibility—and *earning* whatever uses we put the money to—see?"

His adamancy finally cracked. "Oh, shit," he said. "Okay—I'm on board. Happy?"

"Delirious," she said. "And your manhood will grow back to normal in a month or two."

The annual payout from her trust came to three times his salary. They never discussed the disparity.

Her leftover distaste from lunch with Lolly had fled by the time Clara greeted the doorman to their apartment building and hurried to catch the elevator for the pokey twelve-story climb up to her floor. To unwind once inside their door, she kicked off her shoes, tossed her handbag onto the sofa nearest the piano, and sat at the keyboard, accompanying herself while singing a pair of her favorite Schubert lieder in the original German, one of the five languages in which she was fluent.

Her singing voice was sweet, clear, and always on key, but a touch warbly, so she sang only when alone or, diffidently, with Mitch on a long car trip or after they had killed a bottle of wine over dinner. Her piano playing, on the other hand, was assured and energetic—but a touch too athletic for her to have qualified as a performing artist. So she had chosen to sublimate her love of music by accumulating knowledge of its history, theory, and practice. By now, the fifth year of her marriage, she had completed all the course work and the orals for her Columbia doctorate and was devoting herself, when not trying to scare up funds for Lincoln Center, to research for her dissertation. The task was made more manageable by her ownership of a personal, multi-language music library of nearly a thousand volumes, filling a whole wall in the spare bedroom she and Mitch had designated the study.

She had chosen Franz Schubert as the subject for her doctoral thesis because his brief life struck her as having been so poignant. The twelfth child in his Viennese family, he had struggled to survive without benefit of an indulgent patron, earning his bread as a mere songwriter whose serious compositions were rarely performed in his own lifetime of just thirty-one years. To focus her thesis, Clara had decided to concentrate on Schubert's Ninth Symphony, called "The Great" because it was so much longer, more complex, and accomplished than any of his other works, and right up there with Beethoven's best symphonies.

Mellowed by her piano fix, Clara slipped out of her street clothes and into her running shorts and shoes and headed for the treadmill in the corner of the study. En route, she picked up her iPod, dialed up Schubert's "La Truite," and stuck a notepad on the instructions panel to jot down any insight that came to her while chugging away on the exercise machine. Before boarding it, she lifted her phone receiver and retrieved the single message left for her. It was Mitch, at his breeziest and most winning.

"Hi, you gorgeous, long-stemmed tulip," he said. "Guess I forgot you were chowing down today with the lovely Mrs. C. Hope it went okay. Just remember—you don't have to genuflect on my account. She's Harry's problem, not ours. Speaking of whom, something has come up that Harry wants you in on—for actual consultant's pay. Off what I've heard, though, it sounds like a bad joke, but I'll know more by the time I get home. Here's a hint—take a quick look through your library, in the Beethoven section, and see if you can find anything about Ludwig ever being in Switzerland. Love ya." Click.

She stretched her long limbs for a few minutes while pondering Mitch's curious message, then mounted the treadmill with a sigh and flipped on the iPod to soothe her Lolly-tattered nerves. As the belt began to move, she remembered that Schubert had participated in Beethoven's funeral procession. What turmoil might have overtaken Franz, she wondered, if he had known he would outlive the fallen colossus by just twenty months? Would he have hurried to finish the *Unfinished*? And if he had, would the work have been any more affecting or better loved? She doubted it. Even incomplete, it remained the most delicious fragment in all of music.

She strode on, ramping up the treadmill's speed until it was in sync with the *allegro giusto* of the "Trout" finale. Go, Franz, go.

HE EMERGED FROM THE PARK at Eighty-First Street, strode down Central Park West past the Natural History museum, and turned onto Seventy-Seventh heading for the river. The traffic lights were with him, and he maintained his rapid pace as he swung onto Riverside. Each time Mitch came home, even after two years of living in the building, he was freshly pleased with its location near the downtown end of the drive. True, the wind whipping off the river could turn the street bitter cold in winter, but their apartment's unobstructed Hudson view, ten-foot ceilings, elegant crown moldings, and generous layout more than compensated.

Greeted as usual by a flood of Clara's favorite music pouring out into the foyer, Mitch paused for a moment with his key still in the lock, trying to identify the composer. Debussy? No—Ravel? No, no. Satie? Close. Now he had it— *Poulenc!* She craved the French modernists, F. P. in particular, she had told him, for the way he coursed between jittery atonality and poignant, almost achingly melodic sweetness.

Still in her running shorts, often a signal of further disrobing to follow soon after his arrival, Clara welcomed him with an artfully coordinated hug and kiss, more than dutiful but less than urgent. They were not, after all, newlyweds. "What's the big news at your shop?" she asked and arranged herself cross-legged on one of the living room love seats. "From your message, I'm guessing there's been an Elvis sighting on the Matterhorn, climbing arm in arm with Beethoven. Am I close?"

"Closer than you'd think." Mitch smiled and sat beside her. Trying to mask his disbelief in the implausible saga of the *William Tell* Symphony, he recounted Jake Hassler's visit to the C&W premises in four or five sentences and watched her eyes grow wider with each one.

"Wow!" she said softly but without a dismissive peal of laughter. "Now that's a showstopper." Her brow furrowed. "Was this fellow a madman, do you think—or just your textbook con man?" Clara studied his face as he hesitated before answering. "Wait—don't tell me you masterminds think he's neither one—"

Mitch shrugged. "Well, the guy came prepared, anyway," he said. "The composition books sure look like beatup old music manuscripts—and there was a marked-up copy of Schiller's play about Tell—and our visitor was far from a smooth operator—he seemed pretty earnest, actually, though that could well have been part of the con. Or it's entirely possible he's being set up by some people over there." He reached into his jacket pocket. "Oh, I brought this along for your enlightenment," he added and handed her his copy of the Nina Hassler letter. He watched her eyes drink in the astonishing revelation—or fabrication—with rapid shifts of focus.

"*Incroyable!*" Clara cried at the end and dropped the document onto the cushion beside her. "It's a wonderful—story."

"But totally absurd, you mean?"

"Well—I don't know. It has a certain coherence, I'll have to admit."

"Yes—perhaps too much, is what I'm thinking," he said. "It should be more disjointed—maybe less consciously *composed*—"

"Not necessarily—it says she was writing this for posterity—for any future members of her family, or possibly anyone else, who might find it someday—so this Nina would likely have been quite deliberate in writing it to explain herself—and her story." Clara's mind started shifting gear as she began dissecting the letter's contents. "The thing is," she mused aloud, "I can more easily believe that Beethoven composed such a thing than I can swallow the idea that he just threw it away like that. It's almost inconceivable—"

"But Nina claims—oh, there apparently was a Nina, by the way, according to the Zurich records office—that he thought it was crap, so why keep it?"

"A composer of Beethoven's genius would almost surely have figured that out long before he got so far into it."

Mitch was pleased by her immediate absorption in the matter. "Unless—unless he'd been plugging away in the hope he could fix it and—and finally, when he was ready to head home to Vienna, he decided to cut his losses, so he told Nina to trash it for him. Or—or—what about this? Maybe his hearing, or non-hearing, deceived him—he was getting treatments—they no doubt distracted him, maybe even caused him pain. Or maybe there were extenuating circumstances—as the Nina letter implies—that reference to the *Tell* manuscript being 'too dangerous' for him to proceed with—whatever the hell that was about—"

She looked into his eyes. "You sound a little manic, sweetheart. You're not letting your imagination run away with you, by any chance..." It was more a caution than a dismissal.

"Hardly," he said. "It's just that Harry—supreme skeptic that he generally is—let it be known after we met with this Hassler guy and his lawyer that he thinks it's just possible Cubbage & Wakeham has been blessed with a divine deliverance—and the house could run up a very big score with it. Unless, of course, we take the bait and wind up the laughingstock of the cultural world; Harry recognizes the risk. He asked me if I feel up to the challenge of authenticating the manuscript—or dismissing it as a fraud, with the accompanying risk that another auction house will certify it, presumably because it discovers stuff that we missed and makes a fortune off the commission while we stand around in the cold during the world premiere performance of Beethoven's Tenth." Mitch tried to sound lighthearted. "At the end, Harry added, in his intimidating fashion, 'This could make or break your career with us, Mitchell—I hope you understand that. So if you're at all uneasy about taking on this thing, given your still-limited experience as our authentication honcho—and that music isn't exactly your field of expertise—just say so, and we can bring in someone else.'"

"That sounds like a threat. Why does he have to be such a bastard about it?" Clara asked.

"It's just Harry's sweet way of putting me on my mettle."

"Frankly, I'm surprised he's excited about this—I didn't think he was the gullible sort."

"He's not—he's just your garden-variety grasping entrepreneur. So he's also open to the possibility that Beethoven may have been sufficiently inspired by the Schiller play to try setting it to music—it makes a certain amount of sense to him, given that the *Choral* Symphony ends so euphorically with the Schiller 'Ode to Joy'—"

"But anyone who knows anything about Beethoven knows that much," Clara pointed out, "and any shady types trying to fabricate a Beethoven symphony might bring in the Schiller connection for that very reason—to make a far-fetched idea seem plausible."

"Maybe," Mitch said, nodding slowly. "But Harry was also impressed when I told him what you said about Schubert's Ninth, his greatest work, not being discovered until ten years after his death, so why not a comparable Beethoven find? He also reminded me about that Shakespeare play—what was it, *Edward the Something*—*Edward the Third*, I think he said—that was found only a few years ago. So he's thinking this *William Tell* Symphony may not be entirely off the wall."

Clara shook her head. "That was quite different," she said. "The Shakespeare play—it wasn't suddenly discovered at the bottom of a dry well in the Hebrides or someplace. Scholars knew about it for three hundred years—they just couldn't decide whether Shakespeare wrote it himself or someone else in his company did. Besides, nobody has said it's *good* Shakespeare."

"Hey, nobody's claiming this *Tell* Symphony is good Beethoven," Mitch said a bit irritably. "That would be putting the cart about fifty furlongs before the horse—I'm not that naïve."

"Sorry, sorry." She reached a hand over and squeezed his upper arm. "Look, here's the main thing you all need to face before getting in deeper. We, the world, know virtually everything about Beethoven's whole life. He left a ton of stuff behind—notebooks, diaries, letters, bills, hundreds of pieces and scraps of manuscript, maybe thousands—all of which scholars have been combing over for two hundred years. How come nobody anywhere has found or heard a word about a *William Tell* Symphony until now? The composition books you saw and the old copy of the Schiller play about Tell may look convincing enough, and this confessional letter by Nina Whatsherface may be very appealing, but it's all just too convenient for something of this magnitude to pop up out of the blue."

"Sure," Mitch said and took her hand, "and that's what I get paid for—not to accept anything at face value. But that's the adventure—always looking for gold in a pile of poop."

Clara studied his earnest expression. "Well, I hate to be a party pooper right at the start," she said, "but I did what you asked and looked through about fifteen of my books on Beethoven's life and work, and there's no mention anywhere about his ever having been in Switzerland." She stopped short. "Well, I see this Nina letter more or less addresses that objection—it says his visit to Zurich was supposed to be a big secret, and I guess that makes a degree of sense—Beethoven wouldn't have wanted to advertise just how desperate he was to cure his loss of hearing—a deaf musician is like a blind painter or a tongueless chef." She tilted her head in a gesture of concession. "Well—okay—so what's the plan?"

Mitch tossed off his jacket and tugged her toward him.

"Ah, that's where you come in, my lovely Miss Tulip. *You* are Step One in the master plan."

"Me? Get serious—and I'm not sure I like you calling me Tulip anymore."

"After seven years? Really?" He looked crestfallen. "I thought it was endearing. Tulips are beauteous—and, you know, highly Dutch."

"I get that—and I liked it for a while—but it doesn't work unless I'm in a playful mood."

"How about Stinky, then? Nothing playful about that—"

She gave his arm a mock punch and broke into a broad smile. "Okay, call me whatever you'd like—now what's this Step One?"

The plan, he explained, was for C&W to undertake a preliminary inspection of the *Tell* manuscript and of the leading biographical and musicological studies of Beethoven and his work and habits to determine if, based on the bulk of the evidence, the alleged symphony was an obvious fraud—"or,"

Mitch added, "conceivably authentic by any leap of imagination. The quality of the composition, other than whether it sounds detectably like Beethoven's work product, is not an issue at the beginning of the process. The point is to determine whether we'd need to organize a thoroughgoing examination of this material by a panel of international experts to make a definitive judgment about its authenticity."

This preliminary survey of the standard Beethoven sources, Mitch added, would try to establish, for example, if there was contradictory evidence that the composer was living somewhere other than in Zurich during the summer of 1814; what other creative projects he was known to have been working on during the several months he was purportedly in Switzerland; the known degree of his deafness at that time and if it would have justified his travel to a foreign country for treatment by a specialist, and whether the musical handwriting in the *Tell* manuscript bore a close similarity to Beethoven's recognized style, including his idiosyncratic markings, tempi, and even ink colors. "There must be books available in any decent music library that include illustrations of sample pages showing what his composition books looked like," Mitch speculated, "which, at a guess, were probably pretty distinctive."

"Extremely," Clara said. "His musical penmanship was horrendous, a notorious muck-up that in many places only he could decipher—which may not have been an accident."

"And how do you know that?"

"I own a copy of the leading study of Beethoven's sketchbooks. As I said, scholars have churned out endless volumes about him—there's practically a whole Beethoven industry out there in musical academia."

"Excellent," said Mitch. "That'll give our preliminary investigator a lot to work with right off the bat." He separated himself from her by half a cushion. "We'd like you to start as soon as possible—and sop up as much historical evidence as you possibly can in one seven-day week—a kind of crash course so at the end you can sense whether this thing is worth our bothering with—and investing in a full-scale effort to authenticate it."

Clara gave him a startled deer-in-the-headlights look. "*Me*? That's ridiculous—I'm just a graduate student. You people need a top-flight scholar to make even the most tentative sort of judgment—and, at any rate, it can't be done in a week if it's worth doing at all."

"You're not hearing me, Clara—we'd bring in all the top-flight scholars we might need, starting with an all-star to head up the study group. But right now we need someone who has advanced musical knowledge, and whose period of concentration includes Beethoven's career and the German Romantics—someone who's immediately available and can keep this thing entirely confidential and is a sufficiently accomplished musician to try to read these composition books well enough to figure out if what they contain *sounds* like Beethoven—at least remotely so—and isn't just a jumble of notes intended to pass as something genuine." Mitch opened his palms toward her. "*Voilà*—you fit the bill perfectly, Madam Emery."

She sat back, dazed. "You're serious, aren't you?"

"Absolutely, hon—and don't be so friggin' modest. You're perfect because you'd have more detachment than a Beethoven specialist—but Schubert had a whole lot in common with him, from what you've told me, and was a great admirer of his. Also—and don't let this go to your head—some people think you're going to make a brilliant musicologist someday."

She couldn't help smiling at his ardor. "So you've nominated me for this great honor?"

"No," Mitch said, "this was Harry's idea, I swear. It would have been unprofessional of me to put you up for it. Harry says it's a no-brainer—and I'm not to take no for an answer."

Clara's eyes narrowed. "I don't much like Harry, if you want to know the truth."

"I'm not sure that's relevant at the moment. Anyway, he thinks you're a knockout—and Lolly, of course, sings your praises to him constantly."

"More's the pity," she said ungratefully. "Anyway, I'll bet the main reason Harry wants me is he thinks I'll work for him on the cheap, being a mere grad student—"

"Not so," said Mitch. "He's authorized me to offer you a stipend of five thousand dollars for one week, during which you'll be expected to bust your lovely buns—on a twenty-four seven basis, if necessary. You'll understand that the *Tell* manuscript has to remain under tight security on the C&W premises, so you'll be allowed exclusive occupancy of the top-floor apartment above our offices for the entire time in case you don't want to waste your energy commuting across town—there's a well-tuned baby grand in the apartment, Harry says—and one of the company vans will pick up and haul over to the apartment any of the Beethoven books or other related ones in your library or any other revealing material you may find up at Columbia—where, if I may be so bold, you should go for a search of the music stacks first thing in the morning." His firm would also assign a staffer to see that she was well fed, at company expense, with gourmet cuisine. "They might even let you go out for an hour's walk every day, but no other recreation. It will be a grind, without a doubt."

Clara tried to sort it all out—the suddenness of the challenge, the enormity of the responsibility, the unjustifiably generous assumption of her knowledgeability on Harry's and Mitch's part, the total disruption of her life for a whole nonstop week... "Is this a command performance?" she asked, already wearied by the prospect of such a Herculean labor.

"At least it's not slave labor," Mitch consoled.

She sighed. "And tell me again why the big rush for such a possibly momentous artistic work? Shouldn't the vetting process be done with great deliberation?"

"Sure—and it will be, if you tell us it's worth the trouble. But meanwhile, we don't want to lose the opportunity. The owner has agreed to let us hang onto it for a month to determine if we're willing to go through an exhaustive—and expensive—full-scale investigation."

A sudden fear of inadequacy engulfed her.

"I'm not sure this is such a hot idea," she said quietly, "however much I appreciate the honor—"

"Hey, it's you who'd be doing us a big favor. So why not?"

"Well," she wavered, grasping for an excuse, "for one thing, I can't just drop everything and plunge into this. I've got commitments all week—work time at Lincoln Center, an appointment at my hairdresser—I need a cut badly—and Madge Engler and I have matinée tickets for that Beckett revival you weren't interested in, and oh! We're supposed to have dinner next Tuesday with your dysfunctional cousin and his bimbo—"

Mitch threw up his hands. "Listen, angel, Lincoln Center will survive without your services for a week—and your hair's just fine," he said, raking a hand through it gently. "And Madge can watch those guys in the garbage cans without you. I'll reschedule with Cousin Ken—and let's face it, his lady friend isn't a bimbo—she's a tart."

"Poor thing."

Clara sat back and weighed her final words of objection.

"Look, I'll be excruciatingly honest with you. I don't think it's a good idea for me to intrude upon your business. It's like the separation of Church and State in your Constitution. This is your arena, and I shouldn't get involved stomping all over your turf. No good can come of it—we could have fights, or at least serious disagreements—and when it's all said and done, I may not come out where you and Harry would like me to. Why do we need discord when we've got such a good thing going between us?"

Mitch paused respectfully before taking up her concerns. "First of all, Harry and I have definitely not prejudged this *Tell* thing—it's just intriguing enough to warrant our serious attention, at least initially. Second, there won't be any fights between us—I respect you too much—and I won't try to sway your opinion one way or the other—"

"You can be a wee bit intimidating, darlin', when you've a mind to—and I don't think you even realize it—"

"And you, darlin'," he said evenly, "are not exactly a shrinking violet. But we like that about each other, so cast that aside. As to your intruding onto my turf—no way. You're not intruding, you're being *invited* to share in my business for a brief engagement, not a long-term commitment—because I need you, and I trust your wily brainpower." And he fell still.

Clara pondered for a long moment. "Well," she said finally, "okay—provided you promise we don't say a word about it to each other the whole week I'm working on it—and until after I make my report. Not even a conjugal visit—"

Mitch grinned at her capitulation.

"Whatever Tulip wants, Tulip gets."

"Tulip has to pee just now, so stuff the endearments for a while."

That night, while they were both having trouble falling asleep, Clara lifted her seething head off the pillow and said, as if still in the midst of their earlier conversation, "The thing that gets me is that Ludwig supposedly told this Nina person that he wanted her to throw out the composition notebooks mainly because they weren't good enough. So I'm wondering what gave that girl—or any of her heirs or some fathead who might come into possession of it someday—the right to bring their contents to public attention—and possibly sharp ridicule because the work is such inferior Beethoven? He apparently made his wishes in the matter known to her. Why don't they deserve to be respected?"

His mind churning as busily as hers, Mitch flipped his pillow over and addressed her anguished concern. "But what if he was wrong? He may have been distracted for a whole lot of reasons we'll probably never know—"

"That's not the point. Shouldn't his wishes prevail, however many years have passed? Doesn't posterity owe Beethoven that much respect—assuming for even a moment this really *is* Beethoven's work—or is all this just about the fucking money?"

The same question had occurred to him on his walk home through the park, but he had not allowed himself to dwell on it. "How do we know," he asked back evasively, "that Nina was telling it straight? There's only her word to go on at the moment."

"But if she's lying about why he asked her to get rid of it, who says she's telling the truth about *any* of this? Maybe she stole it—or schemed to get it away from him—or...or..."

He ran his fingers lovingly through her hair. "I think you're hooked, sweetie. Go to sleep, and you can start unsticking this nasty little wicket first thing in the morning."

{4}

Mitch, a practicing lawyer for five years when he first set foot in Gordon Roth's office, had determined at once that its occupant was one of the less conventional, more irreverent practitioners of the trade— and all the better for it.

Not that Cubbage & Wakeham's house counsel (and administrative vice president) was a rebel or radical, but his disdain for orthodox wisdom often cast him in the role of a contrarian or devil's advocate, with Harry Cubbage's encouragement. "I like thinking out of the box," Harry would say by way of explaining Gordy's value to the company despite his superficial quirks. On his only office wall not taken up by windows or bookcases, Gordy had put up three large photographic posters: on the left, Albert Einstein, in all his shaggy glory, sticking his tongue out at the universe; on the right, a tipsy W. C. Fields, top hat askew and winking naughtily; and in the middle, an upside-down Richard Nixon, fuzzily imaged on the TV screen and captioned with the words of his eloquent disclaimer, "I am not a crook." Hanging on the back of his usually closed office door was a heavily pocked dartboard, a deterrent to drop-in visitors who entered at their peril if they forgot to knock. Below the target, a small-framed sign declared, "Dogs Are Entirely Unnecessary." Stacks of legal papers covered nearly every horizontal surface, the floor included, suggesting the resident wizard was either overtaxed by work or functioning in an intergalactic time warp. What Mitch had also learned since joining C&W was that Gordy Roth was a very competent attorney indeed.

Harry was already enthroned in the tufted leather recliner in the corner that Gordy preferred for meditation, so Mitch took the wicker rocker angled at the front of the lawyer's heaped desk. It had been only five days since Jake Hassler and his spellbinding cedar box had appeared on the C&W premises, but Gordy had already completed his preliminary findings on the problematic legal status of the *Tell* manuscript. The results, he told his two colleagues, were somewhat iffy and did not fully dispose of the matter.

"*If* the starting point of our concern is whether Mr. Hassler is the rightful owner of the property and can legitimately ask us to auction it for him," Gordy began, "I think the answer is yes, so far as his grandfather's will is concerned." All family papers and related personal memorabilia had been bequeathed to Jake and exempted from the lien-holding neighbors' claims against the estate. But that, said Gordy, raised the separable question of whether all such papers were Jake's property to do whatever he wished with them. And in the case of a manuscript attributed to Ludwig van Beethoven but evidently never purchased from him or anyone else, the answer might well depend on whether a legitimate heir of the composer suddenly stepped forth now to claim title.

"So we're not primarily concerned about the Erpf family next door?" Harry asked. "Our friend Jake Hassler says they're pissed—especially this Ansel character, the prodigal son."

"They could file a claim, probably without merit on its face, but it might serve to intimidate Jake and discourage us from proceeding until the courts dismiss it."

"And will they?" Harry asked.

"Odds are. I'd have been far more concerned about some obscure Beethoven relative creeping out of the woodwork until my conversation upstairs yesterday with Clara Emery." Gordy gave Mitch the semblance of a salute. "Clara tells me that Beethoven never married and had no known children, and that the male line bearing the family name seems to have ended when his beloved nephew Karl's grandson died in a Vienna army hospital during the First World War." Gordy glanced out the window at C&W's landscaped courtyard, as if communing for a moment with the forces of nature. "Could some presently unknown relative suddenly materialize and claim title to the *Tell* symphony? Possibly—but that seems even less likely than the manuscript itself surviving our investigation unsullied. It's a worry, certainly, but a minor one."

"So if we decide to go for the whole nine yards and conclude that this miraculously uncovered *Tell* Symphony is genuine, we'd need to anticipate some claimant, wacko or otherwise, popping up to challenge Jake Hassler's title to it—and very possibly killing our chance of auctioning it and recovering our investment."

Gordy nodded with approval of his only client's perceptivity. "Or postponing it till any legal challenge is adjudicated. But I wouldn't let that prospect alone deter us. Nut jobs abound."

Of much greater concern, Gordy said, was whether Jake's de facto ownership of the manuscript gave him—or anyone he might sell it to—the power to obtain copyright protection of the work for commercial use. "Selling ownership of the manuscript itself as a genuine artifact is one thing," he said, doodling hoops on his otherwise blank notepad. "But if holding title to the composition fails to convey an accompanying right to license it for public performance and electronic reproduction and sale—I'm talking about creating zillions of records, tapes, CDs, videos, you-name-it—its value at auction would be seriously reduced. With that right intact, however, you'd likely have the whole music industry salivating buckets and willing to pay handsomely for it at a Cubbage & Wakeham auction."

"And so?" Harry asked, betraying no impatience with Gordy's didactic bent.

"First, the bad news." Newly discovered works of art were not typically afforded copyright protection under American law, Gordy advised them, if they were no longer controlled by the creating artist or his or her heirs. "Which seems to mean, so far as I can tell, all that Jake Hassler owns outright—and is entitled to get paid for—is the manuscript itself, in the form of the two sketchbooks he says he found in the box in his grandpa's attic—and not for any copyrightably protected use or commercial exploitation that might eventually be made of them."

"Oh, shit," said Harry. "What's the good news, counselor?"

Gordy turned away from the window to consult a memo beside his notepad. "It would *appear*—under the rules of our glorious US Copyright Office—that anyone owning a newly discovered work of art is entitled to copyright protection thereof if he, she, it, or they *do* something to it—do almost *anything*, the way I read the language of their byzantine rulings." Under a provision covering what the government bureau called "derivative works from newly discovered works," as Gordy interpreted the legalese, copyright protection could be extended to newly found literary manuscripts if they were subsequently edited or translated. Likewise, for freshly uncovered musical compositions that were afterward arranged and/or orchestrated in order to be performed. "And that applies *even if* what the copyright office calls 'the underlying work'—which, in our case, seems to mean what's in Jake's cedar box—cannot, *in its present form*, be copyrighted."

69

Harry slowly digested the hairsplitting technicality. "That sounds stupid, but good," he said after a moment. "So any commercial bidder for the *Tell* manuscript would have to be prepared to invest whatever it takes to get the work into performable shape—which can then be copyrighted—and turned into gold."

"Correct. And Clara tells me—she's trying to get a realistic take on the present condition of the thing—that it looks as if the manuscript was about forty percent orchestrated before the composer quit on it, leaving the balance of the rough draft in need of editing and scoring before it could be copyrighted and performed." Gordy flipped his doodling pencil aside. "And that, Clara says from her superficial examination of it, is likely to prove a formidable task, given the ultra-messy state of the composition book."

"All in all, that doesn't sound like such hot news to me," Harry complained.

"Because you're not paying close enough attention," Gordy chided. "The disheveled state of the other sixty percent of the manuscript may very well work to our advantage as its vendor, because the more effort that needs to be expended to turn the whole thing into a presentable work, the surer the new owner of the manuscript would be of obtaining copyright protection."

Given Clara's warning about the condition of the unscored balance of the manuscript, it seemed to Mitch that the law might raise more difficulties than Gordy was suggesting. "If there's all that much work to be done orchestrating the manuscript in order to bring it artistically and commercially viable," he asked Gordy, "wouldn't that seriously reduce the chances of the symphony being accepted as authentic Beethoven by orthodox scholars and music critics? They might very well argue that the finished product—however good—is a hybrid reworked by modern repairmen, and not pure Beethoven, and therefore question its legitimacy as part of his oeuvre. Which, of course, would negatively affect the bidding at our auction if the recording companies—to name the most likely group of bidders—knew they'd have to foot the bill for all that editing and scoring before this wonderful new *Tell* Symphony could be eligible for copyright protection and ready to be performed."

Gordy spun sideways in his chair and considered Mitch's speculation. "Very possibly, but that's going to depend on what shape the remaining sixty percent of the music is in. Meaning, I suppose—and I'm in over my head here since I know beans about music theory—it matters to what extent the themes and their developmental lines are decipherable in the main composition book— Clara's take at this point is that the basic musical guts of the work *appear* to her to be there, to exist already, but need to be cleaned up and refined, or culled from among several versions of the same passage the composer may have been

70

noodling with, and then the whole thing can be orchestrated without doing violence to what the composer intended."

Gordy's look turned cautionary. "This is pretty technical stuff, and Clara tells me she's underqualified to make more than a wishful guess about all of this— and she's not just being modest since we've all had a look at the composition book and seen what a mess it is."

It pleased Mitch to hear Gordy taking serious note of Clara's views, tentative though they sounded. But it worried him just how fraught with problems the whole project seemed to be. "What I'm hearing," Mitch said, "is that even with a best-case outcome, we wind up in a catch-twenty-two bind. I mean, if too much rejiggering is required to turn the manuscript into a playable—and copyrightable—work, it's by definition no longer completely original Beethoven. But if too little reworking is done, it won't qualify for copyright and/or be performable—is that it?"

"Ahhh," Gordy said, "I see where you're going—and it's a fair point." He glanced down at the memo on his desktop. "But I think we're all right on that." He scanned the top page at laser speed and then the next. "Yeah, okay—here. It says you can qualify for copyright protection 'by virtue of the original effort expended...*even if no new material is added.*' To me, 'original effort' in this case would mean editing and orchestrating the work."

"I love it when you lawyers start playing your weasel-word games," Harry said. "I think I follow what you're both saying, but where exactly, if I may ask, does that leaves us?"

Gordy sat back. "I'd say we're still very much in the game—if we want to be."

Harry rubbed his chin. "Pretty dicey stuff, though." He tossed Mitch a quick look. "I think it's time for you to pay a visit to our diamond-in-the-rough in the Jersey outback to see if we've missed something about this Jake Hassler."

A SQUAT, RUDDY BLUR OF PURPOSEFUL MOTION, Jake Hassler resembled nothing so much as a spinning fireplug. His navy-blue T-shirt, tucked into faded jeans, advertised "Sylvan Lumber & Hardware" in no-nonsense white block letters. One hand locked onto a cellphone that he was chattering into, the other signing a receipt from a hovering deliveryman, he had a manic busyness about him that seemed to energize the whole establishment.

Mitch edged closer to him, counter by counter, pausing in front of a long row of kegs each holding a different caliber of brads or nails. Backing toward his prey, Mitch sensed that the present owner of the *William Tell* Symphony was every inch in his element. Jake greeted by name, a wave, or a slap on the hand fully half the customers milling about the hardware section of the sprawling store. Peppered by rapid-fire questioning from every side, he was a human whirligig. His aging choirboy face betrayed an underlying gravity that suggested his job meant a lot to Jake Hassler and he was not about to screw it up.

Mitch waited for him to find a few minutes of relative repose in a corner of the garden tools section, where he was leaning against a rack of rakes and shovels and checking off model numbers in a slick-paged order catalogue. "Nice merchandise," he said to Jake. "Looks like the department head knows his stuff."

Jake glanced up, took in Mitch's open-collar polo shirt and birdman sunglasses, and tried unsuccessfully to place their wearer. "Sorry," he said, "you look familiar, but my friggin' age must be catching up with me. Remind me again who you—"

Mitch reintroduced himself, and far from looking as if he'd been ambushed, Jake greeted him cheerfully and ushered him to his disorderly cubbyhole of an office, where he shut the door behind them. "Nobody around here knows about the—you-know-what—and I'd just as soon keep it that way for now." Jake grabbed a stack of order forms off the fold-up chair beside his desk and invited his visitor to take a load off. "Hey, I didn't think I'd be seeing you again so fast, but I'm glad you guys are into it. The sooner, the better, right?"

"Right," Mitch said, then apologized for not having phoned ahead, claiming that he had a few days of business to attend to in Trenton and thought he'd stop by since it was so close. Before long, Jake was saying he wished he could give Mitch the time to go into whatever was on his mind, but since he was up to his eyeballs at the moment, why not come by his house after work—"we'll do some dogs and burgers out back—if you don't mind peasant food." Mitch said not at all, and the next instant Jake dialed his wife to say they were having a dinner guest.

Mitch killed a couple of hours at the little Lambertville library by sifting through back numbers of the local weekly paper in a random search for any mention of the Hasslers or Jake's employer, but found none. A leisurely swing through the sweet-smelling countryside brought him back to his red-meat rendezvous just before six. Daisy Hassler, a curly-haired charmer, greeted him no less hospitably than her husband had, but with a more amusing turn of phrase.

"Jake is definitely into this Swiss thing," she confided after he had wandered off to their basement to get charcoal for the grill, "ever since he got back from the funeral." He kept repeating to her how Switzerland set the world standard for banks, trains, watches, cutlery, and milk chocolate, hosted the planet's biggest food company as well as the Red Cross, UNESCO, and the League of Nations—"I'm not sure he knows the League's been dead since before he was born," she quipped at Jake's expense—and was presently the oldest, still-running democracy on earth. "It's got to the point where every night he flips through the Bean catalogue asking how come they don't carry *lederhosen.*"

Their house, on a quiet stretch of country road going nowhere, was a bare-bones affair about a century old that served as a showcase for Daisy's skill in the decorative arts. Owner of an interior design business run in conjunction with an upscale antique shop in nearby Hopewell, she had enlivened the place with pickled-pine floors, beaded wainscoting, floral print curtains, and stenciled grape vines and cornucopias parading around the top of the kitchen and breakfast nook walls. The furniture was a covey of unrelated antique pieces, the floors covered with oval braided rugs, and the walls draped with appliquéd album quilts. Not Mitch and Clara's style, to be sure, but he appreciated its studied coziness.

Over the cookout supper taken on their small, screened porch, the Hasslers volunteered most of what Mitch wanted to know about them. They were not rich but certainly not poor, thanks to a double income that had allowed them to retire their mortgage a few years back, lease Daisy a Chevy wagon for her business, and send a small gift of cash every now and then to their two grown children. The older, a bachelor son, had overcome a drug habit and a minor run-in with the law—an indiscreet disclosure on Jake's part that drew Daisy's frown. "Mitch here, he'd find out anyway if he snoops around," Jake told her by way of excusing himself. Their troubled firstborn had reformed and now worked on Long Island as a delivery driver for a big construction outfit. Their married daughter was a registered nurse in Albany and expecting a second child in the fall. "It's not that the kids can't get by on what they make," Jake added, "but it's nice we can help 'em out a little."

A devoted family man, from the sound of it, with a pleasing knack for cutting through polite society's pretensions to say his piece, Jake Hassler was growing on Mitch as an amiable character and a most unlikely conspirator in some convoluted international fraud. Yet each new bottle of Sam Adams passing through Jake's lips—Mitch was beginning to lose count of them—revved up a torrent of profane, less-than-comforting revelations. Among these was a big, throbbing vein of resentment toward his customers ("bunch of royal assholes, most of 'em"), his employer ("a prick and a half—and that's on his good days"), his lawyer ("a buttoned-down rip-off artist"), and anyone else he suspected of slighting him as a social or mental cipher.

After a dessert offering of Dove bars, which Mitch regretfully declined, Jake asked him, in the midst of wolfing down the thickly chocolate-coated treat, where he was spending the night—"not that it's any of my friggin' business." When Mitch answered that he would be heading off shortly to check in at the Bon Soir Motel on Route 31, Daisy impulsively urged, "Stay here—we've got two empty bedrooms and a full bath on the third floor."

It was not the sort of gesture made by people with something to hide. Furthermore, Mitch thought, it might serve his purpose to observe the couple closeup for a bit longer, so he accepted the invitation with grace.

Judging by the contents of the small bookcase in the living room alcove that served more importantly as their TV den, the Hasslers' literary tastes ran to Civil War history, the full range of home carpentry, mysteries featuring female detectives, and Tom Clancy state-of-the-art weaponry novels. Their taste in movies—Jake's, anyway, probably—was reflected by a CD of *Independence Day* that he had brought home to play some evening. Having responded at tireless length to all his guest's inquiries, Jake invited him to join them in watching the film, part of the genre of blockbuster movies featuring mindless violence, superfluous profanity, gratuitous sex, and stupefying special effects—the sort of thing Mitch and Clara studiously avoided. But under the circumstances he could not be finicky. As it turned out, he outlasted both Daisy, who, to her credit, slipped away before the film was a quarter over, and Jake, who was snoring away like a balky chainsaw long before the finale.

Unmonitored, Mitch scanned the first floor for any sign of knavery. He had about abandoned the all-but-pointless search when his eye brushed over a book spread face-down on the small round table next to the larger of the two parlor armchairs. Gliding across the room to examine the book, he discovered that it was an English translation of Schiller's play, *William Tell,* published by the University of Chicago Press, no less. The English translation was based on an old German edition of the same play that Jake said he had found in the cedar box in his grandfather's attic trunk. Not the sort of fare, apparently, that the Hasslers usually turned to for pleasure reading. On loan from the Mercer County Library System, the book had been taken out only recently, Mitch could see from the due date stamped on the slip inside the back cover. Interesting. The presence of the volume signaled an intellectual curiosity on Jake's or Daisy's part, or perhaps of both, that he would not have suspected.

"It's heavy going," Daisy said, startling him. She had finished her kitchen chores and come up behind him noiselessly. "I give Jake a lot of credit—he wanted to see what it was all about—since this Beethoven symphony is supposed to be based on this play."

"Makes sense," said Mitch, recovering his nonchalance. "Never read Schiller myself."

"I got through most of it—not bad. I guess Beethoven didn't dig comedy all that much."

"Not from what I hear."

She ran a hand through her hair to tame a wandering curl. "Do you people think—I mean, is there any way of telling for sure if the manuscript is really real?"

Nothing coy about the woman. "It *would* be amazing, wouldn't it?" Mitch said noncommittally. "What do you think?"

Daisy gave her head a saucy tilt. "How on earth would I know?"

"What's your gut feeling?"

Daisy sighed. "Honestly?"

"Sure."

"I'm afraid it's too good to be true—though I guess weirder things have happened." She sat on the arm of the chair beside them. "But it sounds like you people think it's a phony."

Her directness was disarming.

"Not necessarily. It's our professional responsibility to be suspicious, especially with something that's this...extraordinary."

"We get that. But it sure makes Jake edgy. He's got high blood pressure already, and this whole business has his numbers spiking. I mean, it's not as if he went looking for this thing. Jake likes to think of himself as very honest—he told me he was conflicted as hell about what to do with the—with all the stuff in the attic trunk—he phoned me from over there. I guess I was the one who put him up to it—to just take it and not ask any more questions and bring it home— and then we'd sort out what to do with it. He keeps hoping it'll be our winning lottery ticket, so we won't have to work so hard or worry any more."

Mitch studied her pert, pretty face and saw nothing artful behind it. He noted Jake's place in the Schiller book and asked her if he might borrow it overnight. "Might be a good way to fall asleep—and maybe I'll learn something first."

"Yeah—that Willy Tell wasn't any too bright." Daisy tapped the book accusingly. "I mean, what kind of father would let his son be used for target practice? He should've turned on the evil governor or bailiff or whatever that Gessler guy was and zinged him through the neck."

"I'll get back to you on that," he said and headed up to bed with a grateful goodnight.

Absorbing every line took him two hours to complete the play. Schiller was definitely no Shakespeare, Mitch decided five or six pages into *Tell*. For all its heavy-breathing histrionics and clunky exposition, though, the tale of the Swiss yeomanry rising up against the oppressive officers of the Austrian emperor all those centuries long past had a fervent moral idealism that came shining through. But what, Mitch wondered when he reached the end, could possibly have possessed the German-born Beethoven, who he knew had moved to Vienna in hopes of winning fame and fortune, ever to write a symphony celebrating the return of freedom stolen from the Swiss by the ancestors of those very same Austrians who had cordially welcomed the composer into their midst? Might the answer hold the key to whether *Tell* was authentic or counterfeit?

Still dressed when he finished the Schiller play, Mitch went quietly downstairs to replace the book. Guided on his route by a glass-shaded desk lamp that the Hasslers kept on all night, he could hardly help noticing the small stack of opened bills awaiting payment on the desktop blotter. Where was the line between pressing the investigative advantage his hosts had handed him by their hospitality and trespassing on their privacy? Time did not allow him the luxury to philosophize on the question. Instead, he seized the opportunity to thumb hurriedly through the pile of bills, looking for suspicious creditors. None leapt out at him. The telephone bill, on second thought, invited further scrutiny. He slid it out of its envelope and located the pages listing long-distance charges. Just two phone numbers recurred. From their area codes, he guessed that they belonged to the Hasslers' son and daughter. But then he saw it: a single anomalous entry for an overseas number with an unfamiliar national prefix. He took down the number and date of the call on a scrap of paper he grabbed from the wastebasket beneath the desk, replaced the bill in its envelope and the envelope in its previous place in the sequence—between the gas and electric company and Blue Cross statements—and dropped the pile onto the blotter in approximately its former state of random array. Then he made his way back up to the third floor as weightlessly catlike as he could manage. Too many telltale stair creaks testified that he was no feline. And that his detective skills needed honing.

By six thirty, he was up and on his cell phone. It took five rings to rouse his assistant at her home number. He spoke softly, on guard not to be overheard by his hosts. "Sorry to call so early, Miranda—it's Mitch. I need a little help on the double." There was a fuzzy noise in response that he took for at least semiconscious alertness. "Stick your head under the cold water tap and then call Johnny Winks. Ask him to please check with his reverse phone book sources for the name of the party who has the number I'm going to give you—I believe it's in the vicinity of Zurich, Switzerland. Then let him look up the number or numbers there under the name Erpf—that's E-R-P-F—in particular for Ansel or the initial A—but any first name'll do. There can't be more than fifty living Erpfs, and probably just a handful. Ask him to get back to you ASAP—then call me on the cell as soon as you hear."

He gave her the overseas number listed on the Hasslers' phone bill along with one retrieved from his cellphone belonging to Johannes Winkelmann, Geneva-based former Interpol agent, later UNESCO security officer, now arguably the most resourceful private investigator in the German-speaking sector of the continent. Johnny Winks, as everyone at Cubbage & Wakeham called Herr Winkelmann, was a master of the black arts of financial espionage, in particular the simple bribery of well-placed insiders at every data depot from Hamburg to Lugano to Eisenstadt. Mitch had enlisted Johnny in the *Tell* matter earlier in the week after Harry and Sedge Wakeham in London had conferred and agreed to see how the early stages of the investigation played out. As expensive as he was productive, Johnny had already begun nosing around the Erpfs' Zurich neighborhood and poking into their family dynamics.

By the time Mitch had showered, dressed, phoned Clara to see if all was well, and come downstairs for breakfast, Daisy had already left for a decorating job up in Somerset County. Jake offered his guest juice, toasted muffins, coffee, and minimal conversation first thing in the morning, preferring to commune with the *Trenton Times*. Mitch wondered whether his late-night prowling around the house had been detected and resented, or if Jake minded that his city guest had borrowed the Schiller play. Neither seemed likely, so he risked breaking the ice by mentioning that he'd read *William Tell* overnight and wondered what Jake thought of it so far.

"Hey, yeah, I'm pluggin' right along like a snail," he replied, "but I like it so far. Daisy gave up on it when this birdbrain Tell shot the apple off his kid's head—she said he shoulda been shot himself for that." What got to Jake more was Tell's apparent stupidity after he'd managed to split the apple and not his boy Walter's noggin. "What kind of nitwit hides a second arrow under his shirt, lets this Gessler creep spot it, then *admits*—for crissakes—*admits* that the second arrow was meant for Gessler if the boy got hurt? Naturally they haul his ass off to jail. But the Austrians are even dumber. They stick Tell in this boat to sail him across the lake to jail, and when this big storm blows in, they take off Tell's chains and hand him the tiller because he's the strongest bozo on board. So he steers in close to shore, jumps out onto a rock, grabs his bow, which they left conveniently nearby, and shoves the idiot Austrians back out into the lake." Jake shook his head. "I mean, gimme a break, pal."

Having determined that Jake was no subscriber to poetic license, Mitch switched to a more pressing subject.

"By the way," he began in as low a key as he could manage, "I should tell you there's some concern at our office that your connection with Ansel Erpf may be more complicated than you've told us." It was a ploy that seemed worth trying.

Jake took a final gulp of coffee and put his cup down slowly. "What the fuck is that supposed to mean?" he asked with a touch of truculence.

"Let me try to reword it," Mitch backpedaled. "It could be seen by some people as more than strictly coincidental that this fellow living right next door to your grandfather's house just happened to be hanging around with you when this amazing discovery was made—he may even have led you to the attic trunk without your realizing it. And then, lo and behold, he turns out to be a musician who, with a little effort, figures out the big deal in the box and alerts you to it."

Jake frowned. "What—you guys are still thinkin' Ansel knew what was in there and *wanted* me to find it?"

"It's a possibility."

"But why?"

"That's another question."

"But if it was a plant for me to find, why was he so pissed when I took off with it?"

"Maybe because you weren't expected to grab the box and take it home. Maybe they had hoped to use you, deal with you in some way or other, and you fouled up their plans."

Jake's well-scrubbed face was wreathed in bafflement.

"I don't see how."

Mitch's cellphone went off in timely fashion. He answered without seeking privacy out of Jake's earshot. Miranda's message was short and sweet: "Bingo! The number you gave me is for Ansel Erpf's phone, and Johnny says it's unlisted so it cost him a lot extra to find."

"That's fine," Mitch told her. "Please tell Mr. Olmstead I'm tied up with other business, and I'll be in touch next week sometime." He put the phone away and readdressed his host, at pains not to disclose his freshly fed suspicion just yet. "I know it's dumb, but there's one person in our office who even thinks it's possible that you and Ansel—and maybe some people he's in cahoots with—may all be working together and want to use Cubbage & Wakeham to, well, legitimize your big discovery, which may not have been a discovery at all. Or maybe these other operators enlisted Ansel and you to carry out their scheme and cut you both in on it as a payoff for your cooperation."

"That's total bullshit!" Jake cried, steaming now.

"That's what I told them," Mitch said, spreading out the bait, "but then word came in that you and Ansel talked on the phone not long after you got back home, and nobody at our place can figure out why that would be if you weren't somehow in this thing together—instead of at odds over your having taken off with the manuscript."

Jake tossed his newspaper onto the table. "Is that what this is all about?" His already elevated blood pressure was getting a workout. "And anyway, who *says* I spoke to him?"

"Did you?"

"I—well—he called me, actually—"

Mitch folded his hands patiently and deposited them on the table. "Actually, the phone records we've checked show that you called him, Jake—using his private number."

"I did? Yeah, okay—I didn't remember—"

Mitch nodded, trying to ease him off the hook. "Remembering it right would be good."

"Right—okay—I gotcha."

"How did you happen to have his private number if you weren't—aren't—involved somehow with Ansel Erpf?"

Jake's face calmed. "Oh, that's easy—Ansel passed on his number to old man Schacht, my grandpa's lawyer. The way it happened was Ansel's family lawyer talked to Schacht, like we told you people, and besides letting me know the Erpfs were pissed because I took the manuscript, which they figured was rightfully theirs, and left the country, I was invited to phone Ansel if I changed my mind and wanted to work out something—meaning, you know, maybe we'd split whatever a new Beethoven symphony might be worth. Schacht said I should work through him, but, well, I thought maybe it would be better if I talked directly to Ansel to explain why I'd taken the box and blew out of town—and why we need the money a lot—if there *is* any coming out of this whole friggin' thing. So I called him."

79

"And how did Ansel respond?"

"He sounded out of it, like he was stoned or something. He just said, 'Yeah, yeah—you're just a plain crook, Jacob'—stuff like that. I gave up after a few minutes."

Mitch wore his most compassionate face. "Were you just putting Ansel on, or is there some special need you folks have, something you didn't care to share with us at our office last week, that might give us a better read on your whole situation? It's not a good idea to try to bullshit us, Jake, or conceal information if you want us to work with you."

Jake threw up his hands and the next minute was spilling his heart out. He and Daisy had two big problems at the moment, and the Beethoven discovery seemed as if it might be a heaven-sent cure for both. His wife was afraid she might soon lose her business over a lawsuit brought by a client claiming that a foyer chandelier improperly installed by a workman Daisy hired had fallen, narrowly missing her but definitely crushing their beloved family cat dozing on the rug directly under the fixture. Daisy's insurance company was balking over a settlement, so she had hired Owen Whittaker from a good Princeton firm to defend her—"and they get pretty fat fees." On top of which the Hasslers were worried sick about their granddaughter in upstate New York, who had lately been found to have a heart aneurysm. Her family's HMO was unwilling to allow the case to be handled by an out-of-group surgeon in whom the Hasslers' daughter, an experienced RN, reposed the utmost confidence. "Which means we may have to pony up some big bucks to help the family out," Jake said mournfully. "So I asked Whittaker if there was some way—without putting us in deep hock—he could get involved, and he says maybe, if it doesn't ear up his time, the firm would let him handle it on a—whatchacallit basis—contingency—"

"Would you mind our knowing the particulars?"

Jake gave a seemingly guileless shrug. "The deal is he gets fifteen percent of anything we make off the manuscript—and nothing if it doesn't pan out. Which is okay, I guess, but then when I found out the Erpfs were making trouble and might even take me to court for grabbing *their* property—which is a big fat joke if you ask me—I figured Whittaker wouldn't be up for defending us in *two* suits—Daisy's *and* mine—not on a contingency deal, anyway. So I thought I'd call Ansel to ask if maybe his family would settle for, like, ten percent of whatever price I could get for selling the manuscript—which would've meant ten for them, fifteen for Whittaker, and ten for your firm." Jake's pain-pinched expression registered his level of enthusiasm for the deal. "Daisy and I figure that sixty-five percent of something is a lot better than—you know—zippo. But Ansel wasn't focusing when I phoned—and, anyway, his people are rolling in money. It would just be some kinda power trip for them if they really try to come after me." He sighed. "Now you know all our aggravation—see why I didn't want to lay it on you guys?"

Mitch took a final swig of his coffee. "So long as you were trying to make a deal with Ansel and, considering that his family is loaded, why not get your lawyer over there to tell the Erpfs that you were planning to bring the manuscript to us to auction it, but maybe you'd give them first shot at buying it from you instead?"

"Yeah, I thought of that—except Daisy and I—we didn't have a clue about what the thing is worth—I still don't—so Whittaker said maybe an auction through you people was the way to go and not to worry about Ansel and his people until we had to."

Mitch had met his share of accomplished liars, and Jake Hassler did not fit the bill. Still, his story required substantiation; everyone's did. "How unhappy would you be," he asked, "if I said I'll need to phone your daughter—very briefly—just to, well—you can understand—"

"You think I'd make up something like *that?*" Jake demanded. "About my own *granddaughter* having a serious medical situation?"

"Sorry," Mitch said, "but people in difficulty sometimes do or say things they never would otherwise. I'd rather be straightforward with you, Jake, than call behind your back."

"Thanks a bunch." Jake shook his head, more in sadness than anger. "Fuck it—and fuck you guys, too, but I guess you're in a shitty business, dealing with a lot of creeps." He reeled off his daughter's phone number, adding, "But don't mention Beethoven—she's liable to blab it around out of, ya know, excitement—"

Mitch shook off Jake's disclosure and rose from the table.

"I won't be needing to call her now," he said, extending his hand in thanks. "Only if you'd refused to give me the number."

At Daisy's shop, her assistant told him the proprietor was out for the morning on a decorating job. When Mitch said he was with the insurance company handling the claim for "the chandelier accident," the assistant grew wary, said, "Oh, that," and invited him to come back in the afternoon or leave his card. Which was all that Mitch really needed to hear by way of corroborating the other part of Jake's tale of family woes. "Next time I'll call ahead," he said, adding that it was just a routine question, and thanked the young woman.

Back at his New York office, he placed a call to Jake's attorney. "As a lawyer myself," said Mitch, "I'd never dream of asking you about your fee arrangement with Jake Hassler—it's obviously a private matter under lawyer-client privilege. But in this case, it goes directly to your client's veracity—and if his truthfulness is questionable in one area that's easy to check out—the one I'm asking you about—it casts a shadow over the much thornier business of this *Tell* manuscript and the circumstances surrounding it."

"What is it you want to know, Mr. Emery?" Owen Whittaker asked, his use of Mitch's last name suggesting that their relationship was on the brink of turning adversarial. He listened to Mitch replay his breakfast-table conversation with Jake, mulled it for a moment, then said, "You're right—my arrangement with Mr. Hassler is none of your business. But I appreciate your directness in coming to me, so I don't mind confirming what Jake told you about our agreement. I didn't know Jake had tried to work out a deal with the Zurich family, but I don't blame him for having tried, do you?"

"Not in the least—only that's not what I'm mostly concerned about."

"You think he's making things up to cover some sinister connection with his grandfather's neighbors—is that it?"

"We have to consider every possibility."

"I don't know him all that well, Mitchell, but my sense is that you'd have to check out half the human race before finding a straighter-shooting guy than Jake Hassler. I could be wrong, though. Do your thing—we've all got a vested interest in the outcome."

{5}

Afternoon their week apart, except for the nightly one-hour break Clara permitted herself for sharing her delivered dinner with him in C&W's plush top-floor apartment, Mitch was aroused at the sight of her in the tight jeans and loose sweatshirt she favored when working in private. At ten on the dot, she joined him, Harry, and Gordy, already seated in the high-ceilinged company library, handed each of them a printout of her twenty-five-page report, brushed a kiss off Mitch's cheek as she slid past him, and took her seat at the far end of the conference table.

Clara had laid down only two rules for their brief private soirées in the company apartment—no physical contact beyond a brief nuzzle and no Beethoven talk whatever. "I don't want you to direct me, sway me, question me, or anything me," she insisted, "or the deal's off." Mitch respectfully nodded while crossing his heart. As a result, he had no more idea than his two senior colleagues about where her research had taken her.

"I've made just seven copies of my findings," Clara said crisply, "the four in this room and three extras I have in my case here and will give to Mr. Cubbage when we're done. In the interests of internal security, I've deleted this document file from the PC in the apartment that I was told to use to write my report and scrubbed it from the recycle bin as well."

"What a trooper," Harry said approvingly, noting Clara's pulled-together manner and appearance after her marathon research ordeal. "Coffee *pour madame*? Perhaps an IV drip?"

"Just a glass of ice water, thanks," she said, "and maybe a week in Bermuda."

Harry relayed the first half of the request by intercom and cautioned his colleagues not to mention the subject of their meeting while the waterbearing staff assistant was briefly in the room. "And you can dispense with the formalities, Clara—you're among friends. So I would be Harry, this doodler over here would be Gordon, and the other gentleman I call Mitchell but you're free to address any way you'd like except 'Darling'—not businesslike." He smiled and added, "Relax, my dear—only admirers are in the room."

Still standing, she acknowledged his cordiality with a nod and waited while four crystal goblets and a water pitcher were speedily delivered and Gordy half-filled one for her. She took a sip, flexed her neck slightly, and looked toward the other end of the table. "How do you want to do this—Harry? Shall I read all of this aloud and any of you can stop me whenever something's unclear or you have a question? Or shall I synopsize it and then let you review the whole text at your leisure after this meeting?" She was careful to pitch her voice low, Mitch noted.

"Let's spare your vocal cords," Harry said. "We'll all read it to ourselves a paragraph at a time—no subvocalizing, please, gentlemen—and raise any questions or make comments in case we need you to further elucidate us before we move on, with all deliberate speed."

"Fine," said Clara. "And sorry about the length of the report. I thought it better to err on the side of excess than—than to try to—"

"You're a scholar—it's expected," Harry said in tribute. "Curtain up, Clara."

Her report, she explained, was in three sections, dealing with (1) Beethoven's hearing in the summer of 1814 when he was supposedly in Zurich for treatment by an ear specialist, (2) the composer's whereabouts that summer and what he was working on, and (3) the appearance of the *Tell* Symphony sketchbooks compared to certified Beethoven manuscripts. Clara's text began with a short aside to place the challenge before them in historical perspective:

> The seductive notion of a long-lost Tenth Symphony by the undisputed master of that compositional form is something of an old chestnut in classical music circles—probably starting with the posthumous discovery of Schubert's Eighth and Ninth symphonies and further fueled by the similar finding of Mahler's Tenth.
>
> That Beethoven had spoken of and made notes for a Tenth Symphony in the last years of his life is well known. Nearly two hundred years later, the British actor and playwright Peter Ustinov wrote a comedy titled *Beethoven's Tenth*, performed briefly on the West

Coast before it was laid to rest. A few years later, British musicologist Barry Cooper came upon several hundred bars of what was thought to be the first movement of an uncompleted symphony found in one of Beethoven's four hundred or so authenticated sketchbooks. Cooper took it upon himself to complete the movement as he assumed Beethoven had in mind, then got the collaborative work performed by the National Symphony in Washington. The critics by and large dismissed the attempt for its cheekiness, arguing that no one could know how anyone of Beethoven's unrivaled virtuosity might have resolved his musical lines, since unpredictability was an essential ingredient of his music. Researchers have discovered that on some fifty occasions Beethoven started symphonies only to cast them aside. But none of these efforts thus far uncovered amounted to more than a musical fragment.

Harry looked up. "Well, if this Cooper fellow got roasted for working off material that was understood to be authentic Beethoven, wouldn't anyone drawing on the *Tell* sketchbooks face the same sort of criticism—for daring to presume how the greatest maestro of all would have finished a symphony he abandoned?"

Clara nodded. "But Cooper was dealing with just a part of one movement and trying to interpolate a plausible completion. Here we're dealing with what purports to be quite a different thing—all the elements for the entire work appear—*appear*—to be contained in these two *William Tell* sketchbooks, although only about forty percent had been orchestrated by the composer when he allegedly abandoned it. I think Cooper's procedure was far more conjectural."

"But still a worry for us," Harry persisted, "correct?"

"Sure, but a relatively small one *if* your authentication experts conclude that *Tell* is actually Beethoven's work product." Clara clasped her hands on the tabletop in front of her. "All I'm pointing out at the beginning is that the notion of a lost Tenth Symphony by Beethoven has been floating out there for a long time—but none of the posthumously found fragments of his work has risen to anywhere near the level of what we're being asked to believe in this case."

"Which should give us more reason, not less, to question the genuineness of this thing, correct?" Harry asked.

"Absolutely," Clara replied. "The very idea of it would be immensely alluring to a bold—and greatly knowledgeable—counterfeiter. But, that said, such a remarkable discovery shouldn't be ruled out in the abstract. You need to deal with what's at hand."

"Quite so," said Harry and resumed reading the first section of Clara's report, dealing with the genesis of the *Tell* manuscript:

It can be stated unequivocally that by the summer of 1814, Beethoven's hearing had so badly deteriorated as to warrant his undertaking an extended trip to Switzerland or anyplace else in hope of finding a miracle cure. This finding is based on evidence gleaned from some six dozen books dealing with Beethoven's life, letters, diaries, notebooks, and compositional techniques.

Beethoven's loss of hearing began in 1801 when he was thirty-one years old and was sometimes marked by what he described as a "hum and buzz day and night." Initial diagnoses linked the problem to his chronic diarrhea, and he was administered infusions of medicated powders. Subsequent examinations found the presence of what modern science calls otosclerosis, slow growth of spongy bone in the inner ear, causing intermittent, progressive, and irreversible destruction of the auditory nerves, confirmed by autopsy at Beethoven's death in 1827.

His deepening deafness became a chronic source of embarrassment socially and professionally. "I find it impossible to say to people I am deaf," he wrote. "If I had any other profession I might be able to cope with my infirmity; but in my profession it is a terrible handicap." His encroaching isolation brought on lingering spells of irritability, melancholy, and even suicidal thoughts that led others to mistake him for a misanthrope. And yet, miraculously— what else should we call it?—during the decade preceding the alleged creation of the *Tell* Symphony, this man produced no fewer than thirty incontestable masterpieces, including six of the greatest symphonies ever written, and changed the course of musical history.

Beethoven's hearing loss turned precipitous by 1812, and within two years, he could no longer perform in public either as a pianist, who had formerly been regarded as among the very best in Europe, or as a conductor without embarrassing himself. Thus, the anguished composer had reached a point of such desperation that he would likely have considered making a visit to a neighboring country to seek any therapy that could have reversed his hearing loss.

"But what do we know for sure about where Beethoven spent that summer of 1814," Clara's report asked, "and whether he might have gone to Zurich then for such a purpose?"

It was highly unusual, she explained, for the maestro to leave Vienna at any time for any reason—except during summertime when he sought refuge from the heat by staying at a spa in Bohemia or, more usually, in the resort of Baden just twenty-five miles from the capital, where many of his aristocratic and socialite friends repaired for the season. It was over the summer, away from the city's bustle and distractions, that Beethoven was in the habit of sketching out the primary thematic lines of his compositions, which he would refine and score upon his return to Vienna. "Most Beethoven biographers and students of his life have assumed that the composer spent nearly the whole summer of 1814 in Baden," Clara added, starting right after the July 18 performance, given in Vienna for Beethoven's own financial benefit, of his only opera, *Fidelio,* which included for the first time a new overture and other material he had written earlier in the year. But was there any hard evidence that he had in fact been in Baden or, for that matter, had stayed in Vienna or perhaps gone someplace else? "For the years surrounding and including 1814," Clara disclosed, in answer to her own question, the maestro was known to have kept a *Tagebuch*, or diary, that chronicled his activities. But as luck would have it, the diary has disappeared from the Berlin archive in which it once resided, forcing scholars to fill in the details from letters and other scraps of documentation. Let us see what these tell us.

At Baden, he would most likely have stayed in a rented private cottage or at his favorite hotel, the Alter Sauerhof—but there is no surviving evidence that he did either. And while it has long been known that from 1804 until 1815 Beethoven made the fourth-floor flat in the Vienna home of a Baron Pasqualati his main residence, the encyclopedic, well-respected *Beethoven Compendium* states that for September and October of 1814, the maestro's address was simply "unknown."

"Mmmm," said Harry, "the plot begins to thicken."

Clara looked up and saw that the men's eyes were now riveted on her. "Well," she said, "it's somewhat suggestive, anyway." And Beethoven's correspondence from the period in question was equally tantalizing. In a published volume of his collected letters was one missive that scholars dated "Summer 1814," but no more specifically, in which Beethoven wrote to his principal music publisher, "At last my wish is granted, and I go the day after tomorrow for an excursion of a few days"—yet he made no mention of where he was going. "If he had wished to make a clandestine visit to Zurich for health reasons," Clara theorized,

"Beethoven would very likely have been purposely vague about his travel plans, as he was in this case."

In a second letter datelined August 8 from Vienna—"by which time, Nina Hassler's letter has him installed in Zurich," Clara reminded her readers—and sent to Prague, Beethoven asked his attorney there to settle a lawsuit against the delinquent heirs of one of the maestro's prominent patrons. "Why, one may wonder, would Beethoven have been in Vienna at the height of the summer," Clara asked, "when he was customarily at Baden or some other, cooler countryside location? One can speculate that the letter to his lawyer may well have originally been sent from someplace else, possibly Zurich, to somebody in Vienna, such as his confidant—one could, a bit unkindly, call him Beethoven's flunky—a man named Zmeskall, who handled all manner of chores for the maestro, and this fellow Zmeskall could well have forwarded the letter to Prague."

For the first time, Mitch sensed that Clara might have lost a degree of objectivity in the course of her homework. He hesitated a moment, lest he be seen as undercutting his wife's critical faculties, then decided he might be doing her a favor by speaking up.

"Sounds a little like you might be stretching the shoe to make it fit," he remarked.

"You might think so," Clara volleyed, "but my report, if you'll bear with me a bit, refers to another letter to the same Prague lawyer, a man named Kanka, and sent the very same day as the one I just mentioned, that directs Herr Kanka to—and I quote—'for the time being please address letters to me in the following way—to be delivered to the house of Herr Johan Wolfmayer,' accompanied by a street address. Wolfmayer, we know, owned a prosperous drapery business and was a good friend of the maestro. From this instruction to him, one may reasonably infer that Beethoven was out of town—and possibly someplace he didn't want his correspondents to know about."

Clara's report then abruptly changed gears, or at least momentarily appeared to do so.

"We cannot avoid, however, considering one piece of documented evidence that strongly suggests Beethoven remained at home during some of the time that he was purportedly in Switzerland." The chief impediment to the Zurich story was a surviving receipt issued in Vienna on September 1, 1814, and bearing Beethoven's signature in acknowledgment of a draft for 750 florins drawn against the account of Archduke Rudolph. The emperor's younger brother, a gifted pianist and composer of promise, was Beethoven's only student at that period and one of three noblemen who pooled their resources in 1809 to provide the maestro with an annual dole of 4,000 florins in order to sustain his household and keep him living in Vienna at a time when it was under Napoleon's heel. But by 1814, the composer's other two financial supporters were out of the picture, "and Beethoven was in a serious financial bind," Clara wrote. Thus, the funds he could still draw upon from the archduke were of vital importance to him—"and yet the maestro might readily have arranged, by presigning and predating the receipt, for the trusted Zmeskall to present it at the bank on the designated day and deposit the funds in Beethoven's account for him." Indeed, a letter sent by Beethoven to Zmeskall sometime that summer—"scholars are uncertain of the precise date," Clara admitted even while trying to bolster her speculation—had invited this devoted intimate to drop by his flat at eight o'clock that evening, "possibly to discuss with him such arrangements as forwarding his mail and making bank deposits for him while Beethoven was to be away—someplace he may not have revealed to anyone."

Mitch shook his head. "Unless he wanted his loyal pal to come by to play backgammon or just to shoot the breeze with him." Why was she trying to hype such frail evidence? "Sounds like a bit of a reach, Clara," he remarked before Harry or Gordy could call her on it.

"Except," Clara replied coolly, "for indications we have that by the middle of September, when Beethoven was back in Vienna or at Baden, he had been out of touch for quite some time. See the paragraph in the middle of my page fifteen." An authenticated letter dated September 15 to the composer's Scottish publisher began, "Owing to my very many occupations, I have not been able to reply any sooner to your most esteemed letter..." But Beethoven was not known to have been working on much of anything during that period, Clara noted. A few days later, Beethoven wrote in a similarly apologetic vein to another important supporter, Count Linowsky, that, "Unfortunately I did not receive your letter until yesterday." In short, one could plausibly suppose that Beethoven was catching up with mail that had accumulated during his extended absence, perhaps outside of Austria—"conceivably he was in Zurich."

"Okay, you've raised some possibilities," Mitch said with clinical detachment, "but is there any corroborative evidence that Beethoven was in Switzerland that summer—or even had a reason to go there?"

Clara cast him a neutral sideways look. "None at all," she said, "other than the three letters that we're told Jake Hassler found accompanying the *Tell* manuscript in the wooden box in his grandfather's attic—and of course we don't know if they're real or fabricated—your forensics experts will have to try to date them. But I've been able to translate two of the letters, which came from the same person, and they certainly serve to make the Swiss story sound credible."

The two letters, addressed to "My dearest Maestro," were signed by a Zurich music publisher named Hans Georg Nägeli, who eleven years earlier, as Clara had discovered while sifting through Beethoven's published correspondence, had issued three of the composer's piano concertos and, in the process, earned his displeasure because they contained multiple printing errors. Understandably eager to redeem himself in the eyes of the renowned maestro, this Nägeli—"a certifiably authentic person, you understand," Clara stressed—might well have sent the neatly penned letter dated 17 February 1814, imploring Beethoven to visit Switzerland's leading city. Clara's translation concluded:

> ...In the heartfelt hope of prolonging your creative energies and restoring your hearing to its former condition, I pray you will accept my suggestion that you avail yourself of the services of the above named physician. I also know of a gracious and well-bred family who could provide you, at modest cost, with entirely satisfactory lodgings on a quiet square but a ten-minute walk to the physician's clinic. It would be my high honor, furthermore, to serve as your guide and familiarize you with our city and charming countryside as well as to receive you with open arms for dinner at our home whenever you may be in a sociable humor.
>
> Needless to add, all aspects of your visit would remain strictly confidential as I understand full well your natural reluctance to disclose the purpose for it even to those favorably disposed to you in a city like yours, teeming with musicians so envious of your achievements...

"Very nice," said Harry, "and perfectly plausible—which, as Clara properly observes, would be the point of a con artist including it in the cedar box. And what's the other letter from this Swiss publishing bloke all about?"

It addressed the most serious challenge to the believability of the *Tell* discovery—why the composer would have discarded a largely completed work of such magnitude. Clara related that the Swiss music publisher apparently made good on his promise to offer Beethoven the hospitality of his parlor and dinner table, and on one occasion, August 29—determinable from the date on the letter sent to him the next morning—the maestro must have brought along part of the manuscript from his work-in-progress and played excerpts for his trusted admirer's assessment. The two men apparently disagreed about the merit of the work, judging by Clara's translation of the second Nägeli letter:

My dear Maestro,

Mrs. Nägeli and I have both taken such great pleasure in your company of late that I wish to do nothing which might prove in the least irritating and make you less inclined to share your evenings with us. But I would be remiss in the extreme, I sincerely believe, if I did not once again respectfully take issue with your somewhat low opinion of your present composition.

You may say, "Oh, this Nägeli is of Swiss nationality, so he is naturally partial to something titled The *William Tell* Symphony." To be sure, it is flattering that you would apply your genius to such an undertaking and thereby glorify our foremost folk hero—we are, after all, a small land with an unremarkable past. But I esteem your gifts far too highly to stoop to false flattery, and so please, my dear sir, believe me when I beg of you not to discredit this splendid new creation of yours, which so delights the mind's eye as well as the ear.

I fear that the thus far unsatisfactory results of your medical treatments may quite understandably be skewing your usually acute powers of perception when you remark that your interweaving of vocal song and instrumental passages has resulted in too fractured a structure and that the transitional sections are too awkward and abrupt. Not to our ears, dear Maestro…

By now Harry was unabashedly intrigued.

"But why, having invested that much effort in the project," he asked, "and having received such unreserved encouragement from his Swiss publisher, would Beethoven have chucked it the way Nina Hassler's letter says?"

"Obviously the paramount question," Clara granted, "but well beyond the scope of my inquiry. And neither of these Nägeli letters constitutes reliable independent corroboration of what really happened in Zurich—if anything." The third letter, though, found in the box along with various receipts and invoices, signed only "R" and bearing a royal crest at the top of the first page, might well shed light on his question, she told the group. "According to Jake Hassler, this Ansel Erpf fellow tried to translate it for him while he was clearing out his grandfather's house, but Ansel had no more luck than I've had—other than gleaning something about the writer's belief that the *Tell* Symphony might somehow or other prove 'dangerous' if Beethoven proceeded with it. Almost certainly, the letter was sent by his patron and protector Archduke Rudolph—or some forger wants us to believe as much. You'll need to engage a handwriting expert to decipher the difficult German script and a historian to speculate on the 'danger' the archduke feared Beethoven might face if the symphony were completed and performed in Vienna."

Nearing the end of her presentation, Clara considered a question that delved further into the plausibility of the *Tell* saga: What else was Beethoven known to have been working on at the time he was supposedly in Zurich?

"I have found no evidence the maestro was doing any consuming professional work that summer," Clara reported. "If not, this may be significant, especially when one remembers that summertime was usually a fruitful period for Beethoven. The only thing he was known to have done in those months of 1814 was signing off during the first week in August on the autograph score— the musicologists' term for a final draft—on his piano Sonata in E Minor, op. ninety, the sort of busywork he might well have taken with him anywhere he traveled outside of Vienna and addressed whenever he had a few idle moments. That summer, absent any evidence to the contrary that I can find, seems to have been an uncharacteristically idle spell for him."

"Suggesting," Gordy ventured, "his deafness had simply overwhelmed him at that point."

"Possibly," Clara parried, "but his deafness was nothing new—and, after all, he had produced his superb Seventh and highly creditable Eighth symphonies within the previous year, not to mention the *Archduke* Trio and revisions of *Fidelio* still more recently. No, I think either he was exhausted from the cumulative body of brilliant work he had accomplished almost nonstop over the previous decade—or, possibly, he was covertly working on something else."

Gordy nodded.

"Very curious, but strictly circumstantial," he said. "It's hard to turn a vacuum into corroborative evidence."

Clara acknowledged the point. "There's one last bit of evidence cited in my report—on page nineteen—that could help fill the vacuum." It came from the composer's authenticated and published collected correspondence. In February of 1814, Beethoven sent a letter to his friend Anna Milder-Hauptmann, the great soprano of the day, for whom he had written the title role in *Leonore*, as the opera was known when *Fidelio* was first produced in 1805. As if vowing to improve on *Fidelio*, which had never pleased him, his note to Milder-Hauptmann promised that he would "make it my priority to write an[other] opera" for her, one that would presumably provide a new and better showcase for both their talents.

"And that new opera could conceivably have been *Tell,*" Harry completed her surmise.

Clara shrugged. "Well, that would depend on whether we accept as genuine the sketchbooks found in Otto Hassler's attic trunk." It was apparent, she said, even to an eye as untrained as hers, that the first section of the more heavily filled composition book was a rough draft of the opening act of an opera based on the Schiller play—"the names of the characters and the libretto correspond with parts of the text that someone marked up in the copy of the play found in the cedar box," Clara noted. Somewhere along the line, though, whoever composed the work abandoned the operatic form and transformed it into the hybrid form designated "a dramatic symphony" on the title page in the second sketchbook, containing the fully scored first part of the work. "The music becomes mostly instrumental in the new version, with several vocal pieces blended into each movement."

Harry sat back and began chewing on one of the unsharpened pencils he'd snatched from the mugful of them at the edge of his desk. "If you can figure out that much," he said to Clara as they arrived at the end of her report, "what's your gut feeling about the physical manuscript itself? Does it pass your smell test as being the real thing?"

"With all due respect," Clara said after a moment of due deliberation, "administering smell tests is not my thing. And as you'll understand, I didn't have the time or equipment to examine any of these materials except in a cursory fashion. Nor am I qualified to assess the virtuosity of so complex a composition and in such a—I'd almost call it a derelict condition. You'll need to hire people using technical tools that can't be fooled as readily as I can by cosmetic appearances."

Now she looked straight at Harry and avoided Mitch's narrowed eyes. "But in a word—yes, these sketchbooks certainly have the feel and—well, okay—the smell of a genuinely old work, and their appearance is very similar to the sample pages from his manuscripts that I found reproduced in the leading scholarly reference work on the subject."

"And could any or all of that be faked?" Harry pressed.

"I suppose, with an inordinate outlay of time and money and given sufficient familiarity with all things Beethoven. If this is a hoax, the perpetrators have—to my amateur's eyes, anyway—done their homework superbly."

Everyone sat stone still for a moment, weighing the gravity of Clara's conscientious recitation. "And have you any sense," Gordy asked finally, "whether the music in this *Tell* Symphony is good, bad, or in-between?"

Clara threw up her hands. "It's impossible to say—for me, anyway—at this stage. You'll need to enlist a team of eminent musicologists to transcribe, edit, and score the music before any overall aesthetic judgment of it can be ventured with real authority."

"Could you decipher any portion of the music?" Gordy wondered.

"Well, sort of—in a segmented fashion at best—especially since I had only a piano to work with at the apartment, and his symphonies, like most others, don't have piano parts. I can't get a real sense of how the passagework flows and shifts and resolves itself—the manuscript is too disjointed as it stands—the seams still show." But she had been able to hum a dozen or so bars of the melody to the men's chorus in the first movement, Clara said. "One was titled 'What Need of Noblemen,' which comes across as a rousing anthem of the folk origin of the Swiss uprising. And there's a quite touching—almost piquant—quality to the duet in the second movement between Tell and his wife, Hedwig, who fears for his and their son Walter's safety as they head off toward the vicinity of Gessler's nasty troopers. The piece is called 'I See the Avalanche Engulfing You'—not terribly subtle, or, of course, characteristically Beethoven. But then the whole conception of a 'dramatic symphony' attempting an almost literal translation from one artistic form to another would be a departure for him—and thus add to the historic value of the work—*if* it's his."

"And is it, do you think?" Harry asked, casually raising the bottom-line question.

Clara stood her ground. "Mr. Roth—Gordon—asked me a moment ago about whether the manuscript seems to have artistic quality, and the most I'd risk answering is that it could be genuinely affecting music. But that's a far cry from determining at this stage whether Beethoven could have written it." She measured her words precisely. "He *could* have written a great many things—in different styles. He was a monumental genius, as we all know. My assignment from you was to look for any evidence I might be able to detect within a week's time—historical, biographical, musicological, circumstantial, logical, intuitive—whatever—that definitively stamps these manuscripts as fraudulent, or points strongly in that direction, that screams, 'No way could Beethoven have done this.'" She gathered up the pages from her report. "In spite of this entire proposition flying directly in the face of all my rational faculties, I haven't found such evidence. Others might very well—bear in mind I'm still very much a novice in this field."

Harry cleared his throat, leaned forward, and gave her a short salute. "We're grateful, Clara," he said and turned to Gordy. "Please make sure that accounting cuts a check for Mrs. Emery before the day is over." He began to rise from his chair, signaling the end of the session.

"Sorry—one small last question, please," Mitch said, glancing at the library's high, vaulted ceiling and freezing further motion in the room. "This may sound dumb, but am I the only one to find it odd that the Nina letter makes no reference to Beethoven's having brought a servant with him? Wouldn't a man of his eminence, even if financially strapped, have been able to afford at least one personal retainer to take along on his travels—particularly for a trip of that length to a strange city and given his physical handicap?"

He had not directed his question at Clara, but it came out sounding that way.

"That never occurred to me, to be honest," she said, betraying a hint of impatience after nearly two hours of intensive engagement. "But if pressed, I'd guess that paying the room, board, and wages for a servant for that length of time would have seriously depleted the maestro's already drained resources. For all his critical success and popularity for a time with the fickle Viennese masses, Beethoven generally lived hand to mouth—and had to humble himself to gather handouts from the aristocracy. The coachman who might have brought him to Zurich could have attended to his luggage and personal needs during the trip, and Nina and others in the Hassler household—they probably had a number of maids and hired men—could have done all the rest. Her letter suggests she was assigned to attend to his personal needs."

"Makes sense," said Harry, moving purposefully toward the door. "Nature calls."

When they were alone in the room, Mitch reclaimed Clara from her mission, engulfing her with a fierce hug suitable to reunion with a long-lost love.

"So?" she asked while they were still entwined.

"So," he said softly, "you were awesome."

Clara gave a small sigh of relief. "Harry didn't seem to think so. He doesn't exactly gush with praise, does he?"

"Harry," said Mitch, "has a steel rod up his bum."

BY THE NEXT MORNING, the principal concern within the Cubbage & Wakeham executive offices had shifted from whether the *William Tell* Symphony was Beethoven's Tenth to who actually owned the manuscript regardless of its authenticity. The latter question was raised within moments of the hastily scheduled appearance in the firm's library of a baggy-eyed, deceptively soft-spoken visitor whose card identified him as Philippe de M. Saulnier, legal attaché to the Confederation of Switzerland's embassy to the United States. His government, he made clear shortly after the introductions, did not subscribe to the precept that possession is nine-tenths of the law.

"We are most appreciative, gentlemen, of your courtesy in arranging this meeting so promptly," said Herr Saulnier.

There was no polite way of determining whether he was *the* legal attaché for the Swiss embassy or one of many. He could even have been dispatched from the staff of his country's New York consulate and thus be a careerist of low rank as attachés go. But he looked and acted official enough, Mitch told himself, and Gordy, having put in a five-year stint with the US Foreign Service before beginning his C&W career in its London office, had pointed out that in diplomatic circles, subordinates were not infrequently assigned to deliver sensitive messages in order to avoid high-level confrontations and thus leave the parties wiggle room for conflict resolution. Saulnier exuded the politesse of a wiggle-facilitator.

Owen Whittaker, Jake Hassler's attorney, had been the one to propose the joint session with Cubbage & Wakeham's brain trust after the Swiss embassy had phoned him to say there appeared to be "certain irregularities and related concerns" in connection with Otto Hassler's estate and that a meeting with Jake and his counsel might prove constructive. Since Beethoven's name was not mentioned in that initial exchange, Harry was hesitant to become involved prematurely in an international wrangle with a sovereign state as his adversary. But Gordy counseled him, "Since we have no legal exposure in the matter so far, I really don't see the harm in our sitting around the table and trying to thrash things out. We've got potentially very high stakes riding on this property and a client with shallow pockets—let's try to help him, and us, out."

Harry deferred to Gordy as the presiding C&W officer for the occasion, giving him the chair at the head of the library conference table. Harry even assigned Mitch, though now a nonpracticing attorney, to sit at Gordy's right hand and next to Owen Whittaker, while he himself retreated to the far end of the table, allowing the lawyers to have a go at one another up close. Saulnier, seated to Gordy's left, began by advising, in purest Oxbridgean English, that the Swiss Cultural Ministry had received a protest from a prominent Zurich family "in connection with the removal from our country of a certain musical composition that may be of more than passing interest to our citizens." The family's communication with the Swiss government, said the attaché, had been made in confidence—for the time being, at least—in the hope their concern might be allayed by timely intervention through diplomatic channels.

"And what is your understanding about this musical work?" Gordy tested him.

Saulnier phrased his reply in carefully formal language. "Our ministry was told that, in the first place, the composition was inspired by the story of our country's great folk champion, William Tell, and named after him—and that, in the second place, it appears to have been created by the hand of the immortal Beethoven."

Gordy nodded noncommittally. "And what is the problem?"

"The complainant family asserts a preexisting right to the work that Mr. Whittaker's client surreptitiously removed from our country," said the diplomat.

"There was nothing surreptitious about it," Whittaker objected calmly. "Mr. Hassler took the box containing the manuscript and other papers on board the plane after showing its contents to Swiss security and customs personnel at the Zurich airport. He did so in the belief it was his property under his late grandfather's last will and testament. It was a perfectly straightforward act, so we don't accept its being characterized as illicit or in any way involving subterfuge."

Saulnier nodded. "Your client's Zurich counselor has explained it to us in that fashion, of course." He paused and then added matter-of-factly, "From our standpoint, however, Mr. Jacob Hassler took possession of what may prove to be a greatly valuable and historic work of art without first allowing the Swiss authorities to review and probate his grandfather's will."

"The will is uncontested," Whittaker replied, "according to my conversation with the attorney for the Otto Hassler estate."

The diplomat shrugged. "That remains to be determined through the probate process. My government feels that your client acted rashly—by leaving Switzerland in such haste and carrying with him a work of art that he didn't bother to describe as such to our customs examiners."

"But it hadn't been established at the time—and remains to be—whether this manuscript is a bona fide work of art," Whittaker countered. "And your customs people didn't ask my client to identify the nature of the material in the box he brought with him."

Having registered his charges, the Swiss officer switched to a different tack. "And there is the further matter of whether the musical manuscript in question was legally the property of Otto Hassler—and thus whether title to it can pass to his grandson." He turned to Gordy and then Mitch while adding a bit more forcefully, "And even if these matters were resolved in Mr. Hassler's favor, his ability to remove this document from Swiss jurisdiction may conflict with Swiss law regarding national treasures, which would supersede the grandson's claimed right to offer the manuscript to your company for the purpose of auctioning it to the public."

"Whoa, there, Mr. Saulnier," Harry piped up. "What's this about a national treasure? And even if this manuscript turns out to be the legitimate work of Beethoven—whether it's good or bad Beethoven—how would that possibly qualify it as a *Swiss* national treasure?"

Gordy raised a cautionary hand to quiet his boss. "We need to let Mr. Saulnier speak his piece, so we can find out where he's headed and what he expects us to do about it."

"Sorry, champ."

"Thank you," said the attaché. "Our position is simply that this manuscript and the related materials should be returned for safekeeping by the Swiss government while these various matters can be sorted out and resolved. If Mr. Hassler emerges as the legal titleholder to the work and Swiss laws do not intercede, he would then—but only then—be free to contract with your firm to auction the manuscript."

Whittaker shook his head emphatically. "That's a nonstarter," he said. "Mr. Hassler acted well within his rights as executor and sole heir of his grandfather's estate—and then only after having learned from his grandfather's Swiss attorney that there was no competing will known to exist and no other valid claim against the estate except the neighbors' lien on the house itself and its furnishings. The lien provides that my client may remove and keep the Hassler family's personal papers and records, among which this manuscript was found. End of story."

Saulnier retained his staid demeanor even as the exchange grew more pointed. "The Erpf family—the neighbors—argue otherwise. They ask how Jacob Hassler can claim that his grandfather had legal title to what may be the original manuscript of a Beethoven symphony—and they contest that it can be included among the Hasslers' 'family papers' since it never passed into their hands as its legal owners—unless there is documentation to that effect. Is there any?"

Whittaker was caught off guard by the argument. "None that I know of," he said, "but I don't see how that affects—"

"Ah, but it does," said Saulnier.

Whittaker turned to Gordy for support but won only a shrug in return. "Our understanding from the Erpfs' son Ansel," the attaché followed up, "is that, according to the surviving letter of a Hassler ancestor, she chose to keep the manuscript in defiance of her instructions from the composer to destroy it after he left the family's premises. Whether or not that constituted a criminal act on her part is no doubt a moot question at this late date, but surely it did not establish the family's legal title to the property."

Neither Whittaker nor Gordy offered an immediate rebuttal, prompting Mitch to join the fray. "But even if the manuscript did not, strictly speaking, belong to the Hassler family," he asked, "how did the neighbors' lien give *them* the right to claim title to the manuscript?" Mitch turned to Whittaker for confirmation as he added, "The Erpfs hold a lien, as I understand it, only against the house and its furnishings—*not* the Hassler family papers, among which the purported Beethoven manuscript was found."

"But its being there," Saulnier parried, "does not mean it *belonged* there or that it was a legal family possession, allowing Jacob Hassler just to walk out of Switzerland with it under his arm, so to speak."

"Even granting that, which Mr. Whittaker plainly does not," Mitch answered, "how does that put the Erpf family into play as legitimate claimants to the manuscript? Frankly, they sound pretty greedy—almost as if they regret the generosity they had long extended to old Mr. Hassler and are trying now to extract the last ounce of payback from his grandson."

"Yes!" Harry barked and at once subsided.

Saulnier was nonplussed. "The Erpfs feel it would not be unreasonable for them to be rewarded to that extent—given that first, the manuscript had no business being held captive in Mr. Hassler's attic for all that time—"

"But the manuscript wouldn't exist today," Mitch shot back, "if Nina Hassler hadn't disobeyed the composer's instruction to dispose of it. Or so we've been led to believe."

"Be that as it may," said Saulnier, "it was one of the Erpf family members—a highly accomplished musician accompanying Jacob Hassler at the time—who rescued the manuscript a second time from being consigned to the rubbish. Mr. Hassler, who knows neither music nor the German language, couldn't have recognized the manuscript for what it is—or may be."

"That sounds to me," Gordy inserted, "as if both families may have a legitimate claim to ownership." He looked down toward Harry. "Maybe we ought to let these two families work out some sort of joint title to the symphony and then call upon our services to get it authenticated and sold at auction if they so choose."

"What about that, Mr. Whittaker?" Gordy asked.

"I don't think that's what the Erpfs have in mind. From what Herr Schacht, Jake's Zurich lawyer, tells me, the Erpfs may have struck a deal with the Swiss government to seek its intervention on their behalf—which would explain Mr. Saulnier's getting into the act here."

"Is that right?" Gordy asked the attaché.

Saulnier sat back and gathered his thoughts for a moment. "Well," he said in careful acknowledgment, "it's safe to say that my government has an overriding interest in the fate of this work of art if it proves to be genuine. Bear in mind its subject and theme—they are nothing less than a celebration of the spirit of liberty and independence of our people. Surely Americans ought to be sensitive to these values. The work, moreover, was allegedly written within our national borders. And, as I mentioned, we have rather rigid rules against the unlicensed removal from Switzerland of artistic or other works and artifacts that, in the view of our Cultural Ministry, constitute part of our people's proud heritage—and may therefore be justly classified as national treasures. This symphony may very well qualify as such an item."

"But it had not been so designated," Whittaker pointed out, "at the time Mr. Hassler brought it home, believing it to be his rightful possession. So how can Mr. Hassler possibly be accused of acting in disregard, knowingly or not, of the Swiss laws?"

"His premeditation is beside the point," Saulnier replied. "The point is he wasn't entitled to remove the manuscript until these various issues are settled—and therefore it should promptly be returned to Switzerland."

The suggestion provoked Whittaker to slap his open palm down on the tabletop. "That would certainly facilitate whatever deal the Erpfs have proposed to Mr. Saulnier's government—and screw Jake Hassler royally."

"Do tell us about your arrangement with these people," Harry urged the diplomat.

The Erpf family, far from being grasping people, were well regarded in Zurich for their civic-mindedness and generous support of the arts, Saulnier related. The Erpfs had expressed a patriotic interest in the Beethoven work—should it prove authentic—and offered to donate their claim to it to the Swiss nation. "Title to it would be held in trust by our Cultural Ministry until completion of the authentication process," the attaché revealed, after which a fund would be established to receive all revenues from performance rights, recording royalties, and any other forms of licensed commercial use. He looked up from his papers. "For the first twenty-five years, half of these revenues would be used to subsidize the Swiss National Philharmonic—which, incidentally, would be granted the right to give the world premiere performance of the *Tell* Symphony—and the Zurich Conservatory of Music among others of our financially pressed cultural institutions, and thereafter all of the revenues would be so used."

"And what would become of the other half of the *Tell* revenues for those first twenty-five years?" Gordy pressed him.

"Well, that would depend largely on what the Swiss courts decided about whether Jacob Hassler or the Erpf family had the better claim to ownership of the manuscript. Or perhaps, as Mr. Roth has suggested, the parties might agree upon an equitable division of the income—or the court could order another form of compromise."

Harry stirred elaborately at the far end of the table. "Could your government in all honesty, Mr. Saulnier," he asked in his flattest, most nasal tone, "assure Mr. Hassler that he would be best served by surrendering what he feels is his rightful possession to the aggressive claims of a family you paint as paragons of Swiss patriotism—and to Swiss authorities who are likely to be predisposed against an American citizen in this matter?"

"I think, Mr. Cubbage," Saulnier replied, "that you are asking the wrong question. Your interests and Mr. Jacob Hassler's interests do not necessarily coincide. Your firm should not be placed in a position to embarrass itself. Instead, I would respectfully suggest that you need to ask yourselves if there is any point in proceeding with plans for the auction of a work whose legal title is being contested—indeed, everything about this discovery is open to question. And once Mr. Hassler recognizes he has hold of what I believe the criminal element calls a 'hot property' and cannot readily dispose of it for a great fortune, he may well want to avail himself of the legitimizing procedures of Swiss justice."

"And if Mr. Hassler prefers to proceed in what he believes is good faith," Harry asked, "and we choose to investigate the authenticity of the property?"

The Swiss lawyer's pouchy face took on the woeful mien of a basset hound. "Then I suspect the Erpf family and my government would have no recourse except to challenge his claim of ownership within our legal system. Perhaps Mr. Whittaker and your firm will be good enough to review the informal memorandum I've prepared, stating my government's concerns, rather than risk involvement in lengthy and costly litigation—with an unpromising outcome. Mr. Hassler would likely wind up being branded as a rogue owner of the manuscript and your firm's ability to auction it for a sizable price would be fatally compromised."

That sounded confrontational to the American participants. "Fine," Whittaker said matter-of-factly, "you're free to litigate to your hearts' content. But you'll have to bring your action here—in the American courts. I think you'll discover ours is not a venue friendly to foreigners seeking to deprive US citizens of their property rights."

After the meddlesome Swiss official had taken his leave, Harry hung a leg over the arm of his leather swivel chair. "I believe," he said after everyone had deferred to him in silence, "our emissary from Yodeland was sending up what is playfully referred to as a trial balloon."

"Without a doubt," said Gordy.

Harry looked down at Mitch.

"And what do you say we do about it, pal?"

The question surprised him—was it another of Harry's tests to see what he was made of? No, he had evidently been invited to the meeting to help formulate company policy in the matter. But he would try lighthearted modesty first to be sure of his ground. "Me? I'm just the bottle-washer around here."

"We can arrange for that if you'd like," said Harry. "Out with it, Mitchell."

"Okay. I say we let the trial balloon float away and get on with our business."

"Me, too," said Gordy. "They'll never go to court here—and if they do, they'll lose."

Harry nodded and gestured toward Owen Whittaker.

"Thank you, gentlemen," he said.

{6}

Pleasantly surprised to find that Lolly had already arrived and controlled a sweeping view of the Bemelmans Bar from a corner table, Clara smiled a greeting and hurried over.

"You're two minutes and eighteen seconds late, darling," Lolly bubbled after brushing a kiss past her cheek, "but I forgive you—you're still on DPT, aren't you, angel?"

DPT? Daylight—um—what? Pacific Time? No, not nasty enough. Trying to translate Lolly's latest cryptic slur was always a challenge. "What's that?" she asked.

"Dutch People's Time. It's a variation on a well-known racist term."

"How delightful," Clara said. "I'm only half Dutch, though, remember."

"That's all you need. I'll bet you that nobody in Holland knows or cares what time it is."

"They have other virtues. Now hush and tell me what that dreadful thing is you're gulping down? Looks like lemonade or something."

"Exactly—very seasonal—very refreshing."

"Since when are you into wholesome?"

"If you must know, it's half vodka—and it packs a nice little wallop. I've named it a Lollypalooza. Here, let me order you one—lots of Vitamin C."

"White wine spritzer," Clara told the waiter, "light on the ice." She donned a pert look and called Lolly's attention to the scarlet linen bolero from a boutique on London's Sloane Street she had put on just to avoid yet another volley of scorn about her funereal "weekday uniform." "Is this *pizazzy* enough for you?"

"Truly fetching," Lolly approved. "Now we need to deal with your hair. I have this—"

Clara's cell phone went off just then, muffled by her handbag. She shrugged it off at first. But Lolly gestured for her to answer it.

"I won't—it's rude. I carry it only for emergencies."

"Answer it—maybe God's calling."

Clara frowned but did as directed, catching her caller on the fourth ring. It was Mitch, duly apologetic for intruding on a social occasion. "Can you drop by here after lunch, sweetie? We're having a strategy huddle on the *Tell* situation, and we all think your input would be very useful. Sorry about the short notice."

"That's very flattering, but I've got to go up to the Columbia library to prep for a seminar tomorrow afternoon—it could affect whether I get the instructor's job in the fall."

"We don't need you for more than an hour."

"I doubt you really need me at all. There are top-flight academics available who can—"

"We know—and that's partly what the session is about, and why we want you in on this. Harry thinks you speak our language quite beautifully. And *I* need you there, Clara."

"Oh, Lord," she said. "Okay—I'll shoot for three o'clock."

"No problem, I hope," Lolly said, watching her put the phone away.

"No, just a bit of bother. Mitch needs me at the office when we're done here to check on something—to do with music."

"Ah, good, you're being artfully deceptive—but I'll bet I know what it's about."

Clara had no idea how much or little Harry confided in his wife when it came to professional matters. All she knew was that, for the time being, the Beethoven business was classified as strictly hush-hush. "Then you're miles ahead of me," Clara lied artlessly.

"Come off it, darling," Lolly said. "Harry's let me in on this little Swiss development—but cautioned me, of course, not to breathe a word of it to another living soul. He also said that you've been quite helpful in the matter, so I assume he was leaving you off my *verboten* list."

"I see," Clara said, still mindful of her nondisclosure pledge to C&W.

"As a matter of fact," Lolly barreled ahead, "this quite thrilling development has given me a brainstorm I wanted to bring up with you—and only you."

Clara hunched her shoulders as if to register discomfort. "If you must talk about it," she cautioned, "I think we both need to lower our dulcet voices a few hundred decibels."

Lolly took the mild reprimand with good grace and leaned forward so her grating whisper would be audible. "Just imagine, we gather—you and I, I mean—a healthy task force of donors to raise enough money, strictly behind-the-scenes, to make a knockout bid to buy this...this unmentionable but immensely significant musical work at the C&W auction. Then we immediately donate it to the Lincoln Center endowment. The philharmonic, of course, gets to deliver the world premiere performance as the centerpiece of a spectacular benefit program—I'll bet you could sell tickets for ten thousand a pop—and then think of all the bucks that would come rolling in from performance rights and recordings—you know the classical music business inside out—I mean, wouldn't this be huge? We could sell millions and millions of CDs and downloads of this hot little number all around the world, and the Center would get a lovely rake-off on each and every one. And as the guiding force behind the drive, you'd be the golden girl at the place. I'd modestly settle for honorary chairperson of the board—or something else not overly taxing." She eased herself back, beaming in triumph. "There, I've said it, and if you'll stop to think about it instead of giving me that pained, knee-jerk-negative look of yours, you'd see that it's not all that nutty. Really—how often can philanthropic organizations get in on the ground floor of something as thrilling as this? I say we'd attract a whole lot of givers who don't ordinarily deliver—and of course we'd need our elite corps of donors to dig down deep, or we couldn't be serious players at Harry's big auction."

Clara had to work at stifling a laugh.

"Assuming I know what you're talking about," she began, "I don't see how you or I could become involved in any such effort—I mean, given our husbands' connection to—"

"Why not? Money's money—this would be entirely aboveboard, out in the open—our group would be bidding against everyone else. Why should C&W care where the money comes from? It's not as if Lincoln Center would be getting the thing for an inside price, thanks to us."

"Still—somehow it smacks of—well, I think you'd have to ask Harry if he had any objection, or there were any professional rules against such a thing."

"I will *not* ask Harry ahead of time—the whole point of the thing for me would be to floor him—and I don't see how it could in any way embarrass the firm."

"But he might." Clara could tell from the fire in Lolly's eyes that she was seized with the idea, which, even if harebrained, was a lot more constructive than her usual pointless ramblings. "At any rate, I certainly couldn't get involved in any scheme like that—*my* husband doesn't own the business, he only works there. I couldn't risk putting him in a compromising position."

"Now you're just being Goody Two-shoes." Lolly threw down half her spiked lemonade and gave her head a spirited shake. "Okay, let's drop it for now—it's all beside the point, anyway, if this little bugger gets aborted. But if it turns out to be ready for primetime, you haven't heard the last of this from me."

"Whatever you say," Clara soothed. "Now can we eat?"

GORDY ROTH REPLAYED THAT MORNING'S developments for Clara. The meeting with the Swiss government lawyer, far from souring Harry on the problematic venture, had actually galvanized him. The stakes seemed to have grown dramatically, what with an entire sovereign nation—and a rich one at that—interested in the ultimate disposition of the property. "The three of us agree," said C&W's house counsel, flanked by Harry and Mitch, "that we're ready to move to the next level of exploration—and we've got a phone date with Sedge Wakeham in London in a few minutes to lay it all out for him. Sedge, by the way, says he's a great admirer of your father's—they apparently travel in the same artsy-fartsy social set."

"Yes, Daddy mentioned it after Mitch joined the firm," Clara said. No need to elaborate. Her father had described Wakeham as a drunk and a bore but a good soul.

The plan, as roughed out before Clara's arrival, called for the auction house to proceed at once with a three-phase authentication process. Phase one would be to hire an eminent musicologist to undertake an exercise similar to the one Clara had just performed: studying the *Tell* manuscript for a week or so to determine whether he or she agreed that the composition merited expert scrutiny of its every aspect. If so, the musicologist would agree to chair phases two and three of the project. Phase two, if warranted, would call for a specialized forensics team to examine the paper, ink, and handwriting of the two *Tell* sketchbooks to assess the likelihood that they had been composed by Beethoven with materials known to exist in or around 1814. Phase three, assuming its necessity, would be to enlist a five-person panel of the foremost Beethoven authorities, each to be allotted a week to examine the sketchbooks in private, and then the five panelists would assemble, joining the task force chairman, to compare notes and pass ultimate judgment as to *Tell*'s legitimacy and, to the extent possible before the music had been edited and scored, its aesthetic merits. A contract with Jake Hassler, naming C&W exclusive auctioneer of the manuscript, would be signed after stage one to prevent him from accepting a preemptive offer from a buyer before the auction could be held.

To pay for all this, Harry had tentatively set a budget of $4.5 million, the heftiest appropriation for such a purpose in C&W's history. A million would go for the Beethoven experts' fees, travel, housing, and food costs. Then, $2 million would be set aside for the forensics specialists, $750,000 for Johannes Winkelman's services as snoop extraordinaire in Europe, and the rest for legal and other contingency fees. The total prompted Sedge Wakeham, when he heard the numbers, to cry out over the speakerphone from London, "Sounds bloody rich, Harry old boy! Are we really up for our innings in this sort of match?"

As they came tumbling transatlantically out of the squawk box, Sedge's stentorian words had an element of self-parody about them that brought smiles to his New York listeners' lips. Mitch, having met him only once and briefly, wondered if Sedge's tickety-boo delivery might be the result of congenital dementia in the Wakeham family tree or, at the least, serious inbreeding.

"I do believe so, guv'nor," Harry said, mockingly deferential to Sedge, twenty-five years his senior. "If this unimaginable thing withstands our most rigorous authentication inquiry ever, we might wind up bathing in one helluva lot of gravy. And it doesn't have to be a masterpiece—even a spectacular failure by a certified immortal might have considerable marketplace appeal. What I like about it almost as much, though, is the downside. Even if we have to bail out and label it all a jolly fraud, the write-off would be worthwhile for the publicity value alone—we'd be proving anew that nobody puts anything over on Cubbage & Wakeham."

There was silence on the London end for a long moment until Sedge, quavery upper lip stiffening, from the sound of it, asked, "And who gets to run the show for us—a ruddy bunch from Düsseldorf, I suppose? Damn old Jerry owns the classical music franchise, don't he? But I rather loathe the thought of surrendering our flag to them."

Harry looked over at Clara. "He's asking if our top-of-the-line musicologists have to be an all-German crew." He turned back to the speakerphone. "We have Clara Emery here, Sedge—you know, Piet Hoitsma's daughter. She's been helping us out at the beginning—very brainy girl, knows her music, and, I suspect no more of a krautophile than you are, old top."

"Oh, hullo, dear girl—awfully good of you to lend us a hand," Sedge enthused. "You must come by next time you're home visiting, and bring the folks. Haven't seen Piet and—and your dear mother—sorry, can't fetch up her name—in a dog's age. Met your pa in the big war, you know—hush-hush stuff. And bring your hubby. Harry says he's doing bully work for us."

"Right," she said, "will do—without fail. And it's Gladys—my mum."

"Oh, righty-oh. See to it you visit us. Now about Jerry…"

She reined in her whirling emotions, the sharpest being irritation with Mitch for having ambushed her at the last minute to join the high-level conference without a clue about its purpose. Winging it was not her forte. She'd reprimand him in private; now it was showtime. "Yes, well, it will be hard," she confirmed, "to avoid turning to them for major assistance." Like them or not, Clara conceded, the Germans had undeniably invented what the world thought of as classical music and thoroughly dominated it for two hundred years. Not until Berlioz and Chopin came along was their monopoly broken. Accordingly, musicological academia and literature dealing with that period had become the specialty of German scholars and commentators. "Not that there aren't some perfectly fine people elsewhere," she said, "but if you asked me to name the world's ten leading authorities on Beethoven, most would be German or Austrian—a meaningless distinction in this case. But I don't think you people should be totally reliant on them, by any means—after all, art is an international language."

"Then maybe only our top expert—our phase-one person who'll chair the project—needs to be a German," Gordy proposed, "and the panel of authorities brought on board for our intensive phase-three vetting can be an international all-star cast."

"That makes a certain amount of sense," said Harry. "If you had to name the foremost Beethoven scholar alive, Clara, who would it be—a German, no doubt?"

She had to reflect a moment; so many scholars out there publishing, so little time to keep up with the torrent. "There'd be a handful of contenders, by any academic consensus. But if you ask me, there's one who stands head and shoulders over the field—a rather dreadful old warhorse named Emil Reinsdorf, a professor of history and composition at the National Conservatory in Berlin. His trilogy on Beethoven's works is a collection of close textual analyses of the music, and they're bloody brilliant. He's also done dozens of monographs and journal articles on one or another element of the Beethoven canon and is in worldwide demand as a lecturer. If Emil Reinsdorf were to conclude that the

William Tell Symphony was composed by Beethoven, then ninety-nine chances in a hundred Beethoven it was."

"Mmmm," said Harry, proprietary interest aroused. "But what makes him so dreadful?"

Wait, Clara thought before answering, who am I to gossip about an Olympian figure in my discipline? Tone it down, girl, or you'll come across as a schoolyard snitch. "There's a lot of jealous slander in the music world, I'm afraid, and I've never had the pleasure of his acquaintance, you understand—but Herr Doktor Reinsdorf is said by some to be as ill-tempered as he is exacting. Immensely knowledgeable, of course, but contentious by nature. Devours all rivals in the field, and—well, an ego the size of Pomerania."

"How big is that?" Gordy asked.

"Big," she said with smile. "I could check if you'd like."

"He sounds just the ticket, rotter or not," Sedge cracked. "Rather like your people kidnapping the Nazis' ace rocket fellow—Von Braun, was it?—to run your program."

Harry looked doubtful. "I suspect this prima donna would take a fair amount of coaxing, and I don't know that we have the time or inclination for that. How could we land him, Clara, short of handing the swine our whole bank account?"

Clara felt a rush of empowerment. She was being treated as an equal participant at the table. No time to turn squishy.

"First, I doubt that he's purchasable," she said. "It's the tribute to his stature that might appeal to him—"

"I thought that was what the money was for—to buy his stature," Harry said.

Clara was beginning to see what Mitch had to deal with every day. "Actually," she replied, "I don't think I'd try for Reinsdorf—or any German, for that matter—to supervise this project for Cubbage & Wakeham."

"Good girl," Sedge's voice chimed.

"How so?" Harry asked. "If he's the best, and the Germans are the class of the field?"

"Yes, quite," Clara said. "But there are several points on the other side. For one thing, given that the Germans view themselves as keepers of the flame with regard to classical music in general and their great maestro Beethoven in particular, they may react with high resentment because this manuscript—whatever it turns out to be—has fallen into the clutches of an American—not to mention an Anglo-American auction house that might be tempted to pass less-than-totally-disinterested judgment on the legitimacy of the work. Frankly, the more eminent the German authority you approach to chair the investigation, the more likely he is to view you as pillagers. And the Germans, whether or not you care to admit it, might have a point. How would Americans or Britons react if a newly discovered autobiography by, say, Abraham Lincoln or Winston Churchill were suddenly to surface in the hands of what Mr. Wakeham calls 'that ruddy bunch in Düsseldorf'? How delighted would we be about their proprietary claims on it—and then their passing definitive judgment on its authenticity, and finally putting it up on the auction block, so that it might fall into insensitive hands that might exploit it abusively?"

"But isn't that just what we need," Gordy asked, "a German commandant who'd be the ultimate skeptic, the least gullible interrogator, raising the most demanding questions?"

"Perhaps," said Clara, "but I don't think you want a closed mind or all but guaranteed hostility in your chief arbiter. I'd rather you try to enlist one or two eminent Germans and Austrians for your panel of five experts, Reinsdorf ideally among them, but that's quite different from hiring one of them to oversee your entire proceedings. I'd vote for a top-flight American scholar to head the project. The manuscript is in the possession, legal or otherwise, of an American. C&W is an Anglo-American firm, and logistically it will be far more manageable—since you can't risk letting the manuscript go flying around the world—to have an American within easy reach of this building to serve as your presiding guru."

"Grand thinking, young lady," Sedge put in. "Huns make trouble."

Harry saw her point. "So preferably we want the top Beethoven person in the States?"

Clara looked dubious. "To crack the whip over a pride of lions, you probably wouldn't hire another lion, would you?" she asked. The firm might be better off enlisting someone without his or her own axe to grind, but possessed of wide-ranging yet thorough knowledge of eighteenth- and nineteenth-century music, from the late Baroque through the Classical heyday and deep into the Romantic era. "You need someone perceptive who can see both the forest and the trees—someone collegial enough to forge a consensus and not stir a lot of acrimony—and not a rarefied scholar specializing in theory but someone with working knowledge of composition and a practical grasp of performing." As she paused for breath, her face suddenly glowed with an incandescent thought. "And I may have the perfect person for you," she added, "assuming he's obtainable."

HARRY HIMSELF PHONED CLARA, at Mitch's behest since he didn't want her to think it was his doing alone, to ask her to continue as a paid C&W consultant until the *Tell* Symphony had been either fully authenticated or cast aside as a fake. She thanked Harry and said she'd think it over, but she had no desire to go on the firm's payroll, she told Mitch afterward, nor to be exploited by him, however incidentally or unwittingly. "I've got my own work to do," she said, "and you've got yours—okay?"

"But this is a once-in-a-lifetime experience for anyone as passionately dedicated to music as you are," Mitch argued. "I mean, doesn't this whole thing knock you out?"

"Sure—it's utterly fascinating. And I hope you'll keep me posted, if you can without, you know, violating company security." She guessed that Lolly and her indiscreet tongue would reveal whatever Mitch felt constrained to keep mum about.

He looked crushed. "I still need you with me on his, sweetie—I'm in over my head here. And I don't want to wind up getting tossed out of Harry's window."

His confession, she could tell, had cost him several cubits of ego. "That's very wrong and—and extremely underhanded of you, trying to prey on my sympathy like this. You'll have all the expert help you need to make the final call. I'm not your satellite, Mitch. I thought we'd established that."

He threw up his hands. "Have it your way. But at least come with me to try to lock up our main guy. He's your nominee."

Clara narrowed her eyes. "You're making me feel trapped—if I'm not willing to be your crutch in this thing, I'm disloyal. It's bloody selfish of you, frankly."

His sheepish look said he admitted the charge. "Okay—just this final time, then."

She yielded with a scolding frown. "But this is it."

"Absolutely."

On summer break from his academic duties, Macrae Quarles was touring in Provence with his wife when Mitch tracked him down by telephone at his hotel room in Nîmes. There was still a whisper of Kentucky hill country in his soft, reedy speech and a pleasing cordiality that might have well served the often-abrasive Harry Cubbage. Even so, Professor Quarles sounded politely put upon when Mitch explained the nature of the problem confronting C&W, without revealing the composer's identity beyond classifying him as "a major figure." With a honeyed, scarcely perceptible twang, Quarles replied, "This sort of thing comes up every now and then, Mr. Emery. I wouldn't get too worked up about it if I were in your folks' shoes."

"We're trying not to," Mitch assured him, "but this just might be something quite remarkable." It was not a subject to be discussed on the phone, however, he added and expressed the hope that he and Clara—"my wife is an admiring former student of yours, incidentally"—might fly over and impose on him for an hour or two, at the most, a few days later. "I don't think you'll find it a waste of your time, sir."

"Sounds mighty urgent." Quarles cupped the mouthpiece of his phone briefly, then came back on the line. "My wife and I plan to visit some of the perched villages around here this week," he said, "but I guess a few hours with you folks won't unperch them. Come ahead."

On the late flight to Marseilles, Mitch scanned the bio material on Macrae Quarles that Clara had hastily assembled. A product of hillbilly stock, Mac (as even his students were invited to call him) had somehow contrived to prep at Hotchkiss and earn a Phi Beta Kappa key at Amherst, where his student music group, the Double Cues (for Quarles Quintet), performed everything from rag to rock, with blues, bluegrass, swing, and Dixie in between, and turned the large, lumbering young rube into a campus celebrity.

"He has these great gangly arms that hang almost to his knees," Clara noted, "and big, soft hands, so he can play every note on the piano without exerting himself—and can he play!" En route to his doctorate at Juilliard, he wrote— before his twenties were over—three piano concerti each named for a different Kentucky county, an oratorio he called *Requiem for the Flower Children,* and his best-known work, *The Swing Sonata.* Soon sobered by the near impossibility of making a living as a serious composer, Quarles immersed himself in heavyweight scholarship as the core of his career, starting with an expansion of his Juilliard dissertation on polyphony in Bach. It was published by Oxford University Press and received favorably even in the German journals.

As an assistant professor at the Yale School of Music, he turned out his most widely read book, *The Classical Zenith,* a comparative study of Haydn, Mozart, and Beethoven. "But this time," Clara's memo on him related, "the German critics were less generous, dismissing the dense volume as largely derivative—and probably resenting that a mere American had the brass to attempt it." Juilliard brought him back as a faculty stalwart, and he wrote his National Book Award winner, *Virtuoso: The Life and Times of Louis Moreau Gottschalk,* the first full-scale biography of America's first musical genius. After that, Quarles turned to the art of conducting, which he took up in stints with summer festival orchestras and for a sabbatical term with the St. Paul Philharmonic. His latest book, due out in the fall, was *Bravo! Bravo!: Maestros of the Twentieth Century*. Philadelphia's Curtis Institute of Music had just snared him as its associate director, promising that he would assume the top post within a year or two. "Mac Quarles is a perfect bridge figure between the musical traditions of the Old World and the New," Clara summed him up, "on top of which I had him as a guest lecturer one term at Columbia, and he's a total charmer."

His charm was largely in abeyance, though, at their hastily arranged meeting in Provence as he listened expressionless to Mitch's narrative of the Zurich discovery and briefly inspected a pair of double-page spreads photocopied from the two *Tell* sketchbooks to whet Mac's interest. "I'm afraid somebody's been yankin' you fellas' chain," he said, handing back the copied pages.

So much for down-home courtliness. "I'm totally aware of your matchless credentials, professor," Mitch said evenly, "but, with all due respect, how can you be so certain—from just a glance—that this is a fraud?"

"Well, I do feel bad about that, Mr. Emery—your having come all this way. But I sure didn't encourage you. This thing just doesn't sit right to me. You're talkin' about Beethoven here, not Sir Andrew Lloyd Weber, the good Lord help us. An unheard of Beethoven symphony doesn't just come popping outta the pea patch, my friend. I'm just flat-out not up for lendin' credibility to a bad joke like this by getting involved in it any which way—if I'm makin' myself clear to you and your pretty missus."

Mitch could not hide his chagrin. "Abundantly."

"I'm truly sorry, son—and appreciate your thinkin' I was your man."

"Right." Mitch nodded, turned slowly, and began to retreat toward the hotel room door.

Clara was dismayed her idol's peremptory dismissal of Mitch's appeal for consideration. But her husband's turning tail seemed equally baffling. "Mitch!" she called after him.

"C'mon, hon—we're interfering with the professor's vacation," he said over his shoulder.

"But—he's—not—" She wanted to add "giving us the time of day."

"We can just make the noon flight—and the professor can get on with his sightseeing."

Abject surrender was not like him. Wait—ahhh. Now she got it. This was her cue. Time to bewitch this stubborn son of a gun she had so ardently recommended. She geared up her pluck and turned to Quarles. "Have you a minute more?"

"For such a lovely lady—sure."

She managed a quick smile. "Frankly, I felt exactly the same as you, Professor, when Mitchell first told me about this—this absurdity," she said, all earnestness. "It sounded like a complete fairy tale." But, she went on to explain, after examining the material for a solid week to the best of her ability and reviewing some of the notes she had accumulated during the seminar she had taken with Quarles at Columbia, she was far less sure. "I know it's implausible, but there's something going on here—I don't pretend to know what," she said, managing to sound both plaintive and defiant.

Her appeal caused the scholar to retrieve the manuscript photos and scrutinize them again, this time more deliberately and moving closer to the windows for better light. Meanwhile, Mitch reappeared behind him and slathered on the butter. "Our firm feels you're the ideal person to direct the broad musical aspect of our investigation," he said, "and work with a group of international scholars who, quite frankly, may need to be coaxed into cooperating with one another."

"You been told right, Mr. Emery. Bunch of egomaniacs, every last one—except me." Quarles's grin encouraged Mitch to add quickly that chairing the panel of experts would require relatively little of his time. "And, not to be coy about it, you would be extremely well compensated, as would your eminent colleagues."

The news of unspecified largess was not lost on their quarry. But he was far too canny a specimen to leap at the bait. "Now listen, my friends—even if I were half as intrigued as Mrs. Emery by this polecat here," he said, beginning to bend, "I have lots of prior obligations. I just can't bug off on some fishin' trip, no matter what's bitin'."

Mitch replied that C&W needed him for no more than a week, ten days tops, to make an initial assessment as soon as possible, and if he was not satisfied by the end of that time that the manuscript could well be authentic, his mission would have been accomplished. Otherwise, his presence would be required for one day a week for a month while the other members of the expert panel—"entirely of your choosing, bear in mind"—flew in to examine the manuscript, plus an additional week to chair their final deliberations and a few more days to draw up a summary statement of the panelists' findings. For these services, he would receive a fee of $175,000 plus expenses while staying in New York.

The stipend had a certain gravity to it. "Not bad pay, I'll have to admit. Decent hotel?"

"Your choice," Mitch said. "Not the honeymoon suite, though."

Mac Quarles gave a down-home horselaugh. "I guess you folks are mighty stirred up."

"Mighty curious, that's for sure," said Mitch, feeling the tide now running in his favor, "and eager to get to the bottom of this business."

Quarles drifted to the window and watched the traffic beetling along the boulevard below the hotel. "And I get to choose the Beethoven people I want?"

"Yes, sir, if you decide a comprehensive investigation is warranted."

"And if I do, but I wind up not agreein' with my own panel's consensus, what then?"

"That would be up to you. You could issue a ringing dissent—"

"How about I do what you ask, but my name gets left out of it? This should really be the Beethoven people's call. I'm a kinda generalist, anyway."

The professor's defenses were crumbling fast. "But that's exactly why we want you, and not just Beethoven specialists," Mitch pitched still harder. "They may all have their own predisposed attitudes. We want an expert who's above this explicit battlefield. Frankly, by connecting your name to the effort, my firm would be telling the music world that we've approached the crucial authentication issue as conscientiously as possible."

"So no hideout for me?"

Mitch gambled now to close the deal. "We'd be paying you for both your judgment and your reputation—you'd be our brand name, to be perfectly honest with you. But what an immense thrill for all of us—to be in on a discovery of this magnitude, if it proves genuine."

Quarles nodded. "You talk a good game, Mr. Emery. Let me run this by my better half when she gets back to the hotel—I hate to break up our holiday. But it sounds as if Mrs. Quarles is gonna get a nice little Manhattan shoppin' spree out of it in exchange."

HER PARENTS' SATURDAY MORNING CALL from London came as a bit of a surprise to Clara—only because it was out of sequence. Normally they phoned on Monday night for a chat and reassurance all was well with their beloved daughter.

"Nothing wrong here, darling," Gladys Hoitsma explained as soon as Clara came on, "but your father wants to speak to you when we're done."

She could tell them nothing about the Beethoven development, of course, since Harry had clamped a lid on the entire subject until C&W was ready to go public with it, so Clara groped for a few items of trivia to hold up her end of the conversation until her father came on the line with a kindly reprimand. "A little bird has told me," said Piet Hoitsma, "that you and Mitchell are involved in evaluating a possibly remarkable discovery—I won't say the 'B' word just in case Scotland Yard is tapping my line—heaven forbid."

Clara was briefly dumbfounded but quickly put two and two together. "Your little bird wouldn't happen to be named Sedgwick Wakeham, would it?"

"That's the very bird—haven't seen him to talk to for a while except during intermissions at Albert Hall or Covent Garden. He can be a bit of a trial, but very warm-hearted. He had good words about Mitch from his partner, Cubbage, but he surprised me by saying he'd been in on a conference call lately with his New York office and you were sitting in, contributing brilliantly by sharing your musical knowledge and good sense with them. It made me proud, madam."

"Very nice of him to ring you," Clara said, "but I think he was overstating it by half. Still, why would he go into—he told you what the meeting was about? I don't get that."

"Made me swear an oath to keep it under my hat. Old Sedge, though, is a lot shrewder character than he sounds. He wasn't just calling to compliment my daughter. He was on a mission—and my calling you means he's succeeded."

"I—I'm not following you, Daddy."

Sedge had called him, Piet explained, at the urging of Harry Cubbage, out of sorts because neither he nor Mitch had been able to persuade Clara to stay with the Beethoven project.

"Sedge says Harry says Mitch has practically begged you to come on board as a paid consultant but you've said no—and Mitch doesn't want to make an issue of it anymore."

"Sounds about right," said Clara. "It's lovely that they think I'd be of help, but the truth is they can hire all the expertise they need."

"Sedge seems to think, from what his partner has told him, that this could be the biggest payday their company has ever had—if this discovery is for real. And to a man like Sedge—you know, loyalty to the old regiment, God save the empire, and all that—your walking away from this thing is a bit of slap in the face—not just to their auction house but to Mitch's career there."

Checking to see that Mitch hadn't yet returned from his grocery shopping on Broadway, Clara sank onto the living room sofa with a sigh. "Oh, my—this is escalating out of all proportion, Daddy. And I think Mr. Wakeham, old dear that he may be, should keep his nose out of Mitch's and my business. Sounds like they're ganging up on me, and frankly, I don't like it. I've got a career, too—or would like one if I can get my damn dissertation finished."

"Right," her father said, "and I told Sedge as much. But then I had an afterthought. How wedded are you to your Schubert topic for the dissertation—it's all about his Ninth Symphony, correct? And what about it, specifically—that it's so difficult to play—"

"Yes—that and everything else I can dredge up to explain what makes it so marvelous. What are you driving at?"

"How close are you to completing it?"

"I don't know, a year more maybe or a bit longer—there's no timetable. But that's just why I don't want to be snookered into this *William Tell Symphony* project—it'll turn out to be very time-consuming. You don't know the half of it."

"But it sounds incredibly exciting, Clara. Why don't you write your dissertation on this *Tell* Symphony discovery—even if it proves a fake. The whole investigation would make for instructive and fascinating reading—and I'm sure my friend Dickie Montrose at Faber & Faber would love to publish it. It could be a big hit—put you on the map right at the beginning of your academic career. And then you can go back and pick up with the Schubert and have a better chance of getting it published, too."

He spoke with such caring and conviction that she had to pause and consider the idea instead of dismissing it out of hand.

"Well," she said, "I never thought of that."

"Perhaps you should, Clara. I certainly don't mean to be intrusive, but it just seems…"

She was appreciative of his thoughtfulness and smarts—his success as a high-powered corporate executive commanded respect, not to mention her gratitude for all that he and her mother had done for her in life. But it was, after all, *her* life.

"May I be totally honest with you, Piet?" She would call him by his first name only at moments of particular delicacy.

"I should hope so, child."

"I'm afraid if I mix into this whole thing—which is in Mitch's primary business sphere but in my area of advanced learning—we might have rather a row over where it all comes out—if he and I should see it differently. He's quite protective about his turf—it's his form of independence, his impregnable castle, sort of. I'm afraid it all stems from my trust fund—not that he resents my having it, exactly, but, well, it's understandable in a way—"

117

"Hold on, Clara—I was told Mitch is all for your getting into this thing with him—that he values your brain power—likewise Messrs. Cubbage and Wakeham."

"I think Mitch wants me around just so long as I'll back up his judgment—for moral support, more or less. If I dare oppose him, it could bollix things up between us. Do you see?"

Her father did not.

"If you'll forgive me—my turn now to be totally honest—I think you're underestimating Mitch," he said, "or making a lame excuse to escape from the responsibility that comes with this invitation to take part in a potentially historic event. But what a challenge, Clara—it's a superb opportunity—and all opportunities come with risks. I say go for it, girl."

Which is why the next morning she asked Mitch if his offer to her to play his sidekick in the Beethoven venture was still open—"for a salary, you understand, but not an excessive one."

In response to which, he shouted, "Hell yes, you gorgeous creature!" and squeezed her half to death.

An hour later, the two of them packed up all her Beethoven books and hauled them back over to the C&W office in a taxi, to be at Mac Quarles's disposal while he was examining the *Tell* documents the following week. And when Mac reported his tentative findings ten days later, she was again on hand in the company library, this time taking copious notes.

AT THE END OF HIS SECOND DAY on the job, Mac Quarles had issued a bracing caveat based on the derelict appearance of the first sketchbook, containing the rough draft of the *Tell* Symphony.

"Its ratty condition may well testify to its authenticity, friends, but that doesn't make it any less problematic for purposes of analysis," he memoed the C&W brass. The material in the final two movements had to be gone over measure by measure, page by page, and before that could be done, it all needed to be transcribed for legibility. "As is, it's just too hard—too messy, too broken up—which we do know is how Beethoven composed—to get a clear, overall sense of this thing. Right now I'm reduced to calculated guesswork." And even if the manuscript were to be deemed authentic, he added, "sooner or later somebody—or a committee of somebodies—will have to make a series of choices that the composer, whoever it was, chose not to do for the last half of the work." Melodic lines and harmonic treatments had to be resolved,

Mac explained, "and even if the music is all in there, down on paper—and a lot of it is in unconnected pieces—unraveling it and making sure the edited passages jell with the surrounding ones—that's going to require a whole bunch of hard, sweaty, intuitive work."

Harry was confused.

"I get what you're saying, Professor," he remarked, dropping by Mitch's office, "but don't the first two movements, given their relatively clean shape, provide enough sense of the whole for you to form a preliminary opinion on the authenticity issue?"

"Now that's just what I'm fixin' to see to for you fellas." Mac motioned for the C&W security guard to keep an eagle eye on the manuscript while he headed out to lunch. "Anyone for the tuna and egg club at Three Guys? Nothin' half as good in Provence."

After Mac had labored all week, through the weekend, and two days into the following week, the C&W brain trust gathered to hear his tentative judgment. Delivered orally, unaccompanied by a written memorandum, the report started off sounding more upbeat than Mitch had expected and Clara had dared to hope. Just why she was anxious for positive feedback from this formidable academician she had managed to snare for Mitch's employer was puzzling to her; she had never thought of herself as a wishful romantic. Still, miracles were worth chasing after.

"The most striking thing of all for me," Mac began, without beating around the bush, "is the very nature and structure of this composition. Y'see, what I've kept askin' myself is why, if I were a crooked schemer, I'd create something that's such a radical departure from anything else Beethoven had done to that point—or would ever do afterward. You'd suppose just the opposite—that a forger would try to make up a Beethoven symphony very much in his heroic style. Yet that's not at all what we've got here."

Gordy cut in. "But isn't that also a strong prima facie argument against its authenticity?"

"Hang onto your britches, Mr. Roth, while I say my piece." Gordy subsided, and Mac drove home his point. If an imposter had composed *Tell* and put Beethoven's name to it, he had to be one shrewd cookie, thoroughly aware that every symphony the master wrote was markedly different from those that had preceded it and not just a variant on what he had already achieved. "Mr. B was always pushing the envelope, always comin' on with new structural dynamics, unsettling tonal twists, shifts of key and tempi, and unexpected melodic developments, so that he never let you relax, thinkin' you'd already been there. He just loved surprisin' his audience."

Yet as innovative as *Tell* was—with vocal passages daringly interspersed inside a full-scale symphonic work—it did not strike Mac as an implausible departure for Beethoven at that troubled moment in his career. No one else had tried to tell an explicit story in music without costumed actor-vocalists in front of stage scenery. "But, doncha see, that would have been the excitement of the challenge if you're the supreme maestro of the symphonic form," Mac theorized. Each of the four *Tell* movements included three vocal pieces—an aria, a duet, and a chorale—and a short passage from Schiller's text that the manuscript labeled a "dramalogue" to be recited by an actor with a pianissimo accompaniment. The whole unorthodox creation, as Mac read it, was designed to marry a perceptible story line to highly suggestive passagework, with all the driving tension that marked the great Beethoven symphonies—but without disintegrating into some kind of Swiss peasant hoedown or off-putting cacaphony.

"But why," Mitch asked, "didn't he just do an operatic adaptation of Schiller's play?"

"That's not too hard to figure." Mac tilted his chair back. "It's no accident that Beethoven wrote only one opera, and *Fidelio* was an agony for him—he was no damn good at writin' music for singers. He even admitted as much once in a letter, saying that—and I'm paraphrasin' him now—'When sounds ring within me, I always hear the *tutti*'—that's the full orchestra—'because I can ask anythin' of the instrumentalists. But when writin' for the voice, I must continually ask myself, "Can that be sung?"'" And so, Mac speculated, Beethoven (or his pretender) must have decided, after composing a few scenes of an operatic *Tell,* that he had run into the same old problem and settled on a different approach—a *dramatic* symphony, infused with operatic elements. He had the perfect librettist in Schiller himself, and as he started over, this time Beethoven, or whoever, chose passages from the text that allowed him to compose simple, melodic vocal segments in a narrow range and fixed key—"in other words, they're highly singable but don't intrude much on his overall symphonic scheme because they're musical asides, pleasin' diversions that can stand by themselves as songs and yield seamlessly to the next thematic progression. It's an ingenious solution to a problem that we know bedeviled the real Beethoven."

"Mmmm," said Harry, riveted. "Okay—if you say so. But then why William Tell? And why Schiller's play about him? Just because Beethoven supposedly headed for Switzerland to see a hearing specialist? That's not overly convincing to me."

"Oh, I agree," said Mac. "There are plenty of other historical and biographical factors, though, testifyin' to either the brilliance of your forger or the authenticity of the work."

The maestro, titan or not, was very much a child of his time, place, and social station, Mac related. "Like the rest of us, the man put on his drawers one leg at a time." Though neither an intellectual giant nor a political activist, he was fully aware of the revolutionary ferment sweeping across Europe during much of his lifetime. And as a commoner struggling for his daily bread in a world run by preening aristocrats, Beethoven was highly susceptible to the lure of German Romanticism, which sang to him of universal liberty, brotherhood, justice, and the cultural yearnings of the *Volk.*

The liberating precepts of the Romantic Movement were preached to Beethoven, Mac said, by one of his first music teachers who saw in the remarkable young keyboard artist the next Mozart. While the callow Beethoven could be considered a radical only for the departures from orthodoxy in his musical works, he was known to have attended lectures on Kant's iconoclastic moral philosophy, to have read deeply in the avant-garde literature of the period, and been thrilled by news from abroad—republican France, in particular—promising that the age of the divine-right monarchies was coming to an end.

"But that shinin' future had not yet arrived," Mac recounted. By the time Beethoven was establishing himself as a fixture of the Viennese music scene, the Hapsburg reaction had set in under Emperor Franz I. Faced with choosing between pauperism and expediency, young Ludwig opted out of martyrdom and sought the favor of—and commissions from—the entrenched social order. He did not air his political views any more than his contempt for most of his aristocratic keepers; his disreputable social status stemmed, rather, from his bad manners and indiscretion, attributable probably to his hardness of hearing. His crush on Napoleon hit the skids when the Corsican war lover crowned himself emperor—"on account of which ol' Ludwig took Bonaparte's name off the dedication line on the title page of the *Eroica,* his breakthrough symphony," Mac related.

Beethoven's disenchantment spread to encompass all the oppressive regimes and ideologies that ruled his age, Austrian absolutism included. He became an unsparing cynic about his adopted country. The maestro barely paid lip service to Austrian patriotism, refusing to dedicate any composition to his emperor, who repaid this slight by never attending a Beethoven concert or making him an official musician of the Hapsburg court. His only ally there was the emperor's aesthetic younger brother, Archduke Rudolph, who helped keep him afloat.

"All of which may help explain," Mac wound up, "why creating a work celebratin' the exploits of ol' Willy Tell could have appealed to Ludwig right about then."

"So 1814, you think, might have been payback time for the maestro," Harry said.

"That's what I'm sayin'. Five hundred years earlier, Tell and his downtrodden Swiss buddies were rebelling against an occupyin' army of Hapsburg bullyboys from Austria who'd invaded their peaceable little land. Here, have a look at this."

He handed around the translated lyrics, drawn from the text of Schiller's play, to the first vocal piece in the *Tell* Symphony, a duet between a tenor playing the Swiss yeoman patriot, Stauffacher, and a mezzosoprano playing his wife, Gertrud. The *Tell* composer had titled the duet "How Shall a Quiet Shepherd Folk Do Battle?" and written out the words in the spaces between the staves that carried the corresponding music. The duet began with Gertrud's lines:

The folk are weary of the yoke they bear,
For Gessler's insults are endlessly hurled,
And no fishing boat comes here across the water
But brings report of some new mischief done,
Some act of violence by the governors.
So it would be well if those of you
Of firm intent should quietly take counsel,
Debating how to rid us of the scourge,
And believe God won't abandon you
But will show favor to our righteous cause.

"Who knew any of this?" Harry asked rhetorically. "I flunked Swiss History two-oh-one."

Even more to the point, Mac pushed on, "We know that Schiller's play about Tell had been on Beethoven's mind for at least five years."

The news jolted Mitch, who had thus far not heard anything particularly persuasive—only plausible hunches, like Clara's had been. "And how do we know that?" he asked bluntly.

"Several ways." Beethoven had made no secret, Mac said, of his keen admiration for Schiller, whose favorite subject was the heroic defiance of tyrants. The composer's letters and diaries contained many references to the works of Schiller, who, like him, was a native of Weimar. Early in his career, Beethoven had expressed the hope of one day setting the poet's words to music. The opportunity seemed ripe in 1809, five years after Schiller's play *Wilhelm*

Tell had premiered in Germany. The Vienna court theater planned that year to stage one play each by the two foremost German Romantic dramatists, Mac reported, plucking a folded sheet of paper from his shirt pocket and opening it with exaggerated care. According to the memoirs of the eminent pianist and teacher Carl Czerny, who at the time was a devoted pupil of Beethoven and fully familiar with his professional activities—and I'm quoting now—

> …When it was decided to perform Schiller's *Tell* and Goethe's *Egmont* in the city theaters, the question arose as to who should compose the [incidental] music. Beethoven and Gurowitz were chosen. Beethoven wanted very much to have *Tell*. But a lot of intrigues were at once on foot to have *Egmont*, supposed to be less adaptable to music, assigned to him. It turned out, however, that he could make masterly music for this drama also, and he applied the full power of his genius to it.

"Beethoven's *Egmont* Overture is a short, movin', and very sad composition— it may be the best piece of background music ever written for the stage," Mac said. "Also—and this may be critically important for our purposes—it includes two lieder—folk songs—and a spoken monologue requirin' two vocalists and an actor." Mac bolted forward in his chair. "So you see this concept of combinin' instrumental and vocal music in a non-operatic form did have at least an abbreviated precedent in Beethoven's work," he said. "And so what this *Tell* of yours might actually be is an elaboration, at symphonic length and about a similar dramatic subject—heroic resistance to tyrants—of what he'd begun in miniature five years before."

Now *this* was hot stuff, Mitch thought but ventured no opinion. It was Harry who, having gnawed midway down the barrel of one of his chewing pencils, asked, "So where does all of this leave us exactly, Professor?"

"Nowhere *exactly*," Mac replied gently. "I'm surely not givin' you nice folks yes for an answer—far from it. But what I *am* sayin' is that there's enough goin' on here to deserve a white-knuckle investigation by that panel of experts you want assembled after your forensics people have examined this animal from snout to tail."

Then he added a note of scholarly restraint. "Even if this technical crew gives you the green light, let me clue you in on what you may be up against the moment that some pedigreed Beethoven bloodhounds start sniffin' around this thing. There's one damn funny business goin' on right at the start of this composition." The thematic statement opening the *Tell* manuscript, Mac told them, bore a striking resemblance to the famous overture to Gioachino Rossini's opera, *William Tell*, based on the same Schiller play. It was Rossini's last opera, first staged in 1829, which was two years *after* Beethoven's death—"so it's mighty temptin', so long as we're playin' detective here, to suspect the timin' may not have been an accident."

"That's amazing," Clara said. "I didn't see that. Just how close is the music?"

Mac gestured to her to sit beside him. "I think you'll be able to make out some of it in the autograph score in this second sketchbook if you read along with me." He looked up at the others. "Just so y'all're with me, I'm talkin' about what used to be played at the beginnin' and end of the *Lone Ranger* radio and TV shows when I was a kid—you could hear the hoofbeats of his great horse Silver poundin' through a canyon pass, to Rossini's stirrin' strains."

"Wait—are you suggesting Rossini *stole* the theme from Beethoven and waited until he was dead before staging it?" Gordy asked in disbelief.

"I'm only tellin' you what I find in this manuscript." He turned to Clara and, an outsized index finger hovering over the faded manuscript page, cited the similarities in terms too technical for the rest of them to follow. "But Beethoven," he wound up, "or whoever we're talkin' about here with this *Tell* thing, veers off less melodically than the Rossini version, jumps to the dominant, and goes his own way, tryin' to build harmonic tension and instrumental repartee."

Clara nodded tentatively, in awe of her mentor's perceptive powers. "And what does it all mean? How on earth could Rossini have—"

"You tell me, ma'am. It's anybody's guess."

Clara looked deflated. "Do we know if the two men ever met?"

"Haven't had a chance to look into that, but someone ought to." Mac scanned the table. "You've also got a bigtime mystery on your hands in figurin' out why Mr. Beethoven would have junked any manuscript this extensive. The letters by this Nina Hassler and the music publisher Nägeli may hold part of the answer—that the maestro simply felt the whole construct didn't hang together, so why keep chewin' on a bare bone? But you'd have to think there's somethin' more to it—that is, if there's *anythin'* at all to *any* of this." He guessed that the letter signed only "R" on stationery with a royal crest, found in the box with the manuscript and sent to Beethoven in Zurich seemingly by Archduke Rudolph, might prove highly illuminating.

"I've got our German handwriting experts lined up and raring to get at it," Mitch advised the room. As soon as the "R" letter was checked out and translated, it would be sent to Mac.

"See to it, y'hear?" the musicologist wrapped up amiably and hoisted himself upright. "Now I have a plane to catch—a pleasure, gentlemen and lady."

Two days later, on the premise that Cubbage & Wakeham would be better off trying to control news about the *Tell* discovery than risking its leakage and possible, even likely, premature dismissal, the auction house issued a press statement from both its New York and London offices. *The New York Times* reported it as the lead in its Arts section. The writeup began:

NEW YORK—A musical manuscript purporting to be a complete and previously unknown symphony by Ludwig van Beethoven, apparently composed during 1814 and abandoned by him for reasons as yet unknown, is now under tight security guard, according to Harrison E. Cubbage III, president of Cubbage & Wakeham Auction Galleries, located here and in London. The manuscript was recently found in Switzerland, Mr. Cubbage stated, under circumstances that are to be made public "upon completion of an exhaustive investigation of the authenticity of the composition and documents found with it."

No details on the nature of the symphony, its suitability for public performance, or possible plans to auction the manuscript would be disclosed, Mr. Cubbage said, until a team of experts headed by the highly regarded US musicologist, author, and composer, Macrae Quarles, now associate director of the Curtis Institute of Music in Philadelphia, "has addressed all aspects of the claim."

According to the Cubbage & Wakeham statement, an American scholar was chosen to head the investigative effort as a matter of convenience because the manuscript is currently in the possession of an American citizen, a New Jersey resident whose name would be divulged "eventually." It is expected that a panel of international authorities on Beethoven's music will soon be enlisted by Mr. Quarles.

If declared authentic, the work would be the tenth symphony composed by Beethoven (1771-1827), but the ninth if counted in chronological order. Music experts around the world apprised of the announcement greeted it with uniform skepticism. Anna Wertham Hayes, British author of a widely acclaimed 1987 biography of Beethoven, called the news "mind-boggling and fanciful," adding, "We will need to hear a great deal more about it before daring to become excited."

A still harsher view was voiced by Emil G. Reinsdorf, of Germany's National Institute of Music in Berlin, whose books and articles about Beethoven rank him among the foremost experts in the field. "It is almost surely a publicity stunt," Mr. Reinsdorf commented. "I trust a judgment on its authenticity will not be left to the American entertainment industry or to American music academia—it is far too serious a matter to be treated so lightly."

"You and Mac sure called it—about a hostile reception from the experts," Mitch said to Clara as they devoured the article together over breakfast. "And those are two of our choicest prospective panel members."

"Can't say I blame them," she said. "Sounds as if poor *Tell* may be DOA." She looked up from the news article. "The thing is, everybody thinks it's crazy—until they start looking into it seriously, the way Mac and I have."

Mitch nodded.

"I get that. But my trouble is that anyone talented and motivated enough to try forging a Beethoven symphony would also probably know all that stuff that you and Mac have come across and told us about and—well, would set up the scam accordingly—to make it seem circumstantially and historically—and even musically—plausible."

"You mean even though at first blush, it all sounds wild and loony?"

"Right. Maybe it's *supposed* to come across that way at first—which is why, on careful investigation, it all makes a kind of sense. Just like Mac Quarles said—for a forger to have crafted *Tell*, which is almost entirely out of keeping with all his other symphonic works, seems a stupid mistake; perverse, almost. He should have done something altogether in keeping with the Beethoven style and form, but that's exactly the genius of the scheme. A forger would be *expected* to make it sound like classic Beethoven, but that would have been too easy and readily suspect. So he goes for a radical departure, just as Beethoven often did, so it's not perverse at all—it's shrewd in the extreme."

Clara's head hurt. "So you're thinking—what? That this thing may really be genuine?"

"Ask me after the forensics reports are in," said Mitch.

{7}

C lara slept fitfully, perhaps two hours altogether, on the night flight to Zurich. In a semiconscious haze much of the time after the pathetic meal was served and the lights were lowered, she kept asking herself why Mitch had seized her hand during takeoff—something he had never done before—and tightly interlaced his fingers with hers until the plane had cleared JFK and was over the ocean. How could the gesture, given its timing, be anything other than prayerful? Was he telling her this might prove a portentous flight, likely to fix the course of both their lives?

The decision to go to Zurich on short notice had been prompted by a heads-up call from Johnny Winks. C&W's top undercover operative overseas, after ferreting in and around Zurich for a few weeks, had found enough disturbing dirt on the Erpf family in general and on Ansel Erpf in particular to justify a prompt investigation into the circumstances of the *Tell* discovery. "This Winky person," as Clara referred to Johnny, had infiltrated the city's social, financial, and cultural circles and concluded that Ansel was, at the least, a very odd duck—and, at worst, a deeply troubled, frustrated, and combustible character capable of who-knew-what mischief or antisocial conduct. Almost everyone agreed that, on the one hand, Ansel was brilliant and gifted; on the other, he had never gotten his act together, choosing instead to wallow in anxiety, indolence, self-pity, and drugs to escape the demands of adulthood and the price of professional attainment.

"Are you telling us he's a basket case?" Mitch asked Johnny over the phone.

"He's in therapy and heavily medicated, I'm told reliably," Johnny answered. Ansel's behavior was a never-ending embarrassment to his family, his marriage was an open scandal at their social club, his gross insubordination while he played with the Swiss Philharmonic made him notorious in the arts community, and his slanderous tongue would have got him shot in a duel years ago if such an expedient were still lawful. More to the point, Ansel was a composer *manqué* who had tried repeatedly to foist his creations on the local symphony orchestra and then bristled when they were summarily rejected. He was, however, a deft mimic of instrumental and vocal styles, and his local night club act featured comic blends of classical and pop icons—Irving Berlin tunes as if rendered by Bach, Cole Porter standards with a Mozartian lilt, and his showstopping take on Beethovenized Rodgers & Hammerstein, the uplifting ballad "You'll Always Walk Alone, Liebchen."

All of which added up in Mitch's mind to the obvious conjecture that Ansel Erpf might very well possess the technical tools, the creative talent, and the volatile temperament to have written the *Tell* Symphony, then attributed it to Beethoven, then arranged for it to be conveniently "discovered" in Otto Hassler's attic next door. "The problem is," he told Winks, "that it's just too obvious a stunt. Surely he'd know the authorities would be onto him right off the bat."

"The thought," said Johnny, "occurred to me. But you need to pay Mr. Erpf a visit."

Mitch decided not to await the outcome of the forensics investigation already underway. If he could nip the whole thing in the bud as the runaway brainstorm of an idiot savant, his company would be spared a lot of expenditure and notoriety. The pretext for his visit to Zurich was not difficult to establish in a way acceptable to the Erpf family even while they were challenging Jake Hassler's title to the *Tell* manuscript and C&W's oversight of its pending sale.

"This is a routine part of our effort to authenticate the work," Mitch explained in separate phone conversations with Ansel and his sister Margot, "and of course we feel this procedure is in everybody's interest in this case." Once they all knew what they were dealing with in *Tell*, it might be far easier to reach an understanding about its ownership. Why have a spat over a clever forgery?

Margot was satisfied with that—and she promised Mitch her full cooperation. Ansel, though, was combative, asking, "But why should the investigation be conducted under your auspices? Your client—and I used to like Jake Hassler, mind you—is trafficking in stolen goods, and your company, I hope you realize, is doing his bidding."

"We don't quite see it that way," Mitch told him, "but we and our client are prepared to let others adjudicate the matter if it can't be worked out amicably." Meanwhile, his firm was willing to shoulder the expense of getting to the bottom of the discovery—and anyone who found that decision objectionable might, in C&W's view, have something to hide. Thus confronted, Ansel gave way and agreed to an interview two days later. Clara's command of German on top of her fresh commitment to the project recommended her as Mitch's traveling companion.

THEY USED THEIR FIRST DAY IN Zurich to reconnoiter the overgrown old market town, with its curving lakefront, cobbled streets and squares, stoutly timbered dwellings, and hulking public structures, in good repair if short on monumental scale or inventive design. The city also seemed ironically to be a model of up-to-date operating efficiency. Yet its picturesque charm had not been sacrificed to the grosser demands of modernity. The ancient core of the town, bisected by the little Limmat River that emptied into Lake Zurich, was a maze of mellow stonemasonry, meandering alleys, and endless clusters of overpriced shops and precious boutiques.

Ansel Erpf had arranged to meet them at the Turm, a café directly across the Napfplatz, the little cobbled square where his family's residence stood, right next door to the late Otto Hassler's house. They were to have coffee and, if time and the civility of their exchange permitted, a bite of lunch. He had a tennis match at the Platypus Club at two, Ansel said, and he never played on a full stomach.

He was waiting for them at one of the rear outdoor tables under the café's blue-and-white striped awning. Ansel stood up at their approach, a short, moon-faced man with petite features. He had on blue jeans, desert boots, a brown leather jacket, the round wire-frame glasses of a John Lennon clone, and, of all things, a New York Yankees baseball cap. A single braid of light brown hair hung midway down his back. Wrinkle-free save for crow's-feet lines at the outer edges of his peephole eyes, he could have been twenty-eight or twice that age. "It's a souvenir of my last visit to the States—the height of kitsch," he said, doffing his cap to expose a mercilessly retreating hairline.

Mitch thanked him for the courtesy of meeting with them and, as they sat, asked pleasantly for a few sightseeing tips.

"Ah, such fabulous sights to see in our precious, oh-so-pointlessly charming Züri!" He fell back in his chair, as if overcome by the question. "Where to begin?"

"Since when does charm need to have a point to it?" Clara asked pleasantly. "Besides, your city seems to abound in purposefulness."

Ansel's pinpoint eyes bored in on her; he was at once joyfully *engagé* flaunting his barely accented English. "And what purpose would that be, Mrs. Emery? Beyond, I mean, stuffing our wallets? Oh, for sure, we are one shimmering shitload of fat cats, without a doubt—with all our brimming banks and great pharmaceutical houses, all the fancy shops and glitzy jewelers' windows." He reached inside his shirt pocket for a cigarette. "Someone told me we have a thousand jewelers in Züri, and I believe it. They say there are vaults just below the Bahnhofstrasse heaped with precious metals and gemstones." He pushed a Gauloise between his thin lips and lit it with a cheap lighter. "All these riches, you see, have bought us a nice little everything—smartly appointed homes, rigorous schools, spotless clinics, punctual railways and trams, state-of-the-art plumbing and waste removal—to go with our nice little land." He took a swallow of black coffee, cradling the cup and resting his cigarette in the saucer. "Not to mention our unspeakably nice little cultural institutions—have you been to the Kunsthaus, our most eminent art museum? Not a single first-rate work hangs on its walls."

Mitch was briefly jarred by this acidic spiel, likely delivered for its shock value. But hadn't this fellow been advertised as a patriotic Swiss, out to rescue *Tell* for his worthy, if misunderstood, countrymen? He fed Clara a curious look that invited her to keep goading Ansel.

"We spent a couple of hours at the Kunsthaus yesterday afternoon," she told him, "and found a lovely assortment of regional and genre works that serve quite well to illustrate your—"

"Candy boxes and gift wrappings," Ansel cracked and inhaled with a vengeance.

"I doubt the Kunsthaus was ever envisioned as a second Louvre," Clara countered.

"Exactly so! Because we're the boonies. We have a tiresome history, smalltown values, and insular imaginations to match. To be sure, I exaggerate—it's a fine little museum, just as we have a fine little opera house and a fine little repertory theater and—and a no-longer-so-fine little symphony orchestra, ever since it and I went our separate ways." He gave his braid a fierce wag. "There's just no creative juice flowing through Swiss veins, not a thimble of panache. Where are our writers and painters, our poets and composers, our inventors and thinkers?" He contemplated his cigarette ember for a moment. "Poor little rich people."

Mitch sensed it was all rehearsed, an act to stir scorn in unwary outsiders unaware they were being had. By most standards his country was the envy of the world—peaceable, prosperous, and pristine, or more nearly so than anywhere else. So why the extravagant pretense otherwise? Were they just words he savored spouting, a performance that Ansel's troubled psyche could not restrain? Or was this a calculated put-on to divert them from inquiring too deeply into the particulars of the *William Tell* Symphony? Mitch needed to find out.

"If you find Switzerland and Zurich so sad and stultifying, Mr. Erpf," he asked, trying to sound sympathetic, "why do you stay? Surely you have the means and skills to make your way anywhere else in the world if you'd choose."

Ansel folded his arms and rested his elbows on the tabletop. "You see, that's a perfectly intelligent question that only an American would ask. You are famous for your mobility, always restless and ravaging as you go, whereas we Europeans embrace our rootedness. I've seen my share of the world, mind you, and enjoyed the adventure of it, but in the end the Swiss, even the disaffected among us, remain Swiss. We may be stuck in a deep rut, but it's such a nice little rut that it takes both stamina and a degree of madness to try to climb up out of it. In my case, there is an added consideration. How shall I put it tastefully? My family, we have a certain standing in the community—which I have not exerted the slightest effort to enhance, you understand—yet it's there, and I cannot ignore the reality, which brings pleasing advantages, of course, even as it smothers the spirit the same way that this so-called city can be suffocating. It's too small to spread out in, too hard to get lost in, everyone knows you, and your every gesture gets reported—and so one's every thought is conditioned accordingly." He stubbed out his cigarette in the saucer and cut himself short, like a standup comedian whose opening monologue had gone flat. "Forgive me—it's just my morning catharsis. I believe we have other business to explore."

Before Mitch could channel the conversation, Ansel signaled the waiter to bring them menus, highly recommended the trout salad, and began to rail against Jake Hassler. "My little anti-Swiss tirade shouldn't mislead you," he confided. "I'm still enough of a chauvinist to be repelled when one of your countrymen runs off with a manuscript by an icon of European culture—and especially one dealing with the noblest hero in our national folklore. And really, now—what good do you suppose will come out of it once you Americans begin to hype this Beethoven manuscript, or whatever it turns out to be?"

Mitch contemplated their volatile luncheon partner with dispassion for a moment. "You mean how could a nation of frontier savages possibly treat a high-culture god with reverence?"

"Something like that. It's not in your people's character."

"My guess is," Mitch said, trying to avoid a strident reply while hoping to further stir up this smoldering firebrand, "what's really bothering you about the

Tell manuscript is that it was lying around right under your noses for a couple of centuries—quite possibly—and the moment it was pointed out to a typical American yahoo, he knew enough to grab it and head for open water—and probably had every right to do so." Mitch glanced at the menu to mitigate his provocation. "Frankly, I don't blame you for being upset." He looked up at the hovering waiter. "I'll have the mushroom omelet and a glass of the house red—assuming it's Swiss. If not, would you pick it for me, Mr. Erpf?"

Reference to the *Tell* manuscript focused their attention on the Hassler house directly across the square. The five-story building had high ceilings and large, open-shuttered windows that must have kept the interior cool and bright but lacked grace notes of the sort enlivening the carved stone façade of the grander Erpf home to its immediate right. A strip of red-and-white plastic tape was stretched across the Hasslers' doorway, barring entry. Mitch asked the reason.

"The health and engineering departments are afraid the house has been neglected over the years and may no longer be structurally safe." Ansel shrugged with disdain for the bureaucratic mentality. "So they're investigating, even before Otto's estate is fully certified and my family's firm can take title to it. Repairs may prove costly, but I've told my barracuda sister not to worry—if the Beethoven manuscript is authenticated and amounts to almost anything at all, the house will surely become a shrine for sightseers, perhaps tripling in value. Who wouldn't like to own it and be able to say, 'Oh, yes, that's the room where Beethoven's Tenth was composed'?"

Mitch studied him without addressing the rhetorical question. Ansel's body language—the quick gestures, staccato speech, constantly shifting posture—was thick with coiled tension. Were his visitors making him jumpy, or was he in dire need of a fix? Or was this just his normal angst on display? Perhaps all three. "And do you really believe that?" Mitch asked, trying to catch him off guard. "Do you think this whole *Tell* thing is on the up and up?"

Ansel fished for another cigarette and wore a puzzled look. "'On the up and up,'" he parroted. "I thought I knew every American expression—what does it mean?"

"Honest—legitimate."

"I gather, from the context. But the image—why the two 'ups'? What does the repetition signify? I'm fascinated by derivations."

Was this another diversionary tactic? Or was Ansel flustered and just trying to buy time while he cobbled an answer? "I can't help you there," Mitch said.

Ansel gave a dismissive shrug, then draped one leg over the arm of his chair. "Ah, well—as to the up-and-upness of *Der Wilhelm Tell Symphonie*. Like every

132

serious musician, I know my Beethoven, but ever since our little discovery"—he gestured across the street—"I've been reading up on him intensively." The small eyes narrowed to a slit. "What most bothered me at first was why he would have just left the manuscript behind like that instead of destroying it himself. Freud, of course, would have said he was conflicted—driven by whatever reasons he had to set it aside, yet perhaps subconsciously hoping that the daughter of the Hassler house would disobey his wish." He propped his left elbow on its corresponding knee and cupped his chin. "But then I decided his rashness in abandoning the work was not so very mysterious. Creative geniuses, you know, are notoriously quirky sorts—they often do such impulsive and self-destructive things."

Mitch wanted to keep him going on the chance of pushing him into a self-incriminating slip-up. "That's a possibility, for sure. I mean, hadn't Beethoven revealed self-destructive tendencies well before 1814? What was it called—the Heiligenstadt Testament, the letter to his brothers, telling them that the onset of his deafness was driving him toward suicide?"

"Oh, I wouldn't fall for that, necessarily," Ansel said. "He had this deep, self-pitying streak in him—it wasn't only his hearing problem that depressed the man. Everything in his life seemed to have been put there to torture him—and turned him, if you ask me, into a borderline sociopath. You start with his father being a roaring drunkard and then throw in his dear old mum, giving him delusions of grandeur with her hints that Ludwig might have been the love child of the King of Prussia or the Elector of Hesse when she worked as a maid in the court castle." Ansel warmed to his captive audience. "And, of course, there was his unfortunate appearance—he was short, you know—not even my size"—with his massive head that must have made him look top-heavy, his protruding teeth, indelicate nose, pocked cheeks, and whirlpool of untamable hair. Hardly a creature to lure the ladies, "especially of the rich and refined sort he pined after. I think he was fated never to share himself intimately with a woman. Some people have room for only a single passion in their lives, and for him it was plainly his music. And his deafness must have driven him deeper into loneliness and self-sorrow." Ansel emitted a empathetic sigh. "He had nothing going for him in life except his great gift, and you know what they say—talent is a blessing, genius an affliction."

Mitch sensed he had struck pay dirt. It sounded to him as if this homely, isolated, and idle nobody was identifying his own travails with those of classical music's supreme master. Not a confession, to be sure, but a less-than-subtle hint to arouse his listeners' interest. A cellist with the philharmonic, Ansel would naturally have known a great deal about Beethoven's music, life, and psyche, but was it possible for him to have absorbed all of that detailed and intimate knowledge about the man within the few weeks since *Tell* had surfaced—or was it the harvest of a long-running fixation? Too, there was this preoccupation of his with language and its nuances—Ansel seemed to choose each word with precision. Might this acute aptitude have been applied to fabricating the Nina and Nägeli letters found with the manuscript by way of embellishing the tale he had woven to explain *Tell*'s existence? It was a tantalizing possibility. But then why would he risk awakening such a suspicion in his interrogator? A pyromaniac openly playing with fire and daring his onlookers to stop him before he torched again?

"And is that your affliction as well?" Mitch asked with an awkward show at empathy.

Ansel was onto him, replying with a brief peal of dark laughter. "Ah, Mitchell Emery—so you think you detect a stark raving Beethoven complex in me, do you?" Then out poured an account of passionate devotion to his muse and all her siren song, sustained in the teeth of continuous discouragement by his family. His father, he said, had always objected to a career in the performing arts for Ansel as undignified and certain to leave him financially needy. But by twelve he was the youngest and best musician in his *gymnasium* orchestra; by fifteen he was attending the conservatory for both piano and cello lessons and classes in theory. Belatedly his father tried to shove the musical genie back inside the bottle, ordering a cut-off in all lessons for a year and condemning Ansel to apprentice in the family's Limmat Realty offices to learn about property assessments, rent collection, sales and lease agreements, and how to cosset clients.

"It was all too ghastly and tedious," he recounted, but in concession to his unbending father, Ansel enrolled at Zurich University, immersing himself not only in studying music but also German literature and philosophy. Even as he defiantly distanced himself from the Erpf real estate empire, thereby opening the way for his sister Margot to take his place as heir apparent, Ansel gradually withdrew from the university and turned playboy, by day a fixture at the Platypus Club bar and tennis courts, by night a consumer of more than his fair share of drugs readily available through former university companions and at the dives along the Niederdorf strip. Tired of tolerating this desultory lifestyle, his father offered to fund a year of travel and oats-sowing if Ansel would kick drugs and promise to knuckle down to something useful—even serious music—after he came home. One year of subsidized vagabonding stretched into three. On his belated return, he took up with "my divine Lisa," the socialite daughter of another Platypus Club family, powerful people in the pharmaceutical industry—much to the Erpfs' approval—and returned full-time to the conservatory to turn himself into a polished cellist. Eventually he won a job with the Philharmonia Helvetica National, an occupation acceptable to his family, which had long been generous donors to the symphony orchestra. Marriage to Lisa the Drug Princess—as Ansel called her, even to her face—soon followed, and for a time, things stabilized.

The Swiss Philharmonic, as the orchestra was called, was not a place, however, where any gifted and ambitious artist would wish to remain for long, Ansel contended. Its concert hall close by the lake was gloomy, and the orchestra itself was less a fixed ensemble than a shifting pool of mediocre local and imported past-their-prime musicians. Among such company, Ansel stood out as a natural candidate for the principal cellist's chair as soon as it fell vacant. That, though, seemed an eternity away, "and I grew restless," he confessed to the Emerys, "and then my marriage turned into a sour joke—Lisa was twice as spoiled as I was and no more faithful." He endured the situation with mordant humor, taking solace anew in drugs while starting to compose in a haphazard way and inventing his classical-pop music act for gigs at local wine bars.

"My mother's election to the Philharmonic Board, for all her good intentions, served only to complicate matters," Ansel added. After one board meeting, she drew aside Herr Richard Grieder, the aging, worse-for-wear conductor and musical director, and inquired about her son's prospects for becoming principal cellist. Thereafter, Grieder, no doubt supposing Ansel had put his mother up to it, was curt with him and implied that he would never bow to pressure, no matter how generous the Erpfs were to the orchestra. The ultimate indignity came, Ansel lamented, when he had the temerity to submit several of his own compositions for performance by the philharmonic. "The scores were returned to me without a note of regret or even thanks."

After a dozen years of dutiful time-serving, Ansel related, "I launched guerrilla warfare against the stuffy bastards, but Grieder was hopelessly entrenched." His discipline was lax, he could not communicate, his program selections were mired in cliché, and no concert passed without his falling a half beat off tempo for twenty or thirty bars before he woke up to it. "He was, and remains, a gross incompetent, and I said as much to whoever would listen." One day, he did so at a rehearsal after Grieder had unfairly singled out Ansel for criticism. "Then I got up and marched off the stage—probably about three seconds before they were going to pitch me into the lake—and I haven't gone back since."

His marriage had likewise ended on the rocks. "And just as well," he said. "Our parents had pressured us into it—good for our emotional stability, they claimed. Ha! Now I just look after my family's house, smoke three cigars a day in peace, stay up all night with my Artie Shaw records and a variety of lady friends, and do my comedy act whenever I like. Not a bad life."

That Ansel would unburden himself to strangers in this fashion struck Mitch as testimony to the man's fragile emotional state. "Sounds kind of lonely to me," he said. "Not unlike Beethoven's life, now that you've brought it up."

Ansel drew off his glasses, pinched the bridge of his nose, and began to clean the right lens with his napkin. "Perhaps you should show me your psychiatric license before you begin practicing on me," he said without looking up. "As you may know, Mitchell, I'm already well attended to in that department, so spare yourself the effort."

"No, no—I meant only that you're a musician, too, who's faced considerable adversity and pain and have gone largely unappreciated despite your considerable—"

"Genius?" Ansel gave a wry grin, redonned his glasses, then teetered back in his chair and folded his hands together behind his head in a cradling position. "What you say is quite true—and I blame the outcome on circumstances beyond my control more than on any deficiency in my character. But I hardly think that categorizes my case as raving paranoia." He peered across the table. "Now why don't you tell me what you nice people came all this way to find out?"

"Since you ask," Mitch said without hesitation now. "There's a gentleman back in our office who's a suspicious sort—they pay him for that particular trait. He raised the possibility, however farfetched, that you may be the actual composer of the *William Tell* Symphony—and so I've been dispatched to look into the matter. I asked Clara, who is completing her doctoral dissertation on Schubert, to join me."

Ansel's eye-blink rate did not increase. "Ah—now we're getting somewhere."

"Did you?" Mitch asked.

"Did I what—write the *Tell* Symphony and—what—attribute it to Beethoven?"

"Yes."

Ansel gave a derisive snort.

"Such an insult to poor Beethoven," he said, pausing to light another cigarette. "May I ask if this colleague of yours, who I'll assume to be a total ignoramus about musical matters, has examined the manuscript?"

"He doesn't pass himself off as an authority on music. It's just a gut feeling on his part."

"Just so. And yourself?"

"Do I have musical expertise? Only by proximity to my wife. What of it?"

Ansel turned to Clara. "Perhaps Mrs. Emery—since you know music—have you seen it?"

"The manuscript? I have, actually."

"And doesn't the very idea strike you as—I don't know what else to call it other than completely idiotic—to imagine that anyone could sham the consummate artistry of a Beethoven? I suppose it's very flattering to be considered even remotely capable of such a stupendous deception—Beethoven had unique powers, soaring inspiration..." Now his agitation began to show. "And it's obviously a worn old manuscript. Do you mean I would go to the extent of, what, *antiquing* an old composition book and all the rest?" The edges of a tremor in his voice hinted at a rising level of distress.

"I'm not competent," Clara said softly, "to evaluate the manuscript beyond observing certain similarities to Beethoven's compositional techniques. What someone else might be capable of by way of imitation, for whatever reason, is hardly for me to—"

"Wait, wait—I see it all now!" Ansel interjected. "It's known that I play several instruments and can satirize the styles of many composers—and that I've attempted some composing of my own—and that our home is next door to where the manuscript was found—therefore, according to this brilliant line of logic, I must have written it."

"And," said Mitch, unwilling to let the point be lost to mockery, "how better to attract recognition from the world than by tricking yourself out in the guise of a certified superstar and trying to pass off your work as his?"

"I see." Ansel calmed himself. "How thrilling even to be seriously suspected of such a ruse." He leaned forward to engage his inquisitor. "But if one were to contemplate such an unthinkable undertaking, why dream up a work like *Tell*? It's so utterly unlike most of what Beethoven wrote—a 'dramatic symphony' with substantial vocal interludes—"

"Which would help to explain, of course," Mitch replied, "why Beethoven might have chosen to set such an extensive work aside as a noble experiment gone irreparably awry. Quite an ingenious idea for a forgery, if you think about it."

Ansel inhaled deeply and let the smoke out contemplatively in a thin stream. "And my skills are supposed to extend as well to forging Beethoven's sloppy handwriting?"

"Or hired someone else to do it," Mitch replied.

"How—by placing a help-wanted advert in *The Times* or the *Tagblat*?" Ansel paused, eyes widening, and said, "Oh, wait—now that I think about it, I could have hired my dear cousin from Vevey—Sofie Ries. A highly regarded creator of children's books, and her illustrations have a marvelous depth thanks to her intricate cross-hatching." He looked Mitch in the eye. "I suppose with a little practice she could have learned to forge Beethoven's writing."

The man's bravado was a challenge not to be left hanging.

"Did she?" Mitch asked.

Ansel gave a triumphant snort. "Well, you'll just have to ask her," he said. "I believe her number's listed in the Vevey directory. If not, Margot or I have it around somewhere."

Food arrived and broke the tension of their exchange. Ansel poured wine for all of them with a steady hand and said, "Well, thank you for your directness, but I hereby and equally directly assure you—we have a Bible in our house that I'll swear on if you'd like—that I did no such thing as your deranged colleague imagines. And if I *were* capable of it, why would I be wasting my time playing an imposter instead of creating masterful music in my own name?"

On their stroll along the Limmat heading back toward their hotel, Clara let Mitch steep in silence as he processed all they had seen and heard. "I'll bet you're wondering about dear cousin Sofie's connection to the whole story," she finally intruded. "Why on earth would he even bring up her name if she was involved in this thing?"

Mitch dug his hands into his pockets. "Who knows—he seems clever enough to be playing all sorts of games with us."

Clara had a different take on Ansel. "I think you may be too hung up on the coincidence between his being a professional musician and his living next door to where the manuscript was found. Actually, if both weren't the case, the manuscript would have been lost forever after Otto's house was cleaned out."

Mitch nodded. "But that's not one coincidence," he said, "it's two. His occupation and his address. Two coincidences have a whiff of premeditation about them."

Clara liked watching the cogs of his brain whirring. "He could also just be a genuine neurotic telling us more than we want to know about him because he's enjoying all the attention," she said. "I find him rather appealing, actually—in a homeless puppy kind of way."

♪

THEIR LUNCHEON APPOINTMENT the next day was at the Belvoir Park restaurant, a cheerfully retrofitted mansion on a hillside overlooking Zurich's western lakefront. Margot Lenz, who said on arrival that she lived only a few blocks away, bore little resemblance to her brother. Her angular features, a bit too severe to qualify her as a beauty, suggested an Erté *femme fatale* in a smart, dark tweed suit instead of a diaphanous chemise. Her satiny voice was low-pitched, her manner one of deep concern.

"I'm glad you've come," she told them after the briefest of pleasantries. "I'm still hopeful that we can work something out with Mr. Hassler and your company, so I'm going to be entirely candid with you. Our family's privacy has already been compromised by my brother's history, and you shouldn't be under any misapprehension where Ansel is concerned. It was good that you were able to spend time with him yesterday, so you can better sense—" She cut herself short. "I act as our family's unofficial caretaker for him, more or less—my parents are no longer in the best of health and are often away traveling."

"He didn't seem to be in particular need of a caretaker," Mitch said.

"Not in the sense of a nursemaid. But he's been under medication for some years now, and he's rather at loose ends these days ever since he left the philharmonic and his marriage broke up. He's fine much of the time, but if he forgets his medication or thinks he can get by without it, well, that's when the trouble begins. It's one reason he's been living in our family's old home—there's help around to keep an eye on him, just in case."

Five years older than Ansel, she had been acting as his guardian angel all his life, Margot confided over drinks, "for which thankless service I have been rewarded with alternating bursts of unconditional love and bitter resentment on his part. It is not a mission I enjoy."

"Is Ansel—how shall I put it politely—in control of his mental faculties?" Mitch asked.

Margot hesitated before answering. "I'm afraid he's abused himself and his native resources for so long that there's no short answer to your question." What most people would regard as fortunate—to be born into a family with the Erpfs' advantages—had, in Ansel's case, almost certainly worked to his detriment, she implied. "And his basic musical skills came almost too easily to him." But their father's strong opposition to his son's pursuit of a career in the precarious field of music and Ansel's own laggard, if willful, spirit were too problematic for his natural ability to overcome, "and so he's forever wavered between playing the half-hearted rebel and the devoted sybarite. The result is that his career as a serious artist is in shambles, and all he has left is a part-time job as a kind of musical clown at a piano bar."

"But he claims he had reformed and worked earnestly as a cellist with your philharmonic, only to be rebuffed," Mitch related.

Margot shook her head slowly. "Yes—well, with Ansel it's always other people's fault. The truth is, he got bored with the orchestra early on and took to calling it 'this third-rate band in a second-rate town'—not exactly words to endear himself to his colleagues or, when they got repeated, to his superiors. They doomed his hopes of gaining the first cellist's chair, and when our mother tried to patch things up, he blamed her for only making it all worse. He began showing up late at rehearsals and then missing some altogether, phoning in some feeble excuse. They wanted to let him go, but Mother held them off for a time." Margot sighed and attacked her martini in earnest.

"What about Ansel's compositions?" Mitch asked her. "He claims they never gave him a hearing. Has he ever played any of them for you?"

"I've asked, but he's afraid I'm too judgmental about everything where he's concerned."

"Has anyone told you whether he's gifted—or just—more or less delusional?"

"Only his friend—well, they're more like former friends now—Felix Utley. He's a first-section violinist with the philharmonic. He should have been made concertmaster years ago, but he had a run-in with Grieder also. He and Ansel were in the soup together, for quite different reasons. Felix looked after Ansel, always urging him to play it straight and stop clowning and give up his drug habit whenever he fell back into it. He's a very understanding guy." At the Erpfs' Christmas party one year, Ansel showed up with Felix in tow, and Margot got to thank him for his kind efforts. "Ansel told me the day before that the philharmonic had flatly rejected his latest concerto, so I asked Felix privately if he had ever heard or read Ansel's music. He said yes and then shrugged and looked away. 'I've heard worse,' he said, which I think you would have to characterize as damning with faint praise. I suspect Grieder, our uninspired old conductor, and the other powers that be at the philharmonic gave Ansel's creations at least a cursory review and found them wanting. But Ansel can never take no for an answer."

"And his marriage? He claims the family drove him into it."

Margot's frown deepened. "He simply won't accept responsibility for his own actions—and inactions. Nobody told him to marry Lisa—she was too young, too headstrong, and too—well, let's just say that her affair with the tennis professional at our club became common knowledge—was even flaunted in a setting where discretion is greatly prized." All of which served to cast Ansel as a lost soul and shame his family unbearably.

His sister turned toward the window and gazed at the lawn and the floral plantings at its scalloped edge. "It's one reason our parents are out of town so often. And I keep my distance from our club most of the time—it's embarrassing to be the object of sideways glances from the members—and let me tell you, in my business and in a community as tight as ours is, social contacts are all-important."

The woman's anguish could not be doubted. "Not a happy tale," Mitch commiserated.

"No, but perhaps you can see now why this quite extraordinary discovery of Ansel's right next door to our house seems such a godsend—and why our family has chosen to pursue the matter. This goes well beyond the legalities involved."

"Meaning—what? It's a form of therapy for him, and so—"

"Not just therapy—it's become his driving mission in life, though he probably didn't let on as much to you people. He's totally consumed by it—he reads, eats, sleeps, and breathes Beethoven all the time now. Don't you see— here's something of his doing that nobody can complain about. *He* found the *Tell* Symphony—not Otto Hassler's grandson. Jacob would have undoubtedly disposed of the old trunk as worthless. Finally, Ansel has *done* something immensely useful—or so we all hope it proves. It's given him a noble purpose in life just now—and I thought the family ought to stand by him in the matter." Her feeling had been translated into the Erpfs' proposal to the Swiss government— "The subject of the symphony, after all, is of keen interest to our country"—to enlist its help in retrieving the manuscript from America.

"Yes," Mitch confirmed, "a Swiss official explained the arrangement to our firm—quite creative on your part, and I'm not being cynical."

"What probably wasn't mentioned to you, though—and I'm sharing the information with you because you've come to us in a civilized way—is a side proposal we made to Herr Grieder." In return for the Erpfs' kindness in trying to direct a sizable portion of any funds the *Tell* Symphony might generate to benefit the Swiss Philharmonic, as well as the family's insistence that the world premiere of the work be performed by the Zurich orchestra under Grieder's baton, the conductor was to reengage Ansel and, given his good conduct for one year, to appoint him principal cellist. "The fellow they chose when Ansel was passed over is due to transfer soon to the Orchestre de la Suisse Romande. And to patch up his old friend Felix Utley's falling out with the conductor,

Ansel asked that the understanding with Grieder also ensure Felix's long overdue appointment as concertmaster."

"And Grieder agreed?"

"Only after rumbling and grumbling, you can be sure. But the fact is, all of this excitement over *Tell* is Grieder's one last chance, like Ansel's probably, to make a name for himself. His animus to Ansel aside, he's truly a mediocre fellow."

Mitch nodded appreciatively at her rendering of the larger picture. "All of this predicated, of course, on the authentication of the work and its amounting to something special."

"To be sure, which is why we'd greatly prefer that the investigation be carried on over here in a thoroughly disinterested way by the world's most informed experts."

"And why do you assume my firm won't exercise comparable care?"

"Because it doesn't have the resources or the *bona fides* of the Swiss government—which would cherish this work as a potential national treasure." She drained her drink and added, "For you people, I'm afraid, it's just another transaction—it's only about the money."

"My only question," Clara said afterward, as she and Mitch followed the path along the lakefront on the way back to their hotel, "is why she was so forthcoming with us. Europeans tend to be rather more close-mouthed than Americans when it comes to revealing their family's innermost secrets, especially to strangers."

Mitch was untroubled by the woman's openness with them.

"She probably figured we'd already picked up Ansel's sorry past, so she had more to gain by leveling with us—or appearing to—than by being combative or unresponsive. It's a smarter way to try to generate compassion for her brother and get us to see the whole situation from her family's side of it."

Clara bent down for a flat round stone and sent it skimming over the calm lake surface. "I suppose," she said. "And frankly, I sympathize with their unhappiness over the manuscript being in American hands for sale to the highest bidder. It makes our side look rather predatory."

"Not from Jake Hassler's point of view," said Mitch. "Ansel may have been instrumental in recognizing the manuscript for what it is—or might be—but if you buy the story, it was Nina Hassler who rescued the thing in the first place, and two hundred years later, why shouldn't one of her family's descendants be the beneficiary of her foresight?" He paused to watch a swan swoop in for a landing with much noisy wing-flapping and come to an abrupt, squawking halt a few yards from shore. "As to Margot's claim that we're just being mercenary slobs while the high-minded Erpfs got involved only because of Swiss pride and Ansel's delicate emotional condition—I say the lady doth protest too much. Their willingness to donate something they don't own and have at best a dubious claim on makes is less altruism than smart—and inexpensive—public relations for the Erpfs' real estate business. And if the family's sterling reputation at their snooty club has been stained by Ansel's conduct, what better way to polish it than by demonstrating their avid patriotism—which allows them to sic their government on Jake and C&W?"

"A brilliantly cynical diagnosis," Clara said, reaching for his hand and swinging their meshed fingers back and forth as they went. "Once a lawyer," she added, "always a lawyer."

FELIX UTLEY HAD SOUNDED RELUCTANT to meet until Mitch indicated over the phone that he was calling at Margot Lenz's suggestion.

"I don't know how I can help you," Felix said, weariness in his voice at the prospect of discussing Ansel's tribulations, "but if Margot's put you on to me, fine—she's a saint with regard to her brother. Ansel's been a trial for all of us." Since the Tonhalle, where the Swiss Philharmonic played, was around the corner from the Emerys' hotel, Felix had suggested they meet in front of the building after his rehearsal the next morning and take a walk along Lake Zurich. Clara feared her presence might inhibit the men's strolling conversation and elected to jog beside the lake well out of their range.

In his rumpled black suit and open-collar white dress shirt, Felix was a seedier, longer-haired version of Yves Montand, nice-looking but palpably world-weary. Perhaps the rehearsal had left him drained. "Oh, Ansel-Ansel-Ansel—forever Ansel!" he moaned as he and Mitch headed for the lakeside walkway. "He's his own worst enemy—and such a waste. There—I've said it all—now let's talk about global warming. Any other topic would be more soothing."

"I gather that the two of you were close at one point," said Mitch, declining Felix's offer of a cigarette. "Margot said you tried heroically to reform him."

"Yes, well—he was worth trying to salvage," Felix said, cupping the match flame against the breeze off the lake as he lit up. "Everyone could see it when he first came to us. He played with great feeling and precise phrasing; he drew the fullest possible expression from the instrument." He and Ansel soon took to going for coffee after rehearsals and hashing over technical aspects of the works on the program. "He's very knowledgeable about almost every aspect of music, and his versatility was simply remarkable. With persistence, I suspect he could have played almost any instrument for any orchestra in Europe."

"But?"

"But-but-but-but. If only he had had the proper temperament and a shred of political sense."

As the philharmonic's musical director, Grieder was smug and never more than marginally competent, Felix confided. "But the conductor, you see, goes with the territory—something Ansel couldn't get through his head. It's like being on a ship—you may not admire the captain, but the crew must pay him lip service—mutineers walk the plank." Ansel got himself caught up in a vicious cycle of arguable provocation and excessive response that pushed the philharmonic management to the limits of its tolerance—and finally beyond. "If it hadn't been for Ansel's family connections, his antics would have doomed him long before."

"I gather you had your own run-in with Grieder," Mitch probed.

"I assume Margot offered you no details."

"None."

"She's a model of discretion—a wonderful woman, really." Felix funneled a chestful of toxicity out through his nostrils. "I was involved in an affair with our first flutist for some years until Grieder caught on. The problem was threefold—the woman is his niece, she was married at the time, and Grieder was her only child's godfather. He blamed me for being a seducer and took it out on me the only way he could—which was to deny me the concertmaster's title when it opened up. And he's never relented, though the affair ended some years ago."

Mitch nodded. "Tell me about Ansel's composing—Margot says you were unimpressed."

"He showed me a few of his pieces—and what could I say? His compositions tend to be either remorselessly atonal and jarring or a pastiche of derivative styles—he's a gifted imitator, as you may have heard—his club act is amusing. But mimicry does not equate with creativity."

"What did you tell him?"

"I said his work was interesting, though not especially to my taste. I guess that was the beginning of our falling out, really."

The lakefront promenade turned, and Utley pointed out a dark red boathouse as they passed by. An attractive sign identified it as property of the Platypus Club. Mitch indicated he was aware of the Erpfs' membership in the posh club and its high social standing. Then he asked, almost as an aside, "On a scale of one to ten, how likely is it that Ansel himself could have composed this *William Tell* Symphony and then arranged for its attribution to Beethoven—perhaps as a form of revenge against the world for denying him recognition as—"

"Ansel? Please! Minus-fifty on a scale of one to ten—though I've never seen the manuscript, of course. But sight unseen, the very idea is laughable."

"Did he ever discuss this alleged Beethoven manuscript with you?"

"Yes—he actually called me right after they found it—I was surprised to hear from him since we'd been out of touch. I told him it sounded ridiculous, but he thought it looked quite authentic—and the Hassler girl's old letter as well. I asked him if he wanted me to phone up my uncle, who's a music historian—music runs in our family—to see if he'd be willing to examine it, and Ansel said that would be a good idea if only he could get the manuscript out of the American Hassler's hands for a few days. But next thing I heard, it was gone, and Ansel was having a fit—Margot phoned me about it—which is how their proposal to donate the thing to the government got put together." He waved his hand. "Just between us, I was the one to suggest the idea."

Mitch ended his probe by asking if Felix was privy to Ansel's marital woes.

"He didn't confide in me much about that part of his life, but everyone knew the story about his wife's flagrant behavior—it was humiliating for him."

"Surely he isn't the first man whose wife slept with other men."

Felix's eyes widened. "Oh, I thought you understood—it wasn't with a man at all."

"I was told that she'd been carrying on with the tennis pro at the Platypus Club."

"Yes, the pro was a woman. Lisa's lesbianism was no secret around town—except to Ansel, apparently, at least at the time they married. He took it hard—as a reflection on his manhood, Margot told me—and then reacted in typical Ansel style by turning into rather a sexual predator himself, bedding mostly female students from the conservatory. All of which got back to Grieder and only compounded Ansel's status as a misfit."

Mitch, his mental checklist completed, was about to thank Felix for his help when he suddenly remembered something. "By the way," he asked, "do you happen know if Ansel has a cousin named Sofie?"

"Sofie Ries, do you mean? Yes, I met her once in Montreaux—Ansel and I had gone down there for the summer jazz festival. Very talented artist and writer—did children's books, I believe. Poor girl—she was the size of a dirigible. No doubt that contributed to her early death."

All of Mitch's suspicions about Ansel were instantly reinforced. "When did she die?"

"I'm not sure—possibly a year ago, I think Margot said. She and Ansel were very fond of Sofie—they'd take her to Sprungli, our famous patisserie, whenever she was in town and treat her to a box of their melt-in-your-mouth macaroons, even though they knew it didn't do her any good. I think Ansel cared for her because she was an even sadder case than he was." Felix looked over. "What's she got to do with any of this?"

"Ansel mentioned her to me—in passing. He joked that perhaps she had helped him forge the *Tell* Symphony after I asked him point-blank if he was in any way involved in such a scheme. He said I might want to double-check his denial with Sofie."

Felix shook his head. "That's Ansel for you—always playing games. He's a lost soul."

FOR THEIR FINAL APPOINTMENT IN ZURICH, Mitch tried to reach Ansel's *bête noire*, Richard Grieder, music director of the Swiss Philharmonic. Johnny Winks had provided a dossier on the local celebrity, who led a reclusive existence outside the performing arena. He lived, according to the intelligence file, in a large floor-through flat atop a stylish lakeside apartment house, along with a younger partner named Tonio Nostrada, who, in return for being kept, handled all the conductor's living arrangements. It was he who answered Mitch's phone call.

"Herr Grieder is unavailable," his companion said in a vibrant baritone. "May I ask who is calling and with regard to what?"

Mitch explained his position with Cubbage & Wakeham and that he was in town from New York in connection with the newly discovered *Tell* Symphony.

"This is an unlisted number," Mitch was told. "How did you get it?"

"It's my business to reach people whom our firm needs to speak with. Would you be Tonio, by any chance—Herr Grieder's—uh—executive assistant?"

"Not by chance, Mr. Emery. I don't understand what Maestro Grieder has to do with your mission here, whatever it may be. And I doubt he'd care to see you." Tonio sounded more than dutifully protective. "Why don't you tell me what you're after?"

"I'd rather speak with Herr Grieder directly, if you don't mind. My firm's client is in a dispute with Ansel Erpf, and I'm hoping to learn—"

"Oh, him," said Tonio. "A sad case—I'm sure Maestro Grieder will have nothing to say to you about that—that bad actor."

"But I understand he's very gifted musically."

Tonio gave a dismissive laugh. "Marginally. His family tried to buy him a career with our orchestra, but he abused the opportunity and was disrespectful toward the maestro."

"Mr. Nostrada, I appreciate that you're trying to be protective, but I fear you're doing the maestro a disservice. My company needs to hear it from him, not his—best friend."

"Really?" Tonio's laugh rose half an octave. "We're done here, mister." Click.

On the flight home, Mitch and Clara hashed over their impressions. "The main thing I don't get," she said, "is that if Ansel were clever enough to engineer such an elaborate fraud, why wouldn't he have anticipated our assembling all these circumstantial factors and confronting him as the most obvious suspect? Wouldn't he instead have distanced himself from the scene and enlisted somebody else to lead Jake to the attic trunk?"

Mitch had considered the point. "Maybe he figured that we'd figure—I know this is getting a little convoluted now—that nobody foolish enough to invite our suspicion so openly could possibly be the perpetrator of a world-class con. Or maybe he's as totally innocent as he claims, but he's enjoying tantalizing us—just daring us to pin this thing on him. Maybe that's why he brought up his cousin Sofie and urged us to phone her up."

Clara leaned her head on his shoulder. "That's so wonderfully—*twisted*."

"Except I don't really believe that. But somebody or other has pulled a fast one."

She mulled it all for a moment, then asked, "Is that what you really believe, Mitch? Have you already given up on Beethoven—and decided it's a brilliant scam?"

"I didn't say that," he assured her. "I'm just guessing that Ansel probably doesn't have the talent or powers of concentration to pull off such a stupendous caper on his own. He's an aging spoiled brat in a cultural backwater and almost surely lacking the imagination to dream up such a daring fraud. But he sure as hell could be a part of one."

{8}

I just got off the phone with the emissary from *Schweiz*," Gordy reported to the hastily called meeting in Harry's office. "It sounds as if your little sojourn over there may have been useful," he told Mitch. "This Margot Lenz—your Zurich real estate baroness—has a lot of clout with her government's higher-ups. They're offering a deal that would get us out of the Beethoven business relatively unscathed—if that's what we want."

"I don't mind a little scathing," said Harry, "if the payoff is worth it. What's up?"

The Swiss legal attaché Philippe Saulnier had phoned to say that his country, acting jointly with the Erpf family, might consider ponying up a million dollars—$750,000 to Jake Hassler and $250,000 to Cubbage & Wakeham—for the transfer of title to the *Tell* manuscript to the Swiss Ministry of Culture. The payment would be made half on signing of the agreement and the balance when the ministry's authentication process had been completed—whatever the outcome. So either way, fraud or authentic, they pay us."

"Chump change, you mean," Harry said acidly. "And did Mr. Saulnier indicate what they'd do if we aren't receptive to their wondrously ungenerous offer?"

"He said if we don't get back to him within a week, he's going to file in federal court here for an injunction preventing Jake and us from any effort to sell the manuscript—mainly on the ground that Otto Hassler's will hasn't been duly certified by the Swiss courts—or a determination made whether the *Tell* documents belong to Jake or the Erpfs or neither of them. Also, his government will argue it has a vested interest in the work as a potential national treasure that was illegally taken from within its borders."

148

Harry drummed his fingers on the edge of his massive desk, then looked at Mitch. "I wish I had a clearer picture of this Ansel Erpf character—you've made him sound like an inspired maniac who might be capable of anything—even pulling off a spectacular con that could leave us holding the bag."

Mitch nodded. "Ansel is weird, for sure—but no maniac, inspired or otherwise. He's very possibly unbalanced, though—clinically, I mean. You read my report—I think he was toying with Clara and me and getting a charge out of it."

"Okay," said Harry, "but if this weirdo's eccentricities are well known over there, why wouldn't their government have the same concerns that you've raised? Why should they risk official embarrassment by going to bat for him and his family if there's a good chance that this Beethoven discovery is a hoax?"

"Sounds as if they're convinced his connection to the *Tell* manuscript is coincidental," Mitch ventured, "and that a character like him is hardly up to scamming the whole world."

"And why *would* he?" Gordy asked. "What would motivate this guy to try to carry off such a stunt—what's the risk-and-reward ratio here?"

"Hard to figure off one meeting with him," said Mitch. "It could be just an ingenious ego trip—Ansel thinks the world has sneered at him, so he'll show up the world by carrying off an impossible, colossal fraud."

"And is that what you actually think, or are we just bullshitting here?" Harry asked with more than a touch of irritation. "I'm still not clear where you stand on this guy."

"Because we don't know enough yet," Mitch parried, "either about Ansel or our manuscript. Actually, Clara is less worried about Ansel than this mysterious Rossini connection that Mac Quarles has raised. She says it makes no sense that fifteen years after Beethoven supposedly wrote this symphony and then supposedly ditched it, the opening theme music—or something pretty close to it—shows up as the overture to Rossini's *William Tell*—and then he never writes another opera, though he's still young. And then there's this so-called Archduke Rudolph letter, the one in the box with the manuscript. Our handwriting team is almost done fine-combing the German text—and then we may know a lot more about why *Tell* was junked. Meantime, it's hard to credit the whole story, let alone get a clean reading on Ansel Erpf, with all these loose ends dangling." But the first hurdle, Mitch pointed out, was what their forensics team would find. "They've about wrapped the European end of it—they had to send their crew poking around three different archives over there, photocopying Beethoven's papers—and are due back Tuesday. I'm told they'll need two weeks with our manuscript, and then they'll have something definite for us."

Harry still looked antsy. "The expenses on this thing are headed over budget," he told Gordy. "The Veritas people are saying the forensics workup may run twice the estimate. And we hadn't really planned on getting the last half of the first sketchbook transcribed as Mac Quarles says we need to—which could run at least a couple hundred thousand. And if we land in court now with the Swiss government, our legal bill could go to the moon—and their pockets are slightly deeper than ours."

"Then bail out of this thing, chief," Gordy urged. "But I say, even given our legitimate fears, bailing out now would be pennywise and pound-foolish. Admittedly, it's a gamble."

Harry turned to Mitch. "I agree with Gordy," he said. "And if we hang tough, we can't nickel-and-dime the forensics process. If their lab findings don't kill *Tell* outright—and I'm guessing they will—then we've got some breathing room. Our panel of Beethoven experts may even come up with a calculated guess to explain the Rossini connection—and whatever else is still open to question. But for the moment, we need to hold our horses—or quit the race."

Gordy reminded Harry that the house's position had been strengthened by the precautionary language in the contract it had signed with Jake Hassler. Under its terms, the company had been granted two years—long enough not to require a precipitous decision on the authenticity question—to act as exclusive sales agent for the *Tell* manuscript for a 15 percent commission, and here Gordy had inserted the words "whether the sale be made by auction or any other form of purchase, including a preemptive private negotiation." Thus, if the Swiss government wished to buy all rights to *Tell* from Jake, as it had now indicated, C&W could entertain a fair offer for it on his behalf. "But this one isn't it," Gordy said.

"Okay," Harry agreed. "Then I say we politely tell Mr. Saulnier that we would be willing to consider a sale, but they need to get real—say, five million up front, five million more once they're satisfied about authentication, and if it proves a forgery, *tant pis* for the first five. We're ready to bear the risk, and so should they be."

"Is that really our price?" Gordy asked.

"We *are* talking Beethoven here—maybe that's way low. Maybe we should use whatever they'd counter with as a floor and shop it around—maybe to the record companies—and we'd give the Swiss a topping privilege." Harry's hands conjured the air. "Or am I dreaming?"

"You are," Gordy told him. "Nobody else will touch this thing until it's been fully vetted and labeled kosher. The Swiss government is a special case—for them it's a twofer because a couple of iconic figures are involved: their superstar folk hero and the undisputed German-speaking king of symphonic music."

In the end, Gordy was instructed to tell the Swiss attaché that his government's offer was unacceptable but that in principle a transaction could be arranged, provided the Cultural Ministry—perhaps in league with a consortium of private Swiss citizens—wished to make a suitable bid. Short of that, C&W was prepared only to add a nonbinding condition to its auction terms, whereby the winning bidder would be respectfully urged to arrange for *Tell*'s premiere performance to be given in Zurich as a gesture of respect to the Swiss people. This condition, however, would require the Swiss government's prompt certification of Otto Hassler's will and, with it, Jake's title to the manuscript, ending the threat of legal efforts to thwart its sale.

Within forty-eight hours, C&W had its answer. Forget about a purchase for more than the "exploratory" offer price—unless the entire transaction was conditioned on *Tell*'s authentication. But in exchange for C&W's pledged "best efforts" to have the said work first performed publicly in Zurich or another community in Switzerland, its government had decided not to pursue any legal action to recover the manuscript "at this time."

"But they neglected to say anything about certifying Otto's will," Gordy added. "So I told them if they didn't validate the will forthwith, Jake would be filing suit over there against their government—I didn't say when—and telling the world press how the cold-blooded Swiss had been trying to strongarm him into selling out for peanuts. Saulnier said they'd think it over."

ONE OF THE CHANGES Mitch had effected within months of joining C&W was switching its forensics business to the Anglo-American firm of Veritas Laboratories, with offices in Washington, London, and the two Cambridges, with their easy access to top scientists and scholars. Though more expensive than their competitors, Veritas had a notably deeper staff than the firm Harry and Sedge had long relied on. When confronted with a complex case such as *Tell*, Veritas hired the most knowledgeable individuals available for the length of its investigation. To head up the *Tell* field inquiry, they had enlisted a roly-poly Viennese named Stefan Rodewald, the curator of music at the Austrian State Museum and one of the world's foremost experts on Beethoven's manuscripts and papers.

Rodewald flew to New York with a crew of operatives from Veritas's London office, and the team, wearing cotton gloves most of the time, spent ten days poring over the *Tell* manuscript and the other documents found in Otto Hassler's attic trunk, photocopying them, and getting lab tests done on the paper and ink. Finally satisfied, the investigators presented their report in the C&W library to the firm's top officers, reinforced by Mac Quarles, who had taken the train up from Philadelphia; Clara, who made a point of not taking a seat next to Mitch; and Sedge Wakeham, who had asked to be teleconferenced in on the keenly anticipated proceedings.

"It's all pretty much in here," said Rodewald in a choppy, modulated voice as he drew a clutch of ring binders from a locked metal case and handed them out to the assemblage, "but we're going to walk you through it."

Veritas's starting point had been the paper and related physical properties of the *Tell* sketchbooks as well as the several letters found with them and addressed to Beethoven. Carbon dating and other such sophisticated tools had unfortunately been of no use, the Austrian scholar explained, given the relatively recent span—in geological terms—of Beethoven's life. "They help us determine age by millennia but not within the range of just two centuries from the present." What he could say with confidence, however, was that the manuscript paper found in the cedar box in Zurich was handmade of linen on a wire frame, of the type commonly used in Austria and Bohemia in the early nineteenth century. More to the point, it was of a color and texture similar to the fifty or so varieties of paper on which Beethoven was known to have composed.

Equally consistent, said Rodewald, unfolding a paper clip that he fiddled with while he spoke, were the watermarks the laboratory had found. "Researchers have identified fifty-seven different such markings on the paper Beethoven used in his composition books," Rodewald told them. Those on the pages in the two Zurich sketchbooks differed from each other, one composed of the capital initials "GFA" topped by a kind of loosely drawn tiara, the other a row of three crescent moons in descending size order—"but both were among those we have found in other surviving Beethoven manuscripts."

The methodical archivist warmed to his task. The *Tell* sketchbooks had been fashioned, he reported, from twenty-four large sheets known as bifoliums, each folded first horizontally and then vertically, cut on the first fold, and assembled into oblong books of ninety-six leaves of two sides each for a total of 192 pages, measuring roughly thirty-two centimeters wide by twenty-three centimeters high. "Some of the well-authenticated Beethoven sketchbooks we examined were thicker than these, some thinner, but most were about this size and of these dimensions."

Particular note was taken of the markings on the sketchbook pages made by the rastral, the tool used in Beethoven's time to draw the parallel five-line staves across the page in a single sweep. "These staff lines were usually placed onto the paper by the shopkeeper selling the composition books," said Rodewald, "and typically reveal slight but recurring irregularities, seen most often at the ends of lines as the hand lifts the tool from the paper." Here again, the Veritas investigators had found nothing odd or atypical about the way the staves— sixteen per page—were drawn in the *Tell* sketchbooks.

"So far, so good," said Harry, "right?" His blasé façade seemed to be cracking.

"Well, yes and no, *mein herr*," the highly proper curator replied. "Unfortunately, none of this means a great deal, because any determined forger could have obtained paper typical of this period." Blank pages could be found at the back of many two-hundred-year-old books held in major libraries and surreptitiously removed for illicit use, Rodewald expanded. And antiquarian bookshops commonly sold old volumes of the same type with empty pages on which forgeries could be committed. "They can even be obtained from online vendors, with no questions asked."

"Bad show," lamented the ghostly visage of Sedge Wakeham. Even on screen, his baggy eyes looked alert as he followed the session from London.

Rodewald turned to the ink used for composing the *Tell* manuscripts—a more likely indicator of forgery, because tests now existed to gauge roughly how long a particular ink batch had adhered to a given sheet of paper. The inks Beethoven employed, made of finely ground carbon, were very stable and did not attack the paper to which they were applied, in contrast to the aniline inks, introduced a generation after Beethoven's death, which were water soluble and far more likely to run.

"The ink in these *William Tell* composition books, upon chemical analysis, we also found to be made from ground carbon—but it could have been whipped up yesterday, of course," Rodewald cautioned. The carbon-based inks Beethoven was known to have used were of several tints, most often blue, brown, and green, "with an occasional dash of orange or purple." He sometimes used more than one batch of ink at the same sitting or perhaps applied ink of a different color to a given passage when making corrections or revisions. The writing in the Zurich sketchbooks was mostly in a brownish black "with an occasional bit of greenish."

There was no consistent thickness to the nibs of the quill pens Beethoven generally used, Rodewald added, because they were cut by hand, "and often by different hands, belonging mostly to friends of the composer. Usually he wore them down until the flow of ink was far thicker than when he had started using that quill." This same unevenness of applied ink was evident in the Zurich manuscripts. Nor was the laboratory in doubt that the *Tell* sketchbooks had been composed with a quill; the handwriting showed the variations characteristic of quills due to their flexibility and responsiveness to pressure exerted by the writer's hand. But even today, Rodewald warned, anyone with a bit of perseverance could find, buy, or create a quill pen and learn to write with it.

"So what you're telling us so far," Gordy put in, "is that we'd be dealing with a painstaking forger—if there is one."

"Certainly," the Austrian archivist agreed. Still, there were several positive indications, he continued, that the *Tell* manuscript might well have been written by Beethoven himself. The great speed with which he composed at times and his frugal habit of using quills beyond their normal lifespan caused frequent blobs and splatters, which he often failed to clean up with absorbent sand, the blotting paper of its day. When in a creative frenzy, he would often turn to the next leaf without having allowed time for the ink on the previous right-hand page to dry thoroughly, resulting in "offsets," blots in the corresponding places on the left-hand page opposite. At times he wrote passages in pencil and inked them over later when he was ready to include them permanently. "All these features that we typically find in the archival Beethoven materials are present here as well," Rodewald told them with brisk assurance.

The accumulating evidence was formidable, Clara thought, edging ever closer to elation despite herself. She stole a glance at Mitch, who, professionally noncommittal, wore a deadpan mask as he scribbled notes to himself in a loose-leaf binder. Was he really as emotionless as he looked, she wondered, when they were being presented with such largely corroborative findings? Well, if she were on the verge of being carried away, Mitch was probably right to keep cool. Any moment, no doubt, the Veritas team would let its other shoe drop.

But the next words from the staid Viennese archivist proved even more supportive of the authenticity claim. One of the most common errors by forgers, he noted, was due to their ignorance that paper turns more absorbent as it ages, so that ink newly applied to old paper rapidly spreads in a feathery or blurry pattern around the core of the pen stroke. To avoid this telltale effect, adroit counterfeiters had learned to bathe old or antique paper with ammonia hydrochloride or plain old hydrogen peroxide. "What few of them know, though, is that applying either of these compounds raises the pH level—or alkalinity—of the newly applied ink, causing it to coagulate, harden, and break down in microscopic cracks resembling the skin of a reptile," Rodewald explained. "But we found no such cracking on the *Tell* manuscript pages—which suggests that if it's a forgery, it's probably not a recent one."

"Meaning just what, Herr Rodewald?" Sedge's voice boomed out of the video hookup.

"Dr. Rodewald," the scholar gently corrected him. "I meant merely that the totality of our findings does not remove the possibility that some Beethoven intimate or perhaps another knowledgeable contemporary of his could theoretically have created the manuscript. For a modern forger, it would present a far more difficult but not insurmountable challenge."

Clara admired Rodewald's hypercaution; nothing less would satisfy the demanding standards of Germanic scholarship. Her own dreamy musings were causing her to stray into some enchanted realm of wish fulfillment. Enough, she told herself sternly. Yet a moment later, the Austrian superintendent of orthodoxy was feeding her fantasies with a report from the Veritas handwriting experts. Fooling them would surely have proven the most daunting test for any forger. Here the analysis involved two separable aspects—the words of the libretto and the musical language of the scoring. The former lent itself more easily to microscopic scrutiny.

"Normal writing by honest people is rapid and flowing, with a natural smoothness," Rodewald explained, "so the first thing we look for in examining a questionable specimen is the absence of relaxed fluidity—far more likely when a forger is at work. He's often trying too hard to replicate the original and paying too much attention to detail. This stress may result in a drawn or labored look to the letters or a shakiness or slight wavering in the lines—or both—which a trained eye can spot almost immediately." Forged writing, moreover, often left a heavier-than-normal deposit of ink at the beginning and end of strokes, phrases, or sentences because the pen is more likely to be lifted off the page as the writer proceeds at an unnaturally deliberate pace.

"None of these revealing phenomena were observed in the material that the Veritas staff has examined for you," the Austrian asserted. "But now comes the hard part."

He and his co-investigators, Rodewald said, had focused on a number of the characteristic elements in every individual's handwriting: the angles, curves, and joins of the letters; the spacing between words and between capitals and small letters; the length, width, and slant of the looped letters; and especially the formation of the most common of all words, "the" and "of." Their task soon became excruciating because Beethoven's penmanship was notoriously difficult—jerky and tortured, often sloppy, and at times flat-out indecipherable. But thankfully, no other composer's writings had been more closely studied, "so we are fortunate to have a broad basis for comparison."

He directed his listeners to look in their ring binders at photocopied blowups taken from well-authenticated Beethoven letters, all written between 1812 and 1819. The time frame was highly relevant, said Rodewald, because Beethoven's handwriting changed noticeably after 1798. As the composer's health and hearing began to deteriorate and he became emotionally turbulent, his writing suffered—"because our penmanship is not an isolated phenomenon but a reflection of our inner being," the scholar noted. Beethoven's increasing angst was evidenced by many changes in his writing: his letters became larger, the pressure on the hand shaping them shifted from the downstroke to the sidestroke, and the writing grew more rapid, even frenzied at times, and less legible, "particularly in his fallow years after 1812." Line by line, word by word, letter by letter, the Veritas experts examined examples from the lyrics scattered in the *Tell* manuscript, including every *der, die,* and *das* in sight, and compared them to the writing in the certified Beethoven letters from 1812 to 1819.

The close similarity between the two sets of examples presented in her ring binder was striking even to Clara's untrained eye. And nothing was too minute for the investigators' attention. "Note, if you will," Rodewald instructed, "the precision with which, in both the previously certified letters and the Zurich examples, the dot over the letter 'i' is placed—not wandering somewhere in the vicinity, as most of us haphazardly place it. Given the general sloppiness of his writing, this would seem a contradictory element—until one recalls that Beethoven was primarily a composer, for whom the exact placement of notes and signs in relation to a pageful of fixed parallel horizontal lines—a most unforgiving universe—was an occupational necessity."

In short, Veritas had found no writing in the verbal texts in the Zurich manuscripts to be patently un-Beethovenlike. And the same authentic appearance applied, Rodewald said, to the letter purportedly from Archduke Rudolph, found alongside the *Tell* manuscript, when compared with dozens of other surviving letters from him to Beethoven. Likewise, the pair of letters uncovered in the Hassler attic box that were signed Hans Georg Nägeli, the maestro's ardent Swiss music publisher, whose handwriting the Veritas experts had measured against previously known letters to the composer from Nägeli that they had tracked down in German and Austrian archives.

As Rodewald paused for breath, Mitch asked almost offhandedly, "Should we be just a bit suspicious that so far, nothing at all seems suspicious?"

The Austrian drew a handkerchief from a trouser pocket and tidily patted his moist brow—a gesture that surprised Clara, who had thought him incapable of perspiring. "No two cases are ever alike, my friends at Veritas tell me," Rodewald replied, "but you're surely entitled—indeed, well-advised, I should say—to be skeptical. Nevertheless, the findings are the findings—for you to interpret as you choose."

For the most difficult task of all, an examination of the musical portion of the Zurich manuscripts on the C&W premises, Rodewald had engaged his most experienced assistant curators to join him beforehand in a stringent review of Beethoven sketchbooks and autograph scores preserved in Berlin and Bonn as well as in his own archives in Vienna. "And it is only fair to tell you, gentlemen and madam," he confided, "that I approached this project with towering incredulity. The very idea of this *Tell* manuscript seemed a contrived and defiant act of effrontery to lifetimes of dedicated study by scores of musicologists, some of them friends of mine. Still, like some of you perhaps, I was bewitched by the exhilarating possibility, however remote, of a newfound priceless treasure." He panned slowly around the table, appreciative of the hushed attention. "And, based on all our efforts for the past six weeks, I remain so. Let me tell you why."

Beethoven's preliminary sketches typically took the form of a single-line synopsis that would rough out a long stretch of the work—an entire section or even a whole movement. At the beginning of these statements projecting the principal melodic lines, the composer would specify the clefs, key, and tempo to guide himself in all that followed. "After that, he rarely bothered to repeat these vital road markers," Rodewald observed, "thus making the bulk of his sketchbooks nearly impenetrable for anyone but himself." Having framed out a new work, Beethoven would turn to the developmental phase, consisting of melodic, harmonic, and rhythmic elaborations of his core theme—"or theme*s*, plural, in this case," said Rodewald. "It was here, in these detailed studies, that the real struggle of his creative agony was played out—a tortuous evolutionary process of refinement." On paper it was a seething labyrinth of lines and dots and circles, a swirl of stemless notes and cryptic signs, and, at irregular intervals, a scribbled word or letter or number or abbreviation above the notation, all floating upon clef-less staves without a key or time signature in sight. Nor did this pulsating mass advance in a clean linear progression; it was more a series of starts and stops, of disruptions and resumptions, of second thoughts and strikeouts and partial restorations.

"So he had, you might say, his own Ludwigish language," Rodewald quipped, "a most confounding puzzle that we've been solving bit by bit over the past century and a half—and this *Tell* manuscript, rescued, we are told, from a Zurich attic, shows all of the very same complex habits and idiosyncrasies—the same seemingly chaotic battle with himself that we have found elsewhere." Rodewald looked around a final time before taking his seat. In conclusion, "while we cannot tell you for certain that this work was composed by Beethoven in 1814—or any other time—what we *can* tell you is that it jolly well might have been."

"Three cheers!" Sedge boomed from across the pond. "Well, two and a half, anyway."

Back in their apartment, the Emerys aired their clashing inclinations. "I just can't believe," Clara began, "that anybody smart enough to fabricate all of this with such fidelity to every detail would really go to so much bother. I mean to achieve *what*, exactly?"

"Harry agrees with you—he told me as much afterward," Mitch said, mixing them vodka-and-tonics. "But here's Ansel Erpf, right in our faces—a four-star smart-ass with a screw loose—who conceivably could have forged the thing— and for wholly irrational motives."

He squeezed the juice from a wedge of lime into the tall glasses and handed her one. "Unless, of course, we're missing something more obvious—that Ansel, or someone, did it for the money. My sense is that his family had been doling Ansel a tight allowance so he'll keep away from drugs, and maybe this was his perverse way to break free and become financially independent."

Clara studied her drink, stress level rising over Mitch's reflexively negative approach to the mystery. "But the way it's unfolding, who stands to make any money out of all this except Jake Hassler?" she asked. "And by your own readout, Jake isn't savvy or loony enough to become mixed up in a fraud this elaborate."

"Maybe Ansel really is the mastermind, the one with the musical and historical expertise, who made all the counterfeiting arrangements, and Jake is his seemingly innocent front man—and they're in this thing together—and putting us all on beautifully."

"You can't believe that—"

"I could be persuaded to believe almost anything at this point," Mitch said, eyes narrowing. "I'm pretty well persuaded that Jake was never supposed to find the manuscript—no one figured he'd come to his grandfather's funeral and search through the attic. Maybe it was planted there to be found by the Erpfs' staff when they took title to the house, and they'd—they'd—maybe Ansel thought he could cash in on a counterfeit Beethoven symphony of his own creation—or maybe he sold his sister on it as a way to keep the family business from going bust—though Johnny Winks says it isn't—or maybe a way for them to become national heroes and restore their social standing—"

"Nice try, pal," Clara said, dropping onto one of the love seats and ruminating on his flights of fancy. "But the thing you're ignoring, sweetie, is that a team of world-class investigators just examined the manuscript under a microscope, literally, and told us there's little reason to doubt its authenticity. Why isn't that good enough for you? Why shouldn't we proceed with Mac Quarles's panel of Beethoven scholars to try to evaluate the music itself—whether it's good Beethoven or putrid Beethoven that deserved to be junked? But you seem so damn negative, Mitch—I know it's your job to be super-suspicious, but it's almost as if you can't bear the thought that seemingly out of nowhere, here comes a providential addition to the world's highly limited supply of sublime beauty—if that's what it proves to be."

Mitch weighed her passionate concern. "Listen, I'll be every bit as thrilled as you if it turns out to be legitimate—"

"I don't believe that, Mitch—I think we're coming at this thing from two very different perspectives—and isn't that why you practically dragooned me into working with you on it?" Clara felt beaten down by his icy objectivity while she kept looking for the rainbow. "Maybe I'm just in your way here," she said.

"*Au contraire.* Look, I love your—what did Wordsworth or Coleridge or somebody call it?—'willing suspension of disbelief.' I just can't afford to suspend mine."

"Sounds as if you're saying I'm off in fantasyland."

Mitch gave an emphatic shake of his head. "Not on your tintype."

"Well, maybe I am," she said, waving off his demurrer. "But I'm worried about you—you're letting your imagination dry up. You need to leave some space for miracles to happen."

THE SPEED WITH WHICH the German government was informed of the forensics findings in the *Tell* matter startled and troubled Mitch and his senior colleagues. "The Jerries are coming," Gordy told him, "as our illustrious London partner would put it. Tomorrow afternoon—a big schnauzer from their embassy. Fall in at fifteen-hundred hours."

The news was not entirely unanticipated. Two days after the Veritas team had packed up, Johnny Winks called Mitch to advise that his sources in Berlin had heard that the Federal Republic's Ministry of Culture had been fully debriefed on C&W's *Tell* forensic findings. "Your mole," Johnny reported, "was an assistant to Herr Rodewald—the fellow claimed he hadn't been paid enough to keep mum. I suspect you'll soon have a visitor from Deutschland packing heat."

The gunsel was flawlessly groomed, exquisitely mannered, fresh off the plane from Washington, and, as his remarks soon evidenced, had lately returned from the fatherland with a full rundown on the status of the *William Tell* Symphony. Chief cultural attaché for the German Embassy, Maximillian Neugebaur arrived in Harry Cubbage's office right on time, his abundant, light brown hair combed straight back with dramatic flair and his pale blue eyes alert with probing intelligence. After clasping hands heartily all around the table and accepting an offer of coffee—"Black, please, if you don't mind"—Herr Neugebaur said his government was appreciative of the opportunity to state its position regarding the newly found manuscript attributed to Beethoven, "who is, as you are all surely aware, very greatly venerated by our people."

"By ours no less so," Harry assured their German visitor. "An immense genius—for all ages—and all humanity."

"Just so," said Neugebaur, taking the seat offered to him directly opposite Harry. "Perhaps, then, I need not belabor the great excitement and deep concern which the announcement from your office stirred throughout our nation after it was reported by the media."

"Excitement and no doubt keen curiosity," Harry jousted, "but why deep concern? Our firm is an exceedingly conscientious one. Your government can rest assured that we are treating the manuscript with the greatest care and reverence."

"The course of its fate, however, is evidently proceeding without the least communication with German officials or scholars." He was aware, Neugebaur disclosed, of the expression of concern registered earlier with C&W by a representative of the Swiss government. "But as a ranking officer in our diplomatic delegation to your country, I have been sent to express a perhaps more serious objection to your activities in this matter, because Beethoven was a German—a citizen of a German state—and as such, we feel a—"

"Excuse me, Herr Neugebaur," said Harry, "but I've been led to understand that he had become a citizen of the Austrian empire."

"An *honorary* citizen of Vienna, I believe," Neugebaur corrected him. "I think it safe to say that he was always German in his soul. Our point is simply that this is not a private matter, as your firm seems to view it. It pertains to the property of a deceased German composer."

Harry turned to Gordy to frame a legally immaculate response.

"Our understanding, sir, is that there are no plausible Beethoven heirs to claim title to this property," C&W's counsel said, striving to cleanse his words of abrasiveness. "Nor is anyone else qualified to do so, including the Swiss neighbors of our client's late grandfather, who seem suddenly to require a substantial reward for their years of unsolicited kindness to him."

His coffee cup sat unattended in front of the attaché. "I think the basic point, Mr. Roth, is that your Mr. Jacob Hassler has no substantive claim to the property—certainly none allowing him to exploit or profit from it—or to ask your company to judge its authenticity. Our view is that this work should be examined in the most careful and responsible manner, in view of the paramount importance its alleged composer occupies in the history of world culture."

"Which is precisely what we're doing, sir—"

"But there is only your word for that, Mr. Roth. We have nothing at all to judge by beyond what you've chosen to reveal about this potentially momentous discovery."

Mitch sensed Gordy's rising gorge and his extra effort to keep it from spilling. "In order to prevent wild rumors and unjustified speculation from spreading," Mitch spoke up as head of the firm's authentication program, "we've apprised the world, as a courtesy, of the existence of this document and stated that we're in the process of trying to determine if it's genuine—and that we'll be making full disclosure of our findings at the appropriate time. Please, sir, advise your government to that effect."

"My government has read your announcement," said Neugebaur, trying to remove any sharpness from his tone, "but it believes *this* is the appropriate time for you to reveal everything and to consult those more qualified than yourselves to judge whether the work is authentic or fraudulent. Your own investigation is necessarily tainted by your vested commercial interest in its outcome."

"Frankly," Harry interceded now, "I take issue with that, Herr Neugebaur. Our company has been around about as long as the German nation—and Cubbage & Wakeham's vested interest is as a vendor of meritorious items of artistic and historic interest. Do you think we've stayed in business this long by purveying fraudulent goods?"

The German saw he had invited the reproach. "I meant no disrespect, Mr. Cubbage. But we're not talking about trust here, sir—it's a matter of competence, and you seem unwilling to defer in the least to German expertise in this area. In Beethoven, we're speaking of one of the most revered figures in a cultural movement spanning two centuries and without parallel in human history—I refer to the German achievement in creating classical music as such. It's one of the glories that our people can point to with the purest pride—and so we are entitled to be deeply involved in the authentication process of this work."

Mindful of Clara's more-than-once-expressed insight that art and patriotism are suspect companions, Mitch was moved to challenge the attaché's remarks.

"Some people, sir," he said in a modulated tone, "don't believe that genius, any more than virtue or evil, has a nationality. Genius is a rare quality of the human species, wherever it arises, and the creative spirit rarely thrives under state auspices. In fact, I'd venture, along with many of my countrymen, that governments are inclined, if anything, to suppress creativity and originality as subversive—and your own government, I suspect, is no more enlightened in this regard than any other."

His polite rebuke won scarcely five seconds of respectful silence before Mitch's haughty adversary lashed back undeterred. "The state, all states, may cater to the lowest common denominator, Mr. Emery, but I don't see the free-enterprise sector, especially in populist America, doing any better when it comes to promoting civilized taste. We have a track record in that area, Mr. Emery."

"You have a track record in many areas," Mitch replied.

"Gentlemen, gentlemen," Gordy separated them verbally. "The point we want to stress to the German government, I think, is that we're going to enlist a panel of the very best experts in the world in order to decide—"

"But you're not the ones who should be making that selection," Neugebaur insisted, "especially judging by your choice to oversee the project—this Dr. Macrae Quarles. He is not taken seriously as a musicologist in Germany."

"Is *any* American musicologist up to your country's standards?" Mitch asked bluntly. "Dr. Quarles is one of our most highly regarded and versatile music scholars."

"Yes—for an American, his works may be competent of their sort, but they don't really approach the rigorous standard met by our scholars. We simply don't think Dr. Quarles is up to the very demanding task you've assigned him."

Precisely what Clara had predicted the Germans would say, Mitch remembered, if anyone other than a German was put in charge of the vetting process. Confronted in person now by the claim, he would not buy it. "What is it, exactly," he asked Neugebaur, "that your government would like us to do?"

The German diplomat sat back and surveyed the room coolly. "Let me try to reverse the question, gentlemen, and ask you for an honest answer. Let us suppose a Bavarian bratwurst salesman were to turn up suddenly with what he claimed was the long lost autobiography of Thomas Jefferson—and then said he would consult the local librarian to verify its authenticity. How would that strike America? I daresay that your whole country would be up in arms, demanding—and with very good reason—that your own peerless Jefferson scholars be brought into the validation process and seeking assurances that fraud was not about to be committed in the name of one of your national icons. Think of Beethoven up on Mount Rushmore…"

Harry turned up his palms toward Mitch, as if to say they were in a no-win dilemma, then glanced at their visitor. "Let me reassure you, my friend," he said quietly to the visitor, "that we're going to be enlisting a panel of international experts, with the German cultural community prominently represented. We'll report their findings in full, exercise our legal and commercial rights accordingly, and the world will be free to make its own judgment about the results."

Neugebaur shook his head. "That's not good enough, Mr. Cubbage. This is not a question of merely legal or commercial rights—this is a moral issue with us. The manuscript should be accessible for inspection by all interested parties and its authenticity determined after objective examination by the most able scholars. That's what we believe the world owes to Beethoven."

"Were we to do what you ask," Gordy replied, "we'd be surrendering all proprietary interest in and rights to the work—anyone could copy it and do what they wished with it. Instead of letting it be torn to shreds and profaned, our firm is making a considerable investment to learn everything knowable about the work, after which we'll—"

The attaché did not care to be lectured to; he broke into Gordy's rationale. "My government's position, Mr. Roth, is that your firm's and Mr. Jacob Hassler's claims to proprietary commercial rights are a fiction—and that your assertion of them is an insult to our people and their cultural heritage." The German turned toward Harry as the only worthy authority figure among his listeners. "The posthumously discovered work of one of the great masters of musical composition does not *belong* to anyone—and if you persist in your claims, my government is prepared to invoke the provisions of the Bern Copyright Convention, of which the United States has been a signatory since 1988." Neugebaur's tone now assumed a steely edge. "This agreement among the civilized nations recognizes the moral rights of the creator of an artistic work, even if—as is perhaps the case here—legal title to it may be in dispute or in the hands of others—in which case we Germans, as the countrymen of the deceased composer, are morally entitled to oversee the disposition of his work and to protect its integrity—how it is treated or mistreated, whether it is artfully orchestrated or brazenly prostituted—or, in this instance, whether it should ever reach the world's ears in view of the composer's reported wishes to the contrary."

Gordy replied with quiet defiance. "And it's our position, Mr. Neugebaur, that your government has no legal standing whatever in this matter—no rights recognized in this country to march in here and demand title, in effect, to this property in the name of some vague, nationalistic kinship to a composer who died a generation before your country existed as a sovereign state. As to your so-called moral claims, some would say that Germany has another century or so of penance to pay before qualifying to invoke such grounds."

The diplomat's demeanor turned from steely to wrathful. "I had assumed that I was dealing with more sophisticated people," he said and turned away from Gordy. "Let me urge you, Mr. Cubbage, to reconsider your firm's options, bearing in mind that you'll find no German academicians willing to serve on your self-certified investigatory panel—our ministry will shortly issue an official caveat along those lines to all our institutions of higher learning. And we are advised that our friends in Switzerland are sympathetic with our views of this matter, as are we with theirs—and are unlikely anytime soon to certify the will of your Mr. Hassler's grandfather, indefinitely blocking your ability to transfer legal title to the work to any would-be buyer."

The gauntlet having been tossed across Harry's desktop, revealing the iron fist beneath it, Gordy and Mitch glanced beseechingly toward their proprietor to deliver a parting blow in C&W's behalf. "Well, many thanks for stopping by, Herr Neugebaur," said Harry, the embodiment of cordiality. "Oh, one last thing—if I may?"

"*Bitte*—" Neugebauer was on his feet now.

"Since your government harbors such powerful feelings in this matter, why doesn't it simply buy the *Tell* manuscript from Mr. Hassler? I'm sure he'd be open to a fair offer. After all, Mr. Jefferson bought one-third of America from

Napoleon and saved quite a lot of fussing. Everything, they say, has its price. Why not a likely masterpiece by a titanic German genius?"

The diplomat, momentarily befuddled by the proposal, pivoted on his heels and said, over his shoulder and halfway to the door, "I'll be sure to relay your thoughtful suggestion to my ministry. Good day, gentlemen."

{9}

News reached Mitch two days later about the remaining critical piece of evidence found in the cedar box with the manuscript—the letter allegedly addressed to Beethoven and signed just "R." The Veritas forensics team had now corroborated that its author was almost certainly the composer's friend, patron, piano and composing pupil, sole protector at the Hapsburg court, and frequent correspondent, Archduke Rudolph of Austria, the emperor's kid brother. Once his convoluted handwriting had been deciphered, the translated German text was sent to both Mitch and Mac Quarles, as the latter had requested, to be put into historical context. The following afternoon, Mac came lumbering excitedly through Mitch's doorway, waving his translated printout of the archduke's letter. "I think maybe we've got our elusive critter caged," he said.

Harry and Gordy joined them within the hour, along with Clara, whom Mitch had corralled by cellphone and summoned to the parley. "Let us return, friends, to that memorable year of 1814," Mac buoyantly opened his analysis, "so you can see the whole hog. Be warned, though—it's not a particularly pretty animal."

That year, the musicologist related, Beethoven had been on the verge of defecting from Vienna and imperial Austria. He had told friends he was thinking hard about going to live elsewhere, most likely back to Germany, while admirers in London and Paris were urging him to move to their cities. As the war clouds began to part after twenty-five years of revolution and bloody turmoil across the continent, tastes were shifting in Europe's music capital, and Beethoven had fallen out of favor with the Viennese public. Added to his sagging popularity

166

were the maestro's endless problems with his hearing, his finances, and his brothers and their families, all of which left him in a foul mood.

"And so he had every reason to be receptive," as Mac painted this predicament, "when his kindhearted Swiss publisher urged him to visit Zurich to have his tragic hearing impairment treated." And after having nearly been commissioned five years earlier to compose music for a local production of Schiller's *Tell* but lost out to a lesser but likely more congenial competitor, he may now have gone straight to his bookcase or a bookseller for a copy of the play—"perhaps the very one," Mac guessed, "that turned up in Otto Hassler's attic trunk. 'What a jim-dandy idea for an opera,' Mr. Beethoven might have told himself, admiring its theme of liberty that was churnin' through his heated brain just then as peace was finally restored across Europe."

But it was peace that came at a high price. The forces of political reaction, led by the resurgent Hapsburgs under their crafty minister-in-chief (and soon-to-be de facto ruler), Clemens von Metternich, were already gathering, as statesmen from the coalition of nations that had at last cut down Napoleon prepared for the Congress of Vienna that autumn. The aim of the great conclave was to redraw the map of Europe and reapportion the balance of continental power. Metternich, Mac explained, was demanding restoration of the old order and, above all, eradicating the revolutionary drive for unification of the German-speaking peoples. That dream had long been inflaming the minds and hearts of student radicals and subversive reformers opposed to the repressive regimes ruling the multitude of principalities from the Baltic to the Alps. "And a unified Germany," Mac added, "would have greatly reduced Hapsburg Austria's clout."

Beethoven, though, suffering from a profound sense of dislocation and ever more deeply sunk in his own angst-racked inner world, was distracted from the nationalist conflicts of the moment. And so, likely rationalizing that high art was above petty politics, the maestro plunged earnestly into his adaptation of *Tell*—"if we're to accept the evidence Jake Hassler found in Zurich," Mac theorized. Yet by that summer's end, despite prodigious labor, Beethoven had apparently abandoned not only the operatic format for *Tell* but the nearly finished symphonic version as well. "But why would he do such a thing? We need to answer that question—or else dismiss this work as somebody's inventive joke on us."

If they accepted Nina Hassler's word for it, "and we have no other," she was asked by the composer to discard the sketchbooks as artistically wanting and told that their very existence posed some sort of danger to him. Mac paused in his recitation and studied the ceiling a moment. "Now what kinda 'danger' could possibly have driven this supergenius of ours to toss out a big ol' symphony in mid-creation like a tub of dirty bath water?" He paused again, then said, "I think we have a plausible explanation."

If Beethoven had been politically astute instead of informed largely by gossip retailed by habitual tavern-goers—"of whom he was one," Mac recounted—he never would have dreamed in the first place of devoting a full-scale musical tribute to William Tell and the Swiss revolt against their Austrian occupiers—and tormentors. Such a gesture of nose-thumbing at the Hapsburgs would likely have been taken as a willful insult, especially at a moment, as Mac put it, "when ol' Ludwig was still hankering after hugs and kisses from their imperial majesties and official recognition as the star composer of the realm," which would have made him, given the supremacy of German music, the foremost practitioner of the art in all of Western civilization. The fact was that Beethoven wished mightily to be insulated from the frowns of the fickle Viennese public, from further need to produce voguish work, "like his god-awful 'Battle Symphony,' a piece of wartime claptrap," and yearned for a plump state sinecure and, with it, garlands and elevation to the pantheon of immortal music-makers alongside Bach, Handel, Haydn, and Mozart.

So after he had impulsively launched his *Tell* project, Mac speculated, it probably began to dawn on the maestro that the fulfillment of his material ambitions might depend now more on his public display of political correctness and the obsequious behavior it entailed—never exactly his strong suit—than on his artistic merit, which was never in dispute.

"In short, Brother B smartened up," said Mac. Belatedly mindful of the combustible political climate, he asked himself whether his presentation of a major new symphony commemorating the heroic rebellion of the downtrodden Swiss against their Austrian rulers—*even though it had happened five hundred years in the past*—might be received by Vienna's upper crust as a traitorous attack on the still-intact and still-repressive Hapsburg regime.

To help him answer the question, Mac argued, Beethoven would naturally have turned to his uniquely placed ally at the palace, in whom he had often confided his still-unrequited hopes for the crown's official recognition as court composer and the subsidy that came with it. "And this, according to your forensics experts," said Mac, handing around copies of the translated document, "was how Archduke Rudolph replied to him in a letter sent to Zurich":

2 September 1814

My dear Beethoven,

May I first reiterate to you the great joy with which I welcomed the honor you bestowed upon me this past April with the first performance of your B-flat piano trio named "The Archduke" after your greatly devoted pupil? It is not the first work by which you have honored me with the dedication, but it is the one I most prize. All the more reason for my acute distress upon the receipt of your most recent letter with its disclosure of your present composition.

It cannot have escaped your notice that, with the blackguard Bonaparte now sent away to Elba and licking his highly deserved wounds, Hapsburg blood is once again coursing freely and nourishing a renewal of our national pride. Even as this is our beloved Austria's glorious moment in the sun, so, too, may it be—if my wishes are heeded—for her most illustrious musical genius. I hope and fully expect that your works will be the most prominent of all that mark the season of celebration to begin at our capital this autumn. The plan being forwarded in this regard would start, at the gala gathering of crowned heads and their ministers, with a presentation of your new, improved Fidelio. Your presence and introduction to the notables would of course be expected. Word reaches me that financial as well as ceremonial tributes are at long last to be paid to you—though I cannot speak for our shared hope of your gaining a court appointment, which I have vainly solicited on your behalf. But my confidants tell me there is growing sentiment to bestow upon you another and most rare honor: election as an honorary citizen of Vienna in recognition of your contribution to our national culture.

The value and sincerity of such rewards, it seems to me, are heightened when one takes into account that Maestro Beethoven is not universally beloved at the imperial court. I have been told more than once that your private sentiments, which have been overheard at taverns you frequent, are outspokenly republican. There is, moreover, whispered lamentation that you have never deigned to dedicate a work of yours to my brother, our sovereign liege—an omission made yet more glaring by your repeated tributes of this sort bestowed upon me. When we add to this your famous rough-hewn independence of spirit and insufficiently deferential conduct, which some in my own circle take for impertinence toward their *royal highnesses and their officers, you will perhaps appreciate my deep unhappiness at your having begun an ambitious composition dealing with a subject that can only prove a sharp irritant to the crown.*

My dear valued friend, does this precise moment strike you as an auspicious one to employ your matchless genius in reminding the world of Austria's long-discarded policy of oppression toward our small, sweet cousin-nation to the south? Those who have slandered you out of envy or ignorance will leap at the chance to denounce you for so blatant an indiscretion as lionizing the Swiss rebel leader of yore. All plans to do you honor are likely to cease forthwith. You will be forever labeled an Auslander, unworthy of the palace's kindnesses and recognition this coming season (or ever after).

As your avowed enthusiast and glad patron, I, too, would likely suffer the pain of your disgrace, to the point that I may be forbidden to continue the financial arrangement between us or to welcome you at Schonbrun or even at my home in Baden. The days when I have so proudly stood at your side during social receptions at the Stadt Hotel will become a distant memory. Is this, my dear maestro, what you wish to be the outcome of our friendship?

Let me now confess to you that when, five years ago, your august name was proposed to write music for a staging of Schiller's Wilhelm Tell *at our state theater, I was among that clandestine cabal who saw to it that the idea was dropped in favor of your doing Goethe's* Egmont—*and the result was a small gem. I opposed* Tell *for you then for much the same reason as now, but it is all the more pressing today.*

If you are truly, as you sign yourself in letters, my faithful and most obedient Beethoven, then heed my urgent counsel. There is great danger for the both of us if you persist in this Tell *venture. Any word of its existence or even that it might have been seriously contemplated will be promptly detected by a certain minister and his minions, and worse than mischief will ensue. Please do believe that my only motive is for your genius to be celebrated, not sullied, amidst the general rejoicing of the realm we are soon to enjoy.*

— R.

"That our titan displayed feet of clay on this occasion may not have been commendable," Mac remarked after the others had fully digested the archduke's remarkable letter, "but at least we can sympathize with his fears." That Beethoven totally capitulated in the face of Rudolph's warning was further confirmed, Mac disclosed, by several other documents that the Veritas team had found in the Beethoven archives and attributed to that year, suggesting how abjectly the now vigilant composer was heeding the protocols of discretion as the Congress of Vienna convened. In a letter to Johann Kanka, his attorney, Beethoven pledged, "I shall not write about our monarchs, etc., you can read all about that in the newspapers. I prefer the spiritual realm…" And in a stern diary entry during this period he instructed himself, "Do not show your contempt to all people who deserve it, one never knows when one might need them."

Thus, Mac concluded, the greatest composer of his age, or possibly any age, dishonored his muse in exchange for the rewards of that historic moment when Vienna basked in the continental spotlight. Never again would he mention the *William Tell* Symphony. Instead that fall he produced several insipid cantatas—in particular, the fawning *Der Glorreiche Augenblick* ("This Glorious Moment")—to mark the age's jubilee of peace. The prizes of his Faustian bargain were the ones the archduke had held up for him to glimpse: *Fidelio* did indeed inaugurate the gala concert programs accompanying the Congress of Vienna. The maestro was showered with four thousand florins—a year's living expenses—in tribute money. And the next year he was made an honorary citizen of Vienna after having lived there for twenty-three years.

But there were to be no enduring medals for him. The emperor did not give him a title or appoint him Composer of the Realm, *kapellmeister* of his court, or even the royal organist. And soon Metternich's spies were operating everywhere, trying to ferret out alleged enemies of the state. "The Austrian citizenry, as was their habit," Mac added, "bowed low to its mean regime, and the Hapsburg banner fluttered with renewed glory. End of story."

Mac's interpretation of the purported archduke's letter made perfect sense, Mitch and Clara agreed on their walk home through Central Park. "So Beethoven overreacted to Rudolph's warning," she said. "I mean he was only human, clay feet and all. The funny thing is, now I'm feeling rather better about this whole discovery business—because we're not profaning his genius on aesthetic grounds by going against his wishes in the matter. If he really killed *Tell* for political and mercenary reasons and not because he thought it was bad music, then we're actually righting a terrible wrong—even if he did it to himself, or let himself be cowed into it." She squinted against the still-bright western sky. "That poor man—he must have felt hugely insecure—to be that needy of honors—"

Mitch looped an arm around Clara's shoulder. "Something still bothers me, though," he said. "It's the way these letters in the box all seem to fit together so neatly with Nina's story. How come there weren't any other letters in there— no chatty notes from friends?"

She gave a flippant laugh. "You can't take yes for an answer, can you, mister?"

"It's not that—it just seems too—too—"

"Too good to be true? Why? I think you're forgetting—he didn't want people to know he was in Zurich, so he probably didn't get much mail. And he probably tossed away the pedestrian stuff—and saved the important things, like the Rudolph and Nägeli letters, until he was ready to head home—and since he evidently didn't want to keep any trace of *Tell*, he probably asked Nina to get rid of them, too."

"Maybe," said Mitch. "But it all still makes me edgy."

"You mean because there *are* no rough edges—and because your own forensics people couldn't find any holes in everything they looked at—and now this alleged letter from the archduke also checks out so consistently, therefore the whole business must be contrived?"

"Not *must* be contrived—*could* be contrived—by shrewd and greatly knowing con artists."

Clara shook her head. "Forgive me, Mitch—that's perverted thinking, not just skepticism."

"Possibly," he conceded and let the subject hang for a moment. Then he resumed, "And there's still the Rossini connection—that *does* bother me, the way I know it does you. We need to dig into that more and find a plausible answer before you'll catch me doing any high-fives."

"Right," Clara conceded. "I'm working on it—and so is Mac."

"...AND THEN IN MY BEST JUDY HOLLIDAY VOICE, I asked him the perfect twit question. 'Harry,' I said, 'when you get right down to it, why does it matter who wrote this Beethoven thing? I mean, if it's beautiful music, it's beautiful music—regardless.' You should have seen the look he gave me—as if I were radioactive dog poop. Honestly, when God was handing out senses of humor, he saved a corker for my sweet beau. He thinks sick jokes, pratfalls, and rectal thermometers are the height of hilarity."

Lolly Cubbage on the telephone was scarcely more bearable than in person. Lately, as the *Tell* situation intensified, she would call every few days, seemingly without design but always pumping Clara for the latest news and sharing whatever she was privy to. Harry, she revealed, was growing more excited by the day over the possibility of a major killing when—"he hardly says 'if' anymore"—the manuscript was finally put up for auction.

"Then maybe you shouldn't tease him about it's not mattering who really wrote it," Clara counseled, "or he'll never take you seriously again."

"The man needs to lighten up."

"But selling the genuine article is what his business is all about."

"Point taken," Lolly conceded. "Actually, I think he'd be ecstatic if he only knew how well our little Lincoln Center project is coming along. Did I tell you Penny Gillespie might come in for fifty? Our pledge total is seven seventy-five already, and we're just gearing up."

"It's not '*our* little project,' Lolly—it's yours. You know I'm very much on the fence—"

"I'll bet you sing a different tune—no pun intended—once your lover boy gives the thing his official okay."

"Don't count on it. Anyway, I think you'd be tying Harry's hands—or maybe get him charged with trying to rig the auction. That would kill C&W's reputation."

"Well, that's the last thing I want to do, of course, but I'm afraid you're overreacting, pumpkin. It's not as if I'd be the one doing the buying as a private party—this would all be for the good of Lincoln Center. And who do you think Harry would rather see as the buyer—Lincoln Center or the Maharajah of South Punjab? Oh, and did I mention Penny's bright idea? She says if we're really serious about this thing, we need to form a consortium with a couple of other heavy hitters, like a recording studio or even one of the movie companies—and what a boffo film this would make. Penny's got a first cousin wired in to Dreamworks who thinks the soundtrack CD might rake in even more than the regular recording of the whole symphony."

Lolly's high-powered excitement was apparently contagious. "That may make some sense," Clara allowed, not to be a total wet blanket. "Otherwise, you'd need to raise a small army of big givers—which could get very difficult since nobody's heard a note of *Tell* performed—and probably won't before the auction."

"Exactly what I was thinking," Lolly agreed. "And I have the perfect solution in mind that would work to everybody's interest." Once *Tell* was deemed authentic, why not, she proposed, stage a private performance about two weeks before the auction—"by the philharmonic, of course, at Lincoln Center, of course, maybe in Alice Tully Hall"—of just the first movement as kind of an hors d'oeuvre, so potential bidders could get a real sense of the work? "No press, no critics—attendance by invitation only, which means Harry gets to control the list as he likes—except I'd insist on our being able to invite, say, a hundred or so of the biggest potential givers to our kitty. I'd have to convince Harry each of them would be a possible bidder at the auction, but I'll bet the philharmonic would gladly perform it gratis, just as a historical thing—the very first time any orchestra will ever have played it—especially since the point of the event would be to give our Lincoln Center group the inside track to package a winning bid."

"But that would give you an unfair advantage."

"You're not listening, sweetpea. I *said* other serious potential bidders would be invited as well. I just think we'll be able to top them all if we put it together right."

It was not entirely a crazy idea, Clara recognized, assuming that the music would in the end be judged worthy of public performance. Even the savviest people for the leading record labels, who would presumably be among the most active bidders for *Tell,* would first need to hear at least part of the work performed with the full *tutti* sound; trying to read the score of a complex, never-before-heard Beethoven orchestration in order to gauge its quality would be no easy trick. But dare she encourage Lolly? And shouldn't she tell Mitch, perhaps right away, what Lolly was cooking up, so Harry could stifle it if the whole plan struck him as underhanded? Unless, of course, he chose not to. He just might subscribe to Lolly's argument that nobody was being disadvantaged by her efforts on behalf of Lincoln Center. In fact, her strategy, if seen as no more than a little benign string-pulling behind the scenes, might even get Harry elected to the center's board of trustees. The problem was, telling Mitch about Lolly's ploy would only make him crazy; he'd know he ought to tell Harry about it but couldn't without betraying Lolly's confidences to Clara and possibly dealing a fatal blow to the Cubbages' shaky marital relationship.

"Well," Clara said as neutrally as possible, "it may be an idea worth considering."

"Good girl! Why don't you come help me pull it off—as soon as your involvement in it with Mitch is over? And frankly, I think you should also give up that whole tiresome grind to become a grubby academic and devote yourself instead to socially correct do-gooding—not to mention having a high old time of it." Lolly paused half a beat, then added, "Also having a baby—possibly two. One will do, though—it did for us. Children can be such a bother—"

"Really? I hadn't heard—"

Sarcasm was lost on Lolly Cubbage, mired in her alternate universe of privileged self-absorption. She must have glanced at her Rolex. "Oh, sorry, gotta fly—if I'm thirty seconds late, Dr. Latham makes me wait hours in the stirrups—the rat. But he's cute and cracks such great jokes."

"DON'T WORRY ABOUT EMIL," Rolfe Riker told Mitch over their dessert coffee at the Silver Birch Chalet, Salzburg's best luncheon spot. "His bark's a lot worse than his bite. I can't say the same about that cur of his, though—watch out when he's eyeing you. A very protective beast."

Whether or not he succeeded in enlisting Emil Reinsdorf, the biggest catch of all to sit on C&W's five-member panel of Beethoven experts chaired by Mac Quarles, Mitch was delighted to have snared Riker in his net. Just turned forty, Riker was among the foremost European musicologists of the emerging generation. His book, *The Symphonic Evolution*, on the development of the form from Haydn to Mahler, was considered most illuminating for its dissection of Beethoven's revolutionary contributions to the genre. And he was a German as well, a native of Leipzig, though now a permanent resident of Austria and on the University of Salzburg faculty. "Unlikely as it seems," said Riker, "I'm quite fond of Emil, for all his crankiness. He can be quite engaging when he's not putting you down."

Mitch had allowed himself one month to assemble his panel while a trio of musicologists, selected by Quarles and working under tight surveillance in the top-floor apartment at C&W's offices, was producing a cleaned-up transcription of the *Tell* manuscript, pending further scholarly study and revision. Once the legible transcription was in hand and spot-checked to be sure it accorded with the original messy rough draft, Mac's Beethoven panel would be far better able to assess the composition. It had been agreed that five was the optimum number of participants for the panel of experts, including Quarles as the chair—enough viewpoints for genuine diversity but not so many as to invite wholesale dissension or encourage factions. Each of the four members besides Mac was to receive an honorarium of $50,000 plus expenses for two weeks of effort, the first week dedicated to examining the sketchbooks privately on C&W's premises, the second to meeting with the other panelists to compare notes and try to thrash out a consensus as to the work's authenticity. Unanimity was desirable, of course, but each panelist would be assured the right to file an independent opinion. Mac was to preside as a voting member and write the final report.

He and Mitch, with Clara's concurrence, had decided the proper balance would a German, an Austrian, two from other European countries, and Mac himself, the house American.

A German member, as predicted to C&W by the overbearing attaché from that nation's Ministry of Culture, was proving the hardest to engage. Of the dozen names on the list of eminent German candidates whom Mac had carefully culled and Mitch had deferentially approached by letter and follow-up phone calls, ten declined to meet with him in view of the disapproving advisory issued by the German Cultural Ministry. "They're a very obedient bunch," Mitch reported to Harry, "and rigidly orthodox types, according to Mac." Among the native Germans solicited, only Rolfe Riker, the most junior name on the list, and Emil Reinsdorf at the National Institute of Music (better known as the Berlin Conservatory), the hoariest of the Beethoven sages, had agreed to meet with Mitch.

He had begun his recruitment trip in London, where he and Clara put up at her parents' house while he stalked his first panel candidate, the matronly Anna Wertham Hayes, who lived in Hampstead. Hayes, whose family had fled Austria shortly before the *Anschlüss*, was the author of *Prometheus Unsilenced: The Life of Beethoven*, reputed to be the best twentieth-century biography of the maestro. Now among the gray eminences at the Royal College of Music, she also served as co-editor of its *Journal of Classical Music*, without peer in its field.

"In the unlikely event this manuscript should prove to be authentic," she groused when Mitch took her to lunch at the Dorchester, "I'll have to revise the biography—a pleasure I'd just as soon forgo. So I may prove a singularly testy participant." He assured her such resistance to bedazzlement would be entirely in keeping with the show-me spirit of the inquiry.

"In that case, count me in," she said over her Cointreau-drenched flan. "It all sounds stimulating, the pay is generous—in fact, I'd do it for nothing just to see Emil Reinsdorf turn apoplectic every half hour. The man loathes me—but I'm in good company."

Mitch's next stop was in Denmark to see the gnarled but amiable Torben Mundt, one part gremlin, two parts Peter Pan, who divided his life between professorships at the University of Copenhagen and Lund University in southern Sweden. He was a good friend of Mac Quarles, who told Mitch that Torben's hefty opus, *The German Sound*, was the most insightful piece of critical writing on music he had ever read, witness its translation into twenty-two languages and still counting. It was Torben's judgment even more than Mac's that the addition of the German pair of Emil Reinsdorf and Rolfe Riker would bring ideal strength and variety to the panel—"but you should understand that we're all predisposed to find this *Tell* bonbon a pile of *scheisse*."

"Just as we want it," Mitch asserted and flew off to Salzburg.

Riker had no problem dismissing the German government's attitude toward the *Tell* discovery and its possession by an American as "leftover Junker mentality—it's one reason I've chosen not to pursue my career in Berlin. The conservatory is very much under the Culture Ministry's thumb, and there are still too many around both places living in the past—the glory days of German music, not to mention military might."

Mitch was not cheered by this report. "And Dr. Reinsdorf subscribes to that as well?"

"Not in so many words, of course—and not when he's among foreigners, certainly. The joke among younger people in the field is that Emil is more Germanic than Siegfried—he's hopelessly territorial when it comes to others poaching on German musical expertise. I've heard him describe Anna Hayes's Beethoven biography as 'seven hundred pages of adolescent panting'—and he calls her 'La Blimp.' He can get quite nastily *ad hominem* when he wants to."

"Are you saying that he'll try to dictate to our panel? And do we need that?"

"'Try to dictate,' yes—and yes, you need him, especially if you're hoping to persuade the world that you've got the real goods in your hands. If he says otherwise, it will certainly make the rest of us hesitate, no matter that he's usually on a one-way ego trip."

"How can I persuade him not to snub us?" Mitch asked.

"You're already halfway there," Riker supposed, "or he wouldn't have agreed to meet with you. He's got no worlds left to conquer within his field, you see, so he doesn't have to worry about offending the people in power."

Ten years earlier, it had been different, Riker confided; Reinsdorf had assiduously positioned himself to become elected director of the Berlin Conservatory, the pinnacle of German music academia, yet for all his medals and scheming, he was passed over. The position reopened five years later, but the board of governors wanted a younger man for the taxing job. "Give Emil credit, though—instead of turning into a bitter old man, he jokes about how lucky he was not to have become sucked into all that administrative quicksand—and he's still productive and full of interesting ideas. Get some wine into him, and he'll give you an earful on Beethoven's secret sexuality." Riker grabbed the check before Mitch could. "Treat Emil like a hero—make him feel it's his patriotic duty to keep your panel honest."

WHILE MITCH REMAINED in Europe, recruiting the Beethoven authorities Mac Quarles had selected to make up C&W's elite authentication panel, Clara had returned to New York to attend to new duties assigned her at Lincoln Center and to keep an appointment with her Columbia faculty adviser on the status of her doctoral thesis.

Her supervisors at the city's great performing arts complex had rewarded her élan and diligence by promoting her to a team of fundraisers assigned solely to seek contributions to the Lincoln Center endowment from current patrons and longtime season subscribers. The process, involving luncheons at superior—but not the priciest—restaurants, appointments at the homes of promising prospects, and meetings with donors' attorneys and financial advisers, would entail politesse, patience—and a high threshold for frustration, Clara was told while being assured there was no higher calling among the center's volunteer staff. Her reward was increased from a pair to a set of four superior house seats at any combination of twenty-five performances, whether by the philharmonic, the Met, or the theatrical company at the Vivian Beaumot.

On top of this satisfying news, her Columbia dissertation adviser, Associate Professor Mark Aurelio, was now coming around, Clara was happy to learn, to her proposed change of topic from Schubert's symphonic work, his Ninth in particular, to the unfolding saga of the *Tell* Symphony. Although the professor recognized that Clara could bring an inside vantage point to recounting the story of the discovery of the work and the investigation to authenticate it, he was concerned lest the thesis turn into journalism, something more appropriate to appear in *The New Yorker* or *Harper's*, especially if the manuscript turned out to be bogus. Clara was forced to tell Aurelio that she was unfortunately constrained from disclosing to him any of the findings of the C&W inquiry thus far, but he seemed satisfied by her latest report that the effort was making good headway and its prospects were "promising but by no means certain" in this still-early phase of the process. She agreed to keep pursuing the Schubert study even while the drama over Beethoven's alleged Tenth Symphony was being played out and to advise Professor Aurelio of the outcome as soon as she was able—"If we leave your topic hanging indefinitely, the faculty doctoral committee will be on my back. Neither of us needs that." She understood his veiled reference to the departmental vote to be taken that spring on his tenure status.

The next day, Clara decided to take a midmorning break from her academic reading and note-taking at home and go for a jog in Riverside Park along the narrow greenway beside the Hudson. In good weather, she and Mitch would make the run side by side two or three times a week before breakfast—between Seventy-Second and Ninety-Sixth Streets, up and down twice for a total of about four miles. Other days, when Mitch was at work and her Lincoln Center schedule freed her up, she would bike over to the park at Eighty-Sixth and jog three times around the reservoir, where the going was slower because there were many more runners and walkers but she felt safer because of the company.

With Mitch away, she had cut out the early-morning run along the river—jogging alone amid the sparse turnout of exercisers at that hour made her uneasy. Now and then, though, due to Mitch's or her own scheduling problems, she'd go out solo to Riverside Park at ten when there were more people around and, well, it was right next to their apartment house. On this morning, the last in September, it was perfect jogging weather, just over sixty with moderate humidity and a light breeze off the river, and she was relishing the easy rhythm of her fit body in motion over the broad pedestrian promenade. Her iPod was playing Elgar's *Enigma Variations*, and her heart was beginning to pine for her absent lover, due home after a weekend stay with her parents at their Cotswolds cottage. Her wandering mind refused to settle on any of the clamoring strands that wended through it.

On the third of the four legs of her riverside route, it struck her that she was practically the only runner in sight, though there were a few walkers and an occasional sitter on the benches along the east side of the promenade. There was no runner up ahead of her, but a guy in sweatpants, T-shirt, and sunglasses was trailing her at a distance of perhaps five hundred feet. The gap between them had begun to narrow, she sensed—not surprising since she had set a moderate pace and intended to reserve a burst of energy for the last leg of the run.

As she drew opposite the Soldiers and Sailors Monument at the top of the park incline near Ninetieth Street on the drive, the lace on her right running shoe came loose, and she pulled up at an empty bench to attend to it. Obliquely she noticed that the male jogger, now only about a football field's length behind her, also drew to a halt, seemingly to catch his breath while he looked out at the river and some passing small craft. After a moment, she resumed her run and waited perhaps twenty seconds before glancing over her shoulder as unobtrusively as possible. And there the man was, gliding along smoothly no more than two hundred feet behind her.

Ahead, the park looked deserted, and, growing uneasy now, she sped up to avoid being overtaken. Was he actively pursuing her or just moving along at his own accelerated pace? The latter, surely. She kept losing ground to him the harder she ran, and suddenly she spotted another man to her right, also in running gear, angling down the park slope in her direction, almost as if—it could not just be her imagination—on a course to intersect with her and the runner fast closing in on her from behind.

Dread now seized her and drove her long legs all out. Was this an assault by a pair of rapists working in tandem? It couldn't be a robbery—joggers usually carried nothing more than an ID on them. She could see the man to her right only as a blur now as she lowered her head and kept pumping as hard as she could until finally, she could see a cluster of park-goers joining the promenade from the Ninety-Sixth Street access. Heart pounding, she found shelter in their midst as the two male runners flew past her without a sideways glance. There must have been thirty or forty feet between them the last time she glanced in their direction, suggesting they were not confederates out to do her harm. Still, it had given her a fright. Stupid.

The next day, after her duties at Lincoln Center, she biked over to the Central Park reservoir for her usual three laps around the course. Her brief but intense scare of the previous day now seemed a silly overreaction, but it was nonetheless comforting to be out among a lot of joggers, though annoying as usual when walkers refused to cede them the waterside lane.

Midway through her second lap, near the reservoir's westernmost point, which afforded her a sweeping vista of the Fifth Avenue skyline, Clara became aware of another woman, not quite as tall as herself, pulling alongside and matching her stride for stride for a while. She was wearing a Kelly green T-shirt with "Manhattan College" stenciled on it in white letters, white running shorts with the same green piping, and a white sweatband. The only thing Clara knew about Manhattan College was that it was not in Manhattan. Somewhere up in the Riverdale section of the Bronx, she thought idly. If she were more extroverted, she might have asked the woman to explain the seeming misnomer, but for her to put such a trivial question to a passing stranger was unthinkable.

The stranger, though, did not pass her. "Great weather," she said after another ten or fifteen seconds and without looking sideways at Clara.

Was this an idle pleasantry in the middle of the park in the middle of a lovely New York afternoon, or was it a come-on? "The best," Clara replied disinterestedly and without a lateral look, but imperceptibly slowed her pace in the hope the woman would slide past her. She didn't.

After another short interval, her unwanted accompanist said, "You're Clara, right?" This time she turned toward her, revealing a narrow face and engaging smile. Her question sounded like a declaration of familiarity. An unwanted one.

Must be someone on the Lincoln Center staff she had never taken much notice of or possibly a fellow Columbia scholar or perhaps a secretary in the music department.

"Sorry—do we know each other?" Clara asked politely, picking up the pace again.

"I don't think you know me—I'm Betty—Betty Smith, would you believe?"

"Okay, Betty—but how do you know me?" Clara felt a small stab of alarm, probably a residue from her imaginary run-in the day before with the two male runners along the river. But they had never indicated overt hostile intent—or addressed her by name. Now what was this?

Betty, or whoever she was, kept smiling and looking ahead. "Well, I've seen your picture—some friends showed it to me."

What? Now wait a minute—who *was* this woman? And why did she know Clara's name? And why was she there, insinuating this was a casual encounter? "What friends?"

"Friends who want to speak to you," Betty said. "It's important."

Her anxiety antennae switched on. Speak to her about *what?* Clara was unsure whether to pull up on the spot and demand an explanation or to keep running and tell her to get away or she'd shout for help. Inertia kept her legs moving. She fought to calm herself. Probably a misunderstanding. Only it didn't sound that way. She kept quiet, hoping that silence would end their exchange.

"There's nothing to be alarmed about, Clara," the woman said evenly. "It's a business thing—trust me."

Was it an insurance company pitch? A white-slave recruitment? God in heaven, she asked herself, what have I done to deserve being harassed in public like this?

"Whoever you are or whatever you're up to, would you please leave me alone?" Her panic attack was ill disguised.

"Not until I deliver the message I was sent to give you," said so-called Betty Smith, panting. "Just listen for a minute and don't make a scene, or I'll get sacked for screwing this up."

Christ, now she was accosting her with a plea for sympathy! Was she really a novice at this stalking game or just playing one? "Okay—get it over with," Clara said, pulling up short.

"The people who sent me want to hire you—as a scout—to let them know how William Tell's health is. That's the first part of the message I'm supposed to deliver—it doesn't make any sense to me, but they said you'd—"

The woman cut herself off and waited for a reaction from Clara. When there was none, she continued. "My people also said they would like to buy Mr. Tell and put him to work, if his health permits. Do you get what that's about?"

Clara would not respond. The message, unthreatening on the surface but with an undertow of menace, sent a chill through her. Some people—people who had no business knowing—were up on the whole Beethoven scenario and her professional involvement with C&W's secret authentication proceedings. And they wanted her to betray her own husband's company and let them know if the Beethoven manuscript was real or bogus. What sheer stupidity. What supreme gall. But at least they hadn't kidnapped her—yet. Or were those two guys yesterday in jogging sweats really on her case? Would they have tried for a daylight snatch if the coast had been clear? Her mind raced. "How did you know where to find me?" she asked sharply.

"I was given instructions and your description—with a photo. That's all I know, honest."

Lord in heaven, these creatures had been actively spying on her, they knew her habits and movements, they—they had to be ruthless crooks or something. "Did your friends send a couple of guys out yesterday to find me and give me the same message—or rough me up to scare me into cooperating—or something?"

"Nobody told me that," the woman said as they leaned on the reservoir railing. "I don't think they're into violence. It's a business operation—a big company, I think. And they'll pay you a whole lot of money, Clara. I think you should hear their offer. What do you say?"

"I say tell them to save their money because what they're after isn't for sale—it's going to be auctioned if and when that's appropriate—that's been reported in the media." Clara flashed the Betty person an angry look. "Now get the hell away from me, Miss Whoever You Are, or I'll definitely yell for the cops."

"Hey, calm down—and you don't have to get nasty about it, either, I'm just doing my job. Besides, they know about the auction—I think they want to buy the thing before it gets put up for sale, but they need someone on the inside to tell them if it's worth it."

That was better—not so desperate-sounding. More calculated. Clara turned away and resumed running, nearly at a sprint. "Tell them I'm not interested," she yelled over her shoulder.

"They'll call you tomorrow morning—you should listen to them."

"Get lost!" Clara shouted as passing heads spun around to see what the fuss was about.

She tried to calm herself on the bike ride home. Who could have mentioned her name to whoever these sleazeballs were? Who knew about her involvement with *Tell*? Only Mitch and her parents, who certainly knew enough not to bruit it about. Well, there were the people in Mitch's office, of course, starting with Harry and Gordy, but they'd never—oh, Jesus, there was Lolly, who could have blabbed it to anyone, to any of the friends she's hitting on for her wacky collective bid to benefit Lincoln Center.

But why would Lolly even bring her name up—she was just a minor consultant to C&W. Same with Mac Quarles, who was contractually bound to keep a lid on everything he had to do with *Tell*. Wait—what about Professor Aurelio? He knew she was in on it—and hadn't he just asked her to keep him closely abreast on developments? Could he be some kind of an academic poseur? Or just trying to cash in on one of his students' special entrée to the hottest game in classical music at the moment?

It was all a great muddle—anything and everything suddenly seemed possible. She got home feeling sore and definitely violated. There were demons abroad in the land, and some of them appeared to be on her case. She double-locked and bolted the front door to the apartment.

{10}

His Eminence occupied a third-floor corner office at the Institute of Music in Berlin, a square-block, five-story pile of rough gray stone in the rococo style of the late nineteenth century. The two north windows in Emil Reinsdorf's cluttered lair overlooked the treetops of the Tiergarten, still fully leafed in late summer, while his east windows were perpetually shadowed by the corporate shafts of steel and glass that had risen phoenixlike in recent years of frenetic postwar reconstruction over the rebuilt Potsdamer Platz.

"Once upon a time it was quite serene around here," Reinsdorf said, taking Mitch's hand and directing him to a well-worn armchair, "until the Wall went away and the reconstruction craze came. They've been building a tunnel under the park for years—we've spent millions soundproofing this place. A bunker mentality sets in after a while—if you'll forgive the politically incorrect allusion."

It was the musicologist's only reference to the dark German past, and he did not posture in the least as defender of any master-race *kultur*. Wreathed in his own cigarette smoke, broad shoulders slumped, Reinsdorf was an arresting figure, with a full head of light gray hair cut short in the military manner, a shrubby mustache tobacco-tinged at the bottom, and heavy, horn-rimmed glasses with thick lenses that made his eyes look bleary and elusive. His office was forbiddingly spartan except for the framed drawings of flowers and plants that filled the walls and caught Mitch's eye with their vibrant colors and fluid lines.

"I see you're thinking I should hang portraits of the great composers instead," Reinsdorf said, catching Mitch's peripheral glance and giving a phlegmy laugh. "Yes, well—that's what comes of having a former botanist for a

184

wife. My Hilde decided she'd rather draw than study flora, so she left university to become an artist and nearly starved—until she went to work for a grubby advertising company, the fate I rescued her from. She repaid me in part with these lovely things—we give prints of them to friends at Christmas."

"She's very gifted."

"Unfortunately, the marketplace seems to favor nature's own over man-made floral renderings, however exquisite. Hilde has adjusted." Reinsdorf motioned toward the corner, where a large, black-and-white-mottled bulldog lay beside the radiator. "That's the rest of my family—Scherzo likes it in here despite all my smoke." There was no apology for inflicting the toxic miasma on Mitch's lungs. "Now let's hear all about our maestro's miraculously resurrected Tenth Symphony—which, remember, I've already told the press is a very bad joke."

"Understandably," said Mitch. "And my company fully shared your reaction—at first. But there is an accumulating body of evidence that's hard for us to dismiss lightly." He handed Reinsdorf copies of the forensics report from the Veritas people and the letters from Nina Hassler, Hans Nägeli, and Archduke Rudolph. "Perhaps you might review these overnight."

Reinsdorf nodded, then dropped the papers indifferently on his cluttered desktop. "But first tell me, please," he asked, "why is it that I should lend my name to this bizarre enterprise of yours—which, even assuming good faith on your part, our esteemed national government has decreed would best be conducted under its own supervision—dunderheads that they are?"

Permitting himself a half smile at the subversive crack, Mitch was ready with an answer. "We appreciate your government's concern but believe it's misplaced. We think any patriotic German musicologist invited to examine the evidence should feel conscience-bound to do so—in view of the leading historic role your countrymen have played in creating this art form. And since no one is better qualified than you are to make the necessary judgment—which, after all, should not be left to lesser minds—we're very hopeful that you'll participate quite willingly. And we're prepared, incidentally, to compensate you more than amply for your services."

Reinsdorf drew on the last of his cigarette, then slowly, thoughtfully stubbed it out. "You make several good points," he said and offered no rebuttal. "Come, my Scherzie needs to be walked. We'll have a bite in the park—there's a nice little beer garden I like at one of the ponds. Only don't be offended by the foul smells en route—it's our beloved Turkish immigrants, barbecuing their wretched goat meat on every lawn in the Tiergarten. If Schliemann were still around, he could take them all back to Troy with him."

Over lunch, Reinsdorf recounted his student and junior faculty days at the University of Vienna, when he fell in love with Beethoven and haunted all the places the maestro was known to have lived, eaten, and performed. It was in Vienna where the young scholar wrote the first volume of his *Maestro* trilogy that earned him a professorship at the Berlin Conservatory.

"I moved here very reluctantly—as a non-German, I feared I would always be treated as an outsider. The pace and feeling were entirely different from Vienna, and living in a divided city during the Cold War was no picnic." It was nothing like the heady prewar days of the Weimar Republic, he said, when free-floating Bohemianism had collided with the brutishness of the budding Nazi Reich. In time, though, he grew to feel at home in the divided old capital and became a West German citizen—"pretty much a career requisite." He cut off a piece of his knockwurst and fed it to the quietly slavering bulldog at his feet. "All of which may help explain why this so-called *Tell* Symphony has stirred up so much resentment here. We need our gods badly—the good gods, anyway—and are hopelessly proprietary when it comes to our master composers. So it's been doubly painful to watch others—alien infidels, you might say—pawing through an alleged new cache of Beethoven's holy writ. And suppose it were to wind up in the wrong hands for cheap exploitation?"

Mitch nodded but made no attempt to rationalize either Jake Hassler's making off with the *Tell* manuscript or Cubbage & Wakeham's complicity in helping him try to exploit it. Instead he sat respectfully watching the preoccupied old scholar drain his mug of beer and light a Marlboro. "I've reached the age," he said without a context, "when I look to Beethoven more for guidance in spiritual matters than for sensory satisfaction. Does that surprise you?"

"A little," Mitch said. "I didn't know he was an authority in that area."

"No—not an authority—a believer. He was nearly fifty and had endured— to hear him tell it—far more sorrow than joy in his life when he wrote in his diary, 'With tranquility, O God, I submit...all my trust in Thy unalterable mercy and goodness.'" Reinsdorf looked quizzically at the ember of his cigarette. "This was the same God, mind you, who had bestowed him with the spark of soaring genius and then denied him use of the sensory faculty he needed most to apply that gift. Where was the mercy and goodness in that? Why, I've long wondered, does such a God deserve the loving submission that Ludwig gave him?"

Mitch felt himself turned into the captive ear for a savant's running internal monologue. Was he meant to reply? Was the professor dissing the composer? Or God? Or both—or neither? "Could it be that Beethoven saw his life as an ongoing test," Mitch offered, reluctant to risk a fatuous reply, "rather like Job? I mean that so long as he refrained from cursing his deepening deafness, God would let him keep on creating masterpieces."

A series of dry, wheezy coughs rattled the professor's insides. When the spasm subsided, he replied, "Would that be your definition of a good and merciful God?"

"No, not mine—but it seems to have worked well enough for Beethoven. My limited understanding is that the onset of his deafness more or less coincided with his most fruitful period. Perhaps there was an ulterior purpose to his reverence—forgive my cynical nature."

"Perhaps so," the professor responded. "And may I ask, Mr. Emery, if, accordingly, you've abandoned interest in God's unalterable mercy and goodness?"

Not inclined to reveal his core beliefs—and doubts—to a stranger, Mitch closed down. "Let's just say they seem to be somewhat arbitrarily bestowed. Not that I'm not unappreciative of my life thus far—it's been fulfilling," he said, hoping to leave it there.

"But you nonetheless doubt God's grace as a universal proposition?"

"Let's just say I doubt I'd do as well as Beethoven submitting to a divinity I find capricious about who's worth blessing and who isn't."

"But isn't that the whole point, young man? The only real choice left to us in the end is whether we submit calmly or in anger to the Lord's command of unconditional faith. Defiance gets you nowhere—at least nowhere I've discovered."

They parted amicably after Reinsdorf promised to call Mitch's hotel room early the next morning with his decision.

"I think we may have bearded the lion," Mitch told Clara on the phone to London that night. "I'm not so sure about his bulldog, though."

Word came at 9:05 a.m. "I'm astounded," Reinsdorf began. "You're quite right—it all looks too important—just from what you've given me to read—to dismiss it as I did. I'll gladly participate on your panel. Just give me a few weeks' warning when I'll be needed."

"Great—*wunderbar!*"

"There's just one thing I'll need your help on."

Uh-oh. Was Frankenstein's monster about to surface? "Anything, Dr. Reinsdorf—within reason, of course."

"You need to understand that I'll be vilified—if not crucified—for participating in your investigation."

There was a pause, then: "I need something, Mr. Emery, to cover my derrière, or they'll kick it black and blue."

"Like what?"

"If this thing—this so-called 'dramatic symphony'—should prove authentic, the Berlin Philharmonic must be the first to perform it—and right here."

Mitch's mind reeled. He knew it had gone too well. How exactly had Gordy left things with the Swiss government? "I don't believe I'm at liberty to make that promise."

"Why not? It's only right—and just. Whatever else he was or wasn't, Beethoven was a great German. If the *Tell* Symphony premiere is promised to Berlin—if there ever is a premiere—then I can hold my head up as a defender of our cultural tradition. Otherwise, I'm a traitor."

Mitch phoned Harry and Gordy with the good news / bad news, then asked, "Isn't our commitment to the Swiss pretty iffy—only that we'll recommend to our buyer that the premiere be held there? Their government is still stonewalling on processing Otto Hassler's will, isn't it? So why are we beholden to them? We need this man on our panel, or—at a guess—there won't be any premiere for anyone to worry about."

"We gave our word," said Gordy. "Tell him no can do—maybe he'll cave. Even musicologists have been known to bluff."

"Not this one," Mitch told him and then went back glumly to Emil Reinsdorf.

"How droll," he said dryly. "You've tentatively promised to help arrange for the premiere to be in Zurich—not precisely the world's music capital. It's ludicrous."

"But it's called the *William Tell* Symphony—the Swiss, too, have their national pride."

Silence. And then: "What about this, then, Mr. Emery? Suppose your executives suggest to the Swiss that they're being rather selfish—and that in the interest of historical fairness, the honor of the premiere should be shared among the three German-speaking peoples. The premiere will be held simultaneously in Zurich, Berlin, and Vienna, each with an equal claim to the event. What could be fairer?"

Mitch decided he liked Emil Reinsdorf. He was a pragmatist as well as an ivory tower scholar. "Nothing," he said. "I'll try to work it out."

"Well," Gordy said when he heard the proposal, "I can run it by Saulnier."

"Start with me," said Harry. "I'm not sure it's a good idea. It ties our hands. Suppose a Japanese bidder wants to pay ten zillion yen for the manuscript and hold the premiere on the slopes of fucking Fujiyama? Or an American outfit—maybe one of the entertainment conglomerates—wants to do a global simulcast of the premiere from Carnegie Hall—like Oscar Night, with a billion viewers? Do we refuse their bid because one haughty German bastard has crowbarred us into an all-*Deutsch* extravaganza?"

"But he's *our* bastard," Mitch argued. "Emil could be a major troublemaker if he's not on board. Why don't I tell him we'll try to get the Swiss to buy the three-nation deal, but the broadcast rights have to be reserved for the winning bidder to sell off without restrictions?"

"That's better," Harry said, "but it still narrows our possibilities. I'm not wild about running auctions with any conditions attached to the sale."

"Suppose I ask the Swiss to buy Reinsdorf's proposition," Gordy tried, "and Mitch offers Reinsdorf the same toothless deal we sold the Swiss. Translation: we'll respectfully urge our buyer to go for the triple premiere, but it's not a condition for making a bid."

"Mmmm," said Harry. "Okay, Mitch, you trot it past Emil, and if he's on board, Gordy can try it on the yodelers."

Emil Reinsdorf took the face-saving offer. So, too, forty-eight hours later, did the Swiss, still clinging, nonetheless, to their refusal to probate Otto Hassler's will until the *Tell* authentication issue was decided. Even so, Reinsdorf rose in Mitch's esteem—until his return to London, where he was greeted by an emailed attachment from Johnny Winks consisting of a translated excerpt from the arts section of that week's *Der Spiegel*. It read:

> Prickly scholar Emil Reinsdorf of the Berlin Conservatory this week broke ranks with German music experts boycotting efforts by an Anglo-American auction house to try to authenticate a recently unearthed symphony attributed to Ludwig van Beethoven. Conceding that the investigation ought ideally to be made under the aegis of academicians "and not treated like a commodity by US materialists," Reinsdorf, 63, argued that he had "a responsibility to assure that this manuscript is not the victim of inexpert opinion or the permissive standards presently debasing the arts and much else in contemporary society." In announcing his decision, Reinsdorf, author of the landmark trilogy on Beethoven's work, *Maestro 1, 2,* and *3*, let the cat out of the bag by revealing for the first time that the work in question is called the *William Tell* Symphony, a hybrid vocal/instrumental composition inspired by Friedrich Schiller's 1804

drama. As a condition for his cooperating, Reinsdorf said he had been promised that the premiere public performance of the so-called "dramatic symphony" would be given—if ever—simultaneously in Berlin, Vienna, and Zurich as a tribute to Germanic culture.

"Sly bastard," Mitch whispered to himself and phoned Berlin at once.

"I'm more outraged than you are," Reinsdorf told him hotly before dissolving into a spasm of hacking coughs. "I made no announcement, as the filthy magazine has it—they must have been eavesdropping around our building, where I did mention our arrangement to a few people, as I told you I would have to—a preemptive strike, you might say." He denied claiming the three-city premiere was a certainty, allowing only that it was a distinct possibility. "As to calling your distinguished firm 'US materialists,' that's standard rhetoric around here for any commercial promoters—hardly a slur, I should think. Materialism has its place, as most Germans would be quick to agree."

"*Very* sly bastard," Mitch said on reporting the conversation to his unhappy home office.

"Well, he's your monster now, Dr. Frankenstein," said Harry. "Keep a lid on him."

NO CALL CAME THE MORNING AFTER her encounter at the Central Park reservoir from anyone with a proposition for Clara to betray Mitch and his employer by spilling the beans about the *Tell* manuscript and its chances of being authenticated. Why would anyone think she'd be susceptible to such a blatant enticement? If these people had checked her out the way the approach by this Betty Smith creature suggested, surely they knew the Emerys were not impoverished and that Clara's family was probably worth a tidy sum. Or was that their game? Would they try to grab her and hold her for a fat ransom if she didn't do as they asked?

On due reflection, she decided to quit panicky fantasizing—but also not to tell Mitch when he returned from London on Sunday about her double scare while out jogging without him. All it would do, probably, was make him insist that to avoid further endangerment, she had better sever her formal involvement in the *Tell* investigation, and that was the last thing she wanted now. In truth, she had become as fixated emotionally as Mitch was professionally by the whole mind-blowing mystery.

Among all its vaporous pieces, none remained more mysterious than the Rossini connection. No doubt Mac Quarles's panel of Beethoven experts would address the authenticity issue grain by grain as soon as the transcribed sketchbooks were available for intensive review. How, though, to explain the symphony's abandonment in 1814 but the recurrence of its opening theme as a recognizable variation in Rossini's most famous overture, first heard in public fifteen years later—and two years after Beethoven's death? No clue had been forthcoming from Mac's end.

Clara decided to attack the question head-on. She fished out from her vast CD collection a disk of Rossini overtures, including those from *The Barber of Seville, Tancredi, Semiramide,* and, naturally, *William Tell.* She had always enjoyed the *Tell* overture as alternately rousing and lilting. But now it took on a dimension of intrigue for her.

The whole piece ran just eleven and a half minutes, according to the liner notes inside the plastic holder. While the hushed first half of the work floated about her study, Clara sat staring at the drawing on the front of the slick-paper pamphlet lodged inside the CD holder. It was illustrated, predictably, by a large red apple in the process of being severed by an arrow. When the heralding horns suddenly burst into the soaring section of the music that Mac Quarles referred to as the *Lone Ranger* theme, after the old western adventure series on radio and TV that had adopted the Rossini passage for its musical signature, an impulse drove Clara to tweeze the folded liner notes out of the container and read them. Though brief and in tiny type, the contents of the pamphlet included one startling sentence: "The four sections of the *William Tell* Overture, virtually a miniature tone poem, represent dawn in the mountains, a thunderstorm, the pastoral countryside, and the triumphant return of the Swiss troops (to the music of a quickstep march for a military band that Rossini had written seven years before in Vienna)."

In Vienna! And seven years before the premiere of Rossini's *Tell* opera would make it 1822; Beethoven, at fifty-two, was still very much alive and grousing— and composing. But had the two men ever met while they were in the same city that year? And why would they have? Beethoven was admired everywhere as the aging titan of Western music, without a serious rival among living composers; Rossini was a younger upstart whose operatic oeuvre could hardly have been considered in the same galaxy with that of the supreme music-makers of Vienna. Why would Beethoven have deigned to cross paths with the likes of Rossini, whose gossamer works would likely have been beneath his contempt, assuming they were ever performed in Vienna?

To find answers, Clara camped out the next day at Columbia's music library, a favorite haunt, scouring its stacks for any volume that seemed remotely related to the subject. Unconsciously at first and then with uneasy self-awareness that she was displaying the symptoms of incipient paranoia, she intermittently glanced over her shoulder to be sure nobody was watching her. To be less than vigilant after her two scary jogging episodes would have been foolhardy.

Satisfied nobody was lurking about, she set to work. Her starting point was the index in each of the thirteen Beethoven biographies she found, six of which she owned and had already read, and three on Rossini that were new to her. Her excitement quickened in the course of a two-hour search when she found several references to a meeting the two composers has indeed had in April of 1822, exact date unspecified, at Beethoven's studio. Trying to find out if there was any record of what had transpired during their encounter consumed the rest of the day and half the next morning.

While several of the biographies touched on the meeting, none did so more extensively than Thayer's classic but flawed two-volume work, published in the 1870s, which said Rossini arrived in Vienna for the first time that spring of 1822 at the age of thirty for the presentation of his new opera, *Zelmira*. At the time, Rossini was all the rage in the music capital of the world. His operas had been performed there for several years and met with an ardent reception, *The Barber of Seville* in particular. His airy, melodic music suited the buoyant, sensuous spirit of the post-Napoleonic age and made the dashing Italian composer, with his elegant manners and sparkling conversation, the object of adoration in the drawing rooms of the Viennese aristocracy as well as with the spectacle-craving masses. He and Beethoven were, beyond dispute, the two most celebrated composers alive, but the latter, while still venerated, was old news, souring wine in a crystal decanter, and everything that Rossini was not—ill-mannered, gloom-ridden, and isolated in his soundless world.

Savoring the limelight, Rossini had nevertheless heard enough of Beethoven's music to recognize his immense genius and wished to make the acquaintance of the reclusive maestro. While Beethoven suffered few visitors, fools and savants alike, he did not begrudge the younger man his vogue. He had read and admired the score of *The Barber of Seville* and once described Rossini as "a good scene painter"—a genuine enough talent but hardly on a monumental scale like his own. On at least three occasions long after Beethoven's death (two of them known to Thayer at the time he wrote his massive biography), Rossini told others of his meeting with the supreme maestro. In one account, he recalled,

I had Carpani, the Italian poet with whom I had already called upon Salieri, introduce me, and he received me at once and very politely. True, the visit did not last very long, for conversation with Beethoven was nothing less than painful. His hearing was particularly bad that day and in spite of my loudest shouting [he] could not understand me...

In a second account, Rossini remembered that "between his deafness and my ignorance of German, conversation was impossible. But I am glad that I saw him, at least."

So they had met and tried to converse, but little of real substance had apparently passed between them. That left Clara with not a soupçon of evidence to support her Rossini-stole-the-*Tell*-theme theory. Finally, having nearly lost heart that there was in fact something more to discover, she made yet another run through the stacks and came upon a slender volume, *Beethoven: Impressions by His Contemporaries,* which she had earlier ignored as a worthless miscellany. Now she leafed through it methodically. Midway through it, to her astonished delight, was a third and far more expansive account by Rossini of his meeting with Beethoven. This version, related to Richard Wagner in Paris in 1860 when the German composer called upon the Italian master of their shared musical form, was recorded by a third party who was on hand but did not bother to publish his notes about the meeting until forty-six years later, long after Thayer's encyclopedic biography had been completed. Wagner's exchange with Rossini suggested to Clara, who devoured every word of the account, why the Italian might have been less than forthright in the two earlier disclosures of his interview with Beethoven.

"When I mounted the stairs leading to the poor lodgings of the great man," he recounted to Wagner, "I barely mastered my emotions." Admitted to Beethoven's attic studio, Rossini was struck by "how terribly disordered and dirty" it was and the distressing cracks in the ceiling. Beethoven was bent over correcting printer's proofs when Rossini and the poet Carpani entered unnoticed, and as they waited for him to finish, the younger composer observed "the indefinable sadness spread across his features" while from under heavy brows "his eyes shone as from out of caverns and, though small, seemed to pierce one." When Beethoven raised his head, his greeting was enthusiastic enough: "Ah! Rossini, you, the composer of *Il Barbiere di Seviglia?*" he asked rhetorically in fairly comprehensible Italian. "My congratulations—that is an excellent *opera buffa*. I have read it with pleasure... It will be played so long as Italian opera shall exist. Do never try your hand at anything but *opera buffa*—you would be doing violence to your destiny by wanting to succeed in a different genre."

Carpani, taking offense at the backhanded compliment to his young countryman, interrupted to say—by writing in German in the "conversation book" that Beethoven kept about him for such purposes when visitors arrived— that Rossini had composed numerous serious operas, among them *Otello, Tancredi,* and *Mosè,* several of which Carpani had sent to Beethoven for his examination. To which Beethoven devastatingly replied:

> Indeed, I did go through them, but, you see, serious opera does not lie in the nature of the Italians. For the true drama, they know not enough of the science of music—and how could they acquire that in Italy? In *opera buffa,* none can equal Italians. Your language and your temperament predestine you for it. Look at Cimarosa; how much superior the comic parts of his operas are to the rest. The same with Pergolesi...

Apparently unfazed by this gratuitous insult, Rossini confined himself to conveying "all my admiration for his genius, all my gratitude for having given me the opportunity to express it. He [Beethoven] answered with a deep sigh: 'Oh, *un infelice!*'" (which Clara took to mean, from her rusty Italian, "What an unhappy soul am I!") There followed an exchange about conditions in the theaters of Italy, whether Mozart's operas were performed much there, and what Rossini thought of the Italian opera company in Vienna. "Then, wishing me a good performance and success with *Zelmira,* he rose and conducted us back to the door with the remark, 'Above all, do more of *The Barber.*'"

Descending the dilapidated stairs, Rossini "retained of my visit to this great man an impression so painful—thinking of this destitution and shabbiness— that I could not repress my tears." But Carpani, who knew Beethoven well enough, tried to brace Rossini by remarking, "Ah, that's what he wants. He is a misanthrope, cranky, and can't keep friends."

Rossini, however, was not to be denied his compassion. That very evening, while attending a gala dinner at the palace of Prince Metternich, by then the prime minister and de facto ruler of Austria, Rossini could not rid himself of that dolorous *"un infelice"* Beethoven had uttered, and the Italian grew melancholy when he considered the kindness with which he was treated "by that brilliant Viennese assembly" compared with the way the city neglected its venerable icon. His distress led him, as Rossini told Wagner thirty-eight years afterward,

...to say loudly and without mincing words all I thought of the conduct of the Court and the aristocracy toward the greatest genius of the epoch, about whom one bothered so little and whom one left in such distress. The answer was identical with Carpani's. I asked whether nevertheless Beethoven's condition of deafness was not worthy of the deepest sympathy... I added that this would be very easy by means of subscriptions for a very small amount, if all the rich families pledged themselves, to assure him of an annuity large enough to place him for the rest of his life beyond real want. This proposition obtained support from nobody.

After dinner, the resplendent gathering retired to hear a concert, which included a recently published Beethoven Trio. Although the assemblage paid the maestro's new work almost religious respect, Rossini could think only of Beethoven laboring away in his decrepit attic on a new composition that would "initiate into sublime beauties" the same sybaritic aristocracy that excluded him and "did not worry about the misery of him who had furnished the[ir] pleasures."

Rossini persisted during the remainder of his stay in Vienna in trying to raise money to buy Beethoven a house. While he collected several promises to contribute, "the final result was very meager," and he had to abandon the project. He was told over and over, "You do not know Beethoven. On the day after he finds himself the owner of a house, he will sell it..."

Such a touching tale. And so unflattering to Beethoven, so ennobling of Rossini. That sharp disparity aroused Clara's suspicion. Had Rossini been as achingly sincere as he let on? Or was he perhaps awash in false sympathy and artfully applying the back of his hand to "the greatest genius of the epoch" for having disparaged him as a mere musical buffoon? Why else bother so many years afterward to portray Beethoven to the listening Wagner as an insensitive and improvident boor? Wasn't Beethoven entitled to more respect than that? Or had something else gone on between them? The question persisted maddeningly for Clara. But the more she mulled it, the further a neat explanation receded from her.

When she awoke the next morning, she lay in bed letting her refreshed and roving mind free-associate for a few minutes. And all at once, it was there, whole and obvious. And for her the Beethoven-Rossini puzzle was solved.

Eight years after discarding the *William Tell* Symphony, more from cowardice than conviction, Beethoven—Clara now persuaded herself—must have deeply regretted what he had done. The work, whatever its imperfections and need of refinement, had been conceived as an anthem to liberty, especially in places like imperial Austria and the German confederation, where its absence was being enforced by repressive rulers. But so long as he remained a fixture on the Viennese scene, however much a social pariah and political outsider, Beethoven could not risk resurrecting his *Tell*. The departure from his quarters of the gallant young Rossini, however, had—understandably—stirred anguish in Beethoven, Clara theorized. He was not so devoid of sensitivity that he failed to recognize on reflection the unkind cut, thoughtless rather than intended, that he had dealt his idolizing visitor. Nor was Beethoven by any means bereft of friends, confidants, and hangers-on who brought him the gossip of Vienna. A choice morsel that would surely have been reported to him was word of Rossini's efforts on the maestro's behalf, aimed at improving the material conditions of his existence—a benevolent act that would likely have left Beethoven moved as well as embarrassed. How might he have best responded to this piece of news? The answer sprang full-blown inside of Clara's supple mind; she composed it on her word processor with almost no hesitation.

My dear Rossini,

Word has come to me of the great kindness you have done in the course of your social rounds in this city. They say you ask subscriptions so that my impoverishment may be relieved. This gesture is most generous. Nevertheless, my noble young friend, I must ask you to cease your efforts in my behalf. My circumstances may appear to you less than luxurious, but they suit me well enough. I am, please be assured, in no need of any charity.

Further, I ask your forgiveness for the manner in which my well-intended advice to you—about directing your very considerable talent only toward the creation of opera buffa—may have been spoken. It was wrong of me to have offered the summary opinion that no Italian is by nature capable of a deeper form of musical composition. Your own body of work is proof to the contrary. As evidence of my grief for having offended you, my good Rossini, I attach to this note a leaf that recreates some passagework from a symphonic piece I embarked on a few years ago but set aside for reasons of no interest now. It had begun life as an operatic version of Friedrich Schiller's drama, Wilhelm Tell. It is a task I shall never have the strength or resolve to return to—but one all the more in need of being done these days, and you of all composers, with your popular following, must be the one to accomplish it. Do as you wish with my little offering, given in prayerful hope it may help bend you to the endeavor.

Take pains to destroy this note, and do not trouble to reply, for I am the one who is the more indebted. Know that you have all good wishes, most honored Sir, from your sincere admirer—

—Beethoven

That Rossini would have disposed of such a letter as instructed was entirely understandable, Clara decided. And he seized upon the few dozen measures that Beethoven had delivered to him and transmogrified them, then and there, in Vienna in the spring of 1822, as the liner notes to her CD of Rossini overtures had stated, into the quick-step march that would over time become the most familiar passage in his entire oeuvre, i.e., the *Lone Ranger* signature theme. But out of due reverence (not to mention fear of disclosure), Rossini chose not to develop and present the full version of his own *William Tell* until Beethoven had been pushing up daisies for two years—and never revealed the secret genesis of the opera and the climactic theme of its overture. Oh, yes.

Rereading her text with satisfaction, Clara printed it out and told herself it was surely more rooted in reality than fantasy. And the longer she contemplated the sequence of the documented historical events during Rossini's visit to Vienna, the more plausible she believed her invented resolution to them to be. An hour after Mitch's return from London the next day, she briefed him on the circumstances she had ferreted out of Rossini's interview with Beethoven and its aftermath. Then, with barely contained excitement, she handed him her imaginary letter from the older to the younger composer, which she identified as her English translation of the original. "And you'll never believe where I found it!" she said with a slight theatrical touch.

Mitch scanned the fictive letter with steadily widening eyes. "My God—this is amazing! It all makes perfect sense now." He planted a devout kiss on Clara's beaming mouth. "Okay, hon," he asked, suddenly leery of the perfection of the document, "where *did* you find it?"

"It was just sitting there in the Columbia music library's Rossini archive, in a folder of miscellaneous papers I was going through not very hopefully." Her eyebrows wagged on cue.

"It was?"

She paused, the broke into a sheepish smile. "It wasn't—I cannot tell a lie, not to you, anyway. Not about this, at least. I didn't find it."

"Then what—your fairy godmother appeared with it in her hot little hands?"

"I wrote it."

"*You* wrote it? How? Why? I don't believe it—it reads absolutely authentically."

"It does, doesn't it?" she said proudly. "Because it's entirely possible that's just what happened. And guess what else?" She had gone back to the Columbia library and delved further into the Rossini biographies. "It looks as if Archduke Rudolph was onto something when he urged Ludwig to abandon *Tell.*"

Even twenty years after Beethoven had supposedly put aside his own effort, Rossini's operatic version of Schiller's Swiss saga of liberty felt Metternich's icy hand when it was first mounted at La Scala in Milan, still under Austrian rule along with most of northern Italy. The opera's subject, Clara reported, was deemed so politically sensitive that the Hapsburg-friendly censors required the story's setting to be shifted from Switzerland to Scotland and the hero's—and the opera's—name changed from William Tell to Guglielmo Wallace.

"Wow." Mitch's wonderment morphed almost at once into a frown. "Or is all that also just another invention of your fertile bean?"

"No," she said as solemnly as she knew how, "I swear."

A few hours later, after she had fixed Mitch a ham and mushroom omelet for a late supper, he asked Clara to write up a memo on everything she had learned about the Beethoven-Rossini interaction; in the morning he would email it to Mac Quarles for dissemination to his confreres on the authentication panel. "But please leave off your clever letter—okay?"

"And why is that?" she asked with a trace of irritation.

"Because it's not real. It's fun and ingenious, but it's—it doesn't settle or prove anything. It's strictly—speculative."

"I'd call it highly suggestive. I don't think it's much of a stretch—in fact, hardly at all."

"Clara, sweetie, you're letting this thing carry you away. You *made up* the letter—it can't be shown to a panel of experts as evidence of anything except your informed hunch."

"It's more than a hunch. It's…it's an insight. We can tell them that—blame it on me."

"There's no blame involved because I can't dignify it as a serious document, suitable to be shown to eminent authorities."

"If they're so damn eminent, how come none of them have ever mentioned the Beethoven-Rossini encounter to you?"

"It probably slipped their minds or something. Maybe they are unaware of it, which is why I want your memo on what we know really happened for sure. Listen, it's a judgment call, and my judgment is your letter is OTT."

"Then I'll send it to Mac on my own."

"You don't work for Mac—you work for me, just like he does, and I decide—"

"I don't work for you—I work *with* you. And I'm thinking maybe I won't anymore."

"Clara, you're being petulant."

"I'll have your memo in an hour," she said acidly. "It's three-quarters done already."

WHETHER EMIL REINSDORF was a naïve academician or a sly manipulator was a question hotly debated around Cubbage & Wakeham's offices. There was no dispute, however, about the salutary effect of the German musicologist's self-serving remarks upon joining the company's panel of Beethoven experts. Once his premature and unauthorized disclosure of the name and nature of the newly discovered work was reported in *Der Spiegel* and relayed around the world, inquiries about the *William Tell* Symphony—in particular about when it would be available for inspection and performing—arrived at the auction house at the rate of seven or eight a day, mostly from philharmonics, recording companies, and other enterprises in the entertainment industry. "At least," Harry happily told his colleagues, "we've captured their attention. Dr. Reinsdorf may be a snake but also our best publicist."

This mood of glowing expectations was dimmed by a missile landing at the United States District Courthouse downtown on Foley Square. The weapon took the form of a motion to enjoin any effort by Jake Hassler and/or C&W to sell or otherwise dispose of any or all rights to the *Tell* manuscript and to require its immediate transfer to the Swiss government pending final disposition by the courts of its legal ownership. The moving party in the action, Gordy advised his colleagues, was neither the Swiss government nor the Erpf family doing business as Limmat Realty, holders of the lien against Otto Hassler's estate, but the Erpfs' aging *enfant terrible* and gifted but volatile dropout, Ansel.

His legal papers identified Ansel as "the discoverer" of the *Tell* manuscript and holder of 24.5 percent of the stock of the Erpf family's Limmat Realty firm, which, under Otto Hassler's will, the suit insisted, was entitled to ownership of the work. Accordingly, the Erpfs had promised to donate the composition, tentatively attributed to Beethoven, as a national treasure to the people of Switzerland under an agreement with the Swiss government. In a collateral action filed in Zurich, Ansel had also asked the Swiss courts to probate Otto

Hassler's will "in a timely fashion and end the dilatory tactics being illegally pursued" by his government's Cultural Ministry.

Ansel's US court papers, which characterized Jake Hassler's seizure of the manuscript as "an egregious act of international thievery, not to be condoned by civilized nations," noted that legal action contemplated by the Swiss government and the Erpf family to retrieve *Tell* had been withheld "pending efforts to authenticate the manuscript in question." But recent reports in the media, Ansel's complaint continued, suggested that the rogue holder of the manuscript and the auction house serving as his sales agent had apparently decided to proceed with the sale of the *Tell* composition "like a boatload of camshafts or any other commodity of trade." The US courts were thus obliged to intervene and prevent "an intolerable case of cultural pillage."

"Not to worry," Gordy Roth advised. "We'll move for a summary dismissal—which should be granted promptly." The reasons, he said, were that (1) Otto Hassler's will had not yet been probated, so Ansel Erpf had no legal standing in the matter; (2) Ansel was a minority stockholder of the family company and had probably not been officially authorized to act on its behalf; and (3) C&W had not determined when or whether the manuscript would be auctioned, so there was no legitimate reason to issue a prior restraint order enjoining the firm from doing something it had not yet decided to do.

Before Gordy's reassuring words could be put to the test, Johnny Winks rang in from Geneva with the news that Ansel Erpf had held a press conference the day before on the steps of the Zurich Opernhaus to denounce everyone in sight—Jake, C&W, the Swiss government, his own family, and "rampant, predatory American capitalism"—and announced the immediate formation of a protest movement circulating petitions at all Swiss centers of higher learning and cultural institutions to demand "an end to this gross affront to our nation's honor."

"His piggy little face is on TV twice a day," Johnny reported. "He may call for a declaration of war any minute now, claiming it's about time the Swiss flexed their military might."

With Gordy listening in, Mitch phoned Ansel's sister, Margot Lenz, to try to learn if his legal action had been sanctioned by the rest of the Erpf family or in defiance of it. "Some of both, to be honest," she replied with a renewal of her earlier civility. "I'm not sure whether he's angrier at your concern and Jacob Hassler or at us and the Cultural Ministry."

"Angry at you for what?"

"For not raising the roof with the American authorities—as if we could. Meanwhile, he's making quite a spectacle of himself here as a rabble-rouser and having the time of his life."

"Is all that good for his...emotional stability?" Mitch asked.

"We're not sure—it's not actively antisocial, at least," Margot said almost jauntily. "To be frank, I'm afraid you've rather brought this on yourselves by not properly crediting Ansel for his part in finding the manuscript. He's become very proprietary about it—and is furious at being ignored till now, which may explain why he's taken to posing as a national culture hero."

"If it would be of any consolation to your brother," Mitch offered, hoping to sustain an amicable tone between them, "we plan to give proper acknowledgment of his role in the discovery—once he stops trying to steal the manuscript from Jake Hassler—which, I'm afraid, is what all this outburst on his part looks like from our side of the water. Ansel's claim is based on what children call 'finders keepers'—and unfortunately, the grown-up world doesn't subscribe to that."

Margot weighed Mitch's probe.

"Yes, well, there's always been a childlike element in some of Ansel's behavior. I confessed as much when you visited me, hoping that you would understand him better. Just now, though, my family isn't ready to pull the rug out from under him, even if he may be acting somewhat extravagantly."

"You mean spending the family's money on lawyers?"

"No, no. I thought you understood—well, perhaps you don't, and that's why you've rung me. Ansel's taken these legal measures on his own—he's not impoverished, by any means."

"Well, did you try to discourage him?" Mitch asked.

"To be sure. Our family lawyers told him his lawsuit would probably be thrown out of the American courts and that, at any rate, annoying you people in this way would hardly improve the chances of a friendly compromise if the manuscript were found to be legitimate. But he's got the bit between his teeth." Margot sighed. "We'll do our best to monitor him—and who knows—perhaps your judges will surprise us all."

Ansel's drumbeat soon reverberated across the ocean, and editorial writers in the US picked up on it with a sympathetic ear. Typical among the comments was the cutting appraisal in the *Washington Post*, which editorialized:

> Every schoolchild knows—or used to know before rap became the rage—the heroic tale of William Tell, his devotion to liberty, and his son's bravery. The story remains a vital part of the Swiss national identity,

201

and it deserves to be celebrated by that country in words and song. If the newfound symphonic work glorifying the fortitude of Switzerland's leading patriot and attributed to the immortal Beethoven proves to be authentic, it should rightfully be returned there and not snatched away for private profit by an American whose family has long since emigrated to the New World. Such gross exploitation ought to be discouraged even if the perpetrator is found to be acting within the letter of the law. Otherwise the spirit of international comity is threatened.

Such carping did not escape the attention of *Tell*'s putative owner. "Hey, they're busting my balls, like I'm a rotten no-good crook," Jake Hassler moaned over the phone to Mitch. "Can't you guys do anything about it? Maybe a press release telling them to fuck off or something?"

"Try thinking about it the way Harry does," Mitch bucked him up. "The more attention we draw—of whatever kind—the higher the price the manuscript will probably go for."

"Oh, yeah? I didn't think of that. Daisy'll be thrilled—she's about ready for us to chuck the whole thing and give it to the Goodwill."

"I'd wait a little on that," Mitch advised. "It could still earn you quite a nice nest egg. Maybe a dozen nest eggs."

"Hoo-boy," said Jake.

THE SONG HAS IT RIGHT, Clara thought; New York is an autumnal town. That's when it's fully churning with energy and adventure, its muted colors a sophisticated complement to the city's exuberant yet bittersweet mood. She was glad to be caught up in the whirligig with Hilde Reinsdorf, a stranger appreciative of Clara's attentions as they toured the city's museums and art galleries while their husbands puzzled over the authorship of the *William Tell* Symphony.

It was Emil's assigned week to closet himself with the manuscript, a security guard, and a piano, for whatever use he chose to make of it, while he and his wife stayed as transient guests in the top-floor apartment at C&W's townhouse offices. With time on her hands, Hilde gratefully accepted Clara's offer to show her the town. By tacit agreement, the two women did not speak about the symphony—somehow it seemed off-limits, a sort of military secret, best left to their spouses to cultivate—and concentrated instead on the graphic arts, since Hilde was an accomplished floral painter.

The Berliner, in her millefleur-on-black print dress, belted khaki raincoat, black beret, and high-laced shoes (suited, she said, for walking endless miles), may not have been a fashion-plate, but she knew her art, Clara saw, bustling her all over the city from The Cloisters to the Brooklyn Museum. No place pleased her more than the Morgan Library, where she passed half a day enthralled by the old books, prints, and manuscripts stored there.

For all Hilde's keen aesthetic sensibility, Clara wondered what the woman would wear to the Cubbages' for the dinner party Harry was hosting Thursday night in tribute to their eminent German guest of honor. By way of warning, Clara mentioned the likely problem to Lolly: "I'm afraid the *frau* is not into *haute couture*. She's an academic's wife, and their town was the drab front line for the Cold War all those years."

"What'll we do?" Lolly asked with alarm. "I've got Freddie and Weezie Engelking coming—they're Lincoln Center Gold Circle patrons—and they're down on my *Tell* bidders' list for at least fifty thou. Not a good fit with a pair from Germany's Hundred Neediest Cases. Damn!"

"Could you disinvite the Engelkings? Tell them Emil's got to work instead, so no party?"

"Weezie's the kind who checks out your garbage in the morning to see what you ate last night—she'd find out I lied, and then I'd be toast." Lolly's head worked best under stress. "It sounds as if either we buy Hilde a little something off the rack at Bendel's, or we all show up in dirndls to make her feel at home."

In any event, neither solution seemed to have been necessary. Hilde arrived wearing a smart Escada jacket in grayed lavender with a pale pink silk blouse and black pants—an ensemble scarcely less stylish than Lolly's. Clara could only shrug when her hostess questioned her with arched brows.

Style aside, the evening was all Emil Reinsdorf's. The other guests, including the loaded Engelkings, Gordy and Sara Roth, and Mac and Katie Quarles, hung on the feisty musicologist's every word, delivered with arresting verve. They were just into the cold pumpkin soup drizzled with chives when the table talk turned to an item on that evening's newscast about an Arabic-speaking gay intelligence officer discharged while on duty in Iraq for violating the US armed forces' Don't Ask, Don't Tell policy.

"It's idiotic," said Harry the host. "We desperately need people over there who can talk the local lingo—and what difference does it make if they cohabit with the same sex—or even the same species. With camels, maybe, I'd draw the line…"

The remark evoked nods and gentle laughter. But then Emil Reinsdorf startled the table by dryly commenting, "I'm sure our revered Beethoven would have agreed with you, Mr. Cubbage—he didn't want anyone intruding on his sexual predilections."

"Which were—what?" Harry asked.

"Well—to be blunt—I believe he was not very comfortable with the ladies."

"You're *outing* Beethoven?" an incredulous Lolly asked. "Is nothing sacred?"

"Emil," Hilde said softly, "I don't think that's called for just now—"

"I was only answering Mr. Cubbage, my dear."

Clara, seated across from Emil, found the revelation as gratuitous, and thus offensive, as his wife did, and could not restrain herself from questioning it. "I've never heard that before, Dr. Reinsdorf," she said as politely as possible. "Is it simply your private opinion or an open secret in the upper reaches of musicology?"

"Ah, well—I've piqued your interest. But there's nothing more to it than the obvious." Emil took a slow sip of Lolly's best grand cru French chardonnay. "The documented record fails to reveal, or even strongly to suggest, that our esteemed maestro, in fifty-seven years of life, ever made love to a female—or a male, either, for that matter."

"A celibate, then," Clara suggested, "in love only with his art?"

"So say his usual apologists," Emil replied, "but that's hardly sufficient to cover the matter. I think his carnal instincts—and he no doubt had them—were clear enough." True, the German conceded, scanning the table, there were many letters hinting at the opposite, addressed to women and expressing keen, even passionate, affection. "But these were always women far beyond his social class and safely unattainable." And yes, he added, Beethoven was known to have prowled the demimonde on occasion, at a lusty companion's goading, but such reports were cryptic and without disclosure of particular partners, places, or pleasures. While he was capable of both charming and disarming the opposite sex, he did so in the drawing room, not the boudoir. "In point of fact, nearly all his close companions and confidants were male—likewise, most of his household attendants—and his correspondence with certain men was affectionate and fulsome to a point beyond the conventions of the time."

Clara was confused. Emil Reinsdorf, of all people, she would have cast as the fiercest guardian of Beethoven's reputation. Why was he posing as a detractor of the mainstay of his career? For shock value? To make his hetero self seem superior to the object of his adoration? Or perhaps it was she herself who should be faulted for finding Reinsdorf's characterization almost spitefully defamatory. "But what of Beethoven's famous letters to his 'Immortal Beloved'?" she asked, unable to disguise her level of distress. "Was she, too, a phantom?"

The German scholar withdrew his glasses and began polishing them with his napkin, a gesture in seeming acknowledgment that his indelicacy had put her off.

"Not a phantom, certainly, Madam Emery—those letters are rife with hints of liaisons and deep passion—but his beloved was not necessarily a she. I find neither Maynard Solomon's nor Anna Hayes's biographies conclusive as to the identity or gender of his celebrated sweetheart—and if not certifiably female, only one alternative leaps to mind."

Lolly did not hesitate to voice the table's collective surprise. "But Beethoven's music—it's so...no one composed with more...you know..."

Emil smiled. "*Cojones?*"

"Those would be the ones."

"My dear lady, I am not suggesting Beethoven was a mincing pansy—far from it—or that his sexuality has anything at all to do with the nature or quality of his creative genius." He looked to Mitch and then to Mac Quarles, the latter being his sole professional confederate at the party. "Nor do I find homosexuality an index of weak character—or even of a sadly degenerate love life. Besides, where would the arts be without our gifted gay brigade—Michaelangelo, Proust, Tchaikovsky, your Edward Albee, and Andy Warhol, to name a few recruits?" Emil turned back to Lolly. "And, by the way, Madam Cubbage, Tchaikovsky, too, wrote some thoroughly—may I say it in plain English?—ballsy music, and his sexual preference is not in doubt."

Mitch tried to shift the focus of the conversation. "But this matter has no real bearing, I take it," he proposed to Emil, "on our *Tell* conundrum."

"Is that a question or a statement, Mr. Emery?" came the quick and barbed retort.

"Well...I just...was wondering how it could—"

"Fair enough. We might want to involve Dr. Quarles on that point—bearing in mind the remarkable letter allegedly sent by Archduke Rudolph to the maestro that was found with the *Tell* manuscript. I have long believed that Beethoven's relationship with Rudolph was so extraordinary as to invite speculation about its true nature. Let's be honest—you don't dedicate a dozen inspiring pieces of your music to the same individual unless—well, something very special is involved. More, I should say, than meets the eye."

Mac looked uncomfortable, though less than appalled. "I kinda assumed, after checking into it," he said, "that what was special was the fact that Rudolph was keepin' him afloat financially in those years—and respectable because of that royal connection—so naturally, Mr. Beethoven was very deferential to him. But maybe I missed something—"

"What you say is certainly true, Mac," Emil replied with suddenly collegial familiarity, "but I think there had to be more to it than that." The archduke was the younger man by seventeen years, he pointed out, and in his physical prime, though he suffered from the family curse of epilepsy, "which would likely have made Beethoven more than a little sympathetic toward him, given his own physical afflictions. Then factor in Rudolph's very considerable skills as a musician—by all accounts, he played the piano and composed with genuine accomplishment." Beethoven created an instruction book just for him—something the master composer never did for anyone else. He also entrusted many of his manuscripts to Rudolph for safekeeping in the Schönbrun Palace library. "Finally," the German scholar added, "there is the surviving body of correspondence between the two, which music historians have long chosen to disregard—I believe due to squeamishness."

"I wouldn't call what Rudolph sent to Zurich a love letter," Mac objected mildly.

"No, but it wasn't Rudolph's letters that gave the game away—it was Beethoven's," Emil said. "And I have no trouble, you see, when he writes to the archduke wishing him what he calls 'all the good and beautiful things that can be conceived.' The chap was, after all, his chief provider. But what are we to infer when Beethoven writes Rudolph things like 'your imperial highness is to me one of the most precious objects in the whole world' or assures him 'it is no mere frigid interest that attaches me to you, but a true and deep affection which has always bound me to your highness'?"

"Why can't that be taken," Clara asked, "for the language of platonic friendship? It's a bit syrupy for our tastes nowadays, but might that not be fairer than assuming it's a confession of gay love or, even more troubling, gross flattery that its object would have found transparent?"

"Very well put," the eminent musicologist told the aspiring one. "But you mistake my speculative remark for an accusation, Madam Emery. I was merely observing the biographical facts. The closeness of the two men, at any rate, lends credence to Dr. Quarles's conclusion—based on the archduke's letter to Zurich—that this *Tell* symphony was set aside largely out of deference to Rudolph's special importance in Beethoven's life. I was not dabbling idly in the scurrilous, you see."

"That's a relief," Clara responded with a smile that disarmed the intimidating German and sent a chorus of welcome laughter around the table.

"You're a most able champion of the maestro," Emil remarked to her privately after dinner as the party moved into the living room for aperitifs and coffee. "May I also commend you heartily for the astonishing letter you invented to explain the connection with Rossini's *Tell*—Dr. Quarles circulated it to our panel as a matter of speculative interest. Most creative of you and—but please don't quote me—persuasive."

Surprised—because Mitch had said he wouldn't attach her invention to the rest of the memo she had prepared on the Beethoven-Rossini connection for forwarding to Mac and his fellow panelists—and flattered by the distinguished scholar's praise, she nodded her thanks.

"Do you think, though," she asked him, "that it was just the archduke's appeal to him that caused the maestro to cast the *Tell* aside—for the politics and, well, his personal regard for Rudolph—or might there have been more to it?"

A bemused expression came over Reinsdorf's features. "Hard to say. We know Beethoven was uncomfortable with lighthearted subjects, so his almost playful experiment celebrating a brawny primitive like the hunter Tell may in the end have struck him as rather insipid, compared with, say, his evocation of a brooding tragic nobleman like Egmont."

Clara read a deeper meaning in his comment.

"Then are you saying that you think in *Tell* we're truly dealing with authentic Beethoven—even if it was misbegotten?"

The German turned coy.

"Well, I'll not be rash again—having publicly dismissed this *Tell* piece sight unseen as an obvious hoax. I need to reflect carefully on what I've seen here this week. But I'll say this much—as absurd as I thought the claim was when I first heard about it, now it seems at least as farfetched to me that somebody could perform such an excruciatingly difficult task of fabrication. The perpetrator would have needed a profound familiarity with sophisticated composing techniques. The internal intricacies must all converge—and they more or less seem to here. The alleged circumstances of both the manuscript's disappearance and reemergence naturally invite our suspicion, but they have a kind of coherence not to be sneered at, as I rather did at first."

Clara listened closely, nodded, then confided, "My husband is bothered, though—almost perversely, if you will—by that very coherence you speak of. He marvels that everything seems to fit so well—almost seamlessly."

"But not musically, necessarily—and that's the rub. When I join my august colleagues on your panel here in a few weeks, we'll need to determine, first of all, whether this *Tell* composition is a genuine Beethoven symphony *and*, no less important, whether for all its deviance in form from the rest of his work, it is a triumph—or a monstrosity that he properly aborted."

Just before the party broke up, Hilde Reinsdorf took Clara aside and thanked her again for having served as such a companionable guide throughout the week.

"And, if you'll forgive me for intruding," she added quietly, "I hope a baby comes for you and Mitchell."

The subject had not arisen between them before. "I—but what makes you—"

Hilde saw Clara's uneasiness. "It was the way you kept staring at the *bambini* in all the religious paintings—perhaps I misinterpreted." She put a gentle hand on Clara's wrist. "Emil and I waited—there were so many obstacles—and our country was so wounded and broken—and then it was too late for us. I hope not for you." They kissed on parting.

"There's a sadness about her," Clara told Mitch on the cab ride across town, "but I do like her. I even like Emil, as full of himself as he is."

"You liked Ansel Erpf, too—and you see where that's got us."

"He's a work in progress," she said, "you'll see. Anyway, he didn't write *Tell*—"

"Who did?"

Clara took his hand and, by way of responding, asked him, "You gave Mac my Beethoven letter to Rossini after saying you wouldn't. Why didn't you tell me?"

"I actually gave it to him not to support your theory but to show how all the letters found in the box with the *Tell* manuscript, starting with Nina's, could have been skillfully concocted, like yours. And I didn't want to tell you in case Mac found your letter to be silly. He didn't—he told me just tonight and said he'd call you over the weekend to thank you for all the Rossini stuff. I need you to stay with this thing, babe."

She gave his hand a short, fierce squeeze.

"I think you do, actually."

{11}

The Somerset Hills were washed in coral by the approach of sunset, and the piney air stirred with a mid-October tang as drinks were passed among the guests gathered on Gordy and Sara Roth's cantilevered deck to behold the fading vista. Everyone agreed the spectacle was all the more pleasurable thanks to a pair of large space heaters that neutralized the encroaching chill. The afternoon had been devoted to a microbus tour of New Jersey's Revolutionary War battlefields, organized for the members of Cubbage & Wakeham's panel of experts on the eve of their week-long meeting to decide *Tell*'s life-or-death fate. Also on hand for the outing and the buffet that followed were Jake and Daisy Hassler, the owners—well, claimants, at least—of the luminous, if worse for wear, manuscript that had drawn the group together.

For the benefit of the C&W contingent on hand, composed of Harry and Lolly Cubbage and Mitch and Clara Emery as well as the hosts, Anna Hayes was retelling the traditional version of the maestro's death late in the afternoon of March 26, 1827. According to bedside witnesses, she said, the Viennese sky darkened suddenly a bit after five o'clock and filled with thunder and lightning, which caused the comatose composer to open his eyes a final time. "He looked about him, so the legend goes, clenched his right hand, raised it threateningly—perhaps in anger at the Divinity for calling him away with so many tasks undone—and breathed his last." Hayes's capacious bosom rose and sank perceptibly. "And here we are, all these years later, considering perhaps the most ambitious of those undone tasks."

"Unless, dear Anna," cautioned Emil Reinsdorf, "it wasn't his."

"Not that it matters," Mitch asked diffidently after a moment's pause, respectful of the composer's demise, "but I'm a little curious about that death scene, moving though it is. I've read your book, and I know you call the description hearsay, but what troubles me is how the thunder and lightning could have caused him to open his eyes."

Anna looked puzzled. "Patients have been known to awaken from comas."

"But if his eyes were closed," Mitch persisted, "he wouldn't have seen the lightning—and since he'd been stone deaf for about fifteen years, he couldn't have heard the thunder."

"*Felt* it vibrate, perhaps," Anna suggested tolerantly, "or perhaps it just seemed that way to those present. I'm not vouching for it."

Clara leaned toward Mitch, seated beside her in the gloaming, and whispered, "Give it a rest, sweetie—it's a *legend*, for God's sake. Stop being such a literalist."

Over dinner, Mac Quarles laid out the panel's modus operandi to begin the next morning. The ground rules for their proceedings were simple. Only the five panelists were to be allowed in the C&W library; all officers and employees of the auction house were barred in order to preserve an arm's-length relationship between the experts and those paying them for their services.

The first three days were to be devoted to formal remarks by each panel member, going in alphabetical order, except for Mac, who as chairman would go last and could break a tie if the opinion of the others were divided equally. Panelists were at liberty to interrupt their colleagues' remarks at any time to ask for clarification or challenge an arguable premise. The fourth day was to be reserved for private contemplation and informal exchanges among the participants before the final vote was taken on Friday morning. For historical purposes and the creation of an archive on the authentication procedure, a tape recording was to be made of the discussions, which Mac could consult and quote from as liberally as he chose while writing the final report for the panel to review. Ideally, their judgment would be unanimous, but each panelist was free to file a separate concurrence or dissent.

Mindful of the potential record-breaking revenue from a single item offered to bidders under C&W's gavel, everyone on the auction house staff grew increasingly edgy as the week of deliberations wore on. To track the panelists' progress—or dissension—excerpts from each day's tapes were played in Harry's office that same evening for the firm's high command.

The first panelist to speak was Anna Hayes, assigned the task of framing the central issue. She began by reminding them how radically Beethoven had taken Viennese classicism beyond Haydn and Mozart, "whose work we so admire for its brilliance, subtlety, and masterful technique, yet was emotionally wanting." By contrast, she noted, Beethoven's music was nearly visceral in the way it seemed to convey, by use of disruptive and even disintegrative sound, real-life experience. And, starting with his third symphony, the *Eroica*, he created works that were inherently dramatic "through their melodic and harmonic progressions, hurtling movement, and interplay of moods."

So it was by no means implausible, in Hayes's view, that the maestro could have been moved to compose a "dramatic symphony" around the saga of the Swiss national hero, incorporating narrative through song. "The real challenge for him," as she saw it, "would have been to integrate the vocal pieces within the instrumental passages yet keep them simple enough to be sung—always a problem for him." Here, the panel's redoubtable German scholar pounced.

REINSDORF: But Beethoven didn't compose stories—the drama was all in the unexpectedness of the music itself. And he didn't compose songs—it was beneath his dignity. So how likely is it that he would undertake to do both in the form of this *Tell?* And if so, how can we call it a symphony?

HAYES: Well, it's a symphony if you're willing to be flexible in defining a symphony. Beethoven, after all, had pioneered it by extending the sonata form. But here he had to defer to the vocal pieces, which carry the theatrical burden, without letting the instrumental sections degenerate into mere interludes. So he had to miniaturize the sonata form here in the *Tell*—an innovative departure, to be sure, but innovation is what Beethoven was all about.

REINSDORF: But if you define an apple by saying it can also be an orange, then you might as well discard all classifications as meaningless.

HAYES: Please, let's not turn this into a game of semantics, Emil. Within these *Tell* sketchbooks, we find the composer employing Beethoven's same basic work tools—the succession of developmental increments, the different harmonic progressions, the suddenly shifting keys, *et cetera,* that are chief signatures of his genius.

REINSDORF: Yes, without a doubt, the *Tell* has the ring of *echt* Beethoven. But is the ring enough? Sustaining all his elements is the real test of his genius, not mere snippets, as if we're at a banquet table offering only *hors d'oeuvres*.

"I thought Dr. High-and-Mighty Reinsdorf was lining up on the side of authenticating," Harry said, halting the tape and turning to Mitch. "Didn't he pretty much indicate that to Clara?"

"He didn't go that far. He told me at Gordy's dinner party that he was impressed by the manuscript but not entirely convinced that it was beyond the powers of an inspired faker."

"Sounds like this could get damn ugly," said Harry, restarting the tape.

Anna Hayes did not allow herself to be stampeded by the generalissimo of German musicology. In turning to the rhythmic element in *Tell*, she found further cause for attributing the composition to Beethoven. "Remember," she told the panel, raising her intensity quotient, "how he loved to pound you— as if to say, 'Look here, friend, it's *my* rhythm, not anyone else's. I control it, and I'll break it apart as, if, and when I like, and show you how it can be sped up, slowed down, inverted, doubled in length, hidden in the accompaniment— anything I bloody well choose and in ways you never expected.'"

Hayes, in short, was willing to grant Beethoven poetic license if he indeed were *Tell*'s composer, but to Emil Reinsdorf's way of thinking, that missed the larger point. "Dr. Hayes is quite right about detecting many of Beethoven's principal stylistic elements here, but these are superficial similarities. I am far more struck by how the sketchbook shows the composer continually fine-tuning the first two movements to achieve greater orchestral texture, clearer registration, and richer figuration—he couldn't let go of the thing, a very Beethovian trait."

"That's more like it, Emil!" Harry cheered above the tape. His rooting interest, Mitch now sensed, might end up being a problem when the company's objectivity was ultimately put to the test.

A moment later, though, Reinsdorf was back at it. What was required of the panel, he instructed them, was a precise balancing test to weigh the composer's established stylistic fingerprint—"the stuff that makes Beethoven Beethoven."

TORBEN MUNDT: Excuse me, Emil, but you are preaching to the converted, so—

REINSDORF: Excuse *me*, Torben, but I am making a basic point here—which is that for Beethoven his themes were *not* ends in themselves. The whole essence of his art was the developmental process—how he elaborated on a very brief theme by extending it, bending it, branching it, modulating it, making it leap and arc and curl back on itself, then falter and seem to stumble, then right itself and—how to say it?—*zigzag* off to somewhere else—but never, ever *meandering*—

MUNDT: Beautifully articulated—but your point being—?

REINSDORF: Does the melodic development in this newfound manuscript of ours closely resemble the inimitable Beethoven norm? And I think the answer is—at best—a somewhat limp maybe, which cannot totally satisfy us.

"This son of a gun's trying to kill us!" Harry cried. "I knew he would."

"Relax," Mitch urged. "It could be just a pose. Maybe he's setting up a straw man for the others to push over."

Mundt, the gnarled old Dane, was no more inclined than Anna Hayes to be distracted by Reinsdorf's sniping fire. Dwelling on Beethoven's brilliant use of harmony and counterpoint, "layering his work with new forms of patterning and digressions his listeners had never encountered before," Mundt detected countless such harmonic choices by the composer of the *Tell* Symphony. "Consider, for example, his use here of unsatisfied dissonances in instrumentally rendering the encounter between Tell and Gessler in the third movement."

It was too much for Reinsdorf. "Without a doubt some of the structural polyphony here is characteristic of Beethoven," he condescended. "But let's be honest—none of us can hear the work adequately inside our heads to justify the sort of permissive generosity you're granting it."

"I'm duly chastened," the Dane said dryly.

When it was Reinsdorf's turn to elaborate on his views, he chose to equivocate and repeat his reservations rather than shed any fresh light drawn from his own textual analysis of the sketchbooks.

"Jumping to a rash conclusion serves nobody's purpose," he said, "except perhaps the eager holders of the manuscript who understandably wish to cash in on it."

"Go fuck yourself!" Harry shouted at the tape player.

213

The final—and most junior—panelist, Rolfe Riker, had up to that point deferred in silence to his colleagues, but the young musicologist from Salzburg was not in the least intimidated when his inevitable collision with the overbearing Berliner occurred. Asked to discuss *Tell*'s timbre—how the instruments reacted to one another—Riker noted that Beethoven often favored "jarring combinations to arrest our attention, with a resulting sound sharper and more dissonant than any of his predecessors'. We find this tendency amply exhibited in the work at hand, for all its more conventional use of melody." Citing Beethoven's fondness for using trumpets to stand out above the orchestra, he urged his colleagues to "please witness the difficult intervals he gave the horns here with such telling effect—forgive my poor pun."

> REINSDORF: Yes, Rolfe, but how does all of what you say serve to persuade us that Beethoven himself was the composer and not someone else employing what are without doubt his compositional techniques?

> RIKER: Well, for one thing there is all the forensic evidence—

> REINSDORF: Concluding only that Beethoven might possibly have been the—

> RIKER: With all due respect, Dr. Reinsdorf, you have been tenaciously arguing out of both sides of your mouth all week. When these undeniable stylistic similarities are pointed out, you say, "Oh, well, there's not enough evidence for us to reach a firm conclusion." And when the abundant circumstantial evidence is cited, you say, "Oh, well, someone highly knowledgeable could have cunningly mimicked all Beethoven's composing techniques." A cynic might conclude, sir, that you won't allow facts to intrude upon your preconceived position.

By the end of Wednesday's session, only Emil Reinsdorf appeared to be left on the fence. The following day, Chairman Quarles told the panelists, would be set aside for private contemplation and informal discussions among them. Mac confirmed that he would await the German musicologist's decision at Friday's vote before expressing his own, to be elaborated upon in written form as part of the final report he would be drafting the following week and submit to the participants for their review. The other main question before them, besides on which side Reinsdorf would finally choose to alight, was the precise phrasing of the panel's conclusion: What degree of certitude ought it to express?

Mac Quarles, who had chosen to intervene rarely in the give-and-take, now exercised a more active hand. Each panelist, he said, would be asked to choose from among four options for the group's bottom-line consensus on authentication.

Option No. 1 would state: "I have found insufficient evidence in the course of our examination to conclude that the *William Tell* Symphony was composed by Ludwig van Beethoven." Option No. 2 would state the panelist found that the work "was likely"—or "may well have been"—written by Beethoven. Option No. 3 would say that *Tell* was "very likely" or "probably" written by Beethoven. Option No. 4 would say it was "almost certainly" the maestro's handiwork. The vote was to be taken at ten on Friday morning, the panel's last day together.

MITCH WAS ABOUT TO PICK UP the new Ruth Rendell mystery Clara had bought for them—they shared a fondness for her gallery of bizarre characters—when the phone rang in the Emerys' apartment. It was just before ten Wednesday evening.

"Mitchell, hello—please forgive me for troubling you at home—and so late—but I'm sitting around my hotel room and having a definite problem." Emil Reinsdorf, his accent a trace more pronounced than usual, sounded too coherent to be drunk. Was it his heart?

"Don't worry about me," Mitch told him. "Are you all right?"

"Physically, yes. Mentally, not so well. May I speak freely?"

"Of course."

"I want to be cooperative," Reinsdorf said, "I really do—but I'm having trouble. I have a much more demanding constituency than the others. They seem to think I'm being obstructive—to question a work of such evident quality on narrow technical grounds. But it's far more than quibbling for me. Simple congruence of the elements here is not sufficient for me to justify a label of authenticity—the whole is more than the sum of the parts."

What was the man driving at? Had the accumulated stress of the challenge overcome him? "Aren't there options open to you?" Mitch asked, hoping to calm his agitated caller. "I understood that there are various wordings for the panel members to choose among—conveying different degrees of conviction about the authenticity—"

"It shouldn't be a question of options—this is a matter requiring precision," Reinsdorf replied. "Some of us were put on this earth, Mitchell, for the purpose of preserving standards."

"I respect that, sir, but you have to be fair to yourself. I was once a public prosecutor, and we could ask no more of our jurors than to be convinced beyond a reasonable doubt before voting to condemn the accused—"

"But the question here isn't condemnation, Mitchell—it's whether to sanctify this highly suspect applicant as deserving our enduring certification. It can't be decided by calculated guesswork or by some lax compromise between faith and rationality. There must be a wholeness here, a feeling of rightness about the totality." There was a pause while Mitch heard him drag deeply on a cigarette. "My problem is less with the music, you see—there's ample evidence that it was composed by Beethoven—than with the whole Zurich story. I fear it may be a concoction. Not that we have anything glaring that disproves it. But an absence of negative evidence—all this about our not being able to specify where the maestro was and what he was doing during this period—is a far cry from positive proof."

The man just needed bucking up, Mitch decided. He was being asked to risk his reputation over a narrative of high improbability—his caution on the brink was understandable. "I don't think you're being asked to testify to the circumstantial evidence—we've engaged different experts for that area. It's only the music you need worry over, and there you seem to be—"

"*Only* the music," Reinsdorf repeated with a thick laugh. "I disagree—it is the totality of the evidence that each of us must consider. The problem for me is that my countrymen think it is only they who are entitled—by blood and history and cultural attainment—to judge such a thing as this *Tell* Symphony. If I cooperate with you and the others by going along, I will surely be alienated from our people and my professional standing jeopardized beyond—"

Hadn't they gone down this road before Emil signed on as a panelist? And hadn't he extracted a pledge from C&W, as a special inducement, to recommend the simultaneous premiere for *Tell*, if authenticated, to be held in the three German-speaking countries? What more did he want? "Our President Truman used to say," Mitch ventured, "that 'If you can't stand the heat, stay out of the kitchen.' I don't mean to be impertinent, Dr. Reinsdorf, but I think that principle applies here."

"Too late for that," Reinsdorf said almost curtly. "I'm already in the kitchen and can't get out gracefully. But I'm wondering if it's too late for something else."

"Such as?"

"I understand that when the German cultural attaché met with your firm's officials, Mr. Cubbage invited him to make an offer of purchase."

"Yes, more or less. And Herr Neugebaur seemed a bit offended by the very idea of—"

"But that was before our ministry had any substantial reason to believe the manuscript is authentic. I believe Herr Neugebaur's principal objection then was that German experts ought to be the ones to make that decision."

"Our owners considered his request but decided the issue went well beyond any concern over national pride. All of civilization has an equal stake in the outcome here."

"Our officials see it differently—especially now when there is reason to view the work as genuine. I think they would be quite amenable to—"

"Why would your officials suddenly think the manuscript is genuine?" Mitch got his first full whiff of intrigue. "Your panel hasn't even voted—we haven't made any announcement."

There was a densely pregnant pause, then another quick intake of breath on the other end. The man smoked like an active volcano. "They asked me to keep in touch."

Son of a bitch. "Professor, you were engaged under a pledge of strict confidentiality, not as an agent of the German Ministry of Culture."

"Don't misunderstand, Mitchell, I am not their creature. But I share their pride in German cultural attainments. I want to do my best for all parties concerned. They've assured me that if our panel votes unanimously to authenticate the work, Herr Neugebaur would then act at once to open negotiations with your executives—and offer very liberal terms."

"If your panel is unanimously in favor," Mitch disabused him, "then I suspect our owners would be most unlikely to cancel the auction—interest in the work will soar, and so might the bidding. So I'm afraid the time has passed when a preemptive bid by your government or anyone else can be considered."

"But Jacob Hassler informed me last Sunday—on our bus tour of your revolutionary battlefields—that his arrangement with your firm permits a sale without recourse to an auction."

"Nevertheless, I doubt Mr. Cubbage would consider that now, not with your panel on the verge of—" Suddenly Mitch saw the hand Reinsdorf was playing. "What is it you're telling me, Professor? Is this a negotiation for your vote?"

"Please, Mitchell, do you take me for both an imbecile and an intellectual prostitute?"

"I hadn't. But I find this entire conversation greatly troubling, to be blunt. What is it you want me to convey to my firm's management?"

"That they accept a luncheon invitation for tomorrow that Neugebaur is about to extend to Mr. Cubbage—as a courtesy to my country—to civilization— to Beethoven himself."

Within the hour, Harry phoned to confirm the arrangement—"They're a sovereign country where we conduct business, so it's a command performance, pal"—and invited Mitch along to the meeting, to be held in a private dining room at the Pierre. On their walk down Fifth to the hotel, Gordy lamented their having yielded to what he called the Germans' extortionate tactics. "Now you watch how the nasty Niebelungen try to escalate the game." But Harry held fast to his conviction that they had nothing to lose by hearing Neugebaur out.

The German attaché was far more ingratiating than he had been at their initial meeting. "I am most appreciative for your again giving me your valuable time," he said and then advised that he had come as an unofficial emissary for a group of firms and institutions, including Deutsche Gramaphon, Volkswagen, Siemens, and the Berlin Philharmonic, which collectively wished to purchase the *Tell* manuscript for a fair price. His ministry had held preliminary talks as well with officials of the Swiss and Austrian cultural bureaus, and there was a distinct possibility that the three national governments might facilitate such a transaction with loans against the eventual revenues that worldwide performances of the symphony would produce. "Our hope is that before you schedule the work for auction once your panel has certified its authenticity—assuming it does—but prior to your disclosing as much to the public, you will set a price acceptable to you and your client that our group can quickly raise through commitments from the participating parties."

"Mmmm," said Harry and then downed the first swallow of his Bloody Mary. "That's all splendid, but it would be much cleaner if you just made us an outright preemptive offer by midnight tonight. Under our arrangement with Mr. Hassler, my firm is allowed to consider such a transaction at any time, even before our panel of experts concludes its deliberations—which, as you know, will be tomorrow— and keep the manuscript off the auction block. If your terms are acceptable, fine, we have a deal, assuming the Swiss approve of the arrangement and will promptly probate Otto Hassler's will. If your offer is unsatisfactory to us, your group would of course still be free to participate in our auction—or not, as you choose."

"The problem with that," Neugebaur said after a moment's reflection, "is nobody in our group seems to have a very good sense of what the work is worth in cold, hard cash—and especially in advance of knowing what your panel of experts will decide."

"Yes—well, that's why we undertake the authentication process first," Harry said, "and *then* hold our auctions—to find the limits of what a work of art is worth on the open market. If you care to snatch away the prize without competing against others, you'd have to absorb the risk of trafficking in possibly tainted merchandise."

"To be sure," said the diplomat. "But, to be candid, we have some sense that your experts may not come to a unanimous verdict—and if not, the market value of the work is likely to suffer—considerably." He offered a sly smile. "Therefore, I think there is sentiment among our group to respond to your asking price— if you have one and can tell us now or later today, conditioned, of course, on your panel's final findings—"

"There *is* no asking price, Mr. Neugebaur. You need to understand that we're not an art gallery in that sense—we're an auction gallery. The bidders set the price—we merely state an opening figure and let the public—"

"But suppose," the German cut in, "you did set a preemptive asking price because of the extraordinary nature of this work of art, and even if our group couldn't meet it, they could respond with the best offer they can—and if that still failed to satisfy you, their figure might serve as the starting point for your auction. Then, at the end, our group would hold the right to top the leading bid by ten percent, so that Mr. Hassler and your firm would have nothing whatever to lose by awarding us the inside track."

Harry glanced at his house counsel, who looked lost in thought for a long moment while he framed a response.

"The problem arises," Gordy intervened, "with your accurate use of the term 'inside track.' I'm afraid it smacks of collusion. In our business, we would have to disclose publicly, before the auction, any such preferential arrangement— which would almost certainly have a chilling effect on the subsequent bidding."

The urbane diplomat radiated nonchalance. "I don't pretend to know the subtle dynamics of your business. Nevertheless, we thought you might welcome our initiative. Apparently not—leaving us very little in the way of a choice."

Harry, allergic to threats, scanned the menu before escalating the stakes. "I wonder if hotel crab cakes are trustworthy," he mused before turning to Neugebaur. "Are you implying, my friend, that our firm may suffer consequences if it declines to deal separately with your group and proceeds with our auction as planned?"

Neugebaur tried to look helpless. "It's not that my government has any recourse," he said. "I think your problem is with Dr. Reinsdorf. I can't say for certain, of course, but my impression is that he's inclined to abstain from the vote by your panel of so-called experts. I hear he feels there are still questions and issues that remain unanswered—and are likely to remain unanswerable." The attaché took on a mournful cast. "Unfortunately, without his full endorsement, the legitimacy of the work would be fatally undermined in Germany—and probably throughout the scholarly world. Your auction, I suspect, would then turn into a fiasco."

"Which would be very sad," Harry added, flexing his sarcasm.

"Very," said Neugebaur.

"It would be even sadder," Gordy countered, "if our firm had to disclose before the auction is held that Dr. Reinsdorf, along with his government, had tried to coerce us into a private transaction that we were unwilling to make in exchange for his highly valued—and presumably objective—vote."

"And sadder still," said the unwavering German, "if our government then had to explain that, on the contrary, your firm attempted to purchase Dr. Reindorf's vote to authenticate a work that he believes to be uncertifiable. Perhaps you'll want to confer among yourselves before the Beethoven panel gathers tomorrow." Neugebaur turned aside. "And now, gentlemen, let's speak of pleasanter things—I think the oysters rather than the crab cakes."

THE C&W WAR COUNCIL CONVENED at five that afternoon. At Mitch's insistence, Mac Quarles was informed of the Reinsdorf/Neugebaur tandem ploy and invited to be on hand. Sedge, detectably in his cups, was hooked in by phone from the Wakeham family seat in Surrey. He spoke first, briefly and to the point: "Don't want us to knuckle under to Jerry, come fire, pestilence, or *le deluge*—pardon my French, chaps." And fell silent.

Gordy led off their strategizing.

"Whatever we elect to do or not do about dealing separately with the Germans," he counseled, "Reinsdorf has to declare his position before he knows our decision. Otherwise, we're vulnerable to a charge of conspiring to sway his vote, if not buying it outright."

Harry saw the point. "Suppose, before the panel votes tomorrow, we ask the Germans for an unrealistically high price, even an astronomical one, on a take-it-or-leave-it basis—say, fifty million, off the top of my head. If they take it, we're done, so the issue of Reinsdorf's vote doesn't arise—because we haven't offered any consideration for it, and the whole question of authentication is off the table, at least off *our* table. Then they can make Emil the captain of their own authentication team if they'd like."

Gordy pondered. "That helps, but it doesn't make the problem go away. *Any* deal we'd strike—with the German group or anyone else—would have to be predicated on Emil's assumed agreement to join the other panelists in favor of authentication—because, otherwise, why would anybody pay multi-moola to buy an uncertified Beethoven symphony? So, C&W would have colluded with the German buyers since both we and they would know in advance how Reinsdorf would vote."

"But they'd be paying *us* for the manuscript," Harry objected, "we wouldn't be paying *them* for Reinsdorf's vote—if there is no vote."

"Then how do we explain to the public why we disbanded the panel?" Gordy reached for his notepad and began to doodle. "We simply can't risk opening a negotiation with the Germans without compromising our precious rectitude. They're counting on us to fear—justifiably—that Reinsdorf will fuck us over if we don't play along with them. So we'd be buying into their coercion if we open ourselves to being bribed by a stupendous offer to sell out—which would make us complicit in a corrupted authentication process."

Harry looked glum. "But we've already got Reinsdorf on tape acknowledging to the other panelists a lot of positive things about *Tell* having a definite Beethoven sound, *et cetera*," he argued. "It seems obvious that his objections amount to hokey nitpicking—the bastard was leaving himself an out so he could claim, as he did to Mitch on the phone last night, that he has serious doubts, and then we'd believe he could very well vote against or abstain from the majority in good conscience—effectively nuking the authentication process and costing us a bundle."

"What do you say, Mac?" Mitch asked. "If C&W holds tight and as a result Emil abstains or dissents, has he said enough on the record in your discussions to make him look like a raging hypocrite? I hate to ask—and you can decline to answer—but could you and would you use his own words against him in your summary report if he won't go along with authentication—knowing all you now know about the situation?"

Mac's large frame had seemed to shrink by degrees as the revelations and speculations chased one another around the table. "Gentlemen," he said, slowly righting himself, "I'm appalled—and it's not just on accounta these German slickers." He turned his gaze on Harry. "You sound to me, sir, as if you're readyin' to junk this whole legitimizing process that we've been slogging through for months now just so long as your firm can hit the jackpot behind closed doors. Or am I not followin' you?"

Rebuked, Harry lowered his head and waved Mac on.

"The answer to Mitchell's questions are yes and yes," the Kentucky native rumbled ahead now. "If Emil votes against authentication, he can't retract what he's already said on tape—no matter how he tries to weasel-word his way around it. And yes, my summary would certainly call attention to his self-contradictions—and knowin' what I do, I wouldn't lose a whole lot of sleep over it. Not having him on board with the rest of the panel might cost you a pretty penny, I suppose, particularly if they start beatin' the patriotic war drums over there and try to scare off your bidders. But defying the Germans and Herr Doktor Emil Reinsdorf, who's just tryin' to curry favor with the powers that be in der fatherland, would be the right thing for your respected firm to do—the only thing to do, as I see it. Either this authentication business is aboveboard, or it isn't—there can't be any shilly-shallyin' with its integrity by using the back door to buy the vote of one of the experts who we told the world we went out and enlisted in good faith." He sat forward now and hunched his shoulders, asserting his bulky presence. "I'm gonna stand up in about thirty seconds and leave the room, so you fellas can kick around your options, but if you ask me, you have only one."

Once Mac had left, Harry turned to Mitch. "Well, Quarles is your man— do you buy it?"

Mitch narrowed his eyes and looked at his boss. "I fully appreciate the financial stakes here, but I think Mac is doing us a favor by stating the issue in moral absolutes. He and Gordy are right—Cubbage & Wakeham's reputation is worth a lot more than any short-term profit the firm might realize from the transaction by ditching the authentication process after we've already set it in motion. It would amount to surrendering our position as the ethical leaders of the high-art auction business—and I personally would head for the hills. As for Reinsdorf, I have a feeling about the man—maybe badly misplaced, I'll be the first to concede. I think he sees himself as some kind of cultural warrior, trying to exploit the power position we've handed to him, and if he can come out of this as a hero, bringing Beethoven back alive from the big bad jungle filled with greedy American predators, his life will be complete. So he's trying to wheel and deal with us to the utmost. But if we won't play, I don't think in the end Emil will do the wrong thing. I don't think he's basically corrupt—just badly misguided in his attempt to put himself up on Olympus next to Beethoven—or wherever the hell the gods of music hang out."

"Mmmm," said Harry. "And what if you're wrong, Mitchell, and we refuse to deal with the Germans preemptively, and then not only does Reinsdorf vote against us but, to spite us, they try to kill the auction by claiming we tried to buy Emil's vote—and he nobly refused?"

"We'd have to spill the beans on Neugebaur's attempted power play over lunch with us," Mitch answered, "though I grant you that would come down to our word against theirs."

The heavy silence that followed was broken by a muffled directive from the loudspeaker: "Tell the blighters you tape-recorded Jerry at your luncheon." All eyes turned to the squawk box. "Sedge?" asked Harry. "I wasn't sure if you were—"

"Tell Jerry you've got it all down on tape," Sedge repeated, more clearly this time, "and say that Mitchell was—what do they call it?—wearing a wire at your luncheon, and if they try any more funny business, you'll send a transcript of the tape to every newspaper and broadcast station on the bloofy planet."

Harry looked over at Gordy with raised brows.

"Could we bluff them out of it like that?"

"Maybe," Gordy said, "but I'd want to look into the legality of it." The lawyer wrote himself a note on his scratch pad. "I'm pretty sure you can't tape someone on the phone without his permission." Gordy turned to Mitch. "You worked in a DA's office—the cops use a wire all the time—do they always need a judge to okay it in advance?"

"Supposedly—only we're not the cops," Mitch said. "And I doubt it's a crime to *tell* someone who's made you an incriminating proposition that you've secretly taped the conversation when in fact you haven't. You could call it lying to scoundrels or maybe just fighting fire with fire—but it would certainly give Neugebaur, Emil, and their buddies pause."

"Filthy swine," growled the firm's London partner.

"Thank you, Sedgwick, for your excellent suggestion," said Harry. "Let me ponder all this over a tall Scotch. Are you drinking your mother's good stuff down there, old top?"

"The forty-year-old," came the cheerful reply. "She kept the pure gold locked away from me—couldn't blame the dear gal. 'Night, all."

CLARA HAD DECIDED TO TRY HER HAND at risotto with shrimp and saffron as a special dinner treat for her parents, who were in New York for the week. Half an hour into the task and weary of all the stirring, she welcomed Mitch's return and was enthralled by his account of the escalating *Tell* intrigue. It pained her, though, to hear how the manuscript was being fought over like the prize at the bottom of a rugby scrum. "What's Harry going to do?" she asked, administering her fifth ladle of chicken stock to the creamy porridge.

"The right thing, I hope." Mitch dipped a spoon into the simmering pot and had a taste. "Divine," he announced. "I think you may have missed your true calling, angel."

"*Tu es charmant, mon cher,*" she said, fastening a kiss to his lips while sprinkling a soupçon of turmeric over the risotto. "Anyway, why isn't it an easy call? Sedge Wakeham is right—the Germans aren't entitled to any special consideration."

"Sedge lives in a bubble—way down the rabbit hole. Harry may feel he has to opt for a bird in the hand, possibly a very large, German-speaking bird—and then try to buy off Mac."

"That would be a big mistake—Mac is Mr. Integrity. If Harry tries to buy his silence, Mac will blow the whistle on the whole thing. Harry just needs a little infusion of steel in his spine." Then Clara remembered Lolly's unsanctioned efforts to raise a kitty among Lincoln Center patrons to buy the *Tell* manuscript at the C&W auction. She had never mentioned the scheme to Mitch because Lolly had sworn her to secrecy—neither of their husbands could be told without creating the appearance that they'd helped hatch the Lincoln Center plan; besides, Clara doubted Lolly had the persistence to bring off that big a deal. But if Harry told Lolly about the conniving Germans' attempt to intercede now, would she alert a posse of backers from her Lincoln Center group to come galloping to the rescue and try to snatch the prize away from the krauts? And if so, how angry would Harry and Mitch become when told of Lolly's covert carryings-on, even in a noble cause?

"I've got something to tell you," Clara said. Mitch listened to her account of Lolly's campaign and why Clara had failed to apprise him of it earlier. "I knew you'd either make me make her tell Harry—which she doesn't want to do in the worst way until the thing's a fait accompli," she said, "or you'd feel you had to tell Harry yourself, which might have caused an ugly row in Cubbageland and finished me with Lolly. So I saw no point in speaking up until the authentication issue was settled."

He nodded, took the stirring spoon from her hand, and said, "Go call her—right now. Harry's got to know about it right away—the Germans have to be given an answer by midnight, and she has to tell him. A Lincoln Center bid at the auction engineered by Lolly could be questioned afterward as a setup and hurt C&W badly, couldn't you see that?"

"I told her that. But Lolly's another one down the rabbit hole."

"On the other hand," Mitch conceded, "it could be useful for Harry to know the Germans might not be the only big fish in the game."

As Clara was about to lift the phone from the receiver, it rang and Lolly's voice caterwauled in her ear. "Thank God you're home! You can't believe what's happened!"

"Harry told you about the Germans, and you told him about your Lincoln Center plot—and he's delirious."

"How the hell do you know?"

"I'm psychic. What kind of delirious is Harry—good or bad?"

"If you know so much, smartypants, you shouldn't have to ask. He's orgasmically happy and half drunk already, which is pretty rare. He called me a bad, bad girl but said I've given him the ammo to fight off the Huns. He even loves my idea of the philharmonic doing the first movement of the symphony as a come-on for potential big bidders. He says he didn't think I had it in me—the big lug!"

"Marvelous. Any downside?"

"Oh, that. Yes, well—he says from now on, I am absolutely and totally to withdraw from any dealings with the Lincoln Center group—I'll have to ask Weezie to take over—she'll be just thrilled to bits, smarmy climber that she is. Of course, Harry may wake up in the morning and decide to sell out to the Germans."

"Let's hope not," Clara said and reported back to Mitch.

"Good girl," he said. "Next time, don't keep secrets from me—even for my own good."

"No way," she promised, still certain that unburdening herself to him about the pair of scares she'd braved while out jogging when he was abroad would benefit neither of them.

Piet and Gladys Hoitsma, paragons of discretion, were entrusted with full disclosure of the unfolding *Tell* adventures, up to and including Lolly Cubbage's wayward dickering with Lincoln Center's better angels. As a resistance fighter in his youth against hated Nazi occupiers, Clara's father had never learned to love the rehabilitated German state. An unexpected chance now to deliver a retributive blow for unforgotten brutality was too alluring for him to pass up.

"Is there any reason," Piet asked, "if this *Tell* gemstone is about to be certified, why its sale should be restricted to a private deal between the Yanks and the Boche? Wouldn't Cubbage & Wakeham be still more likely to hold off making a preemptive arrangement with the Germans if the firm knew our people might jump into the bidding game as well as this Lincoln Center crowd that Lolly Cubbage has organized?"

"'Our people' meaning who, exactly?" Mitch asked his kindly father-in-law.

"Exactly who, I couldn't say till I chat things up a bit—but British and Dutch interests, acting in concert and all too glad to keep the property out of German hands."

Piet dug into a pocket for his smartphone, punched a few keys, and reported that he was breakfasting the next morning with Unilever's chairman and three of the company's prime Wall Street lenders; that the Concertgebouw board, on which he chaired the finance committee, was to meet in Amsterdam the day after the Hoitsmas returned to Europe; and that he was scheduled to lunch two days later with Heineken's chief operating officer, a frequent golf partner. "Oh, and the Tillinghasts—Charlie is executive director of Covent Garden—are coming to dinner on the twenty-first. I suspect we could whip up a pretty substantial pot of gold from this bunch to bid for the *Tell* manuscript—and manage to have it paid back within five years—assuming that Mitch and his experts assure us the symphony is the real thing and even half as good as vintage Beethoven. Imagine the global audience for the premiere telecast, performance fees, and all the recording sales!"

"You sound as loopy as Lolly," Clara said with an excited laugh. She turned to Mitch. "Any reason not to encourage Daddy? Neither you nor I would be involved—beyond tonight."

"The more bidders, the better, I suppose, from C&W's standpoint," Mitch said, "so long as the auction is aboveboard and there are no secret conditions."

"Fine," said Piet, swallowing his last spoonful of Clara's triumphant risotto, "let me make just one quick phone call. Raymond's probably back in his hotel room by now—he mentioned that he was turning in early to be fresh for our breakfast meeting with the Wall Streeters."

"Who's Raymond?" Mitch asked his mother-in-law after Piet had slipped away from the table and gone to the study.

"CEO of Unilever," she said. "He doesn't brush his teeth until he checks with Piet. A dear man, actually, but they say he likes to wrestle with saber-toothed tigers for aerobic exercise."

After ten minutes, Piet came back to the dining table wearing a broad smile. "Raymond is up for the idea—thinks it's just the sort of marquee to banner the Unilever name globally. Says he'll talk to the board—and also to Mel Attwood at NatWest—about helping fund the bidding party as soon as he's back in London."

"*Incroyable!*" Clara cried and planted a noisy kiss on her father's brow.

Once the Hoitsmas had left, Mitch phoned Harry to advise him of the possibility that a substantial Anglo-Dutch bid for the authenticated *Tell* might materialize, and Harry told him about Lolly's Lincoln Center initiative; they agreed there was even a chance, Neugebaur's bluster aside, that the Germans might swallow C&W's rebuff of their preemptive buyout maneuver and take part in the full-dress auction—"assuming," Harry added, "your pal Emil doesn't wreck the whole deal."

"There's no telling," Mitch said. "And he's not exactly my pal."

Gordy phoned the German Embassy at seven in the morning and had his call put through to Maximillian Neugebaur's residence. C&W was appreciative of the German interest in the *Tell* manuscript, he said, but was unwilling to enter into a private arrangement for its sale.

MITCH STOOD VIGIL IN THE C&W reception hall, waiting uneasily for the members of the authentication panel to arrive for their ten o'clock meeting. Three of them came on time. Anna Hayes was five minutes late and full of breathless apologies. At 10:15 a.m., Mitch asked his assistant to phone Emil Reinsdorf's hotel room. There was no answer.

Dread pelted Mitch's brain. Had the man worked himself into a fatal frenzy overnight and expired? Or leaped from his hotel room, shameful for having served the fatherland ignobly?

But a moment later, Emil puffed into view, looking haggard and agitated as he stubbed his cigarette out in the foyer ashtray. Nothing in his greeting to Mitch hinted of truculence. They walked to the library together, their silence portentous. Mitch left him at the door.

At the beginning of the meeting, as the tape of the morning's proceedings later revealed, each member was handed an envelope with a check for the balance of the agreed-upon honorarium. Payment in full preceded the vote, so there could be no question of coercion. Mac asked if there were any questions. No one had any. Then he reminded the panelists of their four choices and asked them in alphabetical order to declare their preference, reserving his own vote for last.

Anna Hayes said she thought the *William Tell* Symphony was "probably" written by Beethoven, "but no one can say for certain." Torben Mundt agreed with her but questioned in passing the authenticity of Nina Hassler's letter. "It may be an invention," he added, "to suit circumstances beyond our awareness."

Emil Reinsdorf yielded his turn to Rolfe Riker on the grounds he did not wish to sway the youngest member of the panel. Riker, with a shake of his head and look of disbelief, chose not to quibble over the put-down. The Salzburg musicologist said the work was "probably composed by Beethoven, but the accompanying documentary evidence seems too suspiciously selective for us to conclude with certainty where and when the composition was created."

Emil Reinsdorf, disclosure of his vote now inescapable, coughed thickly, then emitted a single word:

"Likely."

Mac Quarles asked him to please state his position less elliptically for the record. Reinsdorf said he didn't understand.

"We need you to give a complete sentence, sir," Mac explained.

Reinsdorf considered the directive, grunted, and finally said, "I think it's likely that Beethoven wrote this work, though I hesitate to categorize it as a symphony."

Mac nodded his thanks, then said that he, like the first three panelists, thought Beethoven had "probably"—"by which I mean 'more than likely'"—written *Tell*. He turned to Reinsdorf and asked if he would consider joining the rest of them so that their report could conclude with a unanimous finding of probability.

The German shook his head emphatically, paused, then added, "Likely—not probably—no need to go quite as far as the rest of you. I might have chosen 'possibly written by Beethoven,' but that was not among your four options."

"You're free to say whatever you'd like in a dissentin' statement," Mac reminded him.

Reinsdorf shook his head again. "No, I'm satisfied that we have a strong consensus—and willing to be part of it," he said and fell back into a nasty coughing spasm.

The session was over by a quarter to eleven. Since their business had been so speedily concluded, the planned farewell buffet luncheon was cancelled, and, after C&W's executives had come by to shake their hands, the panelists went home.

"But no one gets to shoot an apple off my head," Harry wound up his celebratory report on the authentication panel's vote to a nearly giddy meeting of his entire staff that afternoon, "though possibly an extra-large pumpkin."

"There's been talk of an olive," Gordy piped.

Everyone laughed, even Harry.

{12}

More cheering news arrived at C&W's headquarters hard on the heels of the *Tell* authentication. The US District Court summarily dismissed Ansel Erpf's motion to halt any sale of the manuscript and have it returned to Switzerland, but did so "without prejudice," leaving the door open for a renewed application if further developments warranted.

Gordy Roth found only small comfort in the ruling, which he had anticipated, because uncertainty remained in the form of a potential suit by the Erpfs for title to the manuscript as well as the Swiss courts' delay over probating Otto Hassler's will. The delay meant that Jake Hassler was not yet free to sell the *Tell*, though it also held back the Erpfs from claiming title to the work under Otto's will.

Since everyone had been marking time until the authentication process was completed, C&W now resolved to tie up all loose ends before setting a firm auction date. Accordingly, Gordy transmitted an offer to the Erpf family's attorneys and Swiss legal attaché Saulnier proposing (1) a payment equal to 1.5 percent of the eventual sale price of the *Tell* manuscript, to be divided equally between the Erpfs' realty firm, holder of the lien against Otto Hassler's estate, and the Zurich Philharmonic plus other artistic entities chosen by the Swiss Ministry of Culture; (2) the strongest possible recommendation to the winning bidder at C&W's auction that no public performance of the symphony be given anywhere prior to one on Swiss soil; (3) prominent mention in C&W's forthcoming authentication report of the role played by Ansel Erpf in the discovery of the manuscript—furthermore, Ansel would be rehired by the Swiss Philharmonic, designated first cellist, and introduced from the stage before *Tell*'s premiere performance in Switzerland; and (4) a recommendation that the manuscript itself be housed and displayed at a Swiss cultural institution for six months of every year under suitable conditions of safekeeping, with the Swiss government insuring the owner(s) against theft, damage, or deterioration. In return, C&W asked that Otto Hassler's will be probated forthwith and that the Erpf family and all its members and business entities agree not to challenge Jake Hassler's title to the manuscript and his right to dispose of it however he saw fit.

As a courtesy, Mitch phoned Margot Lenz in Zurich to advise her of the offer and urge her to accept it and press her brother to as well. "I'll do my best," she said, "but Ansel's beyond controlling just now. He's off his medication and touring Europe, trying to stir things up."

Within a week, the Swiss government replied that it could agree to the C&W proposal only if the auction house made its "recommendations" a binding part of any sale of the manuscript. More daunting, the Erpf family lawyers, for all Margot's conciliatory posture and avowed effort to tame her brother's antics, asked that the cash compensation for relinquishing all claims on *Tell* be raised to 5 percent of the gross auction price—with the bulk of the sum to be donated to the Swiss Ministry of Culture.

"No can do, laddie," Harry told Gordy. "Enough nice-nice, let's get cracking over there—we want a mandamus writ, or whatever they've got like it, ordering the probate division of Zurich canton to quit farting around with Otto's will. We've got a business to run. Chop-chop."

All C&W hands now joined in firming up the schedule and ground rules for the *Tell* auction. Its date was tentatively set for mid-March, not quite four months away, in the hope that the legal situation would be sorted out by then; if not, they would have to postpone and reassess the situation. This built-in flexibility was welcomed by the company's director of authentication. For despite the thoroughness of the certifying procedures and the minimal equivocation in the findings by the panel of experts he'd assembled, Mitch Emery continued to be flogged by doubts about the authenticity of the work. There was nothing he could put his finger on; it was just the phenomenal nature of the event that gave him pause. *Tell* was not like some long-lost painting by an Old Master who had done dozens or hundreds of canvases over a lifetime. This was a long, complex symphonic work being attributed to the peerless master of the art form who had produced only nine others, and it diverged markedly in form from the rest. If authentic, this was A Historic Cultural Event.

"Sorry, but I'm not quite ready to sign off on this thing," he told Harry and Gordy. "It's like rolling the dice with destiny. It's good that we have a little extra time before the train leaves the station—we have to keep digging."

"Digging for *what?*" Harry demanded. "We've spent a small fortune answering all the questions—or coming as close as possible. Why the long face? Do you know something all these other brainy characters don't? Speak now, Mitchell, or forever hold your whatchamacallit."

"I can't put it into words, exactly," he replied. "It's just a gut feeling that we're all being had by some diabolically clever bandits, only I can't figure out where the payoff is for them."

Harry was understanding, though impatient to reap rewards on the firm's sizable probative investment.

"Well, you're paid to have gut feelings—keep looking if you like, but try not to bust your department's budget."

Clara was less understanding over his diffidence. "You're not being rational, Mitch," she told him. "You've brought in world-class experts to comb over every detail, and they've done a meticulous job. If you're not willing to take their word for it, why did you enlist them in the first place? Do you think you're smarter—individually—than all of them together? Why not take a victory lap and accept the cheers graciously?"

"Because if the pack of them are wrong, it will ruin Cubbage & Wakeham. My job is to prevent that from happening."

"Does 'the pack of them' include me?" she asked. "Look, I was way more skeptical than you in the beginning, remember? I thought you wanted me at your side in this thing because you trusted me and my judgment—"

"I do—it means more to me than all the others' combined—but that doesn't mean I'm obliged to come out where you do. I never promised you that."

"What is it, then? You think I'm not objective enough for you to rely on—that I'm succumbing to my flighty feminine nature?"

Mitch tried to calm her. "This isn't anything personal, hon—it's not about you and me. We're not in competition here."

"I'm not so sure." Clara turned away from him. "I think maybe you're trying to prove something to me—and there's no need to. Go with the flow, mister."

"Maybe I'm an upstream swimmer by nature," Mitch said with a shrug, "so let's just drop it for now."

The ground rules for the auction provided that potential *Tell* bidders with carefully vetted credentials could examine the manuscript at C&W's offices under tightly monitored conditions during the month preceding the sale date: a ninety-minute observation period per would-be bidder, arranged by appointment; no notes to be taken, no cameras, no electronic recording devices allowed. The strict rules were designed to discourage piracy even by someone with a bionic memory. Still under consideration was Lolly's brainstorm to hold a private recital of *Tell's* first movement, with attendance limited to several hundred individuals or organizational representatives seriously considering a bid at the auction. All media would be barred from the audition and all recording devices scrupulously excluded by means of electronic screening. The exclusive recital, Harry thought, might best be held two weeks before the auction, but he fretted over how to keep hermetically tight security and prevent possible theft of the score when dozens of musicians would be required to perform it. Every rehearsal could degenerate into a police action. Bad vibes.

"But you have to let folks hear a representative samplin' of the music," warned Mac Quarles, still on retainer to C&W after finishing up his panel's report, "if you're expectin' them to make bodacious bids for this big fella—no disrespect intended."

"Mac's right," said Clara, who knew more than a little about the inner workings of the music-recording industry, in which she had worked for five years. "But you might think about scaling down. You could probably shrink the orchestra by two-thirds and still have enough of the *tutti* sound to give potential bidders a faithful rendition. And instead of staging it at Lincoln Center, use a much more intimate hall, like the Mannes School of Music—it's only ten blocks from here—which might minimize the logistical and security headaches."

Harry, impressed, asked her and Mac to explore the possibility and then ordered the preparation of a press kit to reveal the results of the auction house's authentication effort. At its core was the forty-eight-page pamphlet Mac had drawn up to report his panel's conclusions, accompanied by a detailed technical description of the symphony, a full account of its discovery (with a generous acknowledgment of Ansel Erpf's role), a summary of the forensic evidence, a photocopy of two facing pages from the original sketchbook, and a statement by C&W's outside law firm on the nature and extent of copyright protection that would likely be accorded to whoever bought title to the *Tell* manuscript.

The obvious care that had gone into these preparations was rewarded with blowout coverage in the news media. "Scholars Say 'Tell' Symphony More Than Likely Composed by Beethoven," *The New York Times* reported on page one below the fold, and half the newspapers in the world paid comparable attention. *Sixty Minutes* devoted a segment to the newly certified Beethoven's Tenth, Jake Hassler was allotted his fifteen minutes of fame on the *Today Show*, Mac Quarles did star-turn interviews on PBS and National Public Radio's *Fresh Air*, and every other *Tell* panelist was trotted before microphones and cameras. Emil Reinsdorf in particular was hailed all over Germany for his rumored resistance to getting steamrollered into acquiescence during the vetting process. No word, though, was whispered about his collusion with his government's thwarted effort to help German interests purchase the manuscript and prevent it from being desecrated by philistines. The media coverage that excited the keenest satisfaction at C&W's offices was *The Wall Street Journal*'s page-one story, headed "Beethoven Bonanza in the Offing?" which began:

> NEW YORK—The world of longhair music has not been as frenetic since maestro Leonard Bernstein was jitterbugging on the podium at Philharmonic Hall here a generation or more ago.
>
> News that a scholarly imprimatur of authenticity has recently been affixed to a manuscript allegedly composed by Ludwig van Beethoven in 1814 and lost in a Zurich attic until last spring has attracted hundreds of inquiries at the offices of Cubbage & Wakeham, the venerable Anglo-American auction house. The firm hopes to receive bids next March for the work, which purports to be the tenth symphony (but ninth chronologically) by the German-born master.
>
> "We've had an unprecedented number of parties contact us about the 'William Tell' Symphony," reported Harrison E. Cubbage III, the auction house's president, "but we haven't wanted to say much until we were comfortable about the identity of the composer. We are now. This is almost certainly the most spectacular work of art we've ever had the privilege to offer for sale."
>
> Entertainment industry observers think Mr. Cubbage's estimate is not blue-sky wishfulness. With reports circulating that international alliances, made up of major cultural institutions, recording companies, and corporate sponsors with an elite customer base, are now forming to enter bids for the *Tell*, the winning offer could run as high as nine figures. "It's an intellectual property unlike any other ever brought to the marketplace," commented Brooks Bates, arts editor of *The Economist*...

"If this baby is going to be such a huge cash cow, maybe we should just forget the auction," Harry said, casting the newspaper aside, "and go in fifty-fifty with Jake Hassler."

"Not unless," said Gordy, "you first put out a contract on Ansel Erpf—which, being an upstanding member of the bar, is not an option I can actually recommend to you."

"Tempting thought, though," Harry said, reaching for a fresh pencil to gnaw on.

NO SOONER HAD WORD of the C&W expert panel's authentication of the *Tell* manuscript made its bona fide existence a worldwide sensation than fresh complications arose overseas. The disturbing news began with a phone call to Mitch from Johnny Winks, the auction house's undercover troubleshooter.

Richard Grieder, the conductor and music director of the Swiss Philharmonic, was having a hissy fit over Cubbage & Wakeham's decision to play hardball with the Swiss government and the Erpf family in negotiating with them over the rights to *Tell*. Now that it was apparent the auction house would cut neither of them in for a generous portion of the proceeds from the commercial exploitation of the newly found Beethoven work and would not require the winning bidder at the *Tell* auction to hold the symphony's premiere in Zurich, with all the attendant hoopla and prestige accruing to the conductor, Grieder was letting out his unhappiness on Erpf's family by publicly rescinding his offer to restore their gifted problem-child to membership in his philharmonic orchestra. Nor would Ansel's former close friend Felix Utley be designated first violinist and concertmaster, as Margot Lenz had urged Grieder to do. And C&W's latest legal action, filed on Jake Hassler's behalf, to force the Swiss courts to probate Otto Hassler's will was being denounced throughout Alpine country as an egregious affront to Switzerland, its people, and their cultural institutions by denying them any say in the *Tell*'s fate.

These contentious developments so upset Margot Lenz that she telephoned Mitch shortly after he had heard from Winks and asked if any possibility remained of striking a deal with the auction house.

"What sort of a deal do you have in mind?" Mitch asked.

"Perhaps my family would forgo its claim to the manuscript," Margot proposed, "if a substantial cash grant could be made directly to our philharmonic—it's far more needy than our family is. And it might make a great difference to our people's frame of mind if we were promised the right to stage the *Tell* premiere—the symbolism is important to us." Her tone said she was too proud to plead but too distressed to avoid sounding desperate. "I'm afraid for Ansel—he's enlisted a bunch of wild-eyed supporters and—well, he's quite beside himself—and even angrier with me for trying to work out some sort of arrangement with your firm. He says the family is selling out Switzerland's honor and unmanning him in the process. And now this new slap at him by Grieder. It's all a dreadful mess."

After a word with Harry and Gordy, Mitch phoned her back to say that because the cost for the authentication process had proven so heavy, C&W was not in a position to make more than a token gift to the Swiss Philharmonic as a compensatory gesture. "Besides, anything more would look like conscience money. I'm really very sorry."

"I see," Margot said grimly. "Look, I'm frightened about what could happen—Ansel is not a stable person. But I see you have your marching orders."

Five days later, her foreboding seemed to be confirmed. The bombshell came in a FedEx envelope to Mitch from Zurich, containing a copy of a seven-page typed letter apparently from Ansel Erpf to his sister, who had included an English translation and a note that read,

> *Mr. Emery: I think the attached should command your prompt attention. A. is in London, staying at our parents' flat (they are in Provence) while he undergoes treatment for his depression—it is a periodic need, best met at a distance from here. At such times, he is capable of saying and doing things that can appear unbalanced. I fear this is the case here. Please call me if you wish to discuss your firm's and my family's best interests in this matter. —Sincerely, M.L.*

Mitch fell into his office chair and examined the letter. Ansel's acidic voice came bitingly off its pages:

> *My dearest sister (does such ardor stun you?),*
>
> *All is well in Charles St., though the loo is balky—the Brits still have a way to go with their medieval plumbing. Dr. Kohler feeds me the same old meds and warns as always how pointless it all is if I don't stick slavishly to his rules. He makes me yearn for the dear old Zug Clinic, where at least they do not nag. But I prefer Mayfair; the difference is that in London there are ample distractions to dilute my rage—happily on the ebb, I can report, so far as the family goes.*
>
> *All the sad news of late, after glooming me no end, has served to focus my sometime fertile mind on how best to strike back at the Americans. I have a plan. You will at first surely consider it demented. Yet I am*

*convinced it would cause them to cancel their auction and part with Tell,
returning it to us for a modest payment. For my plan to work, I would
have to be—or at least appear to be—willing to face defamation as an
authentic basket case. Since the reigning consensus has already classified
me as such (or nearly so), I suppose it is a small enough sacrifice, though
I am sure the family would as soon avoid the scornful label.*

*My idea is this: I will tell the auctioneers that if they do not abandon
their plan to auction off Tell, I will reveal the truth about the symphony,
namely, that I am not only its discoverer but its true composer! I will
disclose the details of the ten-year project that I embarked upon after
my own compositions had repeatedly been rejected for performance by
the philharmonic and say that I thus hoped to display my virtuosity in
a veiled manner—i.e., by creating a work accepted as recognizably the
product of a universally acknowledged genius.*

*My original intention, I will explain, had been to allow the
symphony to be certified as genuine and performed for a number of
years, winning acclaim of a magnitude I could never have earned in my
own name, before revealing the truth. But now, as I will explain, being
such a decent chap at heart, I have thought better of it—the "expert"
authentication of the work as Beethoven's, recently announced in
New York, has served my purpose well enough. And so I am emerging
from the shadows to confess my delicious little ruse and, having had
my gifts amply validated, to apologize for pulling the wool so tightly
over the eyes of the biggest blowhards in the music world. Think of the
sensation my "confession" will cause!*

Mitch paused, his mind somersaulting. He might have known that Ansel,
jaundiced weirdo that he was, would come up with such an outlandish stunt. But
which was the stunt—was it the demented forgery he had ingeniously fabricated
or was it this convoluted threat to paint the genuine *Tell* as a sham and anoint
himself its creator? Either claim, though, could severely jeopardize the C&W
auction by casting a pall over the legitimacy of the manuscript. Unless, of course,
Ansel's story was perceived as so preposterous that the firm could simply issue a
brief statement dismissing his "admission" as sadly symptomatic of a profound
mental derangement. In a thickening quandary, Mitch read on:

*It all began, I shall proclaim, when, following my weekly custom,
I dropped by one evening to visit with our kindly neighbor, daft old Otto*

Hassler, and have a brandy with him in his foul, airless bedchamber.
Even in his dotage, Otto was capable of lucid memories, one of which
(I shall report) he shared with me that night—a family legend about one
summer long ago when a famous musician, using a false name so his
infirmity would not become known, came to Züri to seek a cure to his
deafness, so fatal to his occupation, and resided in the Hasslers' upper-
story rooms. He departed within two months, frustrated by the failure
of his medical treatments. Although he left no mementos of his stay, the
suspicion grew that their tenant had in fact been the most celebrated
composer of the age.

Ansel would then claim that Otto's story had fired his imagination. Was there any substance whatever to it? And perchance, had their ailing visitor—who could have been none other than *that* composer—pursued his craft while in Zurich and produced a work thematically inspired by his host nation? Ansel would say he decided to look into the possibilities at his own leisurely pace just to amuse himself, gathering up every book on Beethoven's life and work that he could find. Diligent reading over several years, however, yielded no evidence whatever that the composer had ever been to Switzerland. But it did reveal Beethoven's infatuation with the German Romantic movement, his familiarity with Schiller's *Wilhelm Tell*, and that in the summer of 1814 he might very well have made a clandestine trip to Zurich in frantic hope of reversing his deafness. There were also ample historical grounds, Ansel found, to explain why Beethoven might have set aside his symphonic denunciation of Austrian oppression that Tell and his countrymen had rebelled against. "Thus satisfied with the plausibility of all these circumstances, I determined—or so I will assert in my apologia—that I myself would create the symphony about Tell that Beethoven himself lacked the courage to give the world," Ansel wrote Margot. "And I would arrange for its discovery in a place that would appear altogether natural."

To compose *Tell* and render it on paper in a manner faithfully simulating Beethoven's, Ansel would say he'd visited seven archives where the maestro's manuscripts, correspondence, and incidental documents were stored and had used copying machines where possible and his mini-camera behind curators' backs when copying was forbidden. The growing number of publications on Beethoven's compositional techniques added to the abundance of sources he could tap—"and so I passed many a sleepless night utterly enthralled, anatomizing the man's genius at the molecular level, parsing every measure of the *Eroica* and a dozen of his other works of sublime artistry." Then, slowly at first but steadily gaining momentum, he spun out the *William Tell* Symphony as he imagined the immortal maestro might have. "I am perhaps unduly proud of the daring leap my imagination took at this point"—the idea of a hybrid "dramatic symphony" he had hit upon as a manageable format for musically conveying Schiller's drama.

Throughout the years he spent composing *Tell*, according to Ansel's fanciful account, he was also busy researching the art and craft of forgery. Did she know, Ansel's letter asked his sister, that forgeries had been detected going as far back as the Greeks—works attributed to Euripides, Socrates, and Themistocles among others? In recent times, the imaginary diaries of Adolf Hitler had been paraded across the pages of *Der Spiegel* and accepted for a while as authentic. "By far the most common failing among forgers, I discovered, was the tendency by even the most practiced to try too hard, to write too slowly and deliberately, with a resulting quiver of the hand that is detectable under magnification by the trained eye," Ansel disclosed. "Thus, I needed to find a co-conspirator whom I could train and totally trust, someone who had the artistic gift to imitate with great fidelity—and who would share my joy in this rarefied game-playing. I found her in your least favorite of our cousins, dear 'Tub of Lard' (as you nastily called her in our youth) Sofie Ries, whose precise penwork lent such distinction to her books and drawings for children. She relished the scandalous deception I proposed."

To carry off their ruse, only precisely correct materials could be used. Thus, Ansel would explain how, while haunting the archives at the Gesellschaft der Musikfreunde in Vienna, he also made side visits to the antiquarian bookshops in the city, where he found and purchased several quatrofolios dating from about 1800, with their pages empty save for the musical staves ruled across them. In addition, he bought other books of bound blank pages from the same time period to be used for creating the non-musical documents his plot required. His surplus of antique paper, Ansel would say, he burned and then used its carbon residue as the base for the batches of ink that he carefully mixed in various colors and gave to his adored Cousin Sofie, along with a dozen antique quill pens that she practiced with to achieve Beethovenesque writing fluency.

Once he'd completed *Tell* using his own modern composition sheets, Ansel would further confess, it was easy for him to work backward in simulating a sequence of thematic starts and stops and twists and turns and interruptions and resumptions, all flecked with cryptic markings, that typified Beethoven's sketchbooks, by now so familiar to him. For a full year, while Ansel was thus engaged, Sofie would be said to have practiced imitating Beethoven's musical and everyday penmanship with her generous supply of quill pens until she had become adept enough to attempt the forgery without hesitancy in the old blank books Ansel had brought back from Vienna. And to replicate the maestro's habitual messiness, some newly written sketchbook pages would be closed before the ink had dried, creating blots in the corresponding place on the left-hand page opposite. "We didn't miss a trick," Ansel said he would boast, "and had such a grand time of it. And then my Sofie, the dear dirigible, went and died on me."

Otto Hassler was sinking fast by then, and at his death, Ansel was well aware, the house and virtually all its contents were to pass to the Erpfs in repayment for having kept the roof over the old man's head for three decades. Ansel's visit to the Zurich Registry established the certifiable name of Nina Hassler as a contemporary daughter of the house who could have attended the great composer and borne witness to the events attested to in the letter Ansel then crafted over her signature. The similarly invented Nägeli and Archduke Rudolph letters were of a piece with the Nina fabrication, but in their cases there were handwriting models in letters to Beethoven found in archival collections. And so the cedar box, with its entirely fabricated contents, was placed in the Hasslers' attic trunk, its discovery waiting on Otto's imminent demise. The fabulous find was then to be brought forth, hailed as a resurrected Beethoven masterpiece, and proclaimed a national treasure. In time, of course, he had intended to step forward and confess all, stressing—Ansel's letter assured Margot—that "the rest of our family had known nothing of my role in inventing *Tell* and that, indeed, I had relished the prospect of our father's and mother's astonishment on learning that their black-sheep son, who had pissed his life away in dissipation, had created such a stupendously scandalous thing."

The fatal flaw in the plot, the letter wound up alleging, had been Ansel's failure to anticipate the arrival of "that birdbrain American troublemaker, Jacob Hassler. I had not foreseen his greed and recklessness, causing the whole brilliant scheme to founder." The letter ended:

> To be clear, my aim now is to so arouse the fears of the Cubbage people by threatening to tell the tale of my breathtaking subterfuge that they will scuttle to the bargaining table. You and the lawyers may view my scheme as harebrained, but nothing else has moved the Americans to a settlement that honors our family and our nation. If they think I am bluffing or that my revelation will not have disastrous effects on their auction, they will be

disabused before long and eagerly strike a deal returning the manuscript to us. At that time, I will advise them they had been duped and that my threatened disclosures (as outlined above) were only a hoax designed to remove Tell from the hands of American vandals.

Tell me what you think.

Yr not so hateful brother, (signed) Ansel

Mitch sat immobilized, struggling to organize his thoughts. They had known practically from the first that this moonfaced oddball, driven by a complex Swiss movement, might be a ticking time bomb lurking in the closet. But the rest of the C&W management team had lulled itself into believing the bomb was a dud and that, with the expert panel's imprimatur affixed to it, the *Tell* had been insulated against such an incendiary. Plainly they had miscalculated the threat posed by this half-unhinged schemer. But was Ansel bluffing now, or might he really go before the news media with his hokey narrative, even if only as a spiteful gesture? The problem was the richness of detail in his threatened "confession"—it all did more or less hang together. How, though, Mitch asked himself unhappily, could Ansel possibly have concocted such a tale unless—unless—his ruse was the truth? No, that was just too preposterous to contemplate. This nutjob was deep into playing mind games with them. He'd done just enough homework to establish borderline plausibility for his fable. And there was a sizable hole at the core of his so-called confession: Who would believe that feckless Ansel Erpf, aging charlatan, could produce a symphony-length work of such virtuosity that it fooled some of the world's foremost music scholars?

There was a further twist to this unsightly new wrinkle that required even closer analysis. Why had Margot sent him Ansel's letter? Could her cover note be trusted at face value? Why would she have done C&W the favor of a heads-up on her loose-cannon brother's latest connivance? Was she leagued with him in a kind of good cop/bad cop sister-brother act? After all, in forwarding Ansel's letter, she was serving his purpose even if she was not party to his nuttiness.

Calming himself, Mitch phoned Margot for a better fix on her position. She seemed pleased to hear from him, remarking at the outset, "I normally would never have shared such a personal—and troubling—letter, but I'm afraid we both have a problem here."

"Possibly," Mitch allowed, "but frankly, since my firm hasn't been notably conciliatory toward your family and your government, I wonder why we rate your kind consideration?"

The question seemed to surprise her. "I'm sorry, I thought it was obvious. I didn't want your firm to think the rest of our family has anything to do with this nonsense of Ansel's—or to be caught unawares if he goes ahead with his— these preposterous claims his letter threatens."

"Don't you share his objective—trying to shut down our auction?"

"Of course, but this childish sort of game he's up to is hardly the way to do it."

Mitch persisted. "Why are you so sure it's a game? It's a pretty good yarn Ansel says he'll tell the world—there are a lot of details and fine points in there that give me pause—that smack of plausibility—"

"You can't really believe for a moment," Margot cut in, "that there's anything to all that rot he's dreamed up. I'm no detective, but it's obvious that nothing in this so-called 'confession' of his is verifiable. Our cousin Sofie is conveniently in her grave, so Ansel shamelessly invokes her name, poor thing. And the rest of it sounds like a—a Grimm's fairy tale. It's all quite symptomatic of Ansel's condition when he wanders from the straight and narrow—he fantasizes for a time until his medication brings him back to earth. I sent you the letter because there's always the possibility that during an episode of extreme instability, he could actually decide to ring up the media and do what he threatens. That part of it needs to be taken seriously."

"I thought he was under psychiatric care in London."

"Yes, but he's not institutionalized." The way she said it—with an unspoken "yet" implied at the end—left Mitch thinking that the need for such a drastic measure may have long since become evident to her. Margot added that she had called Ansel's attending London psychiatrist, a Dr. Graham Kohler, immediately after receiving the "confession" letter and, as both his sister and legal conservator, sought the latest assessment of his condition. "You may be reassured to learn that at his last session with Dr. Kohler, Ansel was fantasizing about how easily one might steal the Vermeer hanging in Kenwood House in Hampstead." Margot let a grim little sigh escape her. "It's Ansel's overactive id running rampant, I'm afraid, but instead of sex it drives him to fantasies of fraud and larceny. He'll be over it soon enough. But meanwhile, you and your colleagues need to address it."

"And which is it you think we should do?" Mitch asked. "Ignore Ansel's letter as a symptom of dementia or withdraw the manuscript from auction because his so-called confession may be taken for the truth? If *you* believe this 'plan' of his reflects his mental agitation and that his acting it out in public will serve only to turn him—and, by extension, your family—into an object of ridicule, why should *we* fear his threat in the least? Sorry if that sounds cold-blooded, but if Ansel's game is so transparent an attempt to frighten us, why should we offer you and your government more generous terms to stop obstructing our auction?"

Margot weighed the question a moment.

"I was hoping that by being entirely candid, I might appeal to your company's collective better nature—in the wishful belief that you had one. We have a saying in German that you can catch more flies with honey than vinegar. Maybe it doesn't translate well into English."

"Perfectly," Mitch said, "though I've honestly never understood why anyone would want to catch flies. I'll speak with my senior associates and get back to you."

THE LETTER PURPORTEDLY FROM ANSEL in London to his sister in Zurich did not amuse Harry. "This crazy fucker is out to ruin us," he said. "After the German cocksuckers' attempt to blitzkrieg us, my aging heart can't stand many more of these threats. Who's next, the terrorists?"

The co-owner's recent, frequent descent into profanity symptomized the strain he was under, Mitch recognized; after all, the company's reputation and financial health were both on the line, now that C&W had all but formally vouched for the authenticity of Beethoven's alleged Tenth Symphony. That Mitch himself was still not entirely convinced could not even be whispered outside of C&W's inner sanctum. But it was precisely against late-breaking complications like this toxic lightning bolt from Ansel—an allegation, however off the wall, intended to undermine the world's faith in the auction house's due diligence—that Mitch had chosen to stand vigil until his final measure of doubt vanished. "We just need to cope with situations as they arise," he told Harry, "and not overreact one way or the other."

"Here's the thing I don't quite get," Gordy said, looking up after his second reading of the letter carrying Ansel's signature. "What's the sister up to? Is she the real mastermind here, trying to blackmail us into bailing out? She may be into it every bit as much as her brother with this cockamamie letter of his."

Mitch was inclined to give Margot the benefit of the doubt. "My guess is she's trying to act responsibly by flagging us on a situation she can't control. She's hoping we'll be grateful and give ground on a fair settlement with her family and country—period."

"Mmmm," said Harry. "Then why don't we just ignore them? We've invested a bundle in the most demanding experts in the music world, and they certify we've probably got a legitimate golden oldie here to peddle. Is anyone going to care if this equally certified cuckoo comes down from his treehouse and claims he wrote Beethoven's Tenth? Or that he's the Messiah?"

"The trouble is," Mitch argued, "there may be just enough internal coherence to Ansel's story to get him a hearing in the media. It's not that we haven't pretty well proven our case but that it may be hard to absolutely refute his version of it. The guy *is* musically gifted. He *has* composed works of at least some merit. He *was* there when the manuscript was found. And his cousin *was* an artist who just conceivably could have forged the—"

"And the last thing we need right now is to let some cooked-up fairy tale germinate," Gordy agreed. "Raising *any* doubts about *Tell*'s authenticity would likely wipe out our auction. Maybe we really need to strike a deal with this Swiss crowd—"

"I say it's a bluff," Harry countered. "I say sister Margot is in on it— it's a family con—and if we either fold or meet their price with an extorted payoff, we'd be chumps." He straightened his shoulders. "These are the times that try men's souls."

"Maybe," Mitch said in his lowest key, "but part of me is wondering if there's one chance in a thousand that Ansel's 'confession' story is on the level—absurd as that may sound. Maybe the twisted bastard is actually gifted enough to have fooled our academic eminences—"

Gordy nodded. "It's true—history is full of freaky achievements by idiot savants. Maybe we should run this letter of his, no matter how nutty-sounding, past Mac Quarles."

Harry objected. "What the hell is Mac going to say to us—'Sure, fellas, we could have blown it, and this cat could have produced a masterpiece of fakery, so you've wasted your money on us hot-shots'? No way. I say it's time we go out and kick some ass, not kiss it."

"And I respectfully suggest," Gordy counseled, "that we put everything on hold until we know more. I say Mitch heads for London pronto and unannounced and tries to get a read on Ansel. Maybe he didn't even write the letter Margot sent us—maybe she wrote it and forged her brother's almost illegible signature. I don't think we take the sister's word for any of it—there may be a lot of bad blood between them. Maybe he's an eighteen-wheeler wrapped around her neck, and she fakes this letter as the chance to get rid of him. Or if it really came from him, she's eager to let him make a fool of himself so he can be packed off to a loony bin for good."

"Then why tip us about the letter?" Harry asked.

"Maybe she's hoping that, out of gratitude to her for warning us about her brother's imminent 'confession' gambit, we'll fall for it and either buy off the Erpfs and the Swiss culture establishment or sell out cheap to them."

Harry's forehead furrowed. "You friggin' lawyers," he grudgingly yielded. "Okay, okay—let's put Johnny Winks on Ansel's tail for a few days, and then Mitch, you go over there and, maybe more or less casually, you bump into him—take Clara with you, so you're there visiting her parents—and once you've caught up with him, over lunch or drinks maybe, you can see what gives. If all Ansel's after is our attention, we'll give it to him—and official recognition for finding the manuscript. But nobody's going to get away with blackmailing Cubbage & Wakeham."

LONDON IN LATE NOVEMBER is rarely favored by picnic weather. But the short, dank, foggy days greatly facilitated Johnny Winks's task of shadowing Ansel Erpf unobserved for a time before the Emerys arrived to confront him.

The surveillance, though brief, was long enough to gauge the pattern of their prey's conduct. Winks reported to Mitch on the phone that Ansel's daily rounds were unremarkable on their face. Mornings around ten, he would leave the family's flat on Charles Street in Mayfair, drop by Trumper's famed tonsorial parlor on Curzon for a shave and trim, go next door to browse at the Heywood Hill rare and used book shop, pick up copies of the *Guardian* and the *Telegraph* on his walk over to Berkeley Square, visit the NatWest branch there, buy a shirt or something on New Bond Street, and wind up on Conduit in time for his appointment with Dr. Graham Kohler, whose nameplate was posted beside the ground-floor entry to his brick-front office / residence. Afterward, Ansel usually lunched at a busy bistro in Shepherd Market, opting for its quiet second-floor dining room, where he could linger and read his papers.

"I don't think sticking to a rigid routine while undergoing psychiatric care necessarily qualifies someone as mentally unstable," Clara remarked after Mitch filled her in on Johnny's rundown. "He's troubled, for sure, but that's not the same thing. I'm not even convinced that his letter qualifies as lunacy—it's actually not such a daft ploy if it's roused Cubbage & Wakeham enough to send us running over here."

To try to gauge just how erratic Ansel was, they positioned themselves the following midday at an upstairs table at Le Boudin Blanc, Ansel's haunt in Shepherd

Market. At half past one, while enjoying their puréed vegetable soup, they spotted him in a quilted down vest, designer jeans, and a tweed cap as he made his way up the stairs and headed for a table by a corner window. The light, even from the overcast day, was more than adequate for reading the papers he had brought along. He seemed oblivious to the rest of the humming room, except when he looked up to give the server his order from the chalkboard she showed him. After ten fruitless minutes of waiting to be noticed, Clara contrived to drop her emptied wine glass on the floor. The little crash caught Ansel's ear, and he glanced toward them. It took a moment or so after their eyes connected for his face to brighten with recognition; Clara's fingertip wave helped. In another moment he was upon them, looking as pleased as if they were long-lost friends. "Small world, indeed," he said airily. "In town for business or pleasure, may I ask?"

Clara explained about her parents. "And yourself?" she asked with perfect insouciance.

"Oh, a little of both." He gestured toward his table. "Why not come join me by the window—I'm afraid they've stuck you in the tourist section over here."

If Ansel really was trying to blackmail C&W with his confessional letter, Clara thought, there was no hint of it in his demeanor. He was full of small talk about the weather, theater, politics, and the nightmare in Iraq. Only after refilling their wine glasses did he bring up the *Tell*. "I trust you and your company confreres understand why I've played the *agent provocateur* in this thing. For you it's only a business—for me it's a passion, a form of personal rebirth, really."

"I don't think we sensed your degree of patriotism at our earlier meeting," Clara quipped. "If anything, you sounded rather down on your country—as too insular and—how did you put it—'smothering,' I think you said." She smiled to engage him. "Why the radical change of heart? An attack of xenophobia—or an opportune dose of the rampant anti-Americanism around these days? As a European, I can sympathize a bit with the latter." She gestured toward Mitch. "I'm afraid his Uncle Sam has turned into rather a swaggering lout."

Clara had all but invited him to lay his grievance on the table and perhaps even confess the kooky stratagem he had proposed by letter to his sister. But Ansel would not take her cue. Instead he shrugged and said that his presence at the discovery of the *Tell* manuscript had come to seem both providential and personally redemptive, "and so I've stirred a bit of a ruckus—though I don't suppose it will make much difference in the long run. Our side's been battered as of late, and your Yankee juggernaut rolls ahead—as it always does—despite our earnest protests." His tone was more one of resignation than anger or sorrow. Perhaps his meds had kicked in.

Mitch chose that moment to enter the fray. "By the way, this little item was sent to my office recently," he said, producing the copy of the "confession" letter to Margot in the original German that she had forwarded with the translation. "My colleagues in New York have been wondering what to make of it."

Ansel eyed the long letter curiously, took it up reluctantly, and, after checking the signature, began to read, slowly at first and then swiftly. Clara studied his every eye shift. He seemed unfamiliar with the contents—or was giving an awfully good impression of it. After the second page, he paused and glanced up. "It certainly sounds like me, doesn't it?" But there was nothing whimsical in his tone.

"A bit," Mitch allowed. "And that is your signature, isn't it?"

"Or a reasonable facsimile." Ansel read on, his features expressionless. After another two pages, he stopped again and asked, "Where did this come from, if I'm allowed to know?"

"Does it matter?"

"I should think so," Ansel said. "It's apparently addressed to Margot—did she send it on to you?" He didn't wait for an answer. "I'm surprised she didn't phone *me* about it—although that may give you a clue about the somewhat strained nature of our relationship." By now he was no longer managing to mask his distress as he hurried through to the end of the letter. "Very ingenious," was all he said at the end. "Well, do I get to know how you came by it?" Uncoyly he searched Mitch's face, which remained glacial, and then turned imploringly to Clara.

She gave a deferential shrug and gestured toward Mitch, who looked toward the window and asked, "Why is it relevant?"

All wariness now, Ansel methodically lighted a cigarette. "Ah, so our meeting here was not by chance. You've come to confront me with this utterly absurd thing."

"I'm afraid so," Mitch said. "You can see why, I trust."

"I suppose—especially if my dear cunt of a sister sent this to you—"

The word made Clara recoil. "We can do without the epithets if you don't mind," Mitch chided him. "And your sister's covering note expressed great concern over your state of mind."

"Yes, I'm sure—it's one of the preoccupations of her life. Forgive me for seeming less than totally appreciative. We have a history, she and I."

"Why shouldn't she have alerted us to this—proposed—plan of yours?"

Ansel exhaled like a vengeful dragon. "For one thing, she and I are supposed to be on the same side in this battle. For another, there's absolutely nothing wrong with our plumbing on Charles Street, so I'd never have alluded to it in such a letter. And for a third thing, nothing else in its entire contents is true."

He looked hard at Mitch. "And I surely didn't write the symphony—as Margot must know—and as you and I have gone over before, so for me to threaten your company with such a claim, as this letter proposes, doesn't even qualify as a bad joke. Which leaves open the question of why Margot sent this thing to you so unhesitantly without bothering to ask me about it first."

"You didn't write the symphony?" Clara asked softly.

Ansel's eyes widened with disbelief. "But your own experts have confirmed that Beethoven himself almost surely composed it—not some hapless pretender. Yet someone plainly wants you to think I'm suffering from delusions of grandeur—or that I'd even dream of making such a monumentally pretentious claim. And whoever that someone is must be counting on your gullibility—that you'll assume, because I'm under a doctor's care, I'm capable of committing antisocial acts of the sort the letter speaks of."

"And you definitely didn't counterfeit the *William Tell* Symphony," Clara pressed him again gently, "the way the letter says you'd confess to if my husband's company doesn't cancel its auction of the manuscript and return it to Switzerland?"

"Really now, my dear Mrs. Emery—how could anyone be as cracked as this letter suggests its writer is and still manage to create a work of the artistry that your experts have now attributed to the *Tell* Symphony?" He withdrew his cigarette and whirled it in the air, ember up, like a tiny torch. "I thought we had disposed of this nonsensical idea when we met in Zurich." He was struggling to control his anger. "I may be a bit overwrought these days—things have not gone my way ever since I chose to make this *Tell* discovery my preoccupation in life for the time being—but I'm back on my medication and into intensive therapy—"

"Well, if you're being victimized here," Mitch asked, trying to retrieve him from the threshold of rage, "then you need to help all of us by being truthful. Who has it in for you to such an extent that they'd put together this elaborate letter to your sister to make you appear—"

Ansel shook his head and drained his wine glass. "I'll admit, at risk of sounding like a raving paranoiac, that I'm not the most beloved of God's creatures—so I can't say who might be out there with a real or imagined grievance against me."

"There can't be that many people with a deep animus toward you," Mitch challenged him, "as well as enough intimate knowledge of your life and all the particulars of the *Tell* Symphony to have written such a detailed letter. It seems beyond coincidence, for example, that the letter writer speaks of having enlisted your cousin Sofie as an accomplice to the forgery scheme—just as you hinted at when we lunched with you in Zurich." Mitch sat back and adopted a sterner tone. "And why, by the way, did you urge us to contact your cousin Sofie Reis to ask whether the two of you had contrived a Beethoven fraud? You knew the dead don't talk."

Ansel put on an impish face. "It was a taunt—her name just happened to jump into my mind—and maybe I wanted you to go off on a wild goose chase for suspecting me of such an absurd scam. But I see your point about Sofie. All I can guess is that someone else who knows our family membership must have also figured out that in theory, Sofie had the skills to have participated in such an outrage."

Mitch decided this was the moment to reel in his bait.

"Look, the bottom line is that you need to help us here, Ansel, or we can't help you."

He half-turned to the window and looked down on the shopping walkway below. After taking time to weigh answers that may have all seemed problematic to him, Ansel said, without turning back to face them, "If you're looking for the writer of this letter, you might start, I regret to say, with my sister herself—possibly in collaboration with my former dear friend, Felix Utley."

"Why those two?"

"You'll have to ask them. Anything coming from me you'll probably find suspect."

"Try us," Clara urged.

Ansel swung around to face them. "Well, to begin with, they're lovers," he said. "They have been for the past five years or so."

"I see," said Clara. "And how does their relationship have a bearing on your—I don't—"

"Because nobody in the family but me knows about them. Not my dear, clueless parents who would sharply disapprove of such wanton conduct by their married daughter to whom they've entrusted running the family enterprise. Not my two dear nieces whom Margot has thoughtfully parked at boarding school so they won't inconvenience her life or intrude on her frequent liaisons. And especially not my passionless brother-in-law, limp cock that he is—and miserable excuse for a medical healer." He interrupted himself long enough to ask the server for an espresso, then remembered his manners and, with the Emerys' assent, requested a round of them. "The thing is," he then plunged ahead with his explosive revelation, "I don't blame Margot one bit for needing the stimulation—she got herself saddled with a bloody bore of a spouse and a lousy lover in the bargain, but she's stuck by him out of a misguided sense of propriety—and dread of further besmirching the family name—which is why my carryings-on have been such a trial for her." His brow furrowed. "But I do resent her lording it over me as the black sheep in the family when she's deep into her own sneaky antics and howling hypocrisy."

"And let me guess," Mitch said, feeding into Ansel's pathology, "you've hinted to them on more than one occasion, because it's the only weapon you can use against her, that you'll blow the whistle on them—which is why you and Felix are on the outs now—and he and Margot would like you out of the way, permanently institutionalized, perhaps, so they're trying to frame you with this letter, making you look like a raving lunatic."

Ansel gave a slow, confirming smile. "Very well put, Mitchell. Maybe you're not altogether miscast for your profession, after all."

Mitch brushed aside the backhanded compliment. "But isn't it possible that you've got it wrong, and Margot is genuinely concerned about you, and when she got the letter, she believed you'd actually written it and—and she was afraid that you'd—you might—?"

"Then why didn't she call me about the letter, expressing her genuine concern, instead of passing it directly along to you? You don't have to be Conan Doyle to figure that one out."

"Because she knew you'd deny it all if she and Felix created it as a way to have you—"

"Thou sayeth so—I didn't," Ansel answered and gathered up his newspapers.

ZURICH SPARKLED FROM A DUSTING OF SNOW the night before, and out their hotel window, well beyond the wind-whipped lake, the saw-toothed mountains looked edibly frosted. Fifteen minutes late, Felix Utley arrived in a belted black raincoat that was too thin, Clara thought, to shield its wearer against the cold. He also needed a haircut and a shave. His hooded eyes gave him a slightly haunted look that perhaps was part of his appeal to Margot Lenz but left Clara indifferent. His allure, she guessed, probably resided between his legs, if Margot's husband was as sadly dysfunctional in that region as Ansel had cruelly indicated.

Felix accepted the proffered brandy, skipped the cheese sticks, and said icily, "I'll probably be pilloried for consorting with the enemy, but your message said it was important."

Mitch nodded appreciatively. "I'm sorry that your arrangement with Herr Grieder seems to have fallen apart," he said to let Felix know they were familiar with the local repercussions of the *Tell* situation. "We've tried our best to reconcile a lot of competing interests—"

"I don't fault you people—business is business," the visitor said. "Anyway, I didn't particularly want to be concertmaster—the extra pay is hardly worth all the bother, and the honor of it is dubious. It was mostly for my uncle—the great university professor. He and Grieder studied together in Austria, so he keeps trying to pull strings for me, pushing for my advancement. Academicians get excited about petty honors like that. To me it's a lot of crap." Felix lifted his glass in silent toast to the Emerys and took more than a sip. "Well, enough of that—I presume you're here about Ansel's letter. Sad business."

"You know about the letter, then?" Mitch asked.

"Of course—Margot shared it with me. She's terribly worried."

"What do you make of it?"

Felix turned up his palms helplessly. "It's vintage Ansel, I'm afraid— or, rather, Ansel outdoing himself. I don't think he appreciates the consequences of this sort of game-playing. He has, as you see, a rather glaring reality gap."

"He told us he didn't write the letter—and guesses that you and Margot may have written it over his signature."

Felix gave his head a series of small shakes. "Do you begin to understand now why he's undergoing intensive therapy? We've looked out for him for years when nobody else gave a damn what became of him. This whole *Tell* business has totally overwhelmed him—"

"Does that mean that you had nothing to do with the letter?" Mitch pressed.

If Felix's astonishment at the question was feigned, Clara thought, the man belonged on the theatrical stage, not in a concert hall. "Why on *earth* would I do such a thing?" Felix asked.

"Ansel says you and Margot are secret longtime lovers who'd like him out of your way."

Felix's look of exasperation hardened. "I don't see how that's your business."

"I'll take that to mean yes, unless you'd care to—"

"We had a bit of a fling," Felix conceded, "and somehow Ansel caught wind of it. We called it off when we realized how deeply destructive it could become—for her, actually. She has two daughters of an impressionable age. And tongues wag ferociously in this town. But we've stayed good friends—she leans on me to help with Ansel, since I knew him—too well."

"And you stand by what you told me when we first met—that Ansel is incapable of attempting to write a counterfeit Beethoven symphony?"

"That again!" Felix cried. "Are you so entirely ignorant of the creative process as to suppose that being as screwed up as Ansel is heightens one's artistic powers?"

"You have a way, Mr. Utley," Mitch said coolly, "of answering questions with questions. It doesn't inspire my total confidence in your answers, but thanks for your time just the same."

"Seedy sort," Clara remarked on their walk over to Margot Lenz's place. "Looks a bit conspiratorial, too—which I guess is how you know he isn't, since I suppose he'd be at pains to hide it better if he were."

"I think he may be trying to protect Margot," said Mitch.

The hike up the slope to her place was steeper than they'd bargained for, but their view of the lake improved with each step. The sprawling, low-slung apartment building had a dozen units, as indicated by the nest of mailboxes beside the Art Deco entryway. The Lenz flat, which wrapped around two corners of the top floor and boasted a long, railed balcony looking toward the lake, appeared to be the choicest of the lot.

Margot answered the door herself and led the Emerys through an entrance gallery hung with modern art, mostly abstracts in vivid hues and a few sedate landscapes. A spent fire simmered in the rusticated stone hearth that dominated the great room. Clara liked Margot's looks. She had the bearing of a woman of position, braced with self-regard, as if she had paid her dues—without regrets—but still harbored a tenderness behind that formidable façade. Fissures of anxiety lent a solemn cast to her strong features, mirroring the cloudy day that dimmed the view of the lake far below the room-long expanse of picture windows.

"It hadn't occurred to me you'd track him down like a hunted animal," she said even before they were seated, "and confront him with the letter. He called me, crying and screaming that I'd betrayed him to you."

Mitch was neither defensive nor confrontational. "Sorry, but what did you expect me to do about the letter? I'm not a physician—my employers engage me to protect their interests."

"You said you'd speak to them and get back to me."

"I *am* getting back to you—"

Margot glared at him briefly. "That's beneath you, Mr. Emery—"

"You mean you expected our people to read the letter and respond with dread—and perhaps a handsome buyout of all concerned on your end?"

Looking irritated by his direct challenge, Margot declined to answer.

"Ansel tells us he didn't write the letter," Mitch continued.

"I know—Felix called right after he left you and told me the whole story. It's rather devastating—his accusing me of such a thing when I've looked after him for more years than I care to say." She suddenly buried her face in her hands, as if overcome by the realization that the problem had grown beyond her capacity to cope with it.

When her composure returned, Mitch said, "I've three questions—if you can bear them."

"Have I a choice?"

"I'm afraid you're the one who introduced this particular provocation."

"Yes, I suppose that's the case."

"Why did you send me the letter instead of first registering your concerns over it with Ansel himself? Wouldn't that have been the more loving, sisterly way to go about it?"

Margot's tormented eyes narrowed.

"I told you—I called Ansel's doctor in London as soon as I got the letter— that seemed more to the point. I needed guidance on how to handle it. The doctor and I speak frequently—"

"Isn't that rather a violation of doctor-patient confidentiality?"

"It's a fine line sometimes, but Graham—Dr. Kohler—is extremely circumspect. And he knows I'm guided by only one purpose." Margot looked up with a mirthless smile. "Besides, who do you think pays for Ansel's treatment?"

The woman was a total sphinx, Mitch decided. "Are you telling me that Dr. Kohler suggested you send us the letter without first discussing it with Ansel? Wouldn't that just guarantee setting him off as it did?"

"Not if you hadn't gone straight to him with it. I'm the one who feels betrayed, frankly. I deluded myself into thinking we had a sort of *entente cordiale*, you and I—if not your superiors." She fixed her gaze on the fireplace opposite her sofa. "And your second question?"

"There's no delicate way of presenting it, I'm afraid. Ansel says you and Felix are lovers and you resent his knowing it when no one else in the family does, so you want him put away—"

"Yes, yes—I know what he told you." She fought to keep herself from sounding like a scold. "This is a recent chapter in quite an old, sad story, I'm afraid. Ansel's chief enduring delusion is that I want to put him away—as mentally incompetent—so that I alone will inherit our parents' fortune, as if I'm not well enough off already. The fact is, my parents have long since given up on Ansel as a responsible, functioning adult. If it were up to them, I think, he'd have been locked away years ago. I'm the one who keeps hoping against hope that someday, somehow, he'll be 'cured'—which is why I was praying this *Tell* discovery might give him confidence and purpose. My parents, at any rate, adjusted their joint wills years ago, dividing their estate equally but placing Ansel's half in trust for his lifetime—under my oversight. Their fear, of course, was that otherwise he would run through the money in no time and be left impoverished—and needing my charity."

She eased herself back against the pale silk cushions. "Needless to say, Ansel has not been told of this precaution on their part—for fear it would further unhinge him—though, as you perhaps can see by now, it's a necessary arrangement. That's why I'm being brutally honest—and painfully so, I can assure you—so that your company might respond accordingly—and perhaps with some compassion."

"I see," Mitch said hesitantly. "And shall I take that for a denial that you have any possible motive for wanting Ansel institutionalized?"

"None whatsoever—or I'd never have been so open with you in discussing the trust that our parents created to protect Ansel from himself."

"But Ansel seems to think you want him put away as permanently damaged goods, to be ignored if he ever goes to your parents and divulges your relationship with Felix. That might serve to condemn you, I gather, as unworthy of directing your family's affairs and continuing as his—would 'protector' be the word?"

Margot seemed darkly amused. "'Protector' will do, I suppose—but let me disabuse you about Ansel's vile insinuation that Felix and I are intimately involved. We were brought together years ago out of shared concern for Ansel, and so we have stayed—friends only. The rest is Ansel's fantasizing—at which he excels, as you may have grasped by now." She had run out of patience. "Your last question?"

"Since I take it you don't doubt that Ansel wrote the letter to you from London—"

"Who else? It's his way of expressing himself—pitch perfect—"

"Then why would he deny to us that he wrote the letter—if it seems so obviously his?"

"Yes, I've been wondering the same thing since he phoned me. If I'd had any doubts who wrote it, I'd have called him at once to ask who might be trying to embarrass him this way." She looked genuinely perplexed.

"Then again," Clara spoke up for the only time, "his denial may have been true."

Margot threw her a cauterizing glance. "I suppose anything's possible."

{13}

They flew home the next morning after learning that Johnny Winks's investigators had uncovered no new suspects for them to interview—in particular, anyone who both bore a grudge against Ansel Erpf and knew enough about the inner workings of his half-fried brain to have composed the "confession" letter sent to his sister. Johnny's operatives had gone so far as to track down Ansel's ex-wife, Lisa, whom they found sunning her buns and filling her airhead with vintage rock albums on idyllic Santorini in the Aegean, out of touch with her Swiss roots, too rich to still be vindictive toward Ansel and unaware of the *Tell* Symphony—or so she claimed.

One or possibly all of their interviewees had lied to them, Mitch and Clara agreed on the flight home, but they could not tell the white hats from the black hats. Accordingly, *Tell* was still not out of the woods as far as Mitch was concerned. To reach that clearing, he would have to resort to measures he considered somewhere between distasteful and hateful. Ordering Winks and his shadowy crew to tail Margot and Felix for a while was foul and expensive business, but trying to penetrate the files of Ansel's London shrink for a clinical readout on his mental state was downright putrid—and could even prove disastrous, given the possible penalties if the offense were detected. How much would it cost for Johnny's people to bribe Dr. Kohler's assistant for a photocopy of Ansel's file? And how much would it cost Mitch in self-respect?

Seeking expiation in advance, he told Clara his plan over breakfast when they were back on Riverside Drive.

"But that's criminal activity," she said. "We don't do that."

"I don't see what's so bloody awful about our trying to get to the bottom of it all."

"Yes, you do—and you just want me to buy into your turning rogue. I thought you and I were actually civilized human beings who know right from wrong and—and are well enough off not to have to do sleazy things like invading someone's privacy—"

"Determining Ansel's true clinical condition would not involve stealing anything, actually—it would just be a form of self-protection for the firm. And I really don't see how that's any worse than what the cops do—they're allowed to lie to suspects in order to trap them into confessions."

"Sorry to sound sanctimonious, Mitch, but two wrongs never make a right. This isn't like the man I married—Beethoven's not worth selling your soul for."

"Shit," he said and went off to sulk for an hour before leaving for the office.

At which point, as he delivered a perfunctory kiss goodbye, Clara relented. "I'm not agreeing with you, but I promise not to call you a blackguard for doing what you feel you have to do." She rested her head on his shoulder. "But you'll have to do something for me in return."

"What?" he asked irritably.

It had been three months since they had both put aside their last traces of reluctance and agreed to start a family. At first they had gone at it indiscriminately, like wild creatures in heat, but without success. Then, given her age, she took a more scientific approach, closely tracking her days of ovulation and targeting them for morning and evening couplings in the hope that industry would achieve what spontaneity had not. It was proving rather a chore. "We've been shagging overtime and nothing's happened," she said. "I think maybe it's time for you to visit a fertility specialist. Your equipment's easier to check out."

"Isn't it a little early in the game?"

She nipped at his ear. "It's not a character flaw, hon. It's biochemistry. All you do is hand them a lovin' spoonful—in a container, I suppose—and they study it under the microscope to count your little guys and check to see if they're wiggly enough."

"I believe the word is motility."

"Oh, you've been reading up on it behind my back. What a darling!" She grabbed his hand. "You'll do it, then?" Her smile, normally a radiant enough thing, now extended ear to ear.

"Bring us a paper cup, luv," he said in his best Michael Caine East Endese.

AT THE OFFICE, HARRY WAS CRANKY over Mitch's equivocal report on his latest sortie abroad and balked at throwing more money into the pot to explore Ansel Erpf's psychopathology. But in the end, he came around. "There's too goddam much riding on this thing," he decided, "for us to sit back and pray that we're dealing with your garden-variety psycho." It was agreed, though, that Gordy had to be left out of this particular loop if Mitch meant to pursue an extralegal course of action that C&W's house counsel could not be a party to under the canons of judicial ethics.

Sedge Wakeham, C&W's London partner, was another matter altogether. Harry called him to seek his blessing for the nefarious tactics to be employed on British soil and ask for whatever cash had to be disbursed to Johnny Winks for prying into Dr. Kohler's file on Ansel.

"'S not cricket," Sedge admonished. "Shouldn't mix into this sort of nasty business."

"I couldn't agree more, old top," Harry wheedled, "but sometimes there's no choice. Just think of the Opium War and the Raj—nasty affairs, both. Or the Elgin Marbles—they'd be scattered all over the Peloponnesus by now if you chaps hadn't heroically stolen them." He left out the part about Queen Victoria closing her eyes and thinking of England when mounted by Bertie.

It took Johnny Winks a mere forty-eight hours to infiltrate Dr. Kohler's file on Ansel. "The office manager says her folks are about to wind up in the poorhouse," he reported to Mitch, "so she needs every farthing she can lay her hands on, otherwise she'd never violate such a sacred trust. Cost you three thousand quid—I talked her down from five."

Winks, in his beastly way, earned his fee as usual. But Clara was right, of course—this whole thing was warping Mitch, edging him by degrees toward the dark side. The only saving grace would be to get to the bottom of it all on the double. And happily, the bribe to the psychiatrist's assistant and the stakeout across from Felix Utley's apartment behind the Hotel Eden au Lac both bore rapid results.

The faxed file copy on Ansel's psychiatric condition, though largely cryptic, contained the telling comment, "Subject suffers from spells of pathological lying." It seemed corroborative of what Margot and Felix had contended about the authorship of the confessional letter Ansel had denied writing. "But even pathological liars don't lie all the time," Mitch cautioned Harry. "They can be selective about it."

So the question stubbornly persisted: Which part of Ansel's story was true—all, some, or none?

The other intelligence report from Winks's field people, however, complicated Mitch's task of winnowing the truth by appearing to verify Ansel's claim about the ongoing intimacy between his sister and Felix Utley. At 3:30 p.m. on the third day of Winks's Zurich surveillance, who should park her customized Prussian blue Beamer up the block from Felix's apartment house and pay him a visit but Margot Lenz, in dark glasses and a designer scarf hiding her hair.

Mitch and Harry shared this portion of Johnny's report with their lawyer. Gordy proposed a wait-and-see response to the Ansel letter. "The guy hasn't actually done anything yet about his threat—and he really may not have written the thing."

"The trouble with waiting and seeing," said Harry, "is that if Ansel—whatever he suffers from clinically—goes public as threatened, assuming it really *is* his letter, he'll have succeeded in smearing the *Tell* manuscript so badly that it can't ever be fully sanitized—and can't be auctioned as unquestionably authentic—and we come out of this with something a lot worse-smelling than egg on our faces." Why not, Harry asked, beat the other side to the punch—whoever the other side was—by taking away Ansel's threat, real or not? Show the Swiss government the letter, stressing its apparent author's unfortunate history of emotional instability, but still label Ansel what he appeared to be—a sleazy blackmailer—and a horrendous liar in the bargain. Normally, of course, C&W would have a moral obligation to disclose the contents of the alleged Ansel letter, however wacky it was, to any potential bidders, who would be entitled to know about any challenges to the legitimacy of an item on offer. But out of kindness to an obviously disturbed soul and a wish not to embarrass his family and the Swiss people, Harry proposed, "we'd remain silent about this unfortunate incident and its alleged perpetrator"—provided, he added, that the Erpfs dropped their title claim to the manuscript and the Zurich cantonal court promptly probated Otto's will, allowing C&W's auction to proceed on schedule. "And we'll threaten, if they won't go along, to take the story public ourselves to maintain our squeaky-clean reputation."

Gordy paused a respectful moment before demurring. "The thing is, Ansel claims he's being victimized as much as we are, so if we go whining to the Swiss authorities about the letter and their need to bring charges against him for fraud, he could turn around and sue us for slander, and the resulting publicity might achieve exactly what Ansel admits he'd like to accomplish—kill off our auction. We'd be the ones, not Ansel, planting the seeds of doubt about the authenticity of the symphony."

"Whoa-whoa-whoa!" Harry bellowed. "I didn't say we'd actually *make* a public disclosure of Ansel's letter, We'd just lay the threat on the table as a potentially huge embarrassment to the Swiss government and the Erpf family unless they help us out here. It would be a blow to their national pride if the whole idea that the great Beethoven had actually composed a symphony in their honor suddenly goes up in smoke because of this letter. Let the other side, whoever the hell it is who's screwing with us, figure out if we'd actually go through with revealing the letter and then try to debunk it—or not. Let's find out who's willing to call whose bluff."

"It could work, I suppose," said Gordy, "but I wouldn't recommend risking it."

"Duly noted—you're off the hook." Harry turned to Mitch. "This is back in your bailiwick, Lieutenant Columbo—you get the dirty end of the stick since you haven't figured out yet what's really going down here. Just tell Margot Lenz you're sorry but you're under orders to take the letter to the Swiss police even if it means staining her family's name."

Mitch labored to check his temper. "I get it," he said, "and I fully understand your anxiety—the company's reputation and future are at stake here. But I think your counter-bluff strategy could blow up in our faces. It'll only provoke the Swiss if they think we're out to browbeat them into giving up on the *Tell*. Their courts could be pressured into sitting on Otto's will till kingdom come—and their government could call for a worldwide boycott of the stolen *Tell*—and file a criminal complaint against Jake in our courts and name us as accessories—"

"Not if we're bluffing," Harry protested, "and don't go public with the letter."

"But if we bluff and they don't buy it, they'll know we're only paper tigers and will probably come at us all the harder to block the auction. I say we sit tight, as Gordy suggests."

"That's your opinion," Harry snapped, hot at being rebuked by his two subordinates. "And you're both overruled. I'm *instructing* you to do this, Mitchell."

Mitch paused to measure his response. "If you're so sure it's the right step, then I respectfully suggest that you do it yourself. I'm not paid enough to carry out orders that I honestly believe could bring the company down."

"You may not get paid at all if you opt out on this."

"Then so be it," Mitch said and marched out of the proprietor's baroque office.

"Good for you," Clara bucked him up that night. "I'll bet the US Attorney's Office has a staff opening with your name on it."

But the next day dawned with no pink slip in Mitch's office mail or phone message of doom from Harry, so he went back to business, letting the Ansel puzzle hang unresolved.

Two days later, Philippe Saulnier called Gordy from the Swiss Consulate to say that the probate division of the Zurich cantonal court had just rubber-stamped Otto Hassler's will. "We Swiss are not in the business of going out of our way to antagonize the rest of the world," he added. "And I believe the Erpf family has no further plans to pursue the matter. If your firm feels some reciprocal gesture of goodwill is in order, it would likely be accepted."

In passing Mitch the news that the Swiss had caved, rewarding their joint cautionary counsel to Harry, Gordy remarked, "If I had to guess, my money says Margot gave up the ghost because she knew you were up to speed on her love life, and she didn't want to risk having it bandied about. Good work, tiger—and even better for not genuflecting to His Nibs—stress makes him unlovable sometimes."

Clara produced a bottle of Dom Pérignon that night and toasted Mitch for his victory via patience on the Swiss front. "Harry should thank his stars we've got enough fuck-you money—that's Lolly's delightful term for it, by the way, not mine—for you to resist him when he turns into Mr. Hyde." She took another sip of bubbly and rested her head on his shoulder. "Now we just have to stop worrying ourselves silly over the Beethoven. Old Ludwig's temperament may have been a disaster zone, but whatever caused him to compose and then kill off the *Tell* Symphony, no one can convince me he's not the one who wrote it."

"That's still the problem, hon—you're totally invested in it now. I can't afford to be, at least not until I know who wrote the letter to Margot over Ansel's name—and why."

"I don't think it matters anymore. Somebody's just trying to scare us off."

THE THIN, TIGHTLY WRAPPED PACKAGE addressed to Clara bore a return address in Berlin but not the identity of the sender.

"What's this?" Mitch asked, flipping through the mail. "Who do we know in Germany?"

"The Reinsdorfs?"

"Possibly." He handed her the envelope. "Make sure there's nothing explosive inside."

Clara shrugged off the gibe but undid the parcel carefully. Inside was a simply framed, exquisite floral painting in watercolors. The outlines of the plant, an herblike clump of leaves and buds, dense and woolly white, were etched with such precision that the whole effect was one of irresistible tactility. Her impulse was to lift the picture closer and sample its fragrance. "Oh, my," she cried softly. "How perfectly lovely."

The attached note read, "For Clara, a small bouquet of edelweiss—I think often of the kindness you offered during our visit to your shores." It was signed, "Fondly, Hilde Reinsdorf."

Mitch examined the painting with an admiring nod. "Yes, she's quite good—the walls in Emil's office are covered with her work. She was a starving commercial artist when he—"

"Oh, my," Clara said again, this time in a different tone. "Sorry—I just noticed the postscript. She says Emil's in the hospital—'His lung cancer has returned, worse than before, it would appear. Pray with me for him.'" Clara communed with the edelweiss for a moment. "How sad. She never mentioned it when we were together."

Remembering the old scholar's incessant smoking, Mitch was hardly surprised. Still, the news was depressing. Emil Reinsdorf was a lively, brilliant man, and his role on the *Tell* panel was memorable, if less than ennobling. Of Emil's prodigious knowledge, there could not be the slightest doubt. Indeed, word of his serious illness prompted Mitch to consider approaching the musicologist briefly one final time. So long as the "confession" letter from London that Ansel had firmly denied writing remained a mystery, all bets on the *Tell* were perilous, so far as Mitch was concerned. Before it was too late, he had better get Emil's take on the letter, in view of the German scholar's relatively tepid endorsement of the *Tell's* legitimacy. He asked Clara whether it would be callous of him to disturb Emil if he were truly on his last legs.

"Call Hilde and ask," Clara suggested.

Emil's wife, her low voice edged with weariness, told Mitch to send on the London letter, which her husband would no doubt welcome as a momentary distraction from his struggle. With due apologies, Mitch air-expressed the troubling document to the ailing musicologist.

The answer came a few days later while Mitch was at his office desk. Sounding hoarse and drained but still game for disputation, Emil came on the line and instantly denied he was at death's door. "My Hilde is a calamitist," he said, "poor darling. But I've been better. As to your letter writer, he's a good storyteller, Mitchell, but I wouldn't lose sleep over this Ansel fellow. It's all very well for him to explain his elaborate methodology so graphically, but nobody just sits down and composes music like Beethoven."

The nuance of the letter had escaped Emil. "It doesn't say the letter writer actually wrote the symphony—he's just threatening to claim he did so—out of spite because Jake Hassler made off with it, so he wants to devalue the *Tell* and hurt us all financially—unless we hand over the manuscript to the Swiss and let him bathe in glory, at least, for having discovered it."

"I'm afraid that's too muddy for me to sort out," said the musicologist, sounding tired now. "I suspect this Ansel individual—if he really wrote the letter—belongs in an asylum."

Ansel, however, was still very much at large. The extent of the Erpfs' unhappiness over his seemingly incorrigible bizarre behavior was evident from the first of three items in Johnny Winks's stimulating phone report to Mitch later in the week. The assistant in Dr. Kohler's office whose services Johnny had purchased was seeking an additional payoff for a new piece of intelligence: papers approving Ansel's involuntary commitment for institutionalized psychiatric care "for an extended course of treatment" had just been signed by the London shrink and were being mailed off to Margot as her brother's conservator, apparently for processing by the Swiss courts. The papers cited the convoluted "confession" letter about the *Tell* as "the latest episode in an unending pattern of erratic behavior."

"Not to be unkind," Gordy remarked, "but if Ansel gets put away, assuming they can find a Swiss practitioner to consent as well, we're probably off the hook, too, when it comes to any ethical obligation to make a public disclosure of the London letter since its apparent writer is being put away at least temporarily as a certified loony."

Mitch was not elated, however, by the news. "At risk of being tiresome, let me point out that his family's moving ahead with commitment proceedings fully corroborates Ansel's claim that his sister wants to get rid of him. Paranoiacs usually have phantom tormentors—maybe poor, drug-dosed Ansel's got a real one—or several."

Mitch's suspicions over Ansel's pending exile to the not-so-funny farm at Zug Clinic were compounded by a further item of intelligence from Winks. His operatives had kept mucking around in the Margot-Felix affair, which the principals had trivialized as, at most, a bygone fling, contradicting Ansel's claim that it had never ended. What added intrigue to the story was the identity of Felix's lover between his breakup with philharmonic conductor Grieder's married niece, the first flutist with the orchestra, and the onset of his affair with Margot.

According to reports gathered by Winks's crew, Ansel's ex-wife, Lisa, had had enough of his raging infantilism in the form of self-absorption, temper tantrums, and a chronic need for instant gratification. So she floated around Zurich, a defiant adulteress into kinky bisexuality. No lover better suited her vengeful frame of mind than Ansel's former close friend, Felix Utley. Former because Ansel had been quick to take up with Grieder's niece after Felix had cast her aside in the interest of salvaging his career with the philharmonic. It was another way for Ansel to get back at Grieder, and now that Felix had finished using the woman, why should he mind if his close friend took her over? But Felix, brooding Lothario that he was, apparently resented Ansel's insensitivity and retaliated by avidly bedding Lisa, much to her husband's annoyance. "And after Felix has his way with Lisa and boots her," Mitch condensed Johnny's communiqué for Gordy and Harry's benefit, "he turns to a far more formidable lover—Margot, the dominatrix in Ansel's life. Their affair is doubly threatening to the massively insecure Ansel and, according to the scuttlebutt around Zurich, he begins bad-mouthing them all over town, starting at the Platypus Club, where Margot is—or was—a heavy hitter. And, at a wild guess, he threatens to tell Ma and Pa Erpf about sis's infidelity in hopes of bringing her down a peg or two—and getting her off his back. Do you follow my drift here? We're getting whipsawed in a very ugly family feud."

"You may have a point," Gordy conceded, "but I'm not sure we can do much about it,"

"More's the pity," said Harry. "This whole thing is wearing me out."

The last item in Johnny Winks's report, while shedding no further light on Ansel's sanity, introduced a new dimension to the *Tell* puzzle. The week before, Johnny had attended the funeral of a relative at the Old Grossmünster Cemetery on a lakeside slope about ten kilometers from downtown Zurich. By chance it was the one where generations of Erpfs and Hasslers were laid to rest. At the end of the interment service, Johnny wandered among the headstones of the Hassler plot, with no particular purpose in mind, and stopped abruptly in front of a well-worn marker wedged among its neighbors as if space had been grudgingly yielded to accommodate the remains beneath it. The incised writing had been worn away in places by the strafing wind that came up off the lake, but by filling in the lacunae, Johnny could make out the carved lettering:

NINA-MARIE HASSLER
Born 1792, Died 1876
Home Again

Surely this was the grave of *the* Nina Hassler, the very maiden who had rescued the *Tell* manuscript for posterity. Earlier inspection of Zurich cantonal records for 1792 had confirmed the birth of a Nina Christine Hassler to the family of that name living at Napfplatz in that very year. But no record or sign of her death had been found—until Winks noticed the tombstone. Johnny then rechecked at the cantonal registry office, going over every entry for 1876 line by line, but found no mention of a Nina Christine or a Nina-Marie Hassler. Nor did the cemetery association records, hauled out of a warehouse on the outskirts of the city, list any such burial for that year.

The news about the headstone raised more questions in Mitch's mind than it answered. Why had Nina changed—or dropped—the middle name she had been born with? In signing the note describing the Beethoven visit, she had called herself simply Nina Hassler, with no middle name. Where, then, did the "Nina-Marie" come from, and what could it possibly mean?

A still more perplexing question was why, if Nina had outlived Beethoven by nearly half a century, she had not retrieved the manuscript from her family's attic and presented it to the world as a posthumous treasure. Was she afraid of being charged with theft and her account of the great maestro's leave-taking condemned as a lie? After so many years, though, what was the worst they could have done to her? The odds were that, if the work were even half as good as vintage Beethoven, the *Tell* symphony would have been acclaimed as a miraculous rebirth and Nina's family well rewarded. But she had kept her silence. Why?

"I'll bet she thought about it every day for the rest of her life," Clara mused that evening when Mitch told her of Winks's revelations.

"Could be," he said, "if we're sure the letter she left in the Hasslers' attic trunk is real."

"You never give up, do you?" she asked, sounding less exasperated by his mulishness than resigned to it. All their short exchange proved was that they had not morphed into the same person, and likely never would. Maybe not a bad thing, Clara told herself.

CUBBAGE & WAKEHAM'S SENIOR STAFF routinely assembled the week before Christmas to firm up the auction schedule and accompanying workload for the first half of the coming year. At the moment, though, the calendar was clouded by the uncertainty clinging to the *Tell* sale. Mitch still hesitated to sign off on the manuscript, and until his departmental seal of approval was placed on it, the March auction date remained only tentative—unless Harry overruled him.

His lingering qualms stemmed mainly, but not wholly, from the detailed nature of the confessional letter that Ansel had denied writing, Mitch told the C&W planning session, as he had similarly advised Jake Hassler and his lawyer earlier that same week. *Somebody* had written the letter, and whoever it was had expended a great deal of effort to make it sound convincing. Still, describing the modus operandi to pull off a *Tell* hoax was a far cry from hard evidence that anyone could have managed such a masterful forgery.

"What troubles me more," Mitch told his colleagues, "is our reliance on the Nina letter. It's our only evidence for Beethoven's really having been in Zurich in the summer of 1814—along with the Archduke Rudolph and Nägeli letters." Taken together, they dovetailed well enough but had been relied upon by the panel of experts mostly because there was no clinching evidence to the contrary, placing Beethoven somewhere else and doing something else at the time. All three letters could be inventions, beautifully crafted forgeries—"Our forensics people can go only so far," Mitch cautioned. "And if the letters are fakes, what does that say about the *Tell* itself? Not necessarily that it's counterfeit, too—some evil genius could have surrounded the real thing with a cooked-up story, for reasons we don't know, but presumably to make it all hang together in a convincing fashion. I wish we had more to go on—knew more about Nina and her connection to Beethoven."

After the staff meeting, Gordy dropped by Mitch's office to let him know which way the wind was blowing. "Harry gets all your reservations—he's definitely paying attention—and admires the way you play devil's advocate. Me, too—"

"I'm not *playing* anything," Mitch cut in. "I'm doing my job. And if Harry doesn't like the way I'm handling it, he can replace me—with or without severance."

"Take it easy, pal, your stress is showing," Gordy counseled. "Nobody here questions your competence. But Harry is concerned that you want to have it both ways—and you can't vote maybe on this thing forever. In this context, 'maybe' is a no vote, forcing us to pass up the auction and hand the manuscript back to Jake. Hedging your bet that way may be a lot safer—and if the thing blows up and turns out to be a hoax, then you're a goddam hero. And if some other house goes ahead and auctions the *Tell* for a huge score and the music world acclaims it a genuine masterpiece—or even close to it—well, ours would only be a sin of omission, which, Harry and I agree, is a lot less heinous than actively helping perpetrate a fraud."

"Then what's Harry's problem?" Mitch asked.

"Your indecision. If you think the evidence, which seems pretty convincing to most of us, is still too shaky, then say so."

"But that's just what I've *been* saying. Even so, Harry's opted to schedule the auction—it's his shop—but he didn't consult me about it."

"He's *been* consulting you all along—everything's on hold till you get off the dime."

"But who imposed a deadline for deciding this thing? What's the rush? I say the longer we wait and the more certain we are when we auction the manuscript—*if* we do—the higher the bidding will go, and then we can all celebrate." Mitch looked down at his desktop. "If Harry sent you to read me the riot act, please tell him I don't react well to bullying. This thing is too big to deal with impulsively."

On the next to last day of the year, the pressure on Mitch seemed to ease a bit. Word reached C&W's holiday-festooned premises that they seemingly had one less complication to deal with. Winks phoned to say that Ansel Erpf was no more.

Johnny's team had lost track of him for the previous ten days. As it turned out, he had gone to Oia, the Aegean resort village perched atop the northern end of the thousand-foot-high volcanic rim on Santorini, where his ex-wife, Lisa, owned a cavelike dwelling carved out of the cliffside. Ansel's shattered remains were found on the beach approximately where they should have been if he had jumped—or been pushed—from Lisa's terrace. But Lisa was nowhere to be found. The island's small Greek constabulary had not ruled out foul play; the locals, including a contingent of libertarian-minded expatriates, were being notably close-mouthed. More suspiciously, no suicide note was found, according to Winks, who had checked with his contacts on the Zurich and London police forces—not at Lisa's pad nor Ansel's parents' house on Napfplatz nor at their Mayfair flat, where he had been staying lately, nor at the tiny studio he maintained in Zurich's university quarter, where drugs, his undefeated nemesis, were abundant.

The news of Ansel's death hit Mitch with surprising force. Not that he had established any emotional bond with the strange fellow, but during their two encounters, there had been a distinct and appealing vivacity to Ansel Erpf, a sprightliness of thought and expression. For all the testimony about the furies supposedly afflicting him, his seizing upon the *Tell* manuscript as a lightning rod actually spoke well for him despite the legal and public-relations headaches he had caused C&W. Still, Mitch's regret, he was quick to recognize, was fueled less by sorrow over Ansel's demise than by fear that he had taken the truth about the *Tell* to the grave with him.

Margot took two days getting back to him after he had phoned to express condolences and ask, as obliquely as possible, if she harbored even the least suspicion about what appeared to be her brother's voluntary fatal swan dive.

"None at all," she said, her grief firmly under control. "I've been half expecting this—for years, to be honest with you." But she conceded that her family may have unwittingly sped Ansel's self-destruction, if indeed that's what it was. He had found out about the existence of the commitment papers they had submitted to the health authorities. "I gather somebody in Dr. Kohler's office phoned him with word that we were proceeding, at least for temporary hospitalization, and then demanded payment from Ansel for the favor." Putting him away without his acquiescence no doubt struck Ansel as his family's ultimate betrayal—"but it could not be avoided," Margot lamented.

The crowning blow had probably come from his mother, who had let Ansel know in a recent letter that his inheritance would be withheld forever from his direct control and placed under his sister's trusteeship. "His learning about it just now was the height of poor timing," Margot told Mitch. "Ansel called me right after getting Mother's letter and said, more calmly than I'd have expected, that it had been one thing for him to agree to my serving as his conservator while he was in drug rehab, but this trust arrangement was a life sentence that he had not bargained for. Then he called me a few choice vile names, wished me a miserable new year, and rang off. Those were his final words to me." Her steely grip on herself wavered for the first time. "You may find it hard to believe, but I truly loved him—he had this wonderfully mordant wit and talent that he struggled to nourish but in the end our family saw only as a curse."

Ansel's errant suicide letter, postmarked Thera, the main town on Santorini, arrived a week later in, of all places, Mitch's mail. The return address stated simply, "A.G.E., Eternity." Composed in a small, cramped script that trailed off in downward-slanting lines, the rambling letter began with an apology. It begged Mitch's forgiveness for burdening him, "a virtual stranger and mere commercial functionary (though of a superior sort)," with the final communiqué of his life, "but I need to ensure that it is not suppressed by my family, to whom my ending, like my beginning and middle, will prove a source of persistent embarrassment." Who the sender had been of the "confession" letter mailed over his signature, he did not speculate, stating only that it proved "I am surrounded by betrayers of various sizes, shapes, degrees, and locations, not all of them related to me, including that notorious quack of a therapist

267

off Berkeley Square, who has longed to squirrel me away in the nuthatch, and that fat old queen who still presides with off-tempo flourishes over our local philharmonic podium."

The suicide letter included instructions that Ansel's gravestone, "if the family will consent to plant me in its own sacred soil," carry his full name, Ansel Gottfried Erpf, the years of his lifespan, and two further lines below: on top, "Little Esteemed in His Own Time," and underneath, "Saviour of the *William Tell* Symphony."

Mitch seized on the words as a coded message. "Saviour" was not "Composer," which he might well have requested as his parting claim to artistic immortality if he had in fact been its creator. And who could have proven otherwise, given the existence of the "confession" letter to Margot from London despite his denial of having written it? No, Ansel seemed to have been even more certain than C&W's expert panelists that *Tell* was genuine Beethoven. And his discovery of it Ansel apparently saw as his ticket to eternal salvation.

The letter ended with an aside to Margot that registered the full range of his ambivalence toward her. "Ta-ta, dear sis—now Mumzy and Dadalicious are all yours, free of the irredeemable sibling to attend to," it read. "I have not been entirely unappreciative of your occasional spasms of concern for a hapless brother. Shall I see thee in the Milky Way? What a laugh if there should turn out to be an Orchestra Everlasting, with Zvingli playing first fiddle and me the co-principal cellist with Yo-Yo. Retribution at last! Do not let your spouse douse your spark, old girl." It was signed just "A." There was a postscript:

> *Crowning irony: I came here to make my peace with Lisa to tell her I knew what an unlovable brute I must have been. But in character she was not where she was supposed to be. Her cave was empty; neighbors said various scruffy bedmates, boys and girls, have come and gone & last they heard she was in Ibiza making a porn film. What was I thinking when I wed the strumpet? Did I ever think? Non cogito, ergo non sum. Kiss-kiss.*

Before air-expressing the letter to Margot, Mitch phoned Winks to check out her alibi for the day Ansel died, and Felix Utley's as well. If anyone had helped Ansel find eternal rest, they had to be considered among the suspects. But Margot and her parents had spent the holidays together at Napfplatz, while Felix had been in France for the week, auditioning for a place with the Orchestre de Paris.

Margot called him promptly upon receipt of the suicide letter, poorly hiding her hurt that Ansel had addressed his farewell *pensées* to a nonrelative in America. "No," Mitch tried to comfort her, "in the end he was writing to you." And whatever else his final words expressed, he pointed out to her, Ansel had continued to deny having written the confession letter supposedly sent from London as well as having participated in any chicanery involving the *Tell* manuscript.

"OO-LA-LA—TRES SOIGNÉE!" Lolly cooed approvingly of Clara's outfit as she swept into the Cubbages' living room. It was the first time she and Mitch had been invited to his boss's usual New Year's Eve black-tie bash, limited to a dozen couples, none of whom (except the hosts) could be repeaters from the previous year. For the occasion, Clara had bought a black silk spaghetti-strap camisole, black satin pants, and a fitted waist-length black jacket trimmed in ivory lace. A thin necklace of small diamonds set in linked platinum lozenges, a thirtieth birthday gift from her parents, completed the ensemble. "Is it really you, Cinderella, under all that finery?" her hostess teased.

"Don't tell my wicked stepmother," Clara said. "The outfit's rented—except for the Victoria's Secret thong—which I fully intend to model for your guests at midnight."

"Can't wait, darling," Lolly said with a laugh and a hug.

Summoning up her last visit to the Cubbage salon for the dinner party to honor Emil Reinsdorf, Clara reminded Lolly of their shared dread that Hilde Reinsdorf would turn up in a hausfrau frock. "Poor thing's got her hands full now," Clara reported. "Old Emil's smoked himself into an advanced case of lung cancer." In passing, she mentioned that despite all of Hilde's worry and woe, "she sent me the loveliest little floral painting as a thank-you gift."

"That Hilde's something," Lolly said. "And I might as well confess now. That smart outfit she wore here that night—the one with—"

"No—you didn't!"

"I absolutely had to. I pumped you for her size—remember, I asked if she was a regular Brunhild, and you sort of described her height and shape—so I ran right over to Bendel's and had the outfit sent to her hotel, with a note saying I hoped she'd enjoy this little token of appreciation for her distinguished husband's efforts. She called me that night to say thank you but that she couldn't accept such a lavish gift and, anyway, it might compromise Emil's independence of judgment about the *Tell*. So I said okay, just wear the outfit to our dinner party and I'd return it to the store the next day—which of course I couldn't do. The

Salvation Army got it—our accounting department says we may be able to write it off as a three-thousand-dollar business expense."

"Brilliant!" Clara said playfully and then sobered. "I only hope Hilde is left reasonably well-off if Emil doesn't pull through."

"I've heard that all of those European institutional types get fat pensions," Lolly said airily. "She'll be fine—how many shabby dresses does she need, anyway?" She drew closer to Clara's ear. "Speaking of the *Tell,* Harry's torpedoed my big idea, did you hear? No pre-auction recital of the first movement, or even three bars of the thing. He says no matter how small a piece of it is played or how carefully restricted the audience is or how tight the security arrangements, some media parasites are sure to creep in and write it up. And if they bomb it and say the thing should have been left up in that old attic trunk, our auction's a very dead duck."

"Harry's got a point."

"He usually does, the smug rat—but if I let on, I'm dead."

The two women shared no further intimacies until coffee was served in the living room. "Tell me, m' love," Lolly said, cornering Clara, "or don't tell me—how's every *little* thing?"

Pleasantly high, Clara let her inhibitions go for the moment. "Embryo-wise?"

"Uh-huh."

At their last monthly luncheon, Lolly had elected herself coach and cheerleader for the Emerys' procreative activities. "Don't try too hard," she counseled. "It never works that way—they say all the cells and ducts and whatnot can get uptight and reject Mr. Mini-right. Just go with the flow, babe." Gross as Lolly could be, Clara found she could talk to her about the supremely personal subject in a way she would never have thought of doing with her mother or a friend her own age. Still, she hesitated to share her first inklings of desperation, even with Mitch, as fear seized her that they might have to resort to heroic measures—clinical interventions, assaults on her anatomical dignity—to make a baby. Thus, Lolly's words were calming and curiously welcome. But now the subject came up whenever they spoke.

"Nothing new—unfortunately," Clara answered Lolly's New Year's Eve probe.

"Never you mind," said her hearty counselor. "It'll be a fab year for you two adorables."

That night, amid her restless slumbers, Clara decided she would not allow her preoccupation with baby-making turn her into an emotional wreck or derail her professional dreams. The new year, only hours old, would be good to her and Mitch, as Lolly had foretold. She hoped it would be heralded the following week by her scheduled appointment with her doctoral thesis adviser at Columbia to review her stalled application to change her dissertation topic from Schubert's Ninth to Beethoven's Tenth—which is how she now conceived of the *Tell*, without any "alleged" prefixed to it. Time to press her case with Professor Aurelio, who seemed to be dragging his feet instead of promoting her case with his departmental colleagues.

"You're quite perceptive, Mrs. Emery," said Mark Aurelio, a tall, lean, neurasthenically passive academician with a bad beard. He handed Clara back her six-page memorandum applying to the Department of Music's thesis committee for permission to alter her topic. "Your statement makes a plausible case, but I think you can strengthen it in several places where I've made marginal comments. To be frank with you, I'm running into headwinds with my confreres over your request." Clara understood that as an associate professor, up for tenure by faculty vote that spring and assured advancement to the rank of full professor, Aurelio was not eager to buck his senior departmental colleagues or otherwise roil the system.

"Naturally I'll follow your suggestions," she said, "but what seems to be the problem?"

"The whole idea, I'm afraid." However fascinating and seductive the concept of a newly discovered entire symphonic work by Beethoven, its premature acceptance in academia was almost unthinkable, Aurelio explained. "It's not a comment on you in particular—may I call you Clara?" She nodded with a half smile. "It's simply that graduate students can be less rigorous in their standards of acceptance than we grizzled types. This *William Tell* Symphony, which none of us has ever heard performed or seen the music for, is such a stunning development that it demands the most rigorous sort of examination and aesthetic appraisal before it can be considered a suitable subject for a Columbia dissertation. At the moment—unless you care to supply us with a sampling of the text of this amazing find—this so-called symphony is merely a cultural sensation, awaiting authoritative scrutiny. We need more hard information."

Clara was provoked. The man was spouting nonsense. "With all due respect, sir, I'm sure you and the committee are aware that this *Tell* manuscript was painstakingly investigated by a panel of the world's foremost Beethoven experts, and the physical characteristics of the sketchbooks have undergone the most rigorous sort of forensics analysis. I'll go into all of that in my thesis, as I've indicated in this memo—"

"But we only have your word for it, don't you see, Clara? And that entire authentication process is necessarily suspect, because it was conducted under the auspices of your husband's company, which I'm sure is aboveboard and honorable in every way but has a vested financial stake in the work's certification—and subsequent sale to the highest bidder. The vetting process belongs in the hands of disinterested parties without regard for its commercial prospects."

"I can assure you, Professor Aurelio—"

"Mark, please—we don't stand on ceremony in our department."

"I'm afraid that's not the sense I'm getting from your comments, Mark. I can assure you that my husband's firm has insisted upon applying the most rigorous criteria in evaluating the *Tell* manuscript. And, as I'll discuss in my dissertation, the same points you're raising about who should be in charge of the authentication process were brought up by representatives of the Swiss and German governments and their cultural ministries—but they had their own vested and transparently chauvinistic reasons that, to my mind, were no purer than Cubbage & Wakeham's admitted financial stake." She felt her emotions taking control of her tongue and checked them.

"Be that as it may," the professor replied, "the department—this is between us, Clara—views this auctioning off of what should be a priceless work of art as a distastefully mercenary act. What happens if the manuscript winds up in the hands of unscrupulous philistines—people who frankly don't give a damn how the text might be mangled and butchered just to make it more commercially accessible?"

"I appreciate that concern—so does my husband's boss," Clara replied. "But Cubbage & Wakeham didn't solicit the manuscript owner—the gentleman approached the auction house and, I'm told, is in financial need so he's fully entitled to sell it for the highest price it can command."

"Okay, but meanwhile, so far as greater academia is concerned, this *Tell* Symphony is an unknown, qualitatively—it needs to be published and circulated and studied—"

"Of course, Mark—and I'm sure it will be over time—but if that were done first, the owner would lose copyright protection of the text and how it's edited and scored. Which is why I can't append even a page or two of the music to this memo for the thesis committee's enlightenment, however much I'd like to. Look, what I'm proposing for my thesis is an analytical narrative of all these issues you raise—it's the story of a stunning discovery and all it set in motion."

"Just how stunning remains to be seen, I'm afraid," her adviser said stonily. "Besides, you already have a perfectly good dissertation topic, and you're well into the project. Why not finish up the Schubert, collect your doctoral medal, and write about this *Tell* business later when we'll all know more about it?"

"Because I'm on top of it now—I'm watching it all unfold, and it's fascinating. Frankly, and *entre nous*, please, my husband still has doubts about the authenticity of the manuscript, and he won't let it be sold unless they're cleared up. Anyway, I'll do the Schubert right afterward, if that would assuage your committee people."

The professor looked defeated by Clara's resolve.

"Well, if you're so determined," he said, "why don't you revise this proposal a bit as I'm urging, and I'll do my best for you. But meanwhile, you need to keep me posted on developments—we need to be sure this is no hoax."

"Smashing!" she said. "I'm most grateful. When do you need my revised memo?"

"The committee next meets on Friday—can you have it back to me by then?"

"I can do better than that," Clara said, reaching down for her laptop beside her chair. "I've got my memo to the committee on a file in here—and all the supporting material I'll need for the fixes you want. Is there some vacant office around here where I can park for a few hours and do the revisions right now?"

She was accommodated in an office next door belonging to one of Aurelio's professorial colleagues on sabbatical that term. "Take all afternoon, Clara—just send me your edited file and leave a hard copy on my desk when you're done." Aurelio looked pensive as he left her. "I just wish we had a Columbia alumnus with a boatload of gold who could swoop in and offer your Mr. Whatshisname whatever price he wants for his discovery—and then hand the manuscript over to our department for TLC."

"Might be worth a try," she said with an encouraging smile. "But I think the owner is set on auctioning it out of fear he'd be shortchanging himself if he accepted a preemptive offer."

Clara put in an hour and a half revising her memorandum, then decided to take a lunch break and walked over to Broadway for a sandwich. When she came back, she found that the door to the office where she was working had been locked. The problem was solved by an appeal to the secretary in the departmental office who had a set of keys to every member's quarters. "Oh, yes," the secretary said, "Professor Aurelio noticed you'd left the door open when you went out and asked me to lock it as a security measure."

"How very thoughtful of him," Clara said sweetly.

{14}

Jake Hassler's lawyer sounded more animated than usual—giddy almost, for him—when he called Mitch at the end of the third week in January. "We've got something for you," Owen Whittaker told him, "something big. Jake wants to bring it into the city over the weekend."

"Do we get a hint?" Mitch asked.

"Among other things, a new letter from Nina."

Mitch's early-warning system went on instant alert. "I've heard of slow mail delivery, but this is one for the Guinness Book of Records."

Whittaker laughed and then explained. Troubled because Mitch had confessed the week before Christmas that he was still not totally sold on the credibility of the whole *Tell* story due mainly to its reliance on the Nina letter (on top of the as yet unanswered question of who had written the letter from London over Ansel's signature), Jake had begun to brood about whether he would ever realize any serious money from selling the manuscript. The news of Ansel's apparent suicide only deepened his worry and confusion, not to mention guilt because Jake had run off with the symphony after Ansel recognized it for what it was—and ought to have been rewarded for it in some substantial way. But there was no agreement between them at the time of Ansel's demise.

"And then yesterday, Jake got a padded envelope with some documents and a covering note from Ansel—it was apparently sent through an attorney friend of his in London, though there was no return address," Whittaker said. "The note is self-explanatory—it looks pretty legitimate to me. Jake got hold of his neighbor with reading knowledge of German to give us the gist of the items in the envelope—you're in for a treat."

"I could use one about now," Mitch said, at once profoundly skeptical but powerfully eager to see the alleged new evidence. "Can you come here tomorrow—or do you charge overtime for weekend work?"

"How's ten o'clock?" Owen asked.

"Fine—and drive carefully. A lot may be riding on what you bring."

Mitch and Clara rearranged their Saturday plans and met with Jake and Whittaker in the C&W library. Jake had offered to bring along his German-speaking neighbor, but Mitch had assured them that Clara's command of the language would likely serve their immediate needs. The new finds consisted of three documents, two of which Jake said had been tucked together inside the third one, which appeared to be a portion of a diary-like scrapbook. The typed cover letter, on a plain sheet of white copy paper, read:

Dear Jacob,

I am asking a solicitor friend in London to send you these revealing items in the event I am put away or meet some unfortunate and untimely end. After you disgraced yourself by absconding with the wooden box holding the Beethoven manuscript and related papers, I revisited your grandfather's attic and carefully explored again the cluttered contents of the big trunk before Herr Schacht had it sent to your home in N. Jersey. These enclosed items may have been placed in the trunk by someone else long after Nina had put the wood box there and were left nearby but not inside it. I have not sent them to you because we are no longer friends and I have no desire to enrich you with the help of these documents. But if they reach you, it will mean they can no longer do me any good as a "bargaining chip" and so all I ask is that if they help you to make money, you will make sure that the world knows of my essential part in the Tell discovery.

The typed, not handwritten, sign-off read, "Be well, Ansel."

"Why didn't he sign it?" Mitch asked.

"Who knows why he did anything—he was a very strange duck," Jake's lawyer replied. "Maybe he just didn't have a pen handy."

Mitch turned to Jake. "Where's the envelope this stuff came in?"

"It was just a plain padded envelope—no return address. But it had British stamps and a London postmark—I think. No, I'm sure."

"Why didn't you bring it?"

Jake clamped his eyes shut. "I chucked it, I guess—it was all ripped after I opened it." He gave a single, defenseless shake of his head. "Not too swift, huh?"

"But the contents speak for themselves," Whittaker put in to cover his client's blunder.

"Let's see," said Mitch.

They started with the briefer of the two small items, a single half-folded sheet of mildewed paper with neat writing in badly faded brown ink. The heading paragraph stated that a messenger from the Zurich Canton Registry had gone to the Hassler house "on this day, 23 June AD 1818," to urge a member of the family to return with him to the bureau's office to copy the text of a brief notice received in the previous day's post from Vienna, along with a sealed letter addressed to the Hassler residence. Clara translated the text of the notice aloud:

> *The undersigned* Village Clerk of Mittendrinnen-on-Danube *wishes to advise the proper authorities of Zurich Switzerland that the drowned body of a young woman of twenty-five or so years of age was recently found on the shore of the Danube River within our village limits and identified by a local innkeeper as the remains of a lately departed guest at his lodgings—namely, Miss N. Hassler, who had said that she resided at Napfplatz, in the city of Zurich, Switzerland. The deceased was laid to eternal rest without a grave marker in a corner of our local churchyard reserved for those who did not dwell among us. The keeper of the inn has asked me to include a letter to her family that he says Fraulein Hassler paid him to have posted.*

The signature, with rococo swashes and flourishes, read "Karl Olgeschlagger."

"But then how," Clara asked, looking up after she'd finished reading it aloud, "could she have been buried in the cemetery outside Zurich in—what year was it Johnny said?"

"I think 1876," Mitch said with a shrug. "Hell, so as long as we're resurrecting a Beethoven symphony, why not a corpse in the bargain? Read on, sweetheart."

"And here's the letter Nina left with the innkeeper—it's dynamite," Jake said, sliding two folded and yellowed sheets, with a broken wax seal on the outside of the second page, toward them across the conference table, "a real eye-opener. It kinda answers a lot of what's been buggin' Mitch about the whole story."

Clara scanned the letter for a few moments and then, eyebrows arching, began to translate. It was dated 7 May 1818, addressed to the Hasslers from the Hidden Oaks Inn, which the writer said was located at the edge of a Danubeside village not far from Vienna, and "entrusted with the last coins in my purse to the innkeeper who promises me in all earnestness he will post it." She had set out for the Austrian capital, she explained, a month earlier with Marie,

> ...my dear little one, whose existence caused our family such heartache and me much anguish. I came to seek her father, who, unknown to you until now, was our distinguished visitor of four summers ago. With the greatest shame, I must confess that he and I grew intimate over the weeks when the maestro remained in our midst and I served as housekeeper for his quarters. Our bonding brought much happiness to us both and eased his grief over the failed medical treatments he was enduring and the difficulties he was having with his musical composition.
>
> Upon the maestro's departure, he entrusted me with the musical notebooks in which he had been laboring, saying it was too risky to take them back with him to Vienna just then—the reasons were too complicated for him to explain, he said and asked that I watch over them until he sent for the composition books, hinting that he would perhaps ask me to bring them to him myself at his expense when the time was ripe. For safekeeping, I placed his notebooks in the trunk in our attic, where they remain. He left behind, in addition to his composing books and my heavy heart, yet another package, one he did not know of at the time—and the very reason I came hither without his invitation.

Despite the nature of their friendship, Clara read on, translating more freely now, the maestro never wrote to her about the return of his compositions or to ask after her health—or anything whatever—which greatly saddened Nina and left her fearful, upon learning she was to bear his child, that he would not acknowledge its paternity. She nevertheless wrote to advise him of the fact, but he never replied. Thinking that perhaps her letter to him had gone astray, she wrote a second and then a third time, with no happier results. It was then, out of pique, that she wrote the note, dating it just after the composer left Zurich, explaining how he had instructed her to destroy the composition he had been working on during his stay in Switzerland. But believing the maestro was acting rashly and would later regret his command, she kept his workbooks in her own bed chamber. "But in my growing anger," Clara translated more literally now, "I chose, in revenge for his cruel indifference toward me, to keep possession of his composing books as my own property unless he asked me to bring them to him, which I vowed to myself that I would do only if he agreed as well to accept as his own the child I was carrying." Clara paused, moved by the lines she was reciting, and then continued more haltingly:

> *More than three years have now passed since you sent me in penance from our family's loving embrace, to drift with my little Marie, two forsaken souls, and I have grown so weary with this lonely burden that I knew no other solution than to set out for Vienna in quest of the great composer, hoping to renew our acquaintance and presenting him with our precious love child and the fond wish that he would embrace her as well as me.*
>
> *Instead, I was at first denied admission to his atelier, and when I sent word that I would not leave his doorstep until he had seen me, his manservant led us to the maestro. He was not delighted to see me, still less so our daughter, and when I wrote out the nature of my visit in a notebook he kept for that purpose—for his hearing had in no way improved— he angrily denied ever having been acquainted with me and said it was a foul lie to claim my little girl was his and, furthermore, that the very whisper of the idea would ruin his standing in the community, where he was admired as a highly moral person—and he doubted the same could be said for me. When I asked him whether he had resumed work on the musical composition he had left with me to destroy, he grew even more furious and said I must be mistaken since he had never been to Z. in his life and knew nothing of any music he might have mislaid or left behind somewhere. And then I was roughly shown the door, Marie rushing after me—a sad little discard.*

Clara shook her head, grieving over the pathetic scene she had narrated, then read the closing final part of the letter alternating between her own paraphrasing and the author's more affecting words. Her soul could never be repaired, Nina wrote near the end, for just as she had lost the love and regard of her dear mother and father, who had cast her from their home, so too had she lost all illusions that the man she had so much adored from afar would ever mend her wounds and make her whole. "No, he is a vicious rogue, a most inhuman monster," Nina wrote, "and I hereby forsake him forever." The letter to her family ended:

> *Today, knowing you have it not in your hearts to forgive me and accept my child as family, I arranged for Marie to be taken in as a foundling by the holy sisters. Had I begged you to give the innocent creature a place*

among you even while barring me from your door, I fear you would have punished her by repeating with regularity that her father is other than the one I have here named. It is not so. He wronged me, and my only wrongful act in return was to save his music manuscripts and sundry papers against his instruction. Perhaps, at least, since I am denied entry to my own parents' home, you will place this note beside my earlier one telling of the maestro's final hour in Zurich—it is with his composing books and other items he asked me to discard but remain, unless someone has disturbed them, in the cedar box stored in our attic trunk.

Goodbye, may we reunite someday in Heaven, where forgiveness, I pray, shall be within your power and mine.

Your daughter without hope, Nina

Clara's eyes glistened with unspilled tears, Mitch saw as she looked up. It was a heartbreaking, illuminating tale—and quite perfect. Here was the epiphany they had been awaiting to fill out the picture. However unflattering its disclosure of the immortal composer's all too human carnal cravings, the new letter emitted the gleam of truth, as profoundly simple revelation often does. Mitch had before him now another, perhaps better reason besides Beethoven's quarrel with the repressive Hapsburg regime to explain why the *Tell* manuscript had never seen the light of a Viennese dawn. "What an absolute pig he was," said Clara, reading Mitch's mind.

"And so hung up on his righteousness, if we're to believe Nina," he added, "that he'd let a whole symphony go rather than own up to his lusty itch. Hard to believe—but here we are."

Clara moved the letter, which they instantly dubbed "Nina #2," to one side. "This may help explain why the family left the manuscript in the attic all those generations," she offered—out of shame over Nina's conduct and reluctance to muddy Beethoven's glorious name. "I'd say they were a helluva lot more considerate of him than of her, their own flesh and blood. Imagine that poor girl, wandering homeless with a child. I hate to think what she had to do in order to survive."

For all its affecting nature, Mitch began almost at once to have second thoughts about the letter. It seemed to pluck at the reader's heartstrings too adroitly, as if the writer had a literary bent well beyond any that a moderately schooled young woman of her time and place might have acquired. "And I still don't get how all this ties in with the gravestone inscription—if Nina was the mother's name, and Marie was her child's—"

"Oh, you'll love this one, then," said Jake, pushing forward several bound pages from the diary-album that had held the other two items. He passed it on to Clara, who began flipping through it. "Looks like a sort of scrapbook with dated entries—family news, business happenings—the weather—here's a recipe—someone wrote in a joke. I guess any family member had the privilege of putting in whatever seemed memorable—the handwriting changes from item to item." When she reached the long entry for 18 September 1876, she paused to digest the German text, a jumble of names and references that at first meant little to her. Mitch went back to the office kitchen to bring them coffee; by the time he returned, Clara had deciphered the diarist's odd handwriting and allowed her to untangle the gist of the story.

According to the unsigned diarist, writing on the day after Marie's burial, the news of her mother's suicide by drowning fifty-eight years earlier had released a cascade of conflicting emotions within the Hassler household over the family's heartless expulsion of their wronged daughter. When guilt won out over good riddance, a volunteer party of Hasslers inquired at half the convents of Austria before locating Nina's little Marie and bringing her back to the home she had never known. But her presence among the starchy Hasslers proved a ceaseless embarrassment, and the girl was never accepted as more than a marginal member of the family. When she grew up, they assigned her a niche just above housemaid, relegated to a bloodless spinsterhood. That she endured it spoke more to the narrowness of her options, according to the family diarist, than to her strength of character.

Even her death at age sixty-one did not end Marie's lifelong degradation. The heads of the family ruled that, being illegitimate and unbaptized, Marie was not entitled to a grave among them in hallowed ground. Others in the household, though, vexed by this ruling, argued that to heap this final indignity on her long-suffering soul might rain eternal damnation on the rest of the family—not her. "And so we settled upon an awkward compromise," Clara quoted the unsigned diarist's report. To atone for the family's sins against both mother and daughter, they decided to bury Marie in the Hassler plot, but did so unobtrusively, with only a few caring relatives and kindly neighbors attending. No notice of Marie's death was given at the cantonal registry or of her nocturnal interment to the church sexton, normally in charge of burial arrangements. The immediate neighbors, glad to have the long-running scandal laid to rest at last, averted their glance. The gravestone, in order not to attract notice, was made to appear weathered from the first, and it bore a less than strictly truthful inscription. Serving as a monument to both outcast mother and reviled daughter, it was incised with the year of the former's birth and the latter's death, with their names joined—Nina-Marie Hassler—as if their briefly overlapping lives represented a single continuum of heartbreak. Their composite epitaph, "Home Again," was a gesture meant to soothe the family's conscience and drive off its lingering ghosts.

"The bloody hypocrites," Clara said, closing the scrapbook with its damning contents.

Mitch nodded, fingering the album's tattered binding. "But at least all this seems to clear up one mystery—now we know why Winks couldn't find any record of Nina's death or burial."

"I told you there was hot stuff here," Jake said proudly. "You missed one thing, though—there's a family portrait in the back of the scrapbook with the other pictures. Take a gander."

The group picture, with its penned legend, "The Hassler Family of Zurich, 1873" on the reverse side, had been made when photography was still in its infancy and thus suffered from blurring head movements by several of the subjects during the extended exposure time that the old cameras demanded. Among those caught in sharp focus was a woman of forbidding mien in a black dress, standing on the far left of the back row. Mitch bent closer to the dusty album page on which the photo was mounted. "Well, well, well," he said, "what have we here?" He invited Clara to join in the inspection.

The likeness, once pointed out, seemed undeniable: the good cheek bones, the deep-set burning eyes, the broad brow, the strong jawline, the tangled gray hair of a mannish-looking harridan close to sixty. "My God," Clara exclaimed. "Ludwig in drag!"

"That's what we thought, too." Whittaker said. "Of course, there's no caption, so we don't know for sure if that's Marie. But it's certainly food for thought."

AS SOON AS JAKE AND HIS COUNSELOR LEFT, Mitch brought the new documents downstairs to C&W's basement vault room, where the security guard unlocked the thick steel compartment holding the old cedar box still serving as the repository for the *Tell* manuscripts and related documents. Mitch carefully extracted the first Nina letter and examined it closely. To the naked eye, its handwriting looked identical to the style in the second Nina letter—an impression Clara shared a moment later. "I'll have to fly this stuff over in person to the Veritas lab in Cambridge for their handwriting and paper specialists to screen it," Mitch said, "and on the double."

Clara nodded. "And will this new batch of evidence clinch it for you, if Veritas doesn't spot anything fishy?" Clara asked as they set out to walk home across Central Park.

"I don't know—maybe," Mitch conceded. "It sure gives the story a lot more coherence—in strictly human terms. It also pretty much eliminates any pretense that Beethoven didn't think his new symphony was up to his standards, so he was just chucking it."

Still, she detected hesitation in Mitch's voice.

"What's the downside, then?"

"Well, don't you think it's more than a little funny how this new corroborative information surfaces just now—in the nick of time and right after I let it be known to everyone involved with the *Tell* that I still wasn't entirely happy with the Nina story? It's as if there's a workshop of Alpine elves turning out these greatly illuminating documents on demand."

"Aren't you overdoing it, hon? Jake told you what happened—it's a simple explanation."

"Maybe too simple."

He flew to England the following night and stayed in London to await the findings of the Veritas forensics team's microscopic examination of Nina #2 and its accompanying items. Meanwhile, Johnny Winks and his shadowy corps were trying to locate official records to corroborate either the dispatch or the receipt of Nina's death notice that Jake had—almost magically—just produced. Since his in-laws were traveling in the Far East, Mitch took a junior suite at a small hotel in Mayfair and tried to busy himself. Other than a dutiful appearance at Cubbage & Wakeham's Portland Road offices near Regent's Park and an interminable lunch with Sedge Wakeham at his fusty Berkeley Square club, he had time on his hands and Clara on his mind. London in midwinter without her companionship seemed especially dreary.

The skies cleared on Friday morning, inviting him to kill a few hours circumnavigating Hyde Park and then reading the newspapers on a bench beside the Serpentine. While seated there, he noticed a fellow two benches away in a black pea coat and peaked Greek sailor's cap, smoking a pipe and casting an occasional glance Mitch's way. Half an hour later, resuming his walk and pausing to read a ground plaque explaining that the adjacent forsythia beds were named in honor of the park's onetime superintendent John Forsyth, Mitch spotted the same man, still puffing on his pipe, among a group of passersby. And then again several hundred feet behind him, matching his leisurely pace down Embassy Row at the western end of Kensington Gardens. It could not be a coincidence.

Mitch quickened his stride heading back to Mayfair, but after being trailed for another ten or so minutes, he glanced back to find that his pursuer had quit the nerve-racking contest. Relieved, he hurried from the park, had a ham roll and a stout at a Knightsbridge pub, and pondered who had him under surveillance and why. An hour later, on entering his hotel lobby, he had his answer. Two plainclothesmen from HRH's constabulary flashed their credentials and invited him to their waiting car for a trip to New Scotland Yard. "Just routine," Mitch was assured.

"It's not part of my routine," he objected at first. "What's this about?"

"They'll explain at the Yard, Mr. Emery," said the taller of his two attendants.

Belted into the backseat of the unmarked police car next to the shorter but bulkier of his escorts, who was redolent of cigarette smoke, Mitch felt abstracted from the reality of his capture, almost as if it were a theatrical happening staged for his amusement to break the boredom of his stay.

"Sure you have the right Mr. Emery?" he asked. "It's a common enough name. And I'm not in town to bomb Parliament."

Levity was misplaced with these spear-carriers. "We know who you are," the driver said. That was the end of the small talk.

At the Yard, a modern monolith, he was bustled through the lobby and up the elevator to the fifth floor, then down a long, well-lit corridor to a small, windowless room bare except for a table and half a dozen scattered chairs. At one end of the table sat a round metal tray with a full water pitcher and three glasses; at the opposite end was a tape recorder. There was nothing on the gray walls, or any torture devices visible, although, Mitch noted, it seemed the perfect— and no doubt soundproof—setting for a third-degree grilling. "Someone will be along shortly," the taller of his arresting officers said. Then they were gone, and he was left adrift in anxious indignation. So much for British civility.

More than an hour crawled by before the arrival of two higher-ups. The one in charge identified himself as Inspector Riggs and introduced his associate, a younger man in a better suit named Hornsby, who was an assistant to the deputy minister for the Home Office—an indication that the cause of his detainment was a matter of interest to the British government.

"Sorry to have kept you waiting, Mr. Emery," said Riggs, not sounding it. "Care for some water before we get going?"

"Going where?" Mitch asked more waspishly than he knew was in order. "I'd be grateful if you'd tell me why I've been dragged down here."

"Of course," said the inspector, taking one of the two chairs on the far side of the table from Mitch while his colleague leaned against the wall near the door. "You've been brought in—rather unceremoniously, I'm afraid—because of some information we have received concerning your employment activities. The reports, if true, involve irregular conduct which constitutes criminal behavior, both in Britain and on the continent. We've been alerted by Interpol and are looking into these reports with officials in Germany and Switzerland. This is a preliminary inquiry—there may well be others—so it's very much in your interest to be cooperative." Riggs folded his arms across his chest. "Otherwise, we may need to hold you in custody until things are clarified. Do I make myself clear, Mr. Emery?"

As a former law enforcement officer, Mitch knew the man was just going about his business.

"I haven't the faintest idea what you're talking about, inspector," he said with all the calm and as little anger as he could manage. "I'm in Britain gathering information for my firm about the discovery of a manuscript attributed to Beethoven that its owner has asked us to—"

"We know why you're here," said Riggs.

"Okay. And do you also know I'm a licensed attorney and a former prosecutor in the States and am well acquainted with Anglo-American legal procedures? I'm aware of my rights and the limits of your power to detain me without cause and force me to submit to—"

"There's no element of coercion here, Mr. Emery—not yet, at any rate," the inspector cut him off. "You're not obliged to answer, and you're entitled to engage a solicitor before responding if you so choose. We're merely putting you on informal notice that you've been reported as being involved in a number of—"

"Reported by whom, may I ask?"

"Just now, we're the ones putting the questions," Riggs countered coldly. "Let's begin with potentially the most serious of the reports. We're advised that Swiss officials want to question you in connection with the death of Mr. Ansel Erpf, one of their citizens, who was found dead on the beach of an Aegean island—"

"Yes, yes—I know about Mr. Erpf's death. I understood the Greek police were satisfied it was a suicide—he addressed a note to me to that effect before he—"

"So we understand. However, the Swiss police are concerned about the circumstances of his death and believe you may know something about it."

"That's preposterous—I barely knew the man—and he had a long history of emotional instability and drug use."

Inspector Riggs unfolded his arms and tilted his chair back. "Yet isn't it true, Mr. Emery, that you met with Mr. Erpf on several recent occasions, apparently in order to persuade him to stop challenging the authenticity of this *William Tell* Symphony your company plans to auction and to drop his family's claim to title of the manuscript—which he in fact discovered at the home of your client's deceased grandfather?"

Mitch shook his head. "I met with Ansel largely to determine just how much he really knew about the origin of the symphony, its authenticity, and its discovery—that's my job. He was resentful that our client removed the manuscript from Switzerland and was seeking to get it back, that's true. But I didn't meet with him to discourage his efforts. And even if I had tried to, what of it? That's business—there's nothing suspicious or illegal about what we—"

"It goes to motive for wanting him out of your company's way," the inspector shot back. "Furthermore, you made intrusive inquiries about Mr. Erpf's private life, even to the extent of obtaining a copy of his London psychiatrist's records—a serious breach of British law, in case you were unaware—possibly for the purpose of blackmailing Mr. Erpf into stopping his obstruction of your company's financial interests. The Swiss authorities, additionally, are considering charges against you, your firm, and your client for colluding in the unauthorized removal of a national treasure from their country."

Riggs's reference to the violation of Ansel's psychiatric files threw Mitch off balance. Who had ratted out C&W on that—someone on Johnny Winks's payroll with a grievance? Or the secretary in Dr. Kohler's office whom Johnny had bribed to get him Ansel's file and then perhaps been stricken with guilt and went to the police in return for a grant of immunity? But how could snooping in Kohler's files be pinned on Mitch if he only gave the verbal order from New York? Had somebody been tapping C&W's phones, possibly for months? Who would take such wholesale measures to blacken the Cubbage & Wakeham name in an attempt to foil the auction? The German or Swiss culture ministries, maybe partnering? Or had the manuscript become the frantic obsession of some mystical international cabal who saw in it the resurrection of a godlike genius dead for two centuries? Mitch struggled to order his thoughts as an adrenaline rush stoked him for the combat of cross-examination.

"The manuscript had *not* been designated a Swiss national treasure at the time our client removed it from Switzerland," he told the inspector, maintaining an even tone, "in the belief he had every right to do so. As to whether it's a treasure or not, that's precisely what I'm here investigating. Mr. Erpf may have known more about the manuscript than he allowed."

"Did that give you the right to invade Mr. Erpf's privacy," Riggs asked, "and break into his attending doctor's medical files regarding his mental condition?"

"I didn't break into anything," Mitch replied. "And any inquiries we made about Mr. Erpf's condition were addressed to his sister, who has been largely cooperative with my firm—or at least seemed to be." He began to sniff a frame-up unfolding. "If Mrs. Lenz is your informant in this matter, I think you're being used, inspector—"

"And why would that be, Mr. Emery?"

"Because she and her family want the manuscript—they've convinced themselves they have a legal right to it but can't enforce it through the courts, so they may have trumped up this nonsense about me and my company."

"I see," Riggs said and looked over at Hornsby.

"Let's pursue the German issue for a moment," the Home Office representative urged.

"We'll get to that presently," the inspector said, leaning forward, his elbows on the table and hands supporting his head. "We have further information that your firm at times engages the services of an intelligence organization notorious for its use of extralegal methods, including break-ins and bribery to obtain telephone and other records."

Mitch's stress level leaped; hypercaution was plainly in order. "How my firm conducts its business is a private matter," he said. "If you have specific evidence of our engaging in illicit procedures, you should present it to us for a formal response—but not before. I won't participate in a fishing expedition with you, inspector. My belief is that Scotland Yard is being intentionally misled—but why, I can't tell you, beyond guessing that there's unhappiness in some quarters because an American citizen and an Anglo-American auction house control a unique property that they feel rightfully belongs—allegedly for cultural and historical reasons—in other hands."

The inspector's brows arched.

"You're saying you're being victimized in some kind of international culture war?"

"So it would appear," Mitch replied.

"And do you deny that you and others from your firm attempted to bribe one of the members on the panel of Beethoven experts you enlisted so he would vote in favor of the genuineness of this newly found manuscript?"

The evidence of a frame-up by masters of deceit was accumulating. Mitch felt himself begin to flush. This thing could not be laughed off. "I don't know who's been feeding you such a story, inspector, but it's totally unfounded. Our authentication process—which I'm in charge of—is as incorruptible as humanly possible. I'll say no more—except to repeat that I think you good people are being played by some very bad eggs determined to get at us."

"I see," Riggs said again. "We've also been advised that your firm has conspired to rig the planned auction of this *William Tell* manuscript by organizing rival consortiums of bidders in order to jack up its eventual sales price." The inspector rose and began to pace the length of the table and back. "In fact, we're told that your own father-in-law, a highly regarded figure in our financial community, is assembling a group of potential investors for just such a purpose—and that your New York proprietor's wife has acted similarly among her friends who are benefactors of Lincoln Center in order to ensure a lively bidding war that will result in—"

Jesus, Mitch thought, whoever's behind this has tentacles everywhere. Who could know all this shit and feed it to the Brits in such a distorted, incriminating fashion? "Anyone can enter a bid at our auctions," he cut off his inquisitor. "The process is entirely aboveboard—the highest bidder wins—there's no possibility of collusion to fix the outcome."

"So you say," Riggs retorted, "but that wouldn't prevent friends of your firm from working together in groups to bid up the price of whatever you're auctioning and then, when it got steep enough, withdraw from the competition, having forced the winner to substantially overpay for the prize."

The gravity of these collective accusations began to weigh heavily on him now. "If any such phony bids are made at our auctions, they're entirely outside our power to control," Mitch insisted. "But any suggestion that Cubbage & Wakeham has ever attempted to engineer such an abuse of the auction process is a flagrant lie. You're being snookered, gentlemen."

Inspector Riggs stopped pacing and turned abruptly toward Mitch. "I appreciate your passionate loyalty to your company, Mr. Emery, but you need to be aware that if any or all of these reports are substantiated, not only may criminal charges be entered but the Home Office will be forced to lift your company's license to conduct business in the UK."

Their exchange had morphed from an informal inquiry into an adversarial proceeding. Mitch recognized this and shifted gears. "In that event," he said, "I'd like to telephone Mr. Wakeham to arrange for a solicitor before I say another word—and also to speak with people at the US Embassy because I feel there may be international repercussions to whatever is going on here. Is there a place here I can have those conversations in private?"

"We've anticipated your concerns, of course," Hornsby now spoke up, "and taken the liberty of trying to apprise Mr. Wakeham of the situation. Unfortunately, his office tells us he's left for a hunting party at a Scottish estate and is unreachable until his return on Tuesday. We've also learned that your father-in-law is traveling in China at the moment, but perhaps you or your wife knows his itinerary so he might arrange for your legal representation. Otherwise, if you know a solicitor here who's available to represent you, by all means try to reach him—or the Home Office will arrange for a counselor from our legal aid service. As for reaching someone at the US Embassy just now, good luck—they're unlikely to view this matter as an emergency affecting your country's vital interests, so you may not hear back until sometime next week."

Smarmy bastard. Mitch rifled his brain for a London solicitor he knew to be competent enough to come to his rescue; no name surfaced. "And meanwhile?" he asked warily.

"If you're willing to give us a statement directly, I'll start the tape recorder," said Riggs, "and then you can be released, provided you remain in London until further notice. We'd require that you wear an electronic tracking device so we can monitor your movements because, nonsensical as it may sound to you, Mr. Emery, we have to regard you as a flight risk."

"And if I decline to make a statement?"

The inspector shrugged. "I'm afraid you'll have to remain our guest until you can enlist a solicitor. We have holding rooms upstairs—we don't call them cells because they come with a bed, a lavatory, a telephone, a TV, and room service dining, though I'm told the food isn't gourmet quality. The door is bolted on the outside, and your phone will be monitored. No incoming calls allowed, unfortunately—it's not a hotel."

Better to keep a stiff upper lip for the moment, Mitch told himself, than carry on. "Do you have a room with a view?" he cracked.

CLARA WAS ALARMED, ENRAGED, AND FRUSTRATED all at once when he phoned and advised her of his temporary status as a jailbird. What made it worse was that Mitch could not amplify the charges against him, other than saying that they were ridiculous. "The Yard is listening in, hon—I'll fill you in once I'm sprung. Meanwhile, try to locate your father and get hold of Harry wherever he's weekending—Gordy will probably know—and see if either of them can chase down a decent London lawyer for me ASAP."

"Will do," she said gamely, fighting back her shock. "Meanwhile, ask them to give you an extra blanket. And I won't tell a soul you were in the clink until you're out—it'll make a great story over cocktails. I love you, sweetie—and we'll get through this just fine."

Her pluckiness, rather than going to pieces, buoyed him for the two nights and one full day he remained in Scotland Yard's custody. The very possibility, however remote, of his long-term removal from society numbed and chilled him at first. The prospect, given his suddenly altered circumstances, could not be dismissed altogether; life shat on a lot of people who did not deserve it even as it allowed so many sleazy sorts to make off with their ill-got prizes. And he had no appetite for martyrdom, which struck him as just a delusional form of masochism. Surely Harry and Sedge would not let him be put down as a sacrificial lamb to spare their supercilious asses—would they? Well, Clara, anyway, would make her father call in every chit at his disposal to save his son-in-law from claustrophobic madness—right?

Amid his dark ruminations, he tried in vain to unpuzzle who on earth had access to all the twisted information against him that the British police had been given. Inspector Riggs had brought up matters that Mitch supposed only top C&W management and its most trusted hires knew about. Was there a mole on the Cubbage & Wakeham premises, either in New York or in London? Could Johnny Winks be a double agent? Did his operatives feed confidential dirt to Interpol on a retainer basis? And who was trying so methodically to hang them out to dry? None of it parsed.

He turned on TV every now and then but was too distracted to follow much of it except the ever-reliable toilet humor. His mind flitted from subject to subject without settling in any one spot for long. Should he apply for divine intervention to help him out of this dreadful jam? No, the Almighty would see right through his timely discovery of faith and assign him to eternal residence in purgatory for his disingenuous appeal. If the fates liberated him, should he abandon the auction house and its capricious impresario at the first opportunity for a less problematic workplace? Perhaps a Wall Street law firm and go for the gusto of big bucks and power trips that came with a partnership. But he had been freighted with social conscience for too long to turn himself into a steward for the lords of lucre driven by the monomania the job demanded. No, a small-city or suburban firm would probably be better, allowing him to enjoy a more diverse, less compulsive workweek.

What of Clara's career, though? They'd have to settle in or near a college town, which might be good—maybe Ithaca or Charlottesville or their like. Nice family environment—and—and yes, it was time for him to weigh seriously Clara's recent, tentative suggestion that they consider adoption. His sperm testing had checked out normal, her internal plumbing appeared to be in good working order, and yet, still *nada*. Their other options—hormone therapy, artificial insemination, in vitro fertilization, surrogate pregnancy—all seemed, while no doubt sensible alternatives to going childless, somehow distasteful. But since they weren't getting any younger, as Clara reminded him, the subject needed to be resolved. Mentally frazzled at last, he slept, woke, slept, woke…

A little after eleven on the second morning of his involuntary seclusion—by which time he had read the Sunday papers, kindly delivered with his breakfast of porridge and kippers—a guard knocked on Mitch's door to announce that his solicitor was awaiting him in a conference room at the end of the corridor. Good news, finally. But who *was* his solicitor and who had enlisted him? No incoming calls had been allowed. He combed his hair for the meeting.

Dennis Drummond, QC, whose card said his chambers were at Lincoln's Inn Fields, was a tall, lantern-jawed, sixtyish gentleman wearing, Mitch guessed, bespoke Gieves & Hawkes pinstripes. He had thinning silver hair, crooked teeth, an elegant attaché case, and no affect whatever. "I was phoned in the midst of the night," he said, limply taking Mitch's extended hand, "by a partner at my firm who's on close terms with your esteemed father-in-law, and your problem was explained to me. I had to wait till morning to reach the right people in the Home Office—they don't much care to be roused on the weekend. But it's all arranged—or will be within the hour. You're to be released on self-recognizance and my vouching that you'll remain in the city while we try to sort this thing out. I suggest we hold off on further conversation until we've left the Yard—the walls have ears, they say, probably with good reason."

Other than Mitch's voicing abundant gratitude for the gent's speed and efficiency in restoring him to freedom, the two said little on the taxi ride to the cavernous Tate Gallery Annex, the converted power station on the south bank of the Thames, where they found a river-view table in the sleek dining hall. "I don't know what to make of all this," Mitch began after their order was taken. "How the Yard got hold of these so-called reports about the way we've been conducting our authentication process—and the rest of it—is beyond me. At any rate, most of it is a gross distortion, even when there's a grain of truth at the bottom of—"

"I'm fully aware of that," the solicitor assured him.

Mitch was surprised. Drummond had said he was thrown into the breach in the middle of the previous night—that would have made him an exceedingly quick learner. "How so?"

"Because I'm the one who passed on the tawdry information to the authorities."

Something very weird was going on here. "You did—what, exactly?"

"You'll have to forgive me, Mr. Emery. I'm afraid I've misrepresented myself to an extent." The solicitor took a sip from his water glass and patted his lips dry. "You see, none of my firm's partners are on close terms with your father-in-law, but it was a safe assumption on my part that in your distress you would be reaching out to him for legal assistance. Before I contacted our friends at the Home Office and presented myself at the Yard, one of my aides inquired at Unilever and learned that Mr. Hoitsma was abroad, so I was able to proceed with my not-entirely-innocent mission—which, of course, included your rescue."

By this point Mitch was thoroughly confused by what the stranger across from him was saying. It took him only a few moments to explain everything. Among his clients, Drummond related, was a very large Swiss bank that called upon his services from time to time. In this instance, the bank had come into possession of an electronic file revealing the procedures and machinations engaged in by Cubbage & Wakeham while authenticating the lately found *William Tell* Symphony—"and it was passed on to the Private Banking department, which, in turn, thought it might be of interest to one of its wealthiest clients, an Asian gentleman with a quite sizable numbered account in the Zurich office—"

"Hold on—there is no such electronic file," Mitch objected. "I'd be the only person to create and maintain one, and we have no need of it. Most of what we do is by oral exchanges—it's a small shop—there's no written record. So I can't accept what you're—"

"I'm merely telling you what I was told, Mr. Emery," Drummond replied laconically. "May I go on, or would you prefer to remain in the dark?"

"Sorry—let's hear it all."

The bank's Asian client, who Drummond said operated out of Hong Kong and had made his fortune legitimately—"or so I've been advised"—was a fanatic music lover, and the thought of becoming the owner and disseminator of a suddenly unearthed Beethoven symphony had captivated his imagination. But he was also passionately averse to exposing himself during a public auction and a bidding war that might get out of hand, whereas he was more than eager to make a fabulous preemptive offer privately to purchase the *Tell* manuscript outright.

"I don't buy the story so far—the part about our nonexistent electronic file," said Mitch, "but if this Hong Kong fat cat wanted to make a preemptive offer, why hasn't he done so—why antagonize my company by trying to embarrass it with the British police by producing these scurrilous reports that he presumably knows are largely fabricated?"

Drummond nodded.

"Yes, I asked the same question when I was given this material last week and told to have a junior associate present it to Scotland Yard. The answer seems to be inscrutably Asian—though I fear that's a politically incorrect comment to make nowadays." The Hong Kong zillionaire had made several surreptitious approaches to people connected to C&W—"To your wife, actually"—to determine whether the manuscript was authentic and if the auction house would be open to a preemptive offer.

"My wife?" Mitch asked. "Impossible—she'd surely have told me—"

"I'm afraid I can't help you on that score. All I've been told is that these approaches were rebuffed—by Mrs. Emery, as I understand it—and so the Swiss bank's Asian client concluded that your firm and the manuscript's owner were sufficiently greedy to reject any buyout offer in the hope that the auction would yield them a considerably higher reward."

Mitch was baffled. Had Clara really been approached and, for some reason, not told him?

"Well, some Germans approached us more or less in that fashion," he acknowledged, "but I don't know of any Asian gentleman with deep pockets who came to us—"

"You weren't supposed to know," Drummond advised. Having been stymied in his earlier indirect methods, the Asian Croesus bitten by the Beethoven bug opted for coercion as the only effective tactic to gain C&W's undivided attention.

"It may not have been the most gentlemanly approach," said the lawyer, "but his prior success in financial ventures strengthened his resolve. And so I had an extensive memo prepared by our office drawing upon the revelations in the electronic file the bank gave us—which you say doesn't exist—of your company's dubious behind-the-scenes activities and sent it by courier to the Home Office, which promptly passed it on to Scotland Yard for investigation—and thus your compromised condition at the moment."

"But you know much of what you passed on in this memo are lies and distortions?"

"Exactly. And they've had the desired effect, as you've seen." But if C&W and Jake Hassler were now open to the preemptive offer the Swiss bank's secret client was prepared to make for the *Tell* manuscript, Drummond was ready to advise the Home Office that the bank had learned, much to its embarrassment, that the information handed over to the Yard had been badly garbled as an act of reprisal by unnamed individuals enraged because the purported Beethoven manuscript had wound up in American hands. "In short, the dogs will be called off you and your firm the moment a deal is struck with our Hong Kong friend," Drummond wound up. "So I recommend you hear the terms of his offer."

Mitch was dumbfounded by the temerity of the misguided plot. "I don't believe this."

"Nevertheless," said the solicitor, who drew an envelope from his inside breast pocket and consulted the numbers jotted on its front. Payments were to be made of $20 million to Jake Hassler, $10 million to C&W, and $5 million to Mitch personally, all to be deposited in secret accounts at the Swiss bank—"which I presume will also receive a considerable fee on the side for facilitating the sale," Drummond inserted—so the payoffs from the transaction could escape IRS scrutiny. The Hong Kong plutocrat promised to establish a nonprofit foundation to protect the manuscript, see to its being edited and scored in keeping with the highest artistic and academic standards, and then presented in a worldwide tour by a specially assembled multinational orchestra. After which, recordings of the symphony would be released in a global marketing blitz, with the net income from the tour, the recorded version, online downloads, and all future performing rights to be donated to fighting famine in Africa, Doctors Without Borders, and other impeccably humanitarian causes.

"Well, he's thought everything through," Mitch conceded. "But suppose our people think the offer is too low? There's no way of knowing how much the manuscript would sell for at auction, given all the publicity already stirred up—and that our company plans to intensify."

"I've been told to say that the bank's client won't pay a farthing more than I've stated."

Their lunches arrived, but Mitch was too distracted to do more than pick at it. "Well, this is all very fascinating—but insanely conceived. Your bank's Hong Kong customer is a psychopath, if you don't mind my saying so," he told Drummond. "And what's to stop me from telling Scotland Yard everything you've just told me? You'll deny it all, I suppose—"

"Certainly—I was summoned for my services, remember? I'm a QC of unimpeachable standing—and you're a desperate man who'll make up any story that he thinks can get him off the hook, and your company will be seen as a pack of desperados."

Mitch smiled wryly at the conniving lawyer. "Whatever happened to British honor?"

"I wonder myself sometimes. Shocking what we're called on to do for clients nowadays."

Mitch agreed to phone Harry Cubbage straightaway and advise him of the blunderbuss offer. "It's a big decision, as I'm sure the bank you represent—and its overzealous client—will understand," he told the solicitor. "You'll have to give us a few days to ponder the matter, but I can assure you there's no way our company or I—and Mr. Hassler, in all likelihood—would accept payment deposited in a Swiss bank account. It's a blatant form of tax evasion that Switzerland encourages foreign citizens to practice against their own countries' interests —and the Swiss ought to be shamed into banning it or shunned as a nation of international thieves."

Drummond eyed him closely, then began busily attacking the turbot on his plate. "I commend your moral ardor," he said. "Naturally, your people and you are free to accept our buyer's price and pay the resulting taxes in full—the Swiss account option is simply a courtesy offer."

"And what if we don't accept your buyer's price?"

"Then you'll need to arrange for legal representation of your own," said the solicitor, "to fend off whatever charges Scotland Yard chooses to pursue against you and your firm. And I wouldn't count on an early return to America if I were you." When Drummond dropped him off at his hotel, he said, "Pleasant meeting you, Mr. Emery. No need to call me—I'll be in touch."

WHEN MITCH PHONED HIM WITH THE NEWS that could well doom his company, Harry wanted no part of the deal being offered by their depraved Asian suitor through his equally shameless Swiss bank and its contemptible

London solicitor. He was dismayed that their stormtrooper tactics seemed to have co-opted Scotland Yard but even more unnerved by all the internal information about C&W's handling of the *Tell* manuscript that had been fed, in largely corrupted form, to British authorities. "Who the hell else has access to all our little skull sessions?" Harry asked. "There's only you, me, and Gordy. Our support people know only pieces of it—"

"I haven't a clue," said Mitch.

Harry told him to sit tight while he arranged for a top-flight solicitor to take charge of his dealings with Scotland Yard. A moment later, Mitch phoned Clara and briefed her on the sticky situation. And if Scotland Yard was listening in, so much the better, he calculated—it would only add substance to what he had told them: his interrogators were being duped into harassing C&W and threatening criminal sanctions.

Clara listened raptly, emitting an occasional cry of disbelief. "How could these people know all that and twist it against us?" she burst out. "Someone's a traitor, for sure."

"Seems like that," he said and then related the bank's claim that it had somehow come into possession of an alleged electronic file of C&W's confidential dealings and records in the *Tell* matter. Instead of dismissing the story as a transparent lie, Clara reacted with sudden silence. "Sweetheart—are you okay?" he asked.

Her mind had frozen, locked on to the one time she had let her laptop out of her sight. That snake Aurelio! She remembered clearly now his studied detachment when she had first proposed changing her doctoral dissertation topic and ardently explained to him the special insider vantage point she enjoyed as the *Tell* authentication process was unfolding. It might be the biggest event in the classical music world in ages, she had suggested to arouse his interest. As her thesis adviser, the professor had kept resisting the idea and claiming too little was known yet about the legitimacy and merits of the newfound work. But he had nevertheless kept asking her to apprise him of developments, even suggesting that it would benefit her request to change her thesis topic if she could produce a sampling of *Tell*'s text for the music department's appraisal. They were all subtle but in retrospect pointed hints that Mark Aurelio was trying to use her and the Beethoven bombshell to impress his departmental colleagues who were to decide shortly whether to grant him tenure. And she had handed it all to him on a silver platter. And he had apparently passed it on somehow to the people now victimizing Mitch and C&W.

"God in heaven!" she cried. "What an idiot I am! This is all my goddam fault, Mitch—I know just what happened. I could shoot myself for being so thoughtless—"

"What on earth are you talking about?"

"*I'm* the traitor—I've been keeping notes on my laptop—for the dissertation, if they allow me to do it. I've summarized everything I've seen and heard at your office, everything you've told me about what's been going on—how else could I reconstruct a narrative for my thesis? And of course none of it was supposed to be shared with outsiders until well after the manuscript was auctioned. I guess I didn't mention it because I of course intended to show you the whole finished text so you could edit out anything that might prove embarrassing to C&W—"

Mitch was stunned by her confession. "You made a record of *everything* I shared with you? That was all highly proprietary information, Clara—you were told it in confidence—"

"I know, I know," she said, voice quavering, "but I wasn't going to share it with anyone until everything was done and settled. It was just supposed to be raw material for me to draw on when I got to the writing stage. And I always guard my laptop with my life if I ever take it out of the house—like for making notes at the library—"

"So?"

"I know exactly what happened—and I'm mortified that I could have been so fucking careless!"

She explained how she had brought the laptop with her to make notes at the Columbia Library after her appointment three weeks earlier with Professor Aurelio. But first she had to add some material and make some other changes he had requested to strengthen her memo to the departmental committee asking her to change her thesis topic to the *Tell* discovery. Aurelio had provided her with a nearby vacant office to work in, and like a fool, she had left her laptop running while she went out to grab lunch and take a short walk. When she got back, the office she was working in was locked—the departmental secretary told her that Aurelio had passed by, noticed the laptop open and running, and as a security measure, asked her to lock the door till Clara returned.

"That creep must have gone in, locked the door while he was in there, searched my files, and found the one I titled 'Ludwig'—clever, right?—and opened it—and found all my notes on C&W and the *Tell*. He must have scanned it fast and sent the whole file as an attachment to someone—someone who used it to get you and C&W into trouble with the Brits." Someone, she suddenly realized, whom Aurelio must have alerted earlier about her special involvement with the Beethoven find, probably someone or some organized group with money on its mind and menace it was not hesitant to use—someone who had tried to reach out to her. Which would almost certainly explain her scary encounters while jogging along the river and around the park reservoir—episodes she had never mentioned to Mitch out of fear he would have promptly ended her involvement in the seductive adventure to insulate her from further danger.

"But how—and why? How would it help Aurelio?" Mitch asked.

"I'm not sure. Maybe a money kickback for the information he stole from me, or to help his professional advancement—he's up for tenure," she said. "I always thought there was something slippery about him. Only I don't see how I can confront him without risking his wrath, unless I have some firm evidence against the bastard. But I'm sure that's how it happened. God, I'm such a fool. Will you ever forgive me?"

Mitch tried to rein in his chagrin. Clara fully realized her spacey lapse of vigilance. Now was the time for damage control, not berating his cherished partner.

"Okay, hon—what's done is done. Stay close to the phone."

With his cell phone, he reached Johnny Winks at his for-emergencies-only number. On hearing the whole story, including the part about his potential exposure to the authorities, Johnny was riled. "This could put me the fuck out of business, Mitchell, if not in some gulag—you need to give the missus a nasty spanking." Having vented, he recognized the urgent need for a punishing counter-move. "I'll put my American friends right on it—we've got a world-class hacker on board," Johnny said. "But I need this Aurelio bloke's email address quick as hell."

Clara gave Mitch her thesis adviser's contact information, transmitted seconds later to Winks, and the rest unfolded with blazing speed. By Tuesday afternoon, the retaliatory blow was struck against the Swiss bank and its Hong Kong client.

Johnny's star US hacker broke into Professor Aurelio's "Sent Mail" file and, after reviewing 147 outgoing messages in the ten-day period following Clara's last visit to his office, discovered that her strong suspicions were not misplaced. He had forwarded her entire "Ludwig" file to the office of Larry Aurelio, his brother, who proved to be the manager of the Montclair, NJ, branch office of the brokerage firm of Browning & Bryant, lately acquired by Swiss banking leviathan Helvetica Reliance. Mark's covering email message to his brother read:

Hope this may be of additional use to your parent company in the musical matter previously called to your attention. The material was generated by a student whose knowledge of the subject I believe to be unimpeachable. Info should be of interest to the party pursuing this matter. Maybe it will help get you a leg up in the organization, maybe even a piece of the action. Love, big bro Marco.

"Our guess is that the broker brother forwarded the file to Helvetica's private banking department," Johnny told Mitch, "giving the bank, its acquisitive Asian client, and your Mr. Drummond all the ammo they needed to come after you. Nice bit of horseplay. But that's over."

Mitch, still officially restricted to his hotel room, asked, "How come?"

"I phoned the head of private banking at Helvetica Reliance," Johnny said, "and told him who I was—our existence is no secret to the bank's security people— and that unless they backed off this power play, destroyed the file they stole from you, confessed to Scotland Yard they had passed along corrupted intelligence, and told Mr. Got Rocks in Hong Kong to forget about it, I would promptly reveal to the American, British, French, and German governments the names of one hundred of their citizens who hold secret accounts at the bank—and if it wasn't done in two days, we'd turn over another hundred and keep on going. Probably cause a run on their private accounts and lose them billions in deposits."

"But how the hell did you get hold of the names of their secret account holders?"

"I didn't," Johnny said. "But I'm known far and wide as one nasty piece of work, so the bank can't take the chance that I'm bullshitting."

Because of the underhanded manner in which C&W got the goods on Mark Aurelio—and in light of its need to prevent Clara's potentially embarrassing "Ludwig" file from being introduced into evidence—no legal action could be taken against the Columbia professor. But the day after Mitch got home, Clara phoned Mac Quarles to congratulate him on his recent elevation to director of the Curtis Institute of Music. Then, as artfully as possible, she asked if he happened to be on close terms with any of the heavy hitters on the Columbia music department faculty. "I am indeed, Miss Clara," Mac said with his usual gallantry. "My good ol' Amherst roommate Al Yates is finishing a five-year sentence as departmental chairman there this spring."

"Brilliant. Now I have another question if you don't mind. Can unethical conduct be held against an associate professor who's coming up for a vote on tenure?"

"Absolutely," Mac told her. "Why? Somebody hittin' on you up there, Clara?"

"You might say—but I'm in an awkward spot to blow the whistle on him." And she told him the whole sordid story.

"Fear not, dear lady," Mac said. "I'll pass the word."

A week later she received a terse email from Mark Aurelio, advising her that he had accepted a tenured full professorship in Iowa State's Department of Fine Arts to begin that fall. Her doctoral thesis would be supervised "effective immediately" by the incoming music departmental chair. "The doctoral committee, you'll be happy to learn," he added, "has approved your change of topic—good luck with it."

{15}

B y the time Inspector Riggs had dropped by Mitch's hotel room to apologize for the "bit of a cock-up" over C&W's conduct in the *Tell* matter and tell him he was free to leave the country, he had the Nina #2 documents back from the Veritas forensics laboratory, along with their judgment that the items were more than likely authentic. The paper and ink dated from the first decades of the nineteenth century, and the same hand had surely composed the two Nina letters.

Johnny Winks and his people, however, had run into trouble trying to find official records that might corroborate either the dispatch or receipt of Nina's death notice that Jake Hassler had lately produced. At the Zurich Registry, the resident bureaucrats said that no notice of births, marriages, deaths, or commercial transactions was taken if they occurred outside of the canton, no matter that they involved citizens of that jurisdiction. That left only the clerk's office in Mittendrinnen on the banks of the Danube, where the death notice seemed to have originated. But after canvasing the Austrian government's agencies and archives, they could not discover any extant village by that name or any record of there ever having been one.

"The only possibility we've come up with," Johnny reported to Mitch on the phone after his agents' failed search, "is that such a place might have existed before the Danube flooded pretty badly in the early 1830s. There's a couple of newspaper references to the waters having swept away three small riverfront settlements, but no community names were listed. So probably no records survived the flood." It was just conceivable, though, he said, that the middle one of the three little settlements had been known locally as Mittendrinnen.

The untraceability of Nina's Austrian death notice left Mitch irritable. Here was the chance for a real clincher, but the best his crack investigator could manage was no better than a remote possibility. "But aren't the Veritas findings conclusive enough for you, sweetie?" Clara had pressed him after his flight home and ardent embrace of forgiveness for her Aurelio blunder.

"Nope," he said. "Just because they're made of authentically old materials doesn't prove that they're what they seem. They could still be phony—and so could Nina's first letter—and the archduke's letter and Nägeli's—all painstaking, beautifully executed inventions."

Why was he being so damn obstinate? Clara kept asking herself as she shopped along Broadway the next morning. And why did she so want the whole business resolved in a positive way? Nobody could be sure, until the music was finally and properly performed, that it constituted superior artistry, let alone attained the sublime heights of Beethoven's best work, but what a lovely consummation it would be! Was she being, as Mitch more than hinted, a fuzzy-headed romantic about it all? Doubtless, his detached approach was far more sensible and, well, essential where the auction house was concerned.

Her mind skipped about until it focused on the two suicides that had reportedly occurred nearly two centuries apart and had lately become woven into the *Tell* story—Nina Hassler's and Ansel Erpf's. If not for the both of them, Nina as its preserver and Ansel as its recoverer, there would be no *Tell* symphony vexing them now. How sad that the both of them had sunk to a point in their lives where nothing mattered more than putting an end to their misery. Ansel's case struck her as the more poignant, if only for proving that you could be blessed with all of life's material advantages and still wind up a soul bereft. It made her quadruply grateful for the happiness she had found with Mitch—even if no child ever came to further enrich their shared *joie de vivre*.

Finally, she found herself reflecting on Marie Hassler's pathetic life. Did she deserve pity or contempt for remaining within a household that treated her so shabbily? Or might it all really be, as Mitch feared, an invention from top to bottom, and there was no Marie Hassler—and Nina Hassler was no more than a duly recorded name that somebody had decided to exploit. But why? The most plausible answer was the one she had once broached to Mitch—to give the *Tell* discovery a context. She circled back to the Nina-Marie gravestone story. Mitch, incorrigible skeptic that he was, might be right: it was all too neatly packaged. Then all at once she knew what had to be done to validate or finally demolish his doubts. If you could forge documents like Nina #1 and #2, why not a gravestone?

"Call Johnny Winks," she told Mitch excitedly over her cellphone, "and have him take a closer look at the Nina-Marie headstone."

"Why, hon?"

"Because maybe there's nobody buried under it—and never was—which would lend weight to your qualms about this whole thing. Maybe whoever put together the whole *Tell* scam, if that's what it is, was equally capable of installing a make-believe gravestone in the Hassler plot to clinch the whole story."

There was a pause on the other end, then a snicker. "Far out," Mitch said. "Let's go for it—and if it's a dud, we can blame it on you."

He passed on the brainstorm to Johnny and urged him to take along a bottle of detergent and a rag when he revisited the Hassler family cemetery plot and to phone him directly from the gravesite, assuming there was nobody around to object to the minor sacrilege.

"The headstone looks the same as it did to me the last time," Johnny told him from the cemetery the next day. "Old—very old."

"Is the stone anchored solidly in the ground?" Mitch asked. "Give it a little nudge."

"I—that's really not my—hmmm, there is a bit of give there, now that you mention it. But then we've had quite a lot of rain here recently."

"Try the other headstones in the area—especially the older ones—nineteenth century or before—and see if they're the same way."

None of the other older, nearby headstones Johnny pushed against were comparably unstable. And when he briskly applied the detergent to the surface of the Nina-Marie stone, the grime gradually yielded. Not so with the next dozen headstones of comparable vintage when he rubbed them with the cleaning fluid. "Maybe our stone isn't as old as it looks," Winks said. "Maybe we need to find a stonemason to examine it closely."

It took three days to find one willing, even for the generous fee offered, to examine the stone and to poke about the gravesite. "He says he doubts it's been in the ground a hundred and twenty-five years," Winks advised Mitch. "More like a hundred and twenty-five days."

"And the stone itself?"

"The stone itself is old—stones tend to be—but there are signs the surface area with the inscription has been ground down and touched up—and the lettering's possibly been redone and sanded to look old."

"Do you mean it could be a reused old gravestone that someone's fixed up?"

"Could be."

"Yes!" Mitch exulted, telling himself God bless Clara's brains. "Now all we need is a disinterment to see if anyone's under there."

A howl came over the phone. "And how do you propose we do that?"

"Go to the cemetery office. Say it's urgent. Tell them what we suspect."

"They'll tell me to—what's your saying?—go fly a kite. It's hallowed ground, Yank—and I'm not up for impersonating the fuzz on an official grave-opening expedition."

"Then do it without asking. Just bring along a couple of your huskier recruits with long-handle shovels—shouldn't take them longer than an hour or so."

"Mitchell, really now! First Dr. Kohler's office files, now this. Is nothing sacred?"

"Look who's asking," Mitch said with a laugh. "I guess it'll have to be done after dark—and very quietly. When's the next moonless night?"

Winks gave a grunt. "I'll check. And what precisely is it we're to look for?"

"A coffin, to begin with—or some recognizable fragment thereof. It's doubtful there'd be much in the way of remains, but some artifact—anything at all—would help. A hank of hair, a fragment of bone, a piece of a dress, jewelry, a keepsake of any sort. And take photos, so they can't nail you for grave-robbing—only breaking and entering. I used to be a prosecutor."

"You're most considerate, Mitchell."

During the weeklong wait for the moon to wane, Mitch was a study in suspended animation. Much as he would have preferred a fairy-tale ending to the story to gratify Clara and fill the C&W coffers, he had not been hired to validate dreams. He was a certified doubter by profession. And the more fantastic the dream, the more pressing his need to track down every loose end and shed every clinging suspicion. He pounded away for hours on the treadmill in their apartment, his heated brain brimming with possibilities. If only Johnny's crew could unearth a sarcophagus with a well-wrapped Marie mummy inside, it would go far to confirm the whole *Tell* saga, but a few splinters from a casket or shards of a kneecap might serve almost as well. Finding nothing whatever, though, would trigger a red alert and vindicate his hesitancy to buy into the symphony, lock, stock, and timpani.

The arrival of the Nina #2 material had gladdened Harry, but prudence dictated postponing jubilation until the Veritas lab had reported its findings. With these in hand now, Mitch's boss was ready to firm up the tentative auction date for the *Tell* manuscript and step up the surrounding publicity.

"I'm thinking it's time for you to climb down from the fence," Harry told him, "and put your seal of approval on our little gem."

Mitch felt trapped. Until Johnny's diggers completed their ghoulish assignment, no matter what it disclosed or failed to, thereby justifying the trouble and expense of the graveyard transgression, he did not want to reveal it to Harry for fear of being thought extravagant with the firm's money and indecisive about committing to the Beethoven validation. But even more, he told himself, he was dedicated to sparing the firm from rashly allowing itself to fall victim of a spectacular hoax. "I'd like to hold up for a few more days," he said.

"We have to get this show on the road, pal," Harry ruled. "You've got five days.

That afternoon, the CEO of Syzygy Studios, a small, freewheeling record company headquartered in San Rafael, California, called Harry with a preemptive bid of $15 million for the *Tell*, unseen and unheard. "It's a big risk for us," Syzygy's honcho said, "but we can't afford to get into the auction game— and you may not get a better offer."

C&W's deal with Jake Hassler obliged the firm to bring the offer to him. Owen Whittaker advised his client that the buyout would net him around $7 million, no small fortune for a hardware department supervisor at a lumberyard in outermost New Jersey. "Okay," Jake said.

"We don't think so," said Harry, whose firm stood to pocket about $2 million after expenses if it cancelled the auction and grabbed the Syzygy offer. "If a small outfit like this is willing to pay up that kind of money, our auction could bring in four or five times that much—possibly more, though nothing's sure. There's a lot of buzz out there, from what we hear."

Whittaker made Harry agree to a million-dollar guarantee to get Jake to hold his horses.

Three nights later, with Harry's deadline to Mitch looming, a cloud-shrouded moon rose over Lake Zurich while at dusk in Manhattan the Emerys holed up in their apartment, draining a bottle of Chablis while listening to Debussy and anxiously waiting for Johnny Winks to phone.

The ring came shortly before ten New York time, nearly jolting the groggy couple off their loveseat.

"*Les flics* nearly nabbed us at the end," Johnny reported, still short of breath. "And?"

"We dug down ten feet—helluva messy business. Our guys were also scared shitless."

"*And?*"

"*Nada*, Mitch—not a blessed thing down there—just dirt."

♪.

HARRY'S REACTION TO THE NEWS of the empty Nina-Marie gravesite was not quite what Mitch had expected. Far from commending Mitch for assigning Johnny Winks's crew to the daring task—albeit at double the usual hourly rate due to the risk factor—C&W's edgy chief executive was testy about it.

To begin with, Harry thought he should have been consulted before Mitch authorized the substantial outlay, especially since the *Tell* project was already running way over budget. Mitch countered that it was imprudent for the company to stint on this high-stakes venture, and up until the disinterment initiative, Harry had agreed. "But we've got to cap the spending somewhere sometime," he berated his chief of authentication. "Enough's enough."

"I didn't think so," Mitch said. "I thought it was important—and it is."

"Check with me first from now on, like it or not. And as for the vital importance of this empty grave business, I think you're being a wuss. Your caution is commendable, but you're letting it get out of hand. You're finding rattlesnakes under every pebble. Look, that tombstone was probably secondhand when the Hasslers had it re-engraved—they probably did it on the cheap, ordering an old stone ground down for the fresh inscription. And I don't see anything surprising about the grime coming off when the stone was cleaned with a strong detergent." As to when the stone was installed, Harry said, it was a matter of supposition—the stonemason Johnny brought in was making a calculated guess, and he could be wrong. As to the empty gravesite—maybe the Hassler family diarist got it wrong, possibly on purpose. Maybe they didn't bury Marie in the Hassler plot—"maybe they just put up the new stone as a half-assed memorial to the disowned mother and her bastard daughter they'd crapped on all those years and dumped poor Marie's body elsewhere."

"That's a lot of maybes," Mitch objected. "I think we've got a serious problem here."

"I want to get on with this thing. The bidders start coming in here in two weeks to inspect the manuscript—we can't tell them to wait up because we're still trying to figure it all out."

"Why not?"

"It kills the momentum—it raises too many doubts."

"Then maybe we should have waited before announcing our expert panel's findings and scheduling the auction."

"That was my call, Mitch—I run this show, and I thought it was the right one. You've done a fabulous job up to now—don't screw it up at the end by turning into a Nervous Nellie."

"You *pay* me to be a Nervous Nellie."

"Now I'm paying you to back off and enjoy this historic occasion. We've got more than enough evidence to bring the manuscript to the marketplace in complete good faith."

"I don't think so—not yet. There are still too many unanswered questions."

"Because they're unanswerable," Harry said, crossing his arms. "Okay, you're on record as abstaining—and off the hook. But don't expect any medals for it."

If insubordination was not in Mitch's nature, neither was cowardice under fire. Within the hour, Mitch covertly directed Winks to have a rubbing made of the inscription on the Nina-Marie headstone and shown to every stonemason within a hundred kilometers of Zurich to see if any of them had carved it and could identify who had ordered it. "And *mach schnell, bitte.*"

That evening after work, Mitch shared his concern with Clara. "I think Harry's losing his grip over this thing—the enormity of it may just be overwhelming him. Or maybe plain old greed has taken charge of his soul—if he had a soul."

"Is it remotely possible," his devoted devil's advocate asked him, "that you just don't like being called a wuss—and by a Harvard bed-wetter, at that?"

"Childish of me, I know," he conceded. "But I'd just as soon risk his scorn in order to save his firm, and if he doesn't thank me for it, *tant pis.* You and I will survive quite nicely."

The wussification of Mitchell Emery ended with the arrival of the Saturday morning *Times.* As she leafed through the mainsheet while Mitch was reading the business section, Clara paused to dwell as usual on the obituary page—supporting his claim she was an incipient necrophiliac—and let out a pained cry. "Emil's gone," she said. "That didn't take long. Poor Hilde."

"God," said Mitch, pained at the news. First Ansel, now Reinsdorf. He wondered if Emil had met his Maker half as defiantly as his beloved Beethoven reputedly had. "I liked him—in a weird way. Any picture?"

"Yes—and the obituary runs a whole column." She began to scan it. "Uh-oh—"

"What?"

"Emil forgot to mention something to you."

Mitch looked blank a moment. "What—he was a transvestite?"

306

"See for yourself." She handed him the paper.

The photograph was an old one, showing the deceased in dated dark-framed glasses that gave him a decidedly owlish demeanor. The article began:

> BERLIN—Emil N. Reinsdorf, widely regarded as among the world's foremost authorities on Ludwig van Beethoven, died at his home here on Jan. 27 at the age of 64. He had recently fulfilled a controversial assignment as one of five scholars who authenticated the lately discovered "William Tell" Symphony as a composition by Beethoven. Its manuscript is due to be auctioned in late March.
>
> The cause of death was a recurrence of lung cancer.
>
> Dr. Reinsdorf, a professor of musicology for thirty-four years at the Federal Institute of Music, also known as the Berlin Conservatory, was highly admired for his "Maestro" trilogy, close analyses of Beethoven's compositional styles. He also wrote five other books about the great composer and more than one hundred articles for academic journals.
>
> Famous for his bluff, occasionally abrasive personality, Dr. Reinsdorf was a popular and provocative guest lecturer at universities and cultural centers around the world. His books have been translated into twelve languages.
>
> A native of Lucerne, Switzerland, he studied at the Zurich Conservatory and the University of Vienna, where he was awarded his doctoral degree before moving to his academic post in Berlin…

The closing paragraph said the scholar was survived by Hilde, his wife of thirty-eight years, "and a nephew, Felix Utley of Zurich, a violinist with the Swiss Philharmonic."

"Felix!" Mitch's eyes widened. "That slippery fucker."

"Do I smell a hairy rat?" Clara asked. "Possibly a pair of them—feasting on Swiss cheese? Didn't Emil lead us all to believe he was more German than Siegfried?"

Mitch's head began to ache even as it seized on these twin revelations. "I remember now. Felix made some vague reference to an uncle of his—both times I talked to him, as a matter of fact—that he was a professor somewhere. I thought he said in history. Maybe he did mention it was music history."

"I remember at our hotel room. Didn't he say his uncle knew the Swiss Philharmonic conductor—Grieder, the one Ansel detested—from their years together at university, and the uncle kept pushing to get Felix promoted to concertmaster?"

"Yes, but Felix never mentioned him by name—even though he must have known we'd met him while he was serving as one of our *Tell* panelists."

Clara's convictions about the symphony abruptly begin to waver. But maybe it was a simple miscommunication. "Perhaps he didn't think it was appropriate to bring up," she suggested, "or maybe it was just an honest oversight—or irrelevant, the way Emil never bothered telling you he was born in Switzerland, probably because it was something he didn't care to advertise in German academia."

Mitch, though, felt deceived and more worried than ever. How embarrassing that, when recruiting the panel of experts under Mac Quarles's direction, he had not learned Emil Reinsdorf was a native Swiss. Where had Emil's heart and head been during the authentication process?

Mitch had Clara listen in on the bedroom extension while he phoned Felix Utley's home in Zurich. There was no answer, and he left no message. After a moment's reflection, he tried Emil Reinsdorf's number in Berlin. It was answered by Felix, presumably on hand for his uncle's funeral.

"Awfully sorry to disturb you," Mitch said. "My wife and I wanted to express our sincere condolences to your aunt. We hope she's bearing up under—"

"Yes, thanks—I'll pass along your sentiments. She's not taking calls just now."

"Of course." Mitch paused. "I hope you're okay as well."

"Yes, quite—thanks." Felix's impatience was thinly cloaked.

"I had no idea you and Dr. Reinsdorf were related until I just read it in the paper."

"Yes, well, I thought I did mention it to you, actually."

"Never his name or that he was among the world's leading Beethoven scholars."

Felix grasped now that he was being interrogated. "Well, no—one wouldn't normally bring up such a matter or make such a claim. I seem to recall mentioning that when Ansel phoned me about his discovery of the *Tell* manuscript, I offered to ring up my uncle about his having a look at it. I thought it was clear enough in that context—who and what he was. You didn't ask me his name."

That was true, Mitch knew. "But weren't you curious to see the manuscript yourself?"

"Well, yes, of course—I'm a musician." Felix was straining not to sound put upon. "But Ansel told me he was in no position to have outsiders trooping into the Hassler house—that the American grandson might get frightened and— well, you know what happened."

"But why didn't you alert your uncle to the possibility there was an important find—"

"Oh, but I did. Uncle Emil just laughed and said somebody was playing a great joke."

"How could he have been so certain? Why didn't he want to get on the next plane and come look at it? Wasn't Beethoven his life?"

The innuendo, pressing well beyond cordial conversation, drew Felix's curt response. "I've answered your untimely questions, Mr. Emery. Now I trust you'll kindly honor the saying, *De mortibus nihil nisi bonum*—assuming anyone in America knows Latin." And he hung up.

"Sounds as if he may be covering up for Emil," Clara said, back from her listening post.

"And who in the entire world," Mitch asked rhetorically, eyes wide open now, "would have been better qualified—and more favorably positioned—to invent a Beethoven symphony and pass it off as the real thing? And Felix was ideally situated to arrange for the manuscript to be placed in the Hasslers' attic— he and Ansel had been pals for a long time—and sister Margot was his lover— access would have been easy." It all made blindingly simple sense. At last.

Clara was reeling over the sudden obviousness of the arrangement.

"Maybe they were *all* in on it—isn't that what you're thinking?"

"All of them—some of them—none of them—take your pick. Let's stick with Emil for the moment—why would he have done such a thing? What could he have gained by it?"

Clara pondered a while, then wafted her partially formed hunch into the air. "He did it because—just because he could, and nobody else could have— and because he was sick, terminally, and it was sort of a parting display of defiance—because—because he was jealous and thought he deserved the world's acclaim, but nobody outside of academia knew who he was—so this would be his fiendish way to—"

"You left out money," Mitch put in, his excitement spiking. "He'd probably never had a ton of it—his books were too specialized to have sold a lot of copies—so he figured somehow he'd cash in on the *Tell* creation—probably he'd worked out some kind of scheme with Felix and possibly the Erpfs, too, since Felix had been on close terms with both Ansel and Margot—but Jake screwed up the deal by just barging in and taking off with the manuscript—"

"Unless—oh, God, yes!"

Clara was practically tumescent from cerebral stimulation. "Don't you see—Jake's got to be in on it, too, and the whole dispute with the Erpfs was trumped up. It was all a setup to get the manuscript laundered by C&W through an auction. And they knew you people would naturally turn to Emil to be one of the expert authenticators—"

"But Emil was the most reluctant to go along—he was questioning everything."

Clara nodded knowingly. "Exactly—it was a pose."

"So we'd never suspect him?"

"*Voila!*" Clara savored the neatness of the solution—but then fell off the log as fast as she'd jumped on it. "There are a few little flaws in there, of course. To start with, I never heard that Emil composed anything in his life. He'd have needed a collaborator, a very talented one—and Ansel's the only one who might have—well, the only one we know of who was more or less connected to all this. Except, of course, he never composed anything of real distinction, either, so far as we're aware. Also it's pretty hard to imagine Emil scurrying about, attending to the infinite details of such an immensely complex forgery. And Jake Hassler hardly seems the sort to be implicated in a big-time scam with a pack of—"

"Nobody *seems* likely to have been involved—except Ansel, and he's dead."

"Maybe that's *why* he's dead. He couldn't face the music, so to speak."

They groped on and on, chasing their comet tails. Finally Mitch phoned Harry, weekending in Southampton, and ran their astounding theory by him. "Why didn't we know Emil was Swiss-born?" Harry asked. "Why do we need to read about it in the *New York*-fucking-*Times?*"

"I—we—pretty much understood him to be a staunch German patriot," Mitch answered lamely, ready to take his lumps, "and he certainly presented himself that way to us—trying his best to angle the thing for Deutschland. I just pretty much assumed—"

"You're not paid to *assume* things, Mitchell." In the next breath, though, Harry switched his tack. "Listen, if you're trying to convince me that Emil's Swiss connection adds up to a wicked conspiracy, I say you're barking up the wrong Alp. Your whole fantasy is ridiculously out of character—these just aren't the sort of people who get involved in such lunacy—Emil Reinsdorf, least of all. I mean, the guy *worshipped* Beethoven. I admit the idea might just possibly have occurred to Ansel, our deceased certified psycho, but you've told me everyone agrees he could never have sustained that level of creative effort, so let's move on."

Mitch was not about to be cowed.

"You're forgetting about Reinsdorf's connection with his nephew. I want Johnny Winks to try to get us a list of Emil's phone calls for the past year—

there may be a pattern, possibly frequent communication with Felix, that tells us something. I also want a tap on Hilde Reinsdorf's phone, especially as we get closer to the auction date."

"And how many more zillion euros will these little fishing expeditions eat up?" Harry objected. "Besides, if Emil *was* involved in a hoax—an idea that frightens me mostly because it says you're getting carried away by hallucinations—do you think he'd be phoning up his henchmen on his own line? What the hell kind of investigative genius are you, anyway?"

He waited for Harry's smoking tongue to cool, then shot back, "You're burying your head in the sand, Harry. Something's up here."

"Possibly it's *your* head—buried up where the sun don't shine."

For the briefest instant, Mitch wondered if Harry's vehemence was a signal that perhaps even he himself might be involved in some grand connivance with these schemers. All that money was on the table. Why else was Harry chucking caution to the wind? The suspicion fled before he dared dwell on it.

"As soon as we're done here," Mitch declared, "I'm going to call Johnny and ask him to follow up just the way I said—there, you've been advised. If you want to overrule me, fine—you own the joint. But you'll have my resignation first thing Monday."

Had he gone too far? Harry's silence suggested as much. "Is that a threat or a promise?" he finally asked with a dismissive laugh. "You're a bit much—*le grand* Mitchell Emery."

Clara rewarded him with a full-frontal kiss, a long one, after he hung up and then led him back to their boudoir for a half hour's coupling. They rarely lingered in bed Saturday mornings—there was so much else out there beckoning. "I think I need to phone Daddy," she said as they dressed, "about all of this, I mean—before he gets too involved in the *Tell* auction."

"Do that."

"You don't think I'm being disloyal to C&W?"

"Daddy comes first—and you more or less got him into this."

Piet Hoitsma told his daughter that yes, he was still definitely trying to carpenter a joint Anglo-Dutch consortium to bid for the *Tell* manuscript at the C&W auction. "The lawyers have raised some questions—the Bern Copyright Convention and that sort of bothersome detail. But I'm hopeful we'll overcome all of that and be able to make a respectable bid."

"Um, well—you may want to hold up a bit on that—"

"In fact, I ran into Sedge Wakeham at a wassail party over the holidays—he's quite good at wassailing—and allowed that we might be doing some business with his firm before long—"

"Daddy!" Clara broke in, "Mitch and I are terribly afraid it's all bogus—a hoax—"

"What—the *Tell* Symphony?"

"And the whole discovery story."

"Oh, my."

"Mitch is trying to get to the bottom of it, and Harry's behaving rather beastly. I feel dreadful about getting you into this, but I'd hate to see us all wind up looking like total fools."

"Not to worry, darling," his father comforted her. "Tell Mitch to stick to his guns—especially if it gets too dicey and Harry doesn't know enough to bail out."

THE LIST OF PHONE CALLS from Emil Reinsdorf's home over the last year of his life, dredged up by the Winks espionage apparatus from impenetrable computer files at a cost of 6,500 euros, revealed just three conversations between nephew Felix and his uncle, hardly a suspicious total, and none whatsoever with members of the Erpf family, Jake Hassler, or anyone else Mitch and Clara could think of who might be linked in any way to *Tell*. There was one call to Richard Grieder, the Swiss Philharmonic's musical director, but Felix had indicated the two men were old friends, so that contact seemed less than extraordinary. The phone tap on newly widowed Hilde Reinsdorf, costing a further 1,500 euros a day, produced even less evidence of suspicious activity. It was beginning to look as if Harry may have been right—that Mitch was running up the tab in dogged pursuit of phantom villains.

And then, a week before the first would-be bidders were due to begin inspecting the *Tell* manuscript at C&W's offices, Felix Utley telephoned Mitch at his apartment at nine in the evening. That translated to three in the morning Zurich time.

In a halting voice that Mitch attributed to the lateness of the hour, Felix said he was sorry to be calling so inconveniently but circumstances had necessitated it. His personal finances were a hopeless muddle—too many bad investments and mooching friends, too rich a diet of wine, women, and song, heavy debts he could never catch up with—"or you can rest assured I would never approach you in this fashion." He sounded nothing like the assured Felix Utley during their recent phone conversation while he was in Berlin for his uncle's funeral.

"And what fashion is that?" Mitch asked, at once sensing the worst.

"Constructively—and aware that the impending auction of the *Tell* manuscript is certain to bring very substantial returns to your firm. I heard on CNN that you had rejected a preemptive offer of ten million, or something like that, from a small recording company. They said competing international coalitions are in a bidding war that could drive the price way up—maybe as high as nine figures. Someone said there are plans for a world tour to showcase the new symphony with an all-star orchestra, rather like an Elton John or Rolling Stones extravaganza. Sounds enthralling."

"Well, yes—our firm is hopeful there'll be a good response," was all Mitch conceded.

"Splendid—and which I'm sure explains your company's failure to disclose the receipt of my late-friend Ansel Erpf's letter to his sister—the one dealing with his possible forgery of the symphony. We spoke of it at our last meeting in your hotel room here. It would seem to me obligatory for your auction house to make it public out of consideration for your potential bidders—aren't they entitled to be told that Ansel's disclosure may have been genuine and not the ravings of a madman, as you evidently concluded them to be?" His barbed tone hinted that Felix had carefully rehearsed his incendiary approach. Possibly he was reading from a script.

"As you also concluded—and his sister," Mitch pointed out, "and she tried to have him committed as a result—and we kept it all under wraps so as not to embarrass the Erpf family—and Ansel himself—as you perfectly well know."

"I'm afraid that's beside the point just now—"

"All right—what *is* the point, then?"

Felix took a quick swig of something, from the sound of it, before answering.

"The obvious inference to be drawn from Cubbage & Wakeham's withholding Ansel's letter from public knowledge is that you and your colleagues greatly fear it will compromise the outcome of the auction—perhaps even prevent its coming off altogether."

He stopped, as if to gauge what part of the bait he had set out his prey might snatch at.

"Go on," Mitch said.

"Okay. There's one further matter equally troubling, perhaps even more so."

Mitch signaled to Clara to pick up their bedroom phone with care. "Namely?"

"My uncle confided in me that before casting his vote in favor of the authenticity of the *Tell* Symphony, an arrangement was made that assured him a degree of participation in the revenue from the sale of the manuscript. I was shocked, of course, but Emil insisted the understanding was not really unethical because before he made the deal, he'd already made up his mind in favor of the work as a legitimate Beethoven composition. He agreed to the offer, he told me, to protect Hilde, who he was afraid would be left with insufficient funds for a comfortable widowhood after he was gone. He was telling me about it, he said, because as his only surviving blood relative and the heir to whatever was left of their joint estate at Hilde's death, I had a vested interest in the arrangement."

The baldness and implications of Felix's delivery had caught Mitch entirely off guard. All he said in response was, "I know of no such arrangement between your uncle and my firm."

"Perhaps not. Or perhaps you're required to deny it. Or perhaps it was made by your colleagues without your knowledge."

It was a clumsy divide-and-conquer gambit, Mitch recognized.

"You're acknowledging that your uncle didn't say who'd supposedly made this arrangement with him."

"I understood it was a duly authorized representative of your firm."

"But he didn't say that to you, did he?"

"It was implicit, given your vested interest in a sale for some astronomical sum."

"And so you're prepared to make an open declaration to that effect?"

"I am—out of precisely the same concern that I have over Ansel's withheld letter to Margot—both of which the music-loving public, and certainly every would-be bidder for the manuscript, is entitled to be told about. And my two disclosures together, I'm fully confident, would have a seriously detrimental effect on your firm's hopes for the auction."

"I see," Mitch said.

"I trust you understand my situation—"

"Oh, entirely—and your righteous indignation as well. Is there something further?"

"Only that I also trust you'll pass all of this on to your colleagues. And you might indicate to your firm that, in view of my extreme financial duress just now, I'm in need of a prompt response, or I'll have to do what I believe is morally required."

There it was, viciously deceitful and hugely menacing. Mitch could not restrain his wrath. "Your moral obligation to reveal our alleged sins rings a bit hollow, I'm afraid, in view of the absence of any basis in fact for them, as you're fully aware. Ansel's crank letter from London was typed—anyone could have written it—and totally unsupported. The same with your claim that Emil accepted a bribe for his vote in favor of the manuscript."

Felix saw that he had a very balky fish on the line. "Nevertheless, I believe the charges alone would prove highly detrimental to your firm." He paused, then added, "As I said, only my financial difficulties cause me to approach you in this rather distasteful fashion."

Mitch chose to protract the game no longer. "What exactly is it you want, Mr. Utley?"

There was no hesitation. "Just two million dollars. Cash would make most sense—nothing to trace, no way for me to use it as leverage for a second approach to you before your auction comes off. Your people should think of it as a small, prudent investment, not as...a..."

"Shakedown?"

"I'm not familiar with that particular—"

"How about 'extortion'? Or perhaps 'blackmail' would cover it. The Swiss authorities will recognize all three—unless we both agree to forget this conversation took place."

"I doubt you'll go to them. You'd have too much to explain after I advise the media of your company's unethical practices. Your risks are infinitely greater than mine. I'm merely performing a public service. If you claim I've asked you for money, I'll counterclaim that you knew I'd found out about the arrangement you'd made with Uncle Emil and offered me cash to keep quiet about it—and about Ansel's letter to Margot as well. Your word against mine—and you'd look at least as culpable."

He was a more devious scoundrel than Mitch could have guessed. Who would suppose that an accomplished violinist might excel as well as a dexterous con artist? "I think not, Mr. Utley," Mitch replied. "As for your late uncle, whose reputation you seem so eager to blacken, his only imprudent dealing with our firm was his attempt to arrange for the manuscript to be sold—without an auction—to a consortium of German investors in the interest of what you might call cultural correctness. And when we rejected Dr. Reinsdorf's proposal, he accepted our decision with good grace. We attributed his behavior not to bad character but to misplaced patriotism."

"A handy rationalization," Felix shot back, "and frankly laughable—if you'd known Emil at all, Mr. Emery. My uncle harbored a deep resentment of the Fatherland. His Swiss ancestry was held against him by his colleagues at the conservatory. Why do you think he was never seriously in the running for the directorship despite being the most distinguished member of its faculty? He played at being the loyal, even passionate German in order to advance his standing—and who else but a German should be Beethoven's foremost academic champion? So he took out citizenship papers—and lived to regret it. His chauvinist pose in dealing with your firm was almost surely intended to misdirect your attention so that when, in the end, he asked for a financial consideration in exchange for his vote, it was in fact a simple business transaction, to his way of thinking, under the guise of patriotism."

It was Felix's last desperate lunge, Mitch calculated. "Well, so you say, Mr. Utley. But your uncle is no longer around to dispute your charges—a fact that would hardly be overlooked by anyone examining your transparent betrayal of him." His

Felix gave a growl of protest. "My aspersions on his integrity can't harm Emil now. They *can* harm your company, however, and rather severely."

His voice had turned to gravel from the strain of the confrontation. "I'll expect to hear from you by a week from Monday," he said, "or I'll have to make plans accordingly. My press conference would likely be held in New York, and you'd be welcome to attend and refute me. The spectacle would make for marvelous theater and ensure wider coverage. Oh, by the way, the fee I mentioned is nonnegotiable and must be delivered here. I think a mix of dollars, sterling, francs, and euros would work best."

"But notice," Mitch said to Clara afterward, as they tried to calm themselves, "he didn't claim Emil had anything to do with composing the *Tell*. You should be happy about that."

"I'm not happy about any of this, love," she said. "It's all become so hideous."

Harry was even more disconcerted the next morning when advised of Felix's demand.

"But he's bluffing, of course—just like his pain-in-the-ass uncle was."

"I wouldn't be quite so sure," said Mitch. "He sounded desperate enough to do it—and he's not clinically certifiable as unbalanced, the way Ansel was when the London letter came."

The company, they decided, had only two ways to deal with the latest dire threat. Their first option, Gordy contended, was to go straight to the Swiss authorities and tell them about Felix's extortionate game. "Several problems with that, though. For one thing, there's no way we can be sure they'd keep a lid on our accusation—or that, even if they did, Felix won't do precisely what he's threatened—and then, as he told Mitch, it's his word against ours."

"Next option," Harry said with a grimace. "And I hope you're not about to tell me we have to pay off this lowlife."

Gordy turned up his palms in confession.

"Forget that," Harry barked. "Who'd pop up next out of this vipers' nest—the treacherous Margot? Emil's demure widow? Maybe our rube of a client from the Jersey boonies—or Tony Soprano? Maybe it's all a mob scam—"

Mitch—still hoping that the tap he had ordered on Hilde Reinsdorf's phone or Johnny Winks's search for whoever ordered the Nina-Marie tombstone might produce results—saw a third option. "Let's postpone the auction for a month. We can claim we need the extra time to wrap everything up on the authentication end, and meanwhile we're giving more potential bidders an opportunity to review the manuscript. Then I'll get back over there to work more closely with Johnny and try to deal with Felix face-to-face—he's got to be neutralized somehow—and maybe Clara can rev up her feminine wiles and try to get something out of Hilde and Margot."

Harry shook his head fiercely. "No delay, no excuses, no explanations. If we have to bail at the end, then we bail, but nothing should interrupt the process now—it would totally undermine bidders' confidence." He turned to Mitch. "You and Clara get back over there, as you say—I'd start with Emil's widow, she may be our best bet. Have Lolly pick out a dress for her this afternoon—nothing too pricey—and bring it along as a gift for when her period of mourning eases up a little. Maybe she and the scummy nephew are at odds, and she'll turn on him."

CLARA FELT CONSCIENCE-STRICKEN over their thinly varnished pretext for dropping in on Hilde Reinsdorf. Her distaste was compounded by awareness that Johnny Winks's slithery people had been illegally eavesdropping on the poor woman's phone line. But the visit was a professional necessity, not an optional condolence call.

They arrived bearing, as a morale-booster, the smart St. John wool suit that Lolly had chosen for her. Mitch had phoned her several times and gotten no answer, but he knew from Winks's field men that Hilde was at home—just not taking calls. In the end, given their time constraint, they decided to drop by unannounced, with profuse apologies. Better, too, that Hilde would have no opportunity to compose herself beforehand. Her house was a high-stooped, two-family graystone on a short, tree-lined street a few blocks from the conservatory and close by the park. The Reinsdorf apartment occupied the bottom two floors, with its entry three steps below the street level. The instant Clara pushed the bell, the bulldog within went ballistic.

"That would be Scherzie," Mitch said, "pining for his departed master to return home."

Hilde herself was notably more welcoming after she peeked through the curtained glass of the front door and recognized Clara. A short, firm command sent the woebegone bulldog waddling off, his sentry duty fulfilled, and allowed the Emerys peaceable entry. "We tried calling," Clara quickly explained, "and then thought we'd just take our chances—we won't stay long, if you can tolerate visitors at all."

"You're more than welcome," said the gracious widow Reinsdorf. "I'm just trying to, you know, regather my energies and get on with things."

As she led them inside, the Emerys paused in the vestibule, their attention arrested by its stunning walls, painted floor to ceiling in a millefleur design. The *trompe l'oeil* effect left them feeling as if they had been set down amid a meadow of wildflowers. Just as when unwrapping the edelweiss painting Hilde had sent her as a gift, Clara sensed herself instinctively trying to inhale the imagined fragrance of the two-dimensional bouquet. "Oh, how perfectly splendid," she exclaimed. "It must have taken you years."

"Three," Hilde said, pleased by the attention to her artistry. "I did it when we first moved in here—the place needed cheering up—rather as I do, just now. Seeing you both helps."

She served them dry sherry and drier biscuits in the dark-wood parlor and made a game show of pleasure at the gift they had brought her. "We thought it might help a little to take your mind off your loss," Clara said. "It's from Lolly Cubbage and me—she's still sorry you wouldn't accept the outfit she sent to you in New York, and this is my way of thanking you for the wonderful painting you gave me."

Their supply of small talk was soon exhausted, and Mitch had no alternative but to confess they had more on their minds than expressions of sympathy. "I'm afraid your nephew has given us cause for concern," he said and as succinctly as possible spelled out Felix's malevolent threat. "Aside from the discomfort it brings to our company, his claims reflect on Dr. Reinsdorf in a troubling way. I wouldn't have dreamed of disturbing you about this, but my firm is facing a time bind—the auction date for the *Tell* manuscript is only—"

"Yes, of course—I understand completely." Hilde shook her head slowly. "I knew all of this would turn out badly from the start. I urged Emil not to become involved."

Mitch was careful not to pounce. "In the sense that—?"

"*Bitte?*"

"I mean you wanted him not to become involved in—what, exactly?"

"I mean when your firm first approached him to participate in the vetting process. Emil knew more, you see, than everyone else put together about the maestro, and I was afraid he'd find it very difficult to deal with—well, what he considered lesser minds. And so it proved. He was ill at ease throughout the proceedings with your company."

"And Felix?"

Hilde's lips pinched reflexively.

"Whatever my nephew's flaws, outright criminality has not been among them—so far as I know." She sat for a moment, considering how much to reveal. "This is quite a nasty business he's proposing, isn't it? It's brought you all the way here."

"I'm afraid so," said Mitch. "We're hoping you might be able to enlighten us if it's something you can talk about. Mr. Cubbage and our house counsel—you met Mr. Roth at the dinner party—assure me our firm made no secret reciprocal arrangement with Dr. Reinsdorf."

"No, of course—Emil would have marched out in a great fury if you had proposed it and gone straight to the UN General Assembly to denounce you. He could get terribly worked up at times. I can't imagine what's inciting Felix to make such vile charges against Emil—"

"He says it's money—he apparently needs a lot of it to settle his debts and so forth."

"Nothing new there," Hilde allowed and then drew a deeply anguished breath. There followed an unflattering portrait of a nettlesome family relationship—"rather a love/hate sort of thing, I suppose," she said, stemming from the early death of Emil's sister back in Lucerne. Her husband was a philanderer, and when he wandered off, it had seemed for the best—until she fell ill, and Felix was left an orphaned teenager with high musical aptitude. Emil took a close interest in the boy, who stayed in Switzerland, living with his paternal grandparents.

"How close an interest could Emil have taken, living so far away?" Mitch asked.

"Emil would visit with him twice a year. Felix became more or less the son he—we—never had. Emil made sure of his admission to the conservatory in Zurich, opened the door for him when he sought employment at the Swiss Philharmonic—Emil and Richard Grieder had been close as boys and in their student days in Vienna." But as his uncle thrived in the rarefied air at the apex of

German musicology, his hopes that his nephew might follow him to Berlin and perhaps win a place with its great philharmonic were to be forever frustrated.

"Felix never even tried," Hilde recounted. "He was comfortable in Zurich, and although he was gifted, I think he knew—better than Emil—what his limitations were. Emil did his best to promote Felix's hopes of becoming the concertmaster, only Herr Grieder always had some excuse—some obligation to another player or to a member of his board of trustees."

Hilde tried to shake the misfortune from her memory. "I think Grieder never wanted to insult Emil with the truth—that Felix didn't deserve the first violinist's chair, and that he had too much personal baggage. You know all about that, I suppose—"

"His various women?" Mitch ventured.

"And mostly married ones, at that, including Grieder's niece. Felix was rather a predator, I'm sorry to say. Emil didn't want to hear about it. He only cared about the music. He thought Felix had a decent brain and first-rate musical instincts. They'd have great, long discussions about this or that composer or dissect a particular composition whenever he went down to Zurich or Felix came up here to spend Christmastime with us. There was something of a *rapprochement* between them in the later years—they became quite close at the end. Felix would ring up several times a month, just trying to cheer up Emil with any little story."

"Forgive my poor manners," Mitch asked when she was done, "but what about the money? It seems to be what's driving Felix to the point of threatening our firm if we don't—"

"Yes, the money. Always the money."

Hilde poured them all a bit more of the sherry. "Emil gave him gifts from time to time—never anything sizable, though, or so he told me." She gave a wan smile. "Whatever Emil did for Felix in that regard was never enough."

Mitch nodded. "I'm obliged to ask one further question." He waited for Hilde's nod before continuing. "Was there any provision in Dr. Reinsdorf's will for Felix?"

"A bequest, you mean? No, not actually. Emil and I had an understanding that after I'm gone, whatever's left would go to the conservatory and a few of our preferred charities."

"I understood from Felix that the money was to pass to him upon your death."

"I don't know how he could have come by that idea—perhaps he was being wishful."

"Felix said Emil told him so."

"I wouldn't know what Emil told him in that regard—but Emil certainly didn't instruct me to that effect, and there's no mention of Felix in either of our wills."

"But if Dr. Reinsdorf was so fond of Felix, why didn't he make some provision for him in his will? There are no other surviving relatives, I gather. Wouldn't that have been a natural thing to do for a fond uncle—a parting gift to his only blood relative?"

Hilde nodded. "Perhaps." Then she thought further and added, "To be entirely truthful with you, Emil felt Felix was a terrible disappointment—and he was not inclined to rain money on him, even at those rare times when we had any substantial surplus. But money seemed to preoccupy Felix. He had social aspirations—the women he consorted with must have bled him financially. Emil thought Felix was grossly profligate and that the small 'Reinsdorf fortune,' as Emil comically called it, should be used after his death to provide a modest level of comfort for Scherzie and me—and after that, there would hardly be enough to matter." She shrugged. "Felix asked me directly about Emil's will after the funeral and looked unhappy when I told him."

"Revenge may well explain his willingness to betray Dr. Reinsdorf's memory," Mitch suggested, "by approaching us with threats if we don't agree to fatten his bank account."

"Oh, my—he must be in a bad way, though he never let on to me." Hilde offered them a second round of biscuits. "Will your firm bring criminal charges against him?" she asked.

Mitch sensed that the prospect would not have displeased her.

"We haven't determined."

He broke off a piece of the flaky wafer he accepted and studied it a moment, as if searching for insight along its jagged edge. "Incidentally, did you ever, over the past several years, notice Dr. Reinsdorf lingering over a Beethoven score with special attention, I mean?"

Hilde smiled primly.

"Emil was always poring over Beethoven scores—I'm not sure what you mean."

Mitch withdrew the awkward probe with a dismissive wave of the hand. A sideways glance at Clara prompted them to rise, and a moment later they accompanied Hilde and Scherzie for a walk around the corner toward the Tiergarden before parting with warm expressions of mutual gratitude.

"Not much help there, I suppose," Clara said on the way to their hotel, "but I *do* like the woman. I suspect Emil was rather a handful for her to cope with all those years."

"And I suspect," said Mitch, "that likable woman was toying with us just now. She'd have been much angrier at Felix if she wasn't somehow mixed up in it all—with or against him."

Clara was astonished by his unrelenting distrust. "Sometimes you're just horrid, Mitch."

{16}

The urgent voice-mail message from Johnny Winks said that good news was awaiting. He was snowbound in the Tyrol, Johnny grumbled when Mitch reached his cell phone number and learned that his team's search for the stonemason who carved the Nina-Marie inscription on the headstone in the Hassler cemetery plot had finally hit pay dirt. An old-timer whose workshop was beside a quarry close to the Lower River Inn recognized the stone rubbing as his own handiwork, completed fifteen months earlier for a gentleman who declined to give his name but paid in advance with Swiss francs. "The chap insisted the mason use an old stone," Johnny reported, "and dirty the new lettering to look equally old."

"Exactly," said Mitch. "What'd this guy look like?"

"Nothing special—late-forties to mid-fifties—a bit shaggy, longish hair, had a mustache, needed a shave—dark glasses—he took them off for a moment to rub his eyes, but the stonecarver didn't get all that good a look at him—not sure he could identify our guy."

"Clothing?"

"He vaguely remembers a trenchcoat or raincoat—dark, loden green or black, maybe."

"Felix!" Clara cried as soon as Mitch relayed the description. "Don't you remember his beat-up black raincoat? And he's got all that tousled hair. The mustache and dark glasses—those must have been his attempt at a disguise."

"A lot of men own a dark raincoat," Mitch noted.

"Listen, it's just *got* to be Felix," Clara said, undaunted. "He's in this up to his ears."

"Could be Utley," Mitch told Winks. After a moment his bird-dog reflexes kicked in. He politely instructed his indefatigable undercover man to get the best description he could from the stonemason of Felix's telltale mustache, then set up a stakeout at his apartment house in Zurich, put a telephoto lens on him the moment he arrived or left home, make five blow-up prints of his cropped mugshot, find a student artist at the university to draw in five different variations of the mustache—one per photo—and have them faxed back to Johnny. "Maybe then your stonecarver can ID our mystery man."

"Any other trying demands, Mitchell?" Johnny asked. "Perhaps my people can discover a new galaxy while they're waiting for the pictures to be processed?"

"Optional," Mitch said with a warm laugh, too pleased to mind the needling. "We're flying down to Zurich tonight. You can reach me at the Schweitzerhof. Swell work so far, buddy."

They made it in just before a nasty midwinter freeze blew down from the mountains and layered the lakeside city with a dry, drifting snowfall. Clara, in jeans, Shetland sweater, and down jacket with a fake-fur-lined hood, kept puffing out her cheeks like an overworked bellows to stay warm as they struggled around the corner from the hotel to a busy trattoria a few doors off the Bahnhofstrasse. Over a modest bottle of Chianti, they weighed the odds against a gnarled old stonecarver high in the Tyrol being able to finger Felix Utley from a touched-up photograph—and, even if he could, where exactly that would leave them.

Midway into their second glasses of wine, with the carpaccio gone and the rigatoni puttanesca en route, Clara reached over, covered Mitch's ring hand with hers, and without a segue told him, "I'm thinking more about adopting— if nothing's cooking by the end of summer—"

"Me, too," he said, covering her hand with his free one and intertwining it with her long, graceful fingers. It was the third time she had brought up the subject, and he could no longer keep kissing off the idea as a last resort. "But to be honest, sweetie, it still gets me nervous. Who knows what gene pool we'd be diving into?"

She withdrew her lovingly trapped hand and recovered her wine glass. "I mean, all life is a huge gamble, whatever your genes. Some perfectly brilliant people procreate disastrously, and some cretins spawn mutant wizards."

The wine was velvet against her throat. She was debating with herself, really, not him. Brushing back a strand of her fine hair that had worked its way down to just above her bleary eyes, she quipped, "Maybe we should just settle for a pet or two—a collie, maybe, I love collies—though I guess they wouldn't do all that well on Riverside Drive. Possibly an aardvark—you don't see many of them around—and they're so sweet, wonderful companions, I hear…"

Her manic riff ended and her spirits sagged, done in by all the travel, cold, fatigue, alcohol, and synapse overload.

Next day, while Mitch distractedly skimmed *The Magic Mountain,* Clara immersed herself in a book on Swiss folklore she'd bought at a store up the avenue from their hotel and discovered that William Tell was no more a historically based figure than Robin Hood, Till Eulenspiegel, or Father Christmas. "Perhaps that's the problem with the Swiss," she mused. "Their stellar national hero is a myth."

That evening, they attended a concert by the Swiss Philharmonic at the Tonhalle, a short, blustery walk from the hotel. The program—Bartok, Delius, and Beethoven's Seventh—was competently executed, they agreed, but the performance came off as more dutiful than scintillating. Maestro Grieder, well-fed and rosy-cheeked, bestirred himself for the Beethoven, making a sprightly enough run at it. Felix Utley, well groomed for a change, was on hand among the first violins and, like his conductor, displayed more gusto during the Beethoven, Clara's favorite among his symphonies, than for the rest of the program. "Unless I'm just imagining it," she said to Mitch afterward.

The following morning, he played street detective, joining Winks's stakeout team outside of Felix's apartment house. The cold snap had broken overnight, or the outdoor surveillance would have proven brutal work. The assignment had fallen to two of Johnny's brawnier field men who, working out of a VW van, advised Mitch that Felix was at home and apparently cohabiting with a woman of indeterminate age but definitely not Margot Lenz.

Into his second cup of tepid coffee and defying an urge from his brimming bladder, Mitch was rescued from the odious vigil by a phone call to the wheelman. It was Johnny with a short, sweet message: "Utley's your man—probably," he told Mitch. "The stonemason says he's pretty sure from one of the photos of Felix with a mustache drawn on that he was the one who ordered the tombstone, but the old-timer wouldn't swear to it. Almost, though."

"Bravo!" Mitch sang out. "Double bravo! Now let's play this game in reverse. Can you take a headshot of the stonemason on your smartphone and send it back to me real quick? We've got Felix penned in down here, and I want to try bearding him in his den."

Mitch repaired to his hotel for warmer clothing while Winks was carrying out the assignment. By the time the picture of the stonecarver arrived, late-afternoon dusk was encroaching. Winks's men in the van reported that Felix's companion had gone out but that he himself had not been seen. Clara cautioned Mitch as he was leaving the comfort of their hotel that he was about to confront not just a womanizing violinist but a desperate blackmailer.

On the short taxi ride over, Mitch weighed the odds of a violent reception upon ringing Felix's doorbell. He considered phoning up from the street and, with armed guards at his side, inviting his antagonist to come downstairs for a little chat. But Felix was not likely to be coaxed outside in the dark.

He answered Mitch's ring on the intercom with a hesitant but polite enough greeting, apparently hopeful his visitor was acting as Cubbage & Wakeham's courier and had come with a substantial wad of cash to buy off Felix's silence. He asked if Mitch was alone and, assured of it, buzzed him inside.

The walk-up apartment shared the second floor with one other unit in the small, well-maintained building. For a weapon, Mitch carried only his copy of *The Magic Mountain*, a heavy enough projectile but of limited range and deterrent force; inside its front cover he had slipped a printout of Johnny's headshot of the old Tyrolean stonemason who had carved the Nina-Marie grave marker.

Felix's flat was everything its owner was not—expansive, immaculate, and stylish, done in ultramodern, with blond woods, Italian leather, polished steel, and travertine marble. Too posh for a journeyman violinist with a provincial orchestra and no other known income or resources. Three explanations raced through Mitch's mind at first sight of the place: Felix was trafficking in illicit substances, loan sharks were nipping at his heels, or his women had been contributing handsomely to his upkeep. On second thought, all might apply.

"I was just listening to Stravinsky when you rang—shall I turn it back on?"

"Thanks, no. I've left some companions downstairs in a car—I said I'd be only a few minutes—though I can send them on their way if we need longer."

Felix scowled. "I thought you said you were alone."

"I am—as you can see."

The scowl was slow to abate. "I'm not sure what brings you by so unexpectedly. I just assumed we'd transact our business by long-distance phone, except for its conclusion. Is that why you're here? You have something for me?"

"I do," Mitch said blandly, "but it may not be exactly what you have in mind."

Felix gestured him into a vintage Breuer chair. "I was hoping we could dispose of this matter without much *sturm und drang*—what I've asked for should hardly bankrupt your firm."

Mitch sat and ran his eyes around the room, its oversize proportions softened by indirect amber lighting. "The gift I've brought you is a photograph, actually—have a look."

Felix, perched on the arm of the adjacent sofa, took the picture of the stonemason and studied it quizzically for a moment.

"Shows character," he said. "Who is it?"

"He cuts gravestones in the Tyrol. Not an easy fellow to find."

Poker-faced, Felix handed the picture back.

"Am I missing something here?"

"He says he did some business with you not too long ago."

"With *me*? I shouldn't think so—"

"You were in your phony mustache and dark glasses phase at the time."

Felix looked more amused than distressed. "There must be some mistake. At any rate, what is this all about? I thought we had other business to discuss."

"We think it's all the same business."

Mitch leaned forward.

"We know you're a key player in this whole *Tell* thing," he said, "and we're prepared to go to the authorities unless you're ready to tell us everything—in which case we may consider not pressing charges against you. You can have overnight to decide. Meanwhile, we've got people in the street who won't let you go far. In fact, if you try to leave Zurich, we'll alert the police *subito*." He sat back and let his words sink in. "Do I make myself clear?"

By now Felix's eyebrows were undulating. "You must be insane. I don't know what you're talking about, honestly. My approach to you was a straightforward business proposition based on my uncle's arrangement with your firm—"

"There was no arrangement, I can assure you."

"Emil assured me there *was* and promised me that I'd—"

"Well, at least one of you is or was a liar, and I won't debate the question with you."

Felix rubbed his chin and quickly assessed his options.

"Do you want to tell me what this gravestone business is all about?" he tried.

"Save the con, friend—we're onto the whole Nina-Marie scam," Mitch said, savoring his advantage. "Call me at the Schweitzerhof by nine in the morning and let me know if you're ready to spell it out for us—otherwise we go to your police." He rose and headed for the door.

"If you turn me in," Felix said slowly, "I'll have no choice but to perform the public service I promised you on the phone. And not only will I report that you bribed Emil Reinsdorf to vote for the authentication of the *Tell* manuscript, I'll go one better—and you won't like it in the least. I'll tell them the truth about the *Tell*—my version of it, anyway—"

He had caught Mitch's attention and froze his departure in midstride.

"Namely?"

"To start with, I will testify that everything in Ansel's letter from London to Margot—confessing that he himself composed the *Tell* Symphony and then masterminded the discovery of the manuscript—I'll say every word of it is true. I'll explain how he worked on the *Tell* composition for years and showed it to me from time to time for my reaction to its emerging shape—never telling me, of course, what his eventual objective was. I had seen his earlier compositions and given him my assessments, but this effort far surpassed anything he had ever tried before, and its clear evocation of the Beethoven style, worked out within the framework of a musical rendering of the Schiller drama about our national hero—well, I thought it brilliant and kept encouraging him. Only when he pretended to 'discover' his own manuscript in the attic of his next-door neighbors and claim it was *echt* Beethoven did I catch on to his lunatic game."

"And you didn't think to mention any of this to Ansel's sister—your lover?"

"We were never really lovers—just friends, as I told you earlier. For all I knew, she was in on it with Ansel—and maybe the Hasslers' American grandson was, too. But I wouldn't go into that—only that Ansel's letter to Margot was a true confession—and his subsequent suicide, I'll tell the media, indirectly substantiated it."

The room swam in weird amber light. Mitch saw the difficulties presented by his adversary's counterploy. Still, he had to play the hand he'd been dealt. Flattering Felix's wiles might throw him off balance. "Is it true—about Ansel—composing the *Tell*?" he asked softly. "I've had my doubts about its authenticity all along, to tell you the truth."

Felix managed his first hint of a smile since Mitch had arrived.

"Who the real composer is, Mr. Emery, is beside the point. It's the uncertainty I would be introducing into the public's mind about the symphony's acclaimed authenticity that will destroy your firm's effort to cash in on it."

"I get your drift," Mitch said, moving toward the front door again. "You've still got until nine in the morning to come clean with us, including who really composed the symphony. After that, all bets are off."

"Not mine—I'll still be expecting your gift by next Monday." Felix reached for the remote that controlled his CD player and restarted the Stravinsky disk.

♪

"HE'S BOXED US IN," Mitch moaned to Clara back at their hotel, "the smarmy bastard."

"Sticks and stones," she said. "Doesn't it come down to which of you blinks first?"

"He can afford to be more daring—reckless, you might even say. We're supposed to be protecting a respectable business establishment."

She saw the gloom enveloping him and tried to drive it away.

"I don't know about you, sweetie," she said, "but I'm in the mood for a really filthy dirty video—it might clear your brain. I've never seen any porn, actually. There's a charming-looking one featured in a shop window I passed while you were off to the wars—*Yodel Lady Oh-oh-oh!* or something like that—bestiality with Alpine goats, I think it said. Let's send out for it."

Before he could fend off his seductive partner, the phone jangled. Johnny Winks had fresh news. "Your other chicken's come home to roost, old boy."

"Translation?"

"The very friendly Frau Reinsdorf—I think your Berlin visit officially ended her period of mourning. She phoned the States last night—I've just heard the tape. You should, too."

"Play away," he said. "I'll get Clara on the line as well." This is what they heard:

UNIDENTIFIED: H'lo.

HILDE REINSDORF: Do I have Mr. Jacob Hassler's residence?

JAKE: Yup. But he's not buying anything tonight.

HILDE: Would you be Mr. Hassler himself?

JAKE: Would you be the queen of England?

HILDE: Excuse me?

JAKE: Just get on with it, lady—you've got ten more seconds.

HILDE: Yes, all right. This is Hilde Reinsdorf, Mr. Hassler. We met at Mr. Roth's home actually—the dinner party for the panel of experts who examined the manuscript you found? My late husband was Dr. Emil Reinsdorf—I'm sure you'll recall him—from Berlin—

JAKE: I don't think you've got the right party, lady.

HILDE: This is definitely the number Emil gave me—Area Code nine-zero-eight—

JAKE: Okay, what is it you're selling, Mrs. Reinhart?

HILDE: [Pause.] Oh, I think I see—you don't want to speak with me—

JAKE: Do we have something to speak about?

HILDE: Yes, we do, Mr. Hassler—and there's no need to be rude to me.

JAKE: Okay. What's on your mind—*madam?* Is that better?

HILDE: In case you were not aware, my husband told me about his understanding with you. I wanted to let you know that I expect it to be honored in full—in the event you thought his death somehow changed things.

JAKE: [Pause.] I don't know about any understanding with your husband.

HILDE: Oh, but I'm sure you do, Mr. Hassler. I have a memorandum between the two of you—with both your signatures on it.

JAKE: Lady, you must have me mixed up with some other guy.

HILDE: I see. Then perhaps you'll have no interest in the other reason for my calling you, either.

JAKE: Finally!

HILDE: My good-for-nothing nephew—he knows everything, I'm afraid, and was close to Emil—he's become exceedingly greedy. He's threatening to—what is the expression?—blow the whistle on our arrangements if the Cubbage concern doesn't pay him off for his silence. He's a quite proficient liar, and unless he's bought off or stopped—which is not within my power—he'll wreck everything.

JAKE: [Long pause.] What's all that got to do with me?

HILDE: You of all people have the most to lose—and if you lose, I lose as well. Emil explained it to me quite clearly during the last stage of his cancer.

JAKE: [Pause.] Anything else?

HILDE: I understand that there's been a quite substantial offer made by one of the recording companies for the property in question. Perhaps the matter can be reopened at your end—unless, of course—well—I hesitate to say it—

JAKE: Say what, lady?

HILDE: [Pause.] You do something forceful about my vile nephew.

JAKE: Take a hike, lady—and don't call me back, ever, okay?

[*Click.*]

"Wow," Mitch said softly, trying to focus on the mind-blurring evidence of the German widow's masterful duplicity. "Please play the tape for Gordy Roth in New York. I think we're finally getting somewhere, Johnny."

Clara rewarded him with a rapturous embrace. "And don't gloat, you beast!"

"About your precious Hilde? I made a lucky guess."

"Lucky, my foot. I'm just a gullible twit."

"But delectable."

They devoted the next hour trying to fit the pieces together anew. Hilde's deceitful answers during their visit to her home were now a matter of record, even if inadmissible in court. Her outreach to Jake raised two big questions: How much did she know about the whole *Tell* apparatus, and how deeply was she involved in its workings? But what exactly did the tapped phone conversation reveal about a deal between Emil and Jake or Felix's connection to it? And while Jake had admitted to nothing on the phone with Hilde, his credentials as an innocent primitive were now gravely suspect. His end of the tapped exchange strongly hinted he was a far cannier character, if not yet a self-incriminating participant, in whatever racket was now unraveling. The biggest stunner for Mitch was the apparent existence of a written agreement between Jake and Emil. "When Felix spoke about an alleged deal, I just assumed he was referring to an arrangement Emil had supposedly made with C&W," he told Clara, "and had nothing to do with Jake handing over a piece of the action to the Reinsdorfs—or Emil promising to cut Felix in on it after the auction went off. Maybe Emil didn't want Felix to know the whole truth."

"But why," Clara wondered, "would Emil have told Felix about *any* deal he might have made? Just because he was the Reinsdorfs' heir apparent? I don't buy that. There had to be something more going on."

Mitch agreed but had no explanation to offer. "And why did Felix lead me to think Emil's deal was with C&W," Mitch asked, "or threaten to claim it was if we didn't pay him off?"

"That's easy," Clara said. "Because C&W has money, and Felix was angry at his uncle for refusing to promise him a legacy—and if you want my guess, Hilde played dumb when Felix confronted her after the funeral, so he saw himself being shut out of the action altogether—no inheritance and nothing from Emil's deal with Jake—which is why he's turned on C&W to buy him off or he'd force you to cancel the auction." It gushed out in a single, mind-flooding torrent.

"Impressive," Mitch said softly. "If you only had a brain." Then he phoned Gordy and brought him up to speed on the day's startling developments.

The lawyer emitted a long, low whistle. "Well, the tape of Hilde's phone conversation with Jake pretty well explains the call I got this afternoon from Owen Whittaker. Right after she contacted Jake, he must have got in touch with Owen, who tells me Jake has suddenly changed his mind about taking the Syzygy Records offer of ten million, if it isn't too late. I told him it probably was, but I could ask—only how come Jake's getting cold feet over the auction? The guy's already got a million-dollar guarantee from us. Owen said, 'He's a bird-in-the-hand kind of guy.' I said I thought Jake was being shortsighted—but now I see his game. Jake must figure the whole business is about to come unglued, so he'd better grab whatever he can."

"Sounds right," said Mitch. "The thing is, listening to the tape of his responses to Hilde, I can't tell whether Jake really had a deal with Emil—and there's not a clue in there about what it was, *if* it was. You'll have the tape in the morning—listen to it yourself."

"Will do. Now get your backsides stateside, fella—we've got to huddle about whether to pull the plug before the bidders show up."

"I've got to pay just one more visit here," Mitch said, "and then we'll head back."

Gordy was silent for a moment.

"The thing is," he said, "now that I think about it, none of all this byzantine scheming you've uncovered tells us anything about whether the *William Tell Symphony* is bogus or not."

"Roger to that," said Mitch. "*Ciao*, pal."

JUST BEFORE THE APPOINTED HOUR for their revisit to Margot Lenz's apartment, Clara had a phone call from her father advising that Gladys Hoitsma had just slipped on their stairway and broken her hip; emergency surgery was required. Her mother's health and father's angst took precedence over the *Tell* crisis, and she told Mitch, "Go ahead without me—I'm not really needed, and I can't hang up on Daddy." He had badly wanted her on hand for her female instinct appraising Margot's responses—Clara's input from the first had been invaluable to him—but there was no postponing his appointment with Margot.

She appeared rather more drawn than Mitch remembered from their earlier visit. Perhaps it was just the blinding brightness of the midwinter day that afflicted her with a fixed squint as she led him into the living room with its wrap-around picture windows. The glare off the lake caused her to slip on the tinted glasses clipped to the chain around her neck.

He began by apologizing for his renewed intrusion on her privacy but explained that it was his company's responsibility to get to the bottom of all the circumstances surrounding the *Tell* manuscript. "Earlier we pressed you about your brother's possible involvement with the creation of the symphony and his troubled history," said Mitch. "We've now confirmed the nature of your relationship with Felix Utley—sorry, but under these circumstances it's our job to spy—so we need to ask you about his and his uncle's part in this whole Beethoven matter."

Margot nodded assent. "I haven't done very well with the leading men in my life," she reflected after hearing him recite the particulars of Felix Utley's extortionate assault on Cubbage & Wakeham. Her words hinted at victimization but were spoken with a matter-of-factness that did not detract from her grave dignity. Her father, Margot revealed, while a dutiful paterfamilias, had distanced himself from his children as if they were little incubators of vicious microbes sure to do him in. Her brother had been an endearing loon and an infuriating chameleon, whose shortcomings, at least, stemmed more from illness than ill will. The same could not be said of Margot's husband, a desiccated husk who went through all the motions of cohabiting—among them the begetting of their two daughters—with exquisite manners but none of the substance of companionship. An adjunct lecturer in cardiology at the University of Zurich with a few patients, he was away from home three weeks out of four as a consultant for a pharmaceutical giant—"or so he tells me," Margot said. When in town, Dr. Leonidas Lenz made a show of squiring her to upscale restaurants, concerts, the theater, and the Platypus Club—anything to avoid intimacy with his wife, who came to suppose that the cause must be her dwindling charms.

It was inevitable, "and only human," she added without apology, that she would derive comfort and stimulation from her brother's close friend, Felix, a far more attentive and kindred soul than her spouse. "There were times I thought he adored me—even when he was using me, though I was a willing participant at all points."

She turned sharply to Mitch and added, "Do you understand that I had no choice, when you first asked me, but to deny my relationship with Felix? I have two young girls, I run a substantial business, and my aging parents are of the old school—an open marriage to them is no marriage at all. My role as de facto head of our family would have been imperiled if I had not taken every precaution to hide my—our arrangement—"

"Sounds as if your husband would have had little justification for objecting," said Mitch.

"He was skilled at making me feel the inadequacies were wholly on my end," Margot replied, "and, being a slave to propriety, I couldn't risk scandal. Dr. Lenz, not a man of independent means, lives both off me and against me—he made it clear long ago that he would take it out on me emotionally and financially if he ever discovered indiscretions on my part. He felt my brother's antics were the source of quite enough humiliation for one family, though he would never bestir himself, of course, to try to get Ansel the proper medical attention."

"Whereas Felix showed genuine compassion for Ansel?" Mitch inferred.

"Up to a point. My husband thought that our acquaintance was largely concerned with Ansel's problems—and so it was—until Felix displayed and I welcomed a deeper form of caring. It was a new sensation for me." Aside from its novelty, consorting with Felix rather than what she termed "a more socially suitable" lover held two advantages for Margot. He made no objection to the necessarily hermetic nature of their affair, while she, as a high-visibility executive with powerful connections, could keep him under her thumb for a relatively small price. Or so she thought. "Felix, I've only lately come to understand, is a true predator—he knew he could destroy what was left of my marriage and probably bring me down as a businesswoman of rectitude. Promiscuity is not a Swiss virtue. So he's come to assume I'm in thrall to him—which is no doubt why he's attempting to browbeat your firm into paying him off without fear that I'd tell you everything I know if you came to me."

"And will you?" Mitch asked, stirring at the prospect of genuine enlightenment that had eluded him since the beginning of the *Tell* puzzle.

"As best I can—and before it gets worse."

Margot glanced out toward the lake for a time and then began her story, a recital all the more remarkable for its dispassionate self-censure.

One evening two years earlier, Felix had told her—"in strictest confidence"—a tale so improbable that Margot knew it could not have been invented. His Uncle Emil, having long sneered at Felix's musical accomplishments, had recently approached him on a matter of pressing importance. A presentable stranger who claimed to be a lawyer representing unnamed clients had stopped by the Reinsdorfs' apartment with an old manuscript purported to be a long-lost tenth symphony by Beethoven, bearing his signature on the title page and celebrating the exploits of William Tell and his freedom-loving Swiss countrymen. Astonished and incredulous, Emil nevertheless recognized the plausibility of such a work's existence—the maestro, after all, had once been invited to compose incidental music for a Viennese staging of Schiller's drama about Tell—and asked their visitor to relate all he knew about the manuscript's history.

The stranger said he knew little. It had reportedly been hidden for many years at an obscure repository in Czechoslovakia until the Second World War, when Nazi soldiers ransacked the place and, while suspecting the composition attributed to the supreme genius of classical music was a counterfeit, carried off the *Tell* sketchbooks. The two bulky volumes, perceived more as curiosities than precious documents, became underground refugees throughout the war, constantly changing hands for modest sums. In time they reached metropolitan Germany, where they were picked up as a trophy of war by a wealthy industrialist, a favorite of the Reich, who held onto them after peace returned.

The family's second postwar generation, supposing the manuscript was almost surely a sham, chose to dispose of it and hired a friendly attorney to attend to the transaction. Knowing of Emil Reinsdorf's transcendent standing among Beethoven scholars, the go-between brought the ragged manuscript to the Berlin musicologist before any other potential purchaser and offered it to him for 100,000 British pounds. After studying it for a time, Margot related, Felix's uncle concluded that the work was almost certainly the product of Beethoven's hand and, digging deep into his savings, bought it for a quarter of the asking price—for him a considerable investment.

Pondering what to do with his treasure, in need of editing and completed orchestration, Emil decided that its messy condition and murky provenance made the work unsuitable for conventional tests of its authenticity—repair work to cleanse the text and a far simpler and more compelling scenario for its rediscovery would be required. Any traceable involvement on Emil's part, moreover, exposing him as the prime promoter of the find, might cast suspicion on the purity of the work and undermine his standing as the chief arbiter and high priest of Beethoviana. The project had to be carried out at arm's length—and yet under Emil's control. Which, Margot said, was where Felix came in.

Since the symphony was conceived as a tribute to the great Swiss folk hero, what could be more natural, Emil reasoned, than for the work to be found hidden in Switzerland accompanied by a few documents that established a credible link between its presence there and Beethoven's—and, at the same time, accounted for its abandonment? Given all the mechanics and logistics involved in the staggering challenge, he chose his nephew—a skilled, knowledgeable musician and his only living blood relation—to share the secret and a portion of the labor and rewards. While Emil devoted himself to editing and transcribing the painstakingly cleaned-up manuscript, Felix's job was to arrange for bringing the restored *Tell* to the world's attention.

"And that's how I became embroiled in it as well," Margot related. She had once mentioned to Felix that her family held a lien on the Hassler house next door, which would pass into the Erpfs' hands at Otto's death—a disclosure Felix remembered after his uncle had come to him with the *Tell*. The perfect hiding place for the resuscitated manuscript was at hand. After Felix had visited the Zurich Canton Registry and found the birth record of a Hassler family daughter of a suitable age to fit the scenario, Emil invented the Nina, Archduke Rudolph, and Hans Nägeli letters as key elements in the soon-to-be-staged drama of discovery.

"But how could someone of your high intelligence and standing in the community," Mitch challenged her, "permit your family to become mixed up in such a reckless scheme?"

"A good question," Margot conceded. "I let Felix convince me the risk for me and my family was nil. All I personally had to do was place the manuscript and the few other related documents in the Hasslers' attic trunk and let nature take its course." It never occurred to her, she said, to question the authenticity of the manuscript or those "related documents." Emil, after all, was thoroughly acquainted with virtually every detail of Beethoven's life and work, and other experts would be called on as well to judge the legitimacy and merit of the restored symphony. The dormant treasure would be found when Otto died— he was rapidly failing and not expected to survive long—and the household contents would pass into the hands of Limmat Realty, making the Erpfs, as a practical matter, the sole proprietors of Beethoven's lost Tenth Symphony. "Such a heady notion," Margot recalled almost wistfully. For its troubles, her family was to share in the spoils—the Hassler house would become a profitable mecca for music-lovers from all over the world—though the bulk of the revenue was to go to Emil and Felix.

It was Felix, Margot added, who proposed an equitable division of whatever riches might materialize once the manuscript was declared authentic—a process that would, to a greater or lesser extent, inevitably involve Emil Reinsdorf as the world's reigning Beethoven guru. Under Felix's plan, the *Tell* manuscript and ownership rights to it would be donated by the Erpfs, as a gesture of national pride, to the Swiss Ministry of Culture, which would license all performance, recording, and publishing uses of the work. The income from these approved uses would flow into a Tell Fund, to be divided equally for twenty-five years between the Erpf family (and through them, in secret, Emil and Felix) and the Cultural Ministry, which would assign its half to the Philharmonia Helvetica National under the baton of its musical director—and Emil's boyhood pal— Richard Grieder, who would have the honor of giving the premiere public performance of the symphony. And in a side agreement, Grieder was to reinstate Ansel Erpf as a member in good standing of the orchestra, premised on his "appropriate decorum," and promote Felix to concertmaster within two years.

"Felix made it all sound quite irresistible," Margot summed up. There was nothing for her family to lose, no risk of exposure for partaking in any funny business—after all, their coming into possession of the manuscript would have been strictly fortuitous—and there was much to gain by facilitating the discovery of an instant national treasure: enhanced respect for the family's name, business, and philanthropic standing, a good deal of money, and the rehabilitation of Ansel's professional career. What could go wrong?

"But suppose Emil were cracked in the head," Mitch pressed her, "and the manuscript were dismissed by other experts as counterfeit—did you discuss that possibility with Felix?"

"It came up, certainly. But Felix said that was highly unlikely since Emil was indisputably first among the world's Beethoven scholars. And even if worse came to worst, the Erpfs could hardly be accused of trying to perpetrate a fraud—all we'd have done was perform a patriotic act in good faith, leaving the legitimacy of the manuscript for others to decide."

Margot placed the manuscript and its "related documents" in the cedar box inside the attic trunk while paying an afternoon call on bedridden Otto Hassler about a year before he died. "He rarely left his room and was hard of hearing at that point, so there was small risk of his detecting my little side trip upstairs," she recalled. None of the conspirators ever supposed that Jacob Hassler might suddenly appear on the scene for his grandfather's funeral and, with the unwitting assistance of Margot's brother, upset the whole carefully arranged applecart.

Margot tried to salvage the situation by appealing to the Cultural Ministry to intervene on her family's—and the nation's—behalf and proposing to donate the *Tell* manuscript, if it could be recovered from Jake in America, to the people of Switzerland. "I feared it would prove a hopeless quest since you Americans had the advantages of distance and possession," she admitted, "but I had no choice other than to pursue it. In the end, we had to submit to reality and our government's meekness—for which Ansel damned me."

The letter to her from London over Ansel's signature she took to be his perverse form of revenge for her abandonment of the *Tell* fight and Jake's effort to cash in on his brazen theft. "I was sure the letter was from Ansel—why should I have thought otherwise?" she asked. "The writing sounded like his—it looked like his signature—and the half-baked idea the letter proposed, feigning that he himself had composed the symphony, in the hope of forcing your firm to abandon its planned auction, was just the sort of game his lopsided brain was likely to invent." And there was Felix, of course, at her elbow, coaxing Margot to have Ansel hospitalized for sustained treatment so he could no longer bedevil his family and embarrass himself. "I decided to show you the letter before things got out of hand—in case Ansel chose to act rashly as he could do when he was disturbed."

"Didn't Ansel's vehement denial that he wrote the letter give you second thoughts?"

Margot shrugged. "Not at first, of course—it did rather the opposite. Felix was the only other person who knew him well enough—his mannerisms and mental quirks and the whole situation—to have written that letter, but I never supposed he could stoop to such a thing. I knew he was furious at Ansel, though, for having bollixed up the whole *Tell* plan by finding the manuscript and telling Jacob Hassler what it was, so I asked Felix about the letter directly, and he laughed in my face. He said I was at it again, in deep denial of my brother's lunacy and trying to blame it on the rest of the world, just as Ansel did. The meanness of his answer made me begin to realize that I had miscalculated the whole situation. When my brother took his life, still denying he'd written the letter, I finally believed him—but too late. It was the end of my relationship with Felix—I saw that he cared little for me or my feelings—and surely he'd had no pity at all for my brother, otherwise he never would have forged such a letter."

She shook her head in dismay. "And now this news from you—that Felix is nothing but a cheap swindler, trying to squeeze money from your firm by threatening to publicly slander my brother and his own uncle after they're both gone. I have nothing left for him but contempt. I should have come to you long before this, but I was too fearful—after all, I had been Felix's accomplice in planting the manuscript in old Otto's attic after convincing myself that no one could be hurt as a result."

None of her account, Mitch realized with mingled frustration and relief, addressed the overriding issue he still faced: Did Beethoven compose the *Tell* Symphony? Or was the manuscript that passed into and out of Emil Reinsdorf's hands a superb hoax that he'd expertly doctored back to health, able to sustain intense academic and forensic scrutiny?

"Why exactly are you telling me all this?" Mitch asked her. "My firm will have to disclose the whole convoluted story, which may very well doom the chances of the symphony ever being recognized as Beethoven's—let alone ever being auctioned for a fortune—and it's almost certain to complicate your own life. You could be charged as an accessory to an attempted fraud, even if no money actually changed hands."

"But I didn't tell you the symphony was an invention—by Felix's uncle or anyone else. I believe—I've always believed—the account of how Emil got hold of the manuscript. And I considered his cleaning up the manuscript, as far as he got with it before turning it over to Felix to arrange for its "discovery,' to be a devoted exercise of homage."

Margot looked straight at Mitch.

"I've confessed to you because I've had enough," she said decisively. "I'm prepared to tell my family everything about Felix and me—and if it doesn't suit them and I have to lose whatever position and respectability are left to me, so be it. I'll be better off without a sham marriage, and the realty business has lost most of its charms for me."

"Will you testify against Felix if it comes to that—saying what you've just told us?"

"Gladly."

On their drive to the airport, Mitch replayed for Clara his emotionally raw interview with Margot. "Finally," she said, trying to sound positive, "we're getting down to the nitty-gritty."

"Are we?" asked Mitch, growing more dejected by the minute.

"Okay, I was wrong about the Reinsdorfs being pillars of integrity," Clara admitted. "But everything Margot Lenz just told you sounds plausible."

"And why is that?" he asked.

"Because, well, the whole story is so unflattering to her. Why would she paint herself into a corner like that—revealing so many inner feelings—and who could make all that up?"

Mitch shook his head with exasperation over this whole viscous porridge and how it was muddying Clara's ordinarily lucid brain. "We need to think straight here, hon."

"I'm trying to, but it keeps twisting and turning each time we get closer to—"

"First of all, Margot apparently knows only what Felix told her about the *Tell* manuscript—and why should we believe he was leveling with her?" he asked. "Second of all, if he *was* being straight with her and *she* was telling us the truth, then the entire historical background for our authenticated Beethoven symphony goes up in smoke—Emil invented the whole context to make the shoe fit."

Eyeing the elaborate graffiti fouling the walls along the expressway to the airport, he felt the *Tell* was equally corrupted. "Frankly, we're actually losing ground here, buttercup."

"I BELIEVE THE APPLICABLE TECHNICAL term for our predicament," Harry said, opening the C&W war council the next morning, "is 'up shit's creek.'"

"The problem is," Gordy added, "we have five smoking guns—at last count."

With just a week left before the auction was scheduled and the office phones going off nonstop, the precious object attracting the world's attention now appeared to be of dubious origin and fictitious subsequent history. Discovered in a house where it was reportedly created, the symphony could actually have gestated anywhere, it now seemed, and been conceived by black magic—and its foremost (and now deceased) certifier at last report had a vested interest (or several) in its prospective commercial exploitation.

"The best we can hope for," Mitch summarized, "is that Emil Reinsdorf sincerely believed that the *Tell* was composed by Beethoven—and that, by sanitizing its form and tethering it to a plausible time and place, he thought he was accomplishing what no one else had the knowledge and daring to try."

"So—is that good enough for you to greenlight the manuscript for auction?" Gordy asked.

"What do you think?" Mitch asked back.

Harry, near the end of his rope, had turned testier than usual.

"Mitchell, tell me honestly—will we ever get to the bottom of this steaming heap of excrement?"

"I'm not sure. I think we're getting close, though."

"Marvelous," Harry chided, "and meanwhile we're getting our chain yanked six ways from Sunday by these characters."

"Pardon, chaps," Sedge Wakeham rumbled over the speakerphone, "we've no choice but to hold off the crowd of bidders while it's all still topsy-turvy. Give Mitchell the time he needs."

Reluctantly Harry bowed to his partner's elliptical wisdom. More or less. "All right, we'll put everything on standby for two weeks." He turned to Mitch. "Spend whatever it takes—do whatever you need to."

As it happened, he needed to go no farther than his office, where Clara was awaiting him. She was holding the edelweiss painting, out of its frame, that Hilde Reinsdorf had sent her as a gift. "Remember this? I was about to take it to the framing gallery to dress it up a bit."

"Sure. But not now, hon—I've got a million things I need to—"

She put an index finger to his lips. "Turn it over and tell me what you see."

"Da Vinci's last will and testament?"

"Even better. Do it."

He turned the painting over. The sheet of heavy paper looked blank. "So?"

"Look again—try the lower right corner."

There, very faintly, running from the center of the bottom edge to the right side edge at a forty-five-degree angle, were two sets of five parallel lines, the ones closer to the corner of necessarily diminishing length, with dim dots and marks on and between them. Mitch held the sheet still nearer to his eyes. "What are they? If they had clefs, I'd say they were bars of music that had been erased."

"Not erased—just very lightly pressed on—as if this sheet somehow got folded under or over another freshly inked one and the offset rubbed against it, unnoticed. And then it got gathered up and accidentally bound into an old music sketchbook—maybe two centuries ago or so—"

Mitch examined the paper a third time. "Christ, it's about the right page size—the same top decaled edge—similar cream color." He planted a kiss of commendation on Clara's bowed lips and hurried off to the basement to retrieve the object of their collective concern from the company vault. In minutes, he and Clara determined, to the extent the naked eye was able to, that the sheet with Hilde Reinsdorf's floral painting looked identical to the blank pages—in size, tint, and texture—at the back of the second sketchbook found in Otto Hassler's attic trunk containing the partially orchestrated autograph score of the *William Tell* Symphony.

"Emil could have recruited her for his *Tell* project—who could he trust more?" Clara speculated. "I mean, she's a highly accomplished artist—remember the incredible millefleur painting of hers covering their vestibule walls, all the minute touches in the petals and leaves, just like in this edelweiss study. And someone who's mastered that degree of draftsmanship might well be capable of either copying music that Beethoven actually wrote but needed to be cleaned up for legibility—under super-expert supervision—like Emil's—or...or..."

"Or of forging someone else's work—maybe even Emil's," Mitch finished the thought for her, "to make it look as if Beethoven had written it—"

"And when Hilde took time off from the *Tell* project to do a little fun work of her own now and then—like this edelweiss watercolor she did for me—she may have run short of art supplies," Clara hypothesized, "and very, very carefully razored this blank sheet out of the second ersatz Beethoven sketchbook—unless it was the real thing, but she supposed that it would never be missed—"

They burst into Harry's office with their fresh evidence in hand. "I think we're onto something solid," Mitch said, trying—but failing—to suppress a hint of triumph.

"Well, that was fast work," Harry said.

"Fortunately, I'm married to a genius."

"*Un*fortunately," she said, her smile fleeting, "the news doesn't really solve the problem."

Harry and Gordy heard them out, looked at each other, and then in unison pointed the Emerys to the door. "Get back over to Berlin and don't come back without the widow lady's sworn statement about what her husband's real role was in all this *schiess*. There either is or isn't a Beethoven's Tenth—enough voodoo already."

It took another two days to generate a report from Veritas's subsidiary forensics lab in Boston, confirming the paper matchup between Hilde's edelweiss painting and a sample swatch from the second *Tell* sketchbook in the C&W vault. Meanwhile, Mitch drafted a memorandum recounting his long conversation with Margot Lenz at her place and had a copy made of Hilde's taped phone conversation with Jake Hassler, reminding him of his financial obligation to her once the *Tell* auction was held. The items composed what Mitch called his in-your-face kit to lay before the widow Reinsdorf as soon as they could book a flight to Germany.

On their arrival at Tempelhof on a Lufthansa red-eye out of JFK, however, they were greeted at the passport control window by a sleepy inspector who, on examining their documents, was sufficiently alert to buzz for the security police. "Please step over to the side," the Emerys were instructed and within moments were surrounded by a four-man posse, two uniformed and armed German officers and two plainclothesmen who were identified as Swiss security agents.

"You're wanted for interrogation in Zurich, Mr. Emery," one of the Swiss lawmen said calmly, "in connection with the death of Mrs. Lenz four days ago."

Mitch did not have to feign astonishment. "Margot? Yes, I saw her—what?—four days ago at her apartment, yes. But she was fine then."

"But maybe not when you left her," the plainclothesman suggested. "You were apparently the last person to see her alive—the housemaid admitted you and then left for her day off. The coroner's report on her time of death appears to implicate you—"

"In what? What happened to her?"

"She was bludgeoned to death—it may have been a robbery, or the scene was made to appear that way. You'll have to come with us, I'm afraid." The other Swiss agent, apparently in charge of their capture, turned to Clara. "You're free to go about your business, Mrs. Emery."

"I'm not going anywhere," Clara said, "except with my husband. This is an outrage."

Mitch looked into the blank face of bureaucratic rigidity.

"I've done nothing—but I'll be glad to tell you whatever I know about Mrs. Lenz," he said as non-combatively as he could manage. "Why in the world would I be involved in her death? I have no—"

"That's what our police want to ask you. We'll accompany you to the baggage carousel, or do you just have carry-ons?"

Mitch declined to move in the direction he was told. "Why don't you question me right here? I'll tell you all I can—what's the point of dragging me back to Switzerland?"

"It's how we do things in a murder investigation."

"You're telling me I'm a serious suspect in…Margot Lenz's murder?"

"We've told you, as a courtesy, more than you're technically entitled to know."

Mitch looked at Clara and shook his head. "I believe I'm permitted to speak with the American embassy," he said to the Swiss agents, "before I'm abducted by a foreign nation."

"Your transfer to our authority has already been cleared with your embassy," he was told and given a business card. "You're free to use the wall phone over there to speak with a Mr. Henderson, who's available at any time."

"If I resist these gentlemen," Mitch said to Clara, "it will look as if I've got something to hide. You call Gordy right away and ask him to please get his butt on the next plane to Zurich. But you stay here to do what we came for—then join us down there. Nothing bad will happen."

"Oh, God," she said, clinging to him for a moment. "You promise?"

{17}

I'm afraid I'm engaged for the rest of the day," Hilde said cordially when Clara phoned to request an appointment within the hour. "But I'd love a visit with you and Mitchell—perhaps later in the week?"

"I'm here alone," Clara said, "and rather badly pressed for time, I'm sorry to say."

"Oh, I see." A moment's strained silence. "Well, perhaps on your next visit, then?"

"I hate to inconvenience you, Hilde," said Clara, "but it's a matter of some urgency."

"I'm sorry, Clara, am I not making myself clear?" Hilde asked. "I have other commitments—all day."

Aching from Mitch's indelicate seizure and abrupt transfer to the Swiss authorities, Clara was anxious but determined to step in as his understudy and deal with Hilde Reinsdorf—sternly. The woman had betrayed Clara's trust and now had to be held to account. "You can see me now, Hilde, or I can come with the *polizei*. Which do you prefer?"

A longer silence ensued. "I see," Hilde said at last in a now brittle voice. "I...I'll rearrange my appointments, then, if that would suit you."

Scherzo, perhaps sixth-sensing the dread behind his mistress's fretful mood, was even throatier in his unwelcome than on Clara's prior arrival at the Reinsdorf threshold. Hilde had to use visible force to keep the agitated bulldog from catapulting himself at the visitor. "He's very irritable today," she apologized. "That was to be one of my engagements just now—at the veterinarian's. I think

345

Scherzie has an infected tooth—probably because I'm spoiling the poor old fellow with too many sweets."

As soon as they were seated, Clara explained without elaborating that Mitch had been unexpectedly detained, "so he asked me to meet with you again—in the hope that you'll be more forthcoming this time."

Hilde looked perplexed.

"I don't think I'm following you, dear. What is it that—"

"For your own sake," Clara broke in, "let me suggest that you be as candid as you know how. If you are, Mitchell will do his best to prevail upon the principals at his firm not to go to your law-enforcement officials."

"Oh, my," Hilde said coyly. "What horrid thing is it I've done?"

"This won't be any easier for me than for you," Clara said, then reached into her canvas bag, drew out the compromising materials Mitch had prepared for their visit, spread them over the coffee table beside her, and clicked on the pocket tape player.

Hilde appeared startled at the sound of her own voice, imploring Jake Hassler to acknowledge his agreement with her husband regarding the *Tell* manuscript. Scherzie barked sharply as Hilde's eyes reflected what her discerning intellect now fully grasped.

"Tapping someone's phone is quite a serious crime here, you know," she said bitterly after the tape ended, trying to downplay the more serious transgression disclosed by her exchange with Jake. "We don't have the SS here anymore, you know."

"You're free, of course, to notify the authorities," Clara chided her back, "but I'm confident they'll be more interested in learning the truth about Dr. Reinsdorf's scandalous behavior in the discovery and disposition of the *William Tell* Symphony."

Hilde, studying the worn Persian carpet at her feet while collecting her wits, leaned down to stroke Scherzo, who had positioned himself at the side of her chair. She began fussing with one of his crumpled ears, as if to summon the departed spirit of the man who had been master to them both. With her free hand she picked up the forensics report about the paper on which her edelweiss painting had been rendered, soon grasped its finding, and then moved on to Mitch's write-up of his recent extended conversation with the late Margot Lenz. The disclosures in the final document seemed to drain Hilde of all pretense and fully alert her to the peril she was now facing.

"I suppose," she said haltingly, "all of this—all of these things—they leave you thinking the very worst of Emil and me—"

346

"Shall we just say that they're highly suggestive of unacceptable behavior by people who surely should have known better?"

"Oh, yes—yes, I suppose. I can see that." Her posture stiffened. She cast aside Mitch's account of his interview with Margot. "And you no doubt infer from Mrs. Lenz's disclosures that the *Tell* manuscript itself—not only the documents found with it in Zurich—is an invention, and that Emil may have been its perpetrator, and, because of the paper I used for the edelweiss painting, that I was his forger-accomplice. Is that it?"

"Mrs. Lenz never told Mitchell she had any reason to doubt the authenticity of the symphony, based on what Mr. Utley told her about it," Clara said. "But Dr. Reinsdorf's role as the composer—and your own connivance at his request—both seem highly plausible—and that Mrs. Lenz and her family were being used to promote your grand deception."

Hilde managed a thin smile that soon faded.

"I understand, of course, how you might reach such a conclusion—Emil recognized that unfortunate possibility from the beginning. But he felt, under the circumstances, there was no alternative—which was not true, of course. He might instead have been totally forthright when the manuscript came into his possession so providentially, as Felix explained to Mrs. Lenz."

The comment took Clara by surprise. "Forthright in what way?"

"By coming forward with the manuscript immediately after purchasing it and submitting it to a jury of his scholarly peers. But he didn't believe he had any peers in academia or anywhere else on the subject of Beethoven, so he had no desire to risk his judgment that the *Tell* manuscript was genuinely Beethoven's work. Instead, he chose to make that judgment by himself and to arrange all the circumstances of its restoration and discovery—he wanted to be the impresario of Beethoven's Tenth Symphony without letting the world in on the secret—and, incidentally, to make some money for us in the bargain. Lord knows, his faculty salary and the income from his various writings hardly left us well off. He thought he deserved some sizable material reward for all his labors over the years."

Clara sat back in her chair, now thoroughly baffled. "Are you saying that Dr. Reinsdorf took this purported Beethoven manuscript that was dropped into his lap by fate, so to speak, and decided all by himself that it sufficiently resembled the maestro's style—"

"It didn't drop into his lap at all," Hilde cut in. "It was sold to him for a considerable sum—well, for us it was a good deal of money—too much, in my judgment."

"All right, but it sounds as if, after convincing himself the manuscript was actually composed by Beethoven—or might well have been—that your husband then undertook a series of carefully calculated measures, including revisions of the text, to remove as much doubt as possible about Beethoven's being the composer, so that it would be more readily accepted as—"

Hilde's eyes narrowed to slits of resentment.

"You think that Emil *distorted* the manuscript—took liberties he had no right to—that the symphony is—what—false Beethoven?"

Clara couldn't tell if the woman was made of pure brass or desperately putting up a brave front. Or perhaps her refusal to surrender the truth was less stubbornness than failure to recognize the depth of the obsession that had seized her husband. "Is it?" she asked Hilde.

"Certainly not," the widow replied without hesitation. "The *Tell* symphony materialized—it happened just as Mrs. Lenz told your husband, as described in this report on their recent meeting. Emil's judgment may be called into question, but nothing either of us did was meant to be other than completely honorable—and a service to humanity, not to mention the maestro."

"In that case," Clara said, "you'd better enlighten me—fully."

"Yes—I can see that." Hilde raked a hand through her tightly coiffed iron-gray hair. Lost for a moment considering where to begin, she patted Scherzo's slowly heaving flanks. "The fullest explanation, I think, stems from Emil's deep conflict over having abandoned his native land for another one that he felt never duly regarded him." Once underway, her story flowed in a rapid stream.

Switzerland had always been too small a vessel to contain Emil Reinsdorf's aspirations. The lad from Lucerne quickly excelled at the Zurich Conservatory and moved on to Vienna's more demanding stage. But the Austrians and the Swiss were never fond of one another, and Emil, like Beethoven, always felt himself to be an *auslander* among the Viennese. After he began to publish and moved on to Berlin as a *wunderkind* musicologist, Hilde recounted, he found that his Swiss origin was often disparaged behind his back and his countrymen demeaned as soulless mercenaries bereft of national pride or any native aesthetic worthy of the name. In quest of laurels, Emil took on the coloration of his Aryan colleagues, choosing as his foreign-born role model Herbert von Karajan, who had overcome the disadvantages of Greco-Macedonian ancestry to bestride the German music world as director/conductor of the Berlin Philharmonic. Karajan had become a card-carrying Nazi in the Hitler era and afterward exhibited little more than lip-service remorse. For his own ascent, Emil Reinsdorf chose to become an adopted citizen of Germany and a vehement champion of its *kultur.*

Even after he had attained preeminence as a scholar, Hilde recalled, "Emil was never good enough—or German enough—to suit them." He longed for the enhanced dignity, power, and income bestowed by the title of Herr Direktor of the National Institute of Music and twice presented himself as a candidate for the position, only to be twice rejected. "It infuriated Emil—he became a different person," his widow lamented, with his crowning ambition thwarted.

He had been in a deep funk for the better part of a year when *Tell* happened. "It was as if Emil had been put on earth to be there that night," Hilde told Clara, "when this individual appeared at our door—without an appointment, mind you—and presented himself and his story about the Beethoven manuscript, which struck both of us on first hearing as wholly fanciful."

Their visitor, a lawyer named Osterweil—"if that was his true name"—was not at liberty, he said, to identify his client. Nor did he have documentation to support his anecdotal account of how the two sketchbooks had long been stored and later stolen from the ecclesiastical library at Olmütz in Moravia, where Cardinal (formerly Archduke) Rudolph had at one time presided, and sold and resold in the black market during the war-torn Third Reich on the strength of the Beethoven name on the title page. Although supremely skeptical of this hearsay testimony, Emil was of course aware of the maestro's affinity for the works of Friedrich Schiller, so it was by no means inconceivable to him that Beethoven had embarked on such a *Tell* project in operatic form, grew frustrated, transformed it into an experimental symphonic work with vocal sections, and then set it aside for some unknown reason. Emil also knew that as Beethoven's student, friend, protector, and chief patron, Archduke Rudolph had held some of the maestro's manuscripts for safekeeping at the Schönbrun Palace in Vienna and might well have brought them to Olmütz with him when he became a prince of the Roman Church.

Hilde went on: "And so Dr. Reinsdorf asked the lawyer if he could examine the sketchbooks for several days before deciding whether to make a purchase offer—and the gentleman was more than happy to oblige." Emil was disheartened by what he found. The manuscript had been badly fingered over by careless hands for generations. The cover of the old sketchbook was taped together, and many of the sheets had come undone so that the pagination was jumbled. And many pages were a mess, some of them torn, wrinkled, or flaking, some smudged or blurred as if rained upon or otherwise assaulted by liquids, with wine stains and cigarette burns at irregular intervals.

"It had been abused and neglected," Hilde related, "to the point that it brought tears to Emil's eyes."

Nevertheless, the longer he pored over the manuscript, the more Emil was struck by how closely its contents resembled Beethoven's musical handwriting—the stemless notes, the staves without clefs, the curious symbols, all the smudges and drips, the urgent application of pen to paper.

"Anyone else would have given up on it after a single day," Hilde said with muted pride, "but Emil was not like anyone else." By the second day, he had begun to make some sense out of the pagination. By the third day, he grasped that the work had been scored well into the second movement but thereafter it was impossible to decipher in its current form; it needed to be clean-copied, with what were evidently alternate versions of some passages inserted where they belonged. When Osterweil phoned him for a decision, Emil asked for and was given a few more days to complete his assessment. "I couldn't say a word to him throughout that week—he survived on tea, crackers, nibbles of cheese, and his hateful Marlboros."

What kept him at it so feverishly, Hilde said, was not merely the miracle that he had happened on a tenth symphony by his venerated maestro but that the work was a celebration of Swiss gallantry and the love of liberty and independence by Emil's native countrymen. "It was as if his whole life had suddenly come together. Preserving the symphony was his way, I think, of apologizing to the land of his birth for turning his back on it in order to advance his career—and like Faust's bargain with the devil, it failed in the end." Hilde's eyes were brimming now.

On the seventh day, Emil came out of his study and sat beside Hilde to review the matter.

"He said to me, 'Even if I were convinced of it—and I am not yet and may never be—who else will believe this story of a whole Beethoven symphony being stolen and dragged through the mud for so many years? Look at this heap of pages!'" For the unsightly pile ever to be accepted and gain respectability, he said, it would have to withstand intensive scrutiny by elite scholars who had the time and funding to hover over it endlessly—a process that could go on for decades, by which time Emil would long be in his grave. He could not bear to inflict that further ordeal on the fragile *Tell* manuscript, so, never short on hubris, Emil wanted to determine its fate himself. Salvaging the symphony would be his ultimate achievement, the one that would enshrine his name for the ages, forever linked to his exalted maestro's.

But even if he could manage to buy the manuscript for a modest price, Emil knew the undertaking could prove an egregious folly. To bring the *Tell* to life would require a brutal three-step regimen, but one that Emil Reinsdorf was uniquely qualified to attempt. "We'll need to make the manuscript look presentable," he told Hilde. It would have to be cleaned up and made legible enough, even if in Beethoven's customarily messy way, for others to understand it and be able to complete the partial scoring. In other words, they needed to fabricate two new but old-looking sketchbooks *to appear as if* the original manuscript had been lovingly preserved for all those years. Otherwise, Emil reasoned, even if he were to devote all the time required to puzzle the thing out, transcribe it in his own hand, and then bring it forward for public scrutiny while insisting it was a faithful rendering of Beethoven's intentions, he would become a laughingstock—"no reputable scholar would trust it," Emil said.

And that was only the beginning of the challenge. For after having secretly brought the manuscript to life, Emil would then have to invent a plausible scenario to explain the work's creation, abandonment, and rediscovery and produce documents to support the whole story. Finally, a mechanism would have to be found so that Emil and Hilde could realize some material benefits from the ultimate disposition of the work. A greatly devoted husband, Emil fretted because he might leave Hilde little better off than a pauper; the pensions the Berlin Conservatory provided its faculty widows were far from generous. Hilde told him she could survive well enough on whatever was available—there was no need for him to commit a colossal forgery on her account.

"But it will not be a forgery!" Emil shouted at her. There would be nothing false about it. She should think of the newly created sketchbooks as a meticulous restoration, if the term suited her better. The story they would have to spin about the symphony's unknown history would unavoidably be an invention, but only incidental to the thing itself, which he believed—with conviction deepening by the day—to be completely genuine.

"And how will you ever find someone trustworthy enough to help you execute this 'meticulous restoration' of yours?" Hilde asked him.

"But I already have the perfect collaborator, *mein schatz*," he replied, pressing her hand.

She feared that Emil might be turning senile, Hilde confessed to Clara. The whole venture seemed to her absurdly risky, costly, and time-consuming. "But he had made his mind up."

It took Emil more than a year to understand, transcribe, and, in a few places where the manuscript was stained or otherwise illegible, fill in the small holes. By the second year of his labors, Emil felt that he needed professional feedback of a sort Hilde could not offer, and he turned to his nephew in Zurich—"with misgivings on my part that I fully expressed," she told Clara. But Emil, while he regarded Felix as a lazy sensualist, did not doubt his musical aptitude and discerning ear. He was, after all, an experienced violinist with a respectable philharmonic, who he felt, as his only surviving family member, could be counted upon for discretion. Still, mindful of Hilde's concern, Emil hit upon a temporary subterfuge; he pretended to Felix that the *Tell* was his own work, his first serious attempt at composing, and that it seemed fitting for him to render it as a dual tribute—to his greatly beloved maestro, written in a manner intended to evoke with reverence Beethoven's "heroic style," and to his native Switzerland, Felix's homeland, too.

Felix swallowed the story enthusiastically and greatly encouraged his uncle. "I think he was grateful for being treated by Emil with respect, for a change," Hilde reflected. With rising confidence, Emil took the further step, on his next semiannual visit to Zurich, of sharing his venture with his old friend, Richard Grieder, whose perspective as a conductor, even a lackluster one, would be of value. Grieder, too, was taken in by Emil's story of the work as a twin tribute— charmed by it, even—and said after examining the first movement that he hoped someday Reinsdorf's Beethovenesque *William Tell* Symphony might be premiered by the Swiss Philharmonic.

Emil then began bending his brain toward dreaming up "the proper background" for staging the *Tell* discovery. The elements fell nicely into place: Zurich was the right venue for Beethoven's imagined trip to have his deafness cured (and for Swiss heroism to be on his mind); the late summer of 1814 was the right time (since he was not otherwise engaged or accounted for), and the politically repressive climate in post-Napoleonic Austria was a plausible reason for his symphony on an anti-Hapsburg theme to have been set aside by the maestro. Emil's imaginative drafts of the first Nina note, the Nägeli, and the Archduke Rudolph letters followed; all that remained was to find a suitable Zurich household—with a documentable nubile maiden in residence—to fit the scenario.

"I thought the conception quite ingenious—and harmless," Hilde confessed. She even helped Emil embroider the story, which she felt would be more affecting if Nina's relationship with Beethoven were revealed to include a subtle sexual attraction—well beyond the flirtatious or sentimental sort he pursued with the wives and friends of his patrons. Since the resulting love child's existence would have caused a scandal ruinous to the maestro's reputation for rectitude, he would have had to deny fathering the infant and thus could not have reclaimed the abandoned *Tell* manuscript without owning up to his heinous sin. Emil thought it a deft touch and drew up the second Nina letter, with its heart-wrenching farewell rebuke to the family that had disowned her, along with the note from the clerk in a nonexistent Austrian village reporting her death by drowning in the Danube and the entry in an invented Hassler family diary with its equally touching account of the loveless life and unlamented death of Nina's illegitimate Marie.

By now, Clara was equally shocked and enthralled by Hilde's narrative, unable to scoff at or interrupt her story.

By the fourth year, Hilde now hurried on, they had reached the culminating stage of the project—fabricating the *Tell* sketchbooks. After Emil had steeped himself in the literature on the illicit art and craft of forgery, he turned to the only person qualified and trustworthy enough to produce what he termed a "certifiable simulation" of Beethoven's compositional handwriting. At first, Hilde would not hear of it, urging him instead to come forward with his edited, sanitized version of the work and a detailed explanation of how it had evolved— "but it was too late for that." Shortly thereafter, Emil was diagnosed with lung cancer, and all other concerns were put aside during his struggle for survival. His surgery, chemotherapy, and recovery of strength took the better part of a year, but the long interruption served only to harden Emil's resolve to bring the *Tell* to fruition. Sure that he was living on borrowed time, he renewed his appeal to Hilde to apply her artistic skills to creating the ersatz Beethoven sketchbooks.

"It was my dying husband's last request," she explained, "and, as he kept reminding me, I would one day be the prime beneficiary of our joint venture." As an artist, it was to be her own supreme challenge. She studied and practiced for months mimicking Beethoven's inelegant handwriting and slapdash composing penmanship under Emil's rigorous scrutiny.

"Didn't the difficulty of it all frighten you?" Clara wondered with complicitous admiration.

"Of course—I was so nervous that my hand trembled for weeks, and when I overcame my anxiety at last, I wrote in too stiff and deliberate a fashion, lacking the flow of natural writing—which Emil assured me was the undoing of even accomplished forgers." Less trying for her was to simulate the odd handwriting of Archduke Rudolph and the more regular script of Hans Nägeli, photocopied samples of which Emil had found at archives in Germany and Austria.

While Hilde honed her dark art month after month, Emil went about methodically gathering, mostly in antiquarian shops, the ingredients for the rendering process—vintage paper both bound and unbound, quills, the materials for mixing old-fashioned ink, and an early edition of Schiller's *Tell*. With these in hand, he enlisted a graduate student in chemistry to devise a way for doctoring the writing surfaces in the unused old sketchbooks so the ink did not feather when applied to them yet did not crust and crack, telltale signs it had been chemically swabbed to hide the age of the ink. Every page Hilde then copied from Emil's transcribed version of the original manuscript had to be perfected, which meant endless practice. "It was a grinding procedure that could not be hurried," said Hilde. "It greatly tried both our patience."

As his wife labored on, Emil decided he could no longer delay confiding the truth about the *Tell*'s real composer to his two advisers in Zurich. If the manuscript was to be planted there and the discovery scenario played out, both Felix and Grieder had to be in on the secret. His nephew, while distressed at first over having been misled, even if for plausible reasons, soon agreed to become Emil's full-fledged accomplice. It fell to him to arrange the logistics for the staged discovery and to devise some means for extracting money from the sensational rebirth of the *Tell* without giving the game away. Emil, of course, could in no way be suspected of involvement with the resurrected work; his mission thereafter would be to help authenticate it. Informed by his lover Margot of the Erpf family's lien on the next-door Hassler house, Felix hit upon using Otto's attic for the discovery site and Margot and the Erpfs' connections as the conduit for reaping a portion of the riches that the *Tell* would likely generate. It was a steep price to pay the Erpfs, but Felix argued it was the surest way to obtain the Swiss government's imprimatur on the work and to sanitize its profits.

"And what was Felix to get out of it?" Clara asked.

"Emil's gratitude, mostly—but money, to be sure, was always on Felix's mind." Hilde turned up her palms in confession. "When I misspoke to you earlier about the matter, I felt that I had no choice. The truth is, they came to some sort of understanding—Emil never told me the details, only that Felix would receive some share of the money, if only because his paramour Margot would be the front person in dealing with the Cultural Ministry. There had to be trust among them or the whole arrangement was worthless." As an added inducement to Felix, Emil promised to push Grieder even harder to promote him to concertmaster. So heartily did the philharmonic's conductor dislike Felix, though, that he nearly rejected Emil's plea. But on being told authoritatively by his old pal Emil that the *Tell* was authentic Beethoven, he readily forgave Reinsdorf for his duplicitous handling of the matter. For his cooperation, Grieder was promised the world premiere of the symphony and financial support for his orchestra from its revenue stream. In return, all Emil asked from Grieder was silence about what he knew.

"After all," Hilde contended, "it had all been done primarily for art's sake—to salvage an otherwise disreputable work—not for any base motive on Emil's part."

She had woven the tale so compellingly that Clara felt herself torn between fascination and revulsion. Emil Reinsdorf had surely sinned by his massive application of artifice—but not so heinously, perhaps, to deserve condemnation as a criminal. He had paid for the right to own the *Tell* manuscript, be it rogue or genuine Beethoven, and dedicated himself to the excruciating labor of making it presentable in the passionate conviction that he was not committing fraud. Definitive identification of the work's composer, and the finesse of Emil's anonymous craftsmanship in repairing it, he left to other experts to confirm or reject, though he surely did not shrink from complicity in the process when invited to join C&W's authentication panel. "You have a point," Clara admitted, "but I think his zeal was overwrought—and likely misguided by his deteriorating health."

"I don't disagree," Hilde said with some resignation, "but I couldn't deter him."

In the end, Felix persuaded Emil that the second Nina letter about her illegitimate daughter and its related documents might strike too sour a note, so dirtying Beethoven's memory that his infuriated worshippers might go to great lengths to deny the *Tell*'s authenticity. So Emil withheld the Nina-Marie material from the documents that Margot placed in the wooden box in the Hasslers' attic trunk, but he saved them in his bank vault in case they were ever needed to embellish the original Nina tale. As an added precaution, Felix arranged for the carving and installation of the peculiar mother-daughter tombstone in the Hassler cemetery plot, where only Otto remained to be laid to rest.

"And then Jacob Hassler came along to muck up the works," Clara filled in the ending.

"Exactly—and all that backbreaking effort of ours, about eight years' worth, seemed lost to Emil for good. He was terribly depressed."

The Reinsdorfs' spirits revived, however, when Emil was asked to serve on C&W's panel of experts, and it became clear at once that his judgment would prove pivotal. His unique leverage allowed him to compensate for Jake Hassler's heist of the *Tell* manuscript. "Your firm had arranged a sightseeing tour of your Revolutionary War battlefields in New Jersey just before his panel was to begin final deliberations, and Emil found himself brushing up against Mr. Hassler, this grasping American philistine. They were able to discuss the situation—*sotto voce*—and work out a sensible understanding."

"How much of the real story did Dr. Reinsdorf tell Jake?" Clara asked.

"I was sitting elsewhere on the bus, so I can't say for certain," Hilde replied. But each of them needed the other if either was to realize anything from the sale of the symphony, so their agreement was soon committed to paper. They both had something in writing as a protection in case the other failed to perform his part of the bargain—Emil to vote for authenticating the manuscript and Jake to turn over a share of the auction price to him. "It was very risky, of course," said Hilde, "but then the whole undertaking was fraught with risk from the beginning."

The trade-off with Jake struck Clara as inexcusable.

"Didn't it seem to you blatantly immoral for Dr. Reinsdorf to sell his vote in the authentication process by my husband's firm?"

"Not in the least," said Hilde. "Emil's vote was never in doubt, of course. And Jacob Hassler had, in effect, stolen Emil's property from him. And your husband's company has been Mr. Hassler's eager accomplice ever since. Furthermore, your people approached Emil to join in the certification process—not the other way around—and Mitchell's auction house got what it bargained for, so where was Emil's sin?"

When his cancer recurred, it was virulent and inoperable. Still, Emil was almost at peace because it looked as if the *Tell* would survive him—intact and fully legitimized. But he had to contend with two final threats to the *Tell's* acceptance. The first was the letter Margot Lenz received, apparently from her brother, threatening to claim that the symphony was a hoax and that he himself had perpetrated it.

"It infuriated Emil. He could make no sense of it whatsoever," Hilde recalled, "until he realized that it must have been written by Felix. Who else knew all the technical details that the letter mentioned?" Felix's purpose, Emil guessed, was to scare C&W into withdrawing the manuscript from auction and thus encouraging its sale to the Erpf family, so that the original plan to cash in on the symphony could be resurrected. The ploy was not as witless as it first struck Emil, who, in his anger at Felix for allowing the manuscript to be removed from Zurich, had informed his nephew about the income-sharing deal he had reached with Jake. So Emil had phoned Felix from his sickbed, railed at him for meddling by concocting the fake Ansel letter, and then forgiven him.

Her explanation did not satisfy Clara. "Felix told my husband that Emil promised him a part of whatever he would be paid under the arrangement he had made in America."

"Possibly—but I didn't hear their conversation, and Emil never told me about any such promise. I doubt he wanted to reward Felix for letting everything get out of hand in Zurich."

Soon after Emil returned home from the hospital, he had a phone call from Jake Hassler anxiously informing him that C&W was still questioning the Nina story. Emil told him he would think about it, then instructed Hilde to retrieve the second Nina letter, which had been residing in their bank vault along with its supporting documents, and to phone his nephew, asking him to hurriedly compose a typewritten note to Jake over Ansel's name, the same way Felix had earlier concocted the confession letter addressed to Margot from London. Overnight, Felix faxed Hilde the fake cover note to Jake, explaining why the accompanying documents had been withheld previously and were being forwarded now supposedly by Ansel's London lawyer friend who had been asked to do so in the event of Ansel's death or commitment to a mental hospital. Hilde added the new faked Ansel note to the other items Emil had prepared earlier but withheld till then and shipped them to Jake along with instructions to tell Mitch and his C&W colleagues that the material had come from London and, if asked to supply the envelope, claim he had thoughtlessly discarded it. "My Emil was lucid till the end, as you see," Hilde added. "He died very soon after that." She unfolded her hands, which had remained serenely immobile on her lap throughout her long narration, then reached down to stroke Scherzie's squat neck and looked up brightly. "Shall we drink to his health?"

They did. Silently, respectfully. "It's what Americans call a fascinating yarn," Clara said.

"Well, I trust this helps you understand a little better why we—"

Hilde cut herself off, as if assuming she had disposed of the entire matter to Clara's satisfaction.

"Is there anything else, dear? I've tired myself, and no doubt you, with all of this..."

"There is just one troubling thing, I'm afraid."

"*Bitte?*"

"Dr. Reinsdorf was an eminent musicologist," Clara said, "so it's unthinkable to me that he would have tampered to the extent you've described with an original Beethoven manuscript of such importance and priceless value."

"But he didn't tamper with it—as I thought I explained to you," Hilde said, growing irritable now. "It was in a hopeless, unsightly condition when he obtained it from Herr Osterweil—so he and I created a cleaner, more legible reproduction in order to make it comprehensible to the music world. There was no other way for it to be taken seriously."

"Fair enough," said Clara. "Then where is the original? Surely Emil must have preserved it, no matter how derelict its condition. My husband's company must have that evidence if the auction is to proceed as planned."

Hilde bowed her head.

"I was afraid you'd ask me that sooner or later. And I fully understand why." She looked up glumly. "But sad to say, I cannot oblige you—Emil instructed me to destroy the original sketchbooks at his death. He said because they were in such wretched condition, any account he might leave behind of what had happened would never be believed—and that instead, our painstaking restoration of the originals, which by then had been authenticated by your panel of experts, would have to satisfy posterity." She shook her head mournfully. "And I had to honor his instruction."

"Then what about this lawyer who sold you the manuscript—Herr Osterweil? Is he reachable to corroborate the beginning of your story?"

"I don't much care for that word 'story'—it sounds as if you think I've made all this up."

Clara, sensing the woman was about to snap, was uncertain whether to press her attack or relent out of kindness. But she had come there for a reason. "That wasn't my intention, Hilde—it's just a word in common use. Now, please—do you know where this Osterweil is?"

Hilde would not face her now.

"I have no address or contact number. He more or less disappeared after settling up with Emil—by their mutual agreement, I rather think."

"That's unfortunate," Clara said, growing less charitable with each new pat answer she was given. "Do you understand that my husband's company has nothing else to rely on in the way of documentation but your word for all of this?"

"But why would I tell you less than the truth at this late stage?" Hilde asked plaintively. "And now that Emil's gone, I have nothing—and no one—left to protect."

"Except yourself."

Hilde leaned forward to massage Scherzo's neck folds. "I don't matter now," she said.

♪

IN POLICE CUSTODY FOR THE SECOND TIME in a month, Mitch told himself mirthlessly that this had better not become a habit. For him, as a former law officer, to be held under duress as a suspected murderer and transported across an international boundary for questioning was more than infuriating—it was plain absurd. His resentment churned throughout the thankfully short flight—less than an hour's airtime—as he sat wedged between his silent Swiss escorts and began to think about Margot, her austere beauty and quicksilver intelligence, and why her vibrant life had been taken so soon after her painful revelations to him.

The timing of her death, Mitch reflected, could very well have been planned by conspirators out to frame him for the murder, victimizing both Margot and him. But who could have had advance knowledge of his movements and arranged the fatal crime accordingly? And toward what end? No, it was just as likely that he had been in the wrong place at the wrong time. His best hope for swift release was to point the police in the right direction.

The most obvious candidates for the murderer were Margot's ex-lover and her husband.

But what did he know for certain about their relationships with her? Only tangled claims and counterclaims about her and Felix. Mitch had never met Dr. Lenz, the heart specialist, but had repeatedly heard him vilified as a distant spouse and very cold fish. Felix seemed the more likely assailant. By their mutual account, there had been bad blood between him and Margot for some time now, much of it over Ansel. And Margot probably knew about or suspected his promiscuity—and if she was subsidizing his fancy flat and his high lifestyle, she had likely called a halt to the practice and left him, as he had claimed to Mitch, financially desperate. He might even have feared she was about to turn him in to the police as the mastermind behind planting the *Tell* manuscript in Otto Hassler's attic. All of that could have driven him to do her in. All he had to do was show up at her door, and she would have let him in—he likely knew it was the housemaid's day off. And in an instant he could have violently slain her even as he had long and passionately made love to her.

Dr. Leonidas Lenz, from all accounts, was the opposite sort. Tired of being humiliated by her brazen, habitual infidelity, he might have told her it had to end and, when she rebuffed him, he took her life. Or perhaps, long clueless to her trysting, he had lately discovered it and reacted berserkly. Or maybe he had simply grown to hate her as his powerful tormentor, successful in the business world even as he had failed to become successful in the field of medicine.

As their plane taxied toward the Zurich air terminal, Mitch kept flailing for answers. Perhaps Margot had enemies in the business world whose fortunes she had cold-bloodedly reduced by deception, poor advice, or dirty dealing. Or could it have been a simple break-in robbery she fatally resisted? With no answers, he had but one recourse, Mitch told himself: keep calm and don't obfuscate.

The bland sign reading "Government Building 1" over the entrance left him unprepared for the ground-floor lobby of Zurich's central police station just off the Bahnhofstrasse. A broad, bare expanse with no seating, it was a psychedelic vision of baroque ornament, its tile floor, stout columns, interlocking archways, and barrel-vaulted ceiling painted in soft reds, golds, and blues in exquisite floral patterning lit from below by recessed lights that gave a roseate glow to the entire space. It suggested a great entry chamber to a royal pleasure palace more than the access hall to the workplace of a small-city police force. Its inviting warmth was the opposite of the cold, impersonal interior of New Scotland Yard, his other recent holding pen.

The Swiss officer on his right noticed Mitch's bewildered expression as he scanned the artistry of the magical cave. "It's called Giacometti Hall," he was told. "It's very beautiful, yes?"

"Yes. Why such fantastic workmanship?"

"Just for a police station, you mean? Well, why not? Giacometti was Swiss, he needed work, Zurich is a wealthy place—it's very soothing. It makes us proud."

"Was it Alberto Giacometti—or maybe a relative?" Mitch asked with professional curiosity.

"Ah, you know about art. It was Augusto Giacometti, the uncle—also excellent."

Mitch was impressed with the civility of a municipality willing to enlist first-rate artists to embellish its public buildings. Now how civilized would its law-enforcement corps be in dealing with a foreign murder suspect?

Very, it appeared, as he was ushered without haste to a carpeted second-floor interview room with smartly upholstered furnishings and several abstract prints on the wall, like an upscale doctor's office. Awaiting him were City Police Captain Kurt Wydler, Inspector Lieutenant Andres Ackermann, and a Mrs. Kirschner, no first name provided, from the canton prosecutor's office. Mitch was invited to sit on the leather-covered sofa and told that the police had been contacted by Gordy Roth, who was due in Zurich the next morning and had arranged for a well-regarded Swiss counselor to represent the suspect. "If you'd care to answer a few questions before then, that would be helpful to us all," Captain Wydler said, "but no need if you prefer to stay here with us until tomorrow. We don't have your Miranda rights as such or the precise equivalent of your Fifth Amendment, but we know you're a former prosecutor in—which state was it—Maryland?"

"Yes," said Mitch, glad they seemed reluctant to intimidate him. "I want to be as cooperative as possible—I liked Mrs. Lenz and was very sorry to learn what happened to her. All I can tell you is that I went to visit her at her home the day she was killed to clear up some issues about my firm's pending auction of the *William Tell* Symphony—I'm sure you're familiar with some of the controversy surrounding its discovery—"

"We know all about it, Mr. Emery," Lieutenant Ackermann confirmed.

"Okay. I spent an hour with her, our talk was cordial and wide-ranging, and I left. And I can assure you I had nothing whatever to do with—with her awful death. I really don't have anything more to offer you people, and I'm not clear why you need to detain me here—though I must admit it's the most beautiful police headquarters I've ever seen."

"Perhaps the only beautiful one," Captain Wydler said with a smile. "Since we have no extradition treaty with your country, we need to detain you until we've had the chance to question you thoroughly. So far as we know, you were the last person to enter Mrs. Lenz's home before her death. It's our procedure—and she was a prominent citizen—"

"But what possible motive would I have had?"

"We're looking into that, you can be sure." A subdued but perceptible hint of menace in that. "We'll try to make you comfortable overnight—your wife is free to stay with you when she arrives—and we'll resume our interview when you have counsel present." The captain handed him a copy of the Zurich daily paper. "You may want to read the story in here about Mrs. Lenz's death—it's factually accurate as far as it goes. We're not saying a lot to feed public curiosity until we have more to go on."

Mitch took the newspaper with a nod of thanks. "My German is pretty rusty, but my wife is fluent—she'll translate."

Clara looked pleased when she arrived just after 8:00 p.m. and saw that Mitch was not bound and gagged or strapped to a rack. They were left by themselves in the locked interview room, where they were brought ham and cheese sandwiches, a chocolate bar, and coffee and allowed to spend the night in recliner chairs. "Say nothing about your session with Hilde," he whispered to her. "The place could be bugged—in the hope we say something incriminating."

Clara nodded and settled for reading aloud the newspaper account of Margot's death, which was the lead front-page story. The police had made no announcement of what they called "an apparent homicide following a burglary break-and-entry" until three days after the severely bludgeoned body had been discovered and reported to the police by "Mr. Felix Utley, a family friend, who said he had found the Lenz apartment front door open and the victim dead inside." Felix claimed he had an appointment with Margot "to discuss a memorial service for her late brother, Mr. Ansel Erpf, who had died by suicide on the Greek island of Santorini six weeks earlier, and a suitable family gift to the community in his honor." The story noted that Felix had been Ansel's colleague for a number of years as musicians with the Swiss Philharmonic. "Police said there was no evidence that the deaths of the brother and sister were in any way connected," the article added, but pointed out that both siblings were "highly active" in the effort by Swiss nationals to recover "the manuscript of the celebrated *William Tell* Symphony, lately attributed to Beethoven by a panel of international scholars. It was found here last year in the house next door to where Mrs. Lenz's parents, Mr. and Mrs. Hugo Erpf, live on Napfplatz and removed to the US soon thereafter." The victim's husband, Dr. Leonidas Lenz, a consulting cardiologist, had been reached by police in Bhutan, "where he has been on a mountain-climbing trip with several fellow physicians for the past two weeks. He is expected to return to Zurich tomorrow if he can make flight connections."

Mitch shook his head; there went his two leading murder suspects. Felix, to be sure, could have been lying; he might have killed Margot, ransacked the apartment to make it look like a robbery, and then calmly phoned the police afterward to pretend he had found her body. And Dr. Lenz could have arranged for a contract killing of his wife while he was on the other side of the world with an incontrovertible alibi.

Clara read Mitch's drawn face. "At least there's no mention of you or your supposedly having been the last person known to have seen Margot," she said. "I think that's a good sign, sweetie—they must know you couldn't have had anything to do with it."

"Right," he told her and then placed a cautionary index finger over his lips.

A long, silent night followed.

Gordy, the proverbial sight for sore eyes, was admitted to the Emerys' room a little after ten the next morning, more rumpled than usual but very much on his game. "You kids look like hell," he said. "Cheer up—we'll get this taken care of." He caught Mitch's apprehensive look as he cupped an ear and pointed to the walls, ceiling, and table lamps. "Oh, yeah," Gordy said. "They assured me the place isn't wired, so I'm afraid we'll have to take them at their word."

Gordy had been a whirlwind since Clara called him in a panic from Tempelhof right after Mitch was taken into custody. "So," he reported now, "here's where we are. The leading criminal lawyer in Zurich is skiing this weekend in Zug—he'll be back Monday and meeting me at my hotel at eleven—he and the canton prosecutor are best buds. Harry's been in touch with his second cousin's husband, who happens to be the Undersecretary of State heading up the European Desk—he's talking today to our ambassador in Bern, who'll be instructed to approach the Swiss Ministry of Justice about your situation and say that unless they have some firm evidence linking you to Margot Lenz's death, they can't lock you up. Meanwhile, our friend Johnny W. has his people fanning out around town, shaking the underworld grapevine—talking to snitches, drug pushers, fences—anyone who might have heard anything about the killing."

Gordy's news about Felix was mixed. The police had reviewed Margot's bank records and discovered she'd been writing him monthly checks of 5,000 francs for years, "so they're not buying Felix's assurances that he and Margot were just casual pals. Plus she stopped writing him checks three months ago, suggesting a change in their arrangement—and a possible provocation for him to strike back at her. Unfortunately, Felix asked to take a polygraph test, Chief Inspector Ackermann tells me, and the results suggest he had nothing to do with Margot's murder. Ackermann wants to know if you'd also be willing to take a lie detector test."

Mitch was alarmed by the question.

"There's a reason the tests are not admissible evidence in the States," he told Gordy, whose legal expertise did not include crime detection. "The results are notoriously unreliable—some people get very jumpy taking them and give false positive readings, and some can control their emotions and fool the machine. I don't want to bet my life or freedom on whether my involuntary nervous system has a good or bad day."

"Whatever you say, Mitch—but I wouldn't count on its going over too well."

Late in the afternoon, following a day of deafening silence from the police, Ackermann appeared in a loden green blazer bearing the crest of his sports club and told the Emerys they were to be transferred within the hour to the nearby Widder Hotel, where Gordy had booked them all rooms. Mitch was to be interrogated on Monday about issues that he had allegedly gone to Margot's apartment to discuss shortly before she was killed.

"I'll do my best to be helpful, of course" Mitch said to Lieutenant Ackermann, hoping to sound as cooperative as possible. "But I honestly doubt I can be of much use in your investigation—my exchanges with Mrs. Lenz dealt only with the extent of her involvement in the discovery of the *Tell* manuscript."

"That sounds to us," the lieutenant replied, "as if your firm has had suspicions of fraudulent activity on somebody's part—possibly Mrs. Lenz or her late brother—or Mr. Utley, who we now have reason to believe was the victim's longtime gigolo. And fraud is criminal activity, and so is murder—these are the possible connections we need to explore with you."

"The manuscript issue is strictly a business matter," Mitch countered, "and the details are private information. We are not a public company or agency."

Ackermann was unimpressed.

"This is a murder investigation—there's no such thing as private information when we need to account for a savage killing of a leading citizen. So while you're thinking things over, you're to remain within the confines of Zurich city until we resume our conversation on Monday." The lieutenant pivoted on his heels. "Have a nice weekend."

{18}

At liberty within the city limits while under round-the-clock police surveillance, Mitch and Clara braved the winter wind off the lake to oxygenate their tired lungs. They viewed the stained-glass windows and listened to the choir during Sunday morning services at the Grossmünster, then rode the tram up to the Zurich zoo for a diversionary outing before attending to their unfinished task of determining the truth, all of it, about the *William Tell* Symphony. Was it Beethoven's Tenth, Emil Reinsdorf's First, Somebody-or-Other's Forgery, or still possibly even Ansel Erpf's nose-thumbing defiance of a world that never understood him?

It was four in the afternoon, with darkness already encroaching, when Mitch phoned Felix Utley to ask for a final audience at his apartment. "So long as you're not wearing a wire," he said, sounding dead serious, "or have any hit men with you." In view of the peril Clara had been exposed to during her earlier jogging encounters, Mitch insisted she stay in their hotel room just in case Felix tried to act up—and to let Lieutenant Ackermann know if he didn't return soon.

It was evident from the outset of the session that things had changed since their earlier confrontational meeting at his flat. Both of them were now subjects of interest in the police investigation of Margot's slaying, and neither could afford a misstep by flying off the handle.

The shaggy-headed musician listened closely to Mitch's playback of the final round of disclosures to him and Clara by Felix's lately slain mistress and his still very alive Aunt Hilde. By the end of Mitch's delivery, Felix saw that his clumsy attempt at a million-dollar shakedown of C&W had backfired. But he would not allow himself to be vilified, he insisted, by lies and half-truths. "You need to understand two things about my aunt," Felix said, trying to sound more sorrowful than vindictive. The first was that she disliked him profoundly. The second was that for all her painterly gifts, Hilde had always been a classic German *küche-kirche-kinder* hausfrau, "only there were no *kinder,* so her sun rose and set on Uncle Emil—he could do no wrong by her—he was brilliant and faithful and never struck her—what more could she ask? And if he ran off the track at the end, it had to be someone else's fault." He poured Mitch and himself shot glasses of cognac.

"Off the track in what sense?" Mitch asked.

"The whole *Tell* thing—in hindsight—was clearly an immense error in judgment on his part, but, Emil being Emil, he was a force of nature, and he roped us all in, starting with Hilde herself. She sees that now and knows we all should have stopped him. But she's trying to make you believe Emil's only mistake was confiding in me, entrusting the manuscript to my care, and holding me responsible for everything that went wrong. And she never wanted me to share in the rewards—if there ever were any."

The reason his aunt disliked him so, Felix said, was not hard to grasp. In her eyes, he was a rival for Emil's affection who never went away—not far enough away, at any rate, to suit her. "I once overheard her tell Emil that I'd been a leech on their marriage for nearly forty years. My real sin was admiring him more than he deserved." When Felix chose to remain in Switzerland instead of joining him in Berlin, his uncle had accused him of cowardice, fearing to compete against Europe's finest young musicians. "I doubt it ever occurred to him what failure might have done to me," Felix mused. "We traveled in different galaxies, you might say."

Which brought Felix to the *Tell* saga. "You can't begin to understand it without realizing what an egomaniacal old bastard Emil truly was." It wasn't enough for his uncle to become the world's leading Beethoven authority; he needed to be seen as a great man in his own right—"and that hunger drove him nearly delusional in the end. In a way he really thought the *Tell* was as much his own accomplishment as Beethoven's."

Felix sat staring into his cognac, trying to reconstruct the twisted skein of events.

"I was utterly blown away when he first brought it to me on one of his visits about six or seven years ago." His uncle had devoted his entire career to anatomizing harmonic structure and delighting in like drudgery that for him unlocked the mysteries of musical genius. "And suddenly here he was, showing me this thrilling piece, with its extraordinary charm and power, and claiming it was his own creation!" Felix shook his head, as if to exorcise the jarring memory. "I couldn't believe he'd pulled it off—nobody becomes an instant composer, particularly in such an inventive way and on such an ambitious scale." He wondered if his uncle was playing a joke on him, but Emil assured him he had been slaving over the work for years and had progressed inch by painful inch. And when he revealed the daring notion behind the effort—to attempt what Beethoven himself had flirted with but never begun, namely, putting Schiller's *Tell* to music, and trying to simulate the maestro's "heroic style" as closely as he could—"it struck me as raging egomania. But then Emil was nothing if not full of himself."

Felix's skepticism was overcome when his haughty uncle invited his assessment of the composition. "He was telling me, for the first time, that my opinion mattered to him." Felix's investment in the project deepened when his uncle swore him to secrecy; until Emil's Beethoven symphony was presented to the world in all seriousness, he might be mercilessly mocked by envious colleagues in academia. What gave Felix pause, he said, was that his uncle had also opted to confide in his old friend Richard Grieder. Even before running afoul of the Swiss Philharmonic's conductor, Felix had found Grieder to be a shallow character who had parlayed modest talent and imposing looks to win an unassailable perch atop his country's music establishment. The only thing Grieder and he had in common—besides affection for the conductor's niece— was Emil's fondness for teasing them both as hopeless provincials.

One day shortly after Emil had first apprised them of the existence of his grand undertaking, Grieder summoned Felix to his apartment to solicit his thoughts about what the conductor called "this *William Tell* madness of your dear uncle." Although he'd encouraged Emil's effort to evoke the grand Beethoven style, Grieder struck Felix as envious of his old friend's swollen ambition and eager—beyond Emil's earshot—to mock it. "It reeks of kitsch, dear boy," Grieder pompously told Felix. "Do we let him go on, or do him the favor of candor —and risk his eternal wrath?" Felix shook his head. "Grieder just couldn't grasp what Emil was trying to accomplish," he said, "whereas I thought it was a gorgeous conception but had grave doubts Emil was capable of sustaining it."

When his uncle was struck down by cancer and finally confessed the truth about his acquisition of the *Tell* manuscript from a stranger knocking on his door, Felix found the revelation even more fantastic than Emil's original claim that he had composed the work himself. At first he suspected that the old rascal had indeed written it but was so frightened of being laughed at that he was now trying to palm it off as genuine Beethoven—and what a masterful ruse! Who else could pull off such a colossal deception? But it all made a crazy kind of sense when Emil explained to him the sorry condition of the two original sketchbooks when they had come into his possession in dire need of exacting restoration before being delivered to mankind.

After being told the full story, Grieder did an about-face when he and Felix spoke again in private. "Richard, that old windbag, leaped at the news and said he had known all along that the *Tell* was far too dazzling to have been Emil's creation."

"But if it was authentic Beethoven," Mitch asked, "why did your uncle need to reach out to you and Herr Grieder—even assuming you're both far more than competent musicians?"

"He said he needed confirmation, as he went along refining the manuscript, that the music was truly masterful—feedback from people he could trust to keep a monumental secret."

The real challenge for Felix came when his uncle prevailed upon him to help stage the discovery of his restored *Tell*. Grieder and he ought to have urged him to play it straight, Felix conceded, but Emil by then was too deeply committed to his plan and very fearful he would be blamed for having laid his profane hands on holy writ. Moreover, the material rewards Felix claimed he was promised—a quarter of Emil's profits and renewed pressure on Grieder to make him concertmaster—overcame his qualms. Grieder was similarly seduced by Emil's assurances of the fame and fortune that had eluded him; the *Tell*'s world premiere by the Swiss Philharmonic would cure that. He even bowed to Emil's insistence that he make Felix concertmaster—"and then, at the first opportunity, please notice, he broke his word, treacherous ponce that he is."

"Your aunt insists she doesn't know about any financial arrangement that Emil made for you to share the payoff from *Tell*," Mitch prodded.

"So she says—perhaps became Emil found it convenient to blame me when Jacob Hassler ran away with the manuscript." Made to feel guilty, Felix dreamed up the Ansel letter from London, hoping that if it would scare C&W enough to cancel the auction, allowing Margot's family to buy back the manuscript cheap from Jake. It was the only way for any of them to make money from the thing, Felix had calculated, never suspecting that Emil had struck his own deal with Jake. In the end, after Mitch had sent him the Ansel letter in the hospital, Emil figured out who its real writer was, relented enough to apprise Felix of his arrangement to share in Jake's take from the auction, and told C&W that the letter claiming Ansel had written the *Tell* was preposterous. "And he promised I'd benefit someday from his share of whatever the manuscript sold for—which I assumed meant I'd be a beneficiary under his will."

"But nothing was ever put in writing between the two of you?" Mitch asked.

"He was my uncle—how could I ask him for that? I had to trust him." Whether Emil ever told Hilde about his promise, Felix said he never knew. "But maybe you can see more clearly now—without awarding me a medal—why I tried to lean on your company after Hilde told me at the funeral to forget about any inheritance. I would not call her a doting aunt."

Nor, he insisted, had Margot Lenz's animosity toward him been justified. Their ardent affair had foundered, in Felix's view, when it collided head-on with her chronic ambivalence toward her half-mad brother. "I was forced to point out to her, on more than one occasion, that he was a nasty piece of work. She was lying to you if she tried to convince you that I was the sole author of the letter Ansel supposedly sent her from London."

"Then who did write the letter?" Clara asked.

"Margot and I, together—taking pains with every word. If she wasn't a party to it, and it wasn't intended from the first for your company's eyes, why do you think she was so quick to send it on to you?" Felix turned up his palms to stress the obvious.

"Then why hide from us her own part in writing the letter and blame it all on you?"

"Because by then she was in denial that the letter may have driven Ansel to do away with himself—which was certainly not our intention." The collateral purpose of the letter, besides trying to confuse C&W enough to call off its auction, was to get Ansel institutionalized as paranoid and delusional, "which he certainly was." Margot's dirty little secret, Felix charged, was that even though she complained bitterly about the burden, she subconsciously *wanted* to keep her brother in a dependent state. Ansel's accidental disruption of the *Tell* scheme messed up things so badly that his situation became unmanageable. He was unemployable as a musician, on drugs once again, and living off the family dole while publicly badmouthing its members. Worst of all from Margot's standpoint, Ansel was threatening to use her affair with Felix as leverage to dislodge her control of Limmat Realty and was even hinting that he would get his act together sufficiently to participate in the family business. "Ansel's involvement in the *Tell* situation offered an opportunity to get him out of the picture," Felix confessed. "I'd been urging her for some years to have him hospitalized—for however long it might take to repair him fully—but she always said she didn't have the heart for it and, anyway, he'd never forgive her." That was when Felix proposed drafting the Ansel "confession" letter from London.

"But surely you must have known he'd suspect one or both of you," said Mitch. "He said as much to us when my wife and I met him in London—suggesting he wasn't all that addled."

"Oh, Ansel could be perfectly lucid for long stretches, especially when he was medicated. But his underlying pathology wasn't being dealt with. Our purpose was mainly to get him help—the letter was meant to demonstrate his pressing need of it. The beauty of it was that the louder he protested that he hadn't written it, the crazier it made him seem."

"The beauty of it," Mitch noted acidly, "may have helped drive him off a cliff."

Felix gave a hardly persuasive nod of contrition. "Sadly."

Mitch returned his shot glass to the table. "Well, I'm sorry to inform you there won't be any million dollars in hush money coming your way from Cubbage & Wakeham," he told Felix. "Nor, I suspect, will you ever become concertmaster of the Swiss Philharmonic."

"You may be wrong about that—not that it much matters anymore. Grieder's just announced his retirement, in case you haven't heard."

AT TEN MONDAY MORNING, Gordy came by their hotel room to report that Chief Inspector Wydler was showing no signs of relenting in his insistence that Mitch disclose every last detail about his encounters with Margot Lenz, her brother, and anyone else concerning the authenticity of the *Tell* manuscript and the circumstances of its discovery.

"I think you'll just have to tough it out for a few days longer," Gordy added. "Our hotshot local lawyer is due by my room a little later, and we'll get a better read on the law of the land. Meanwhile, Johnny Winks's people are still scouring the town for any leads that might link up to Margot's killing."

Mitch and Clara used the interlude to pursue their final, still untapped source of enlightenment regarding *l'affaire Tell*—Richard Grieder. A vibrant male voice answered Mitch's phone call and, after a brief, unheard colloquy on the other end, advised, "The maestro will be glad to see you. Three o'clock, please—ring three times."

The music director's expansive fourth-floor flat was directly across the street from the philharmonic's Tonhalle headquarters. The Emerys arrived ten minutes late by intention, not wanting to signal urgency about their mission.

"I'm surprised you haven't come by for a visit before this," Grieder greeted them in a plummy baritone. "As a matter of fact, your call anticipated my coming to you with slightly soiled hands and a full heart—now that I've formally cut my ties with the orchestra, as you likely know." He guided them through a white-marbled foyer to the snow-white living room. "But let me assure you I never intended to allow your auction to be held under false pretenses."

He had the jaunty look and manner of a thickset boulevardier with a suspiciously unseasonable tan and blown-dry white hair that swooped and swirled after much cosseting. His pearl-gray, Italian-cut blazer screamed pricey and may have been retrieved from the cleaners only a few hours before by Tonio, his strapping, chisel-chinned, and considerably younger companion. Mitch focused his line of inquiry—surely the last he could undertake to solve the whole *Tell* riddle if he hoped to remain employed by Harry Cubbage—on the disclosures by Felix Utley, inviting the conductor to confirm or correct them.

"About what we would expect, eh, Tony?" Grieder said blithely. "Typical of Utley to try to savage me by playing fast and loose with the truth." Felix had never forgiven him, he said, for breaking up his rather brazen affair with Grieder's happily married niece, the mother of two, being carried on right under the conductor's nose and in plain view of the orchestra. "Pity he's not half so accomplished an artist as he is a womanizer," Grieder sniped.

The remark drew an assenting whoop and girlish cackle from Tonio.

"Then why did you keep him on?" Mitch asked.

"Oh, he's a competent enough musician—and then there was dear Emil, always hovering and nagging me to advance Felix. But he didn't deserve it—rather the opposite, on grounds of depravity." The aging dandy folded the fingertips on his left hand into its palm and examined their cuticles intently. "In fact, I've just signed his notice of dismissal from the orchestra—did he mention that? It's one of my final acts as music director—it was very satisfying. They may not have told him yet." Was it any wonder, he asked, that Felix had accused him of being an active co-conspirator in the reprehensible game that he and his uncle had been playing with this *Tell* symphony? "It's all an outright fraud, in my opinion, and Felix perfectly well knows it."

"A fraud—how, exactly? Because Emil counterfeited it—and there never was a stranger who appeared out of the blue and sold him the beat-up manuscript?"

"Who can tell?" Grieder cried. "He kept changing the story—"

"But you deny being implicated in any way?" Mitch pressed him.

"If you mean did I engage in any fraudulent activity, certainly not! But was I culpable for failing to speak up and shame the supremely eminent Professor Reinsdorf, the *eminence gris* of the German music world? I plead guilty."

He had been acquainted with the *Tell* project for some years and with its instigator since boyhood, Grieder acknowledged. They had attended the same schoolhouse in Lucerne, shared university digs in Vienna and dreams of becoming famous concert artists, and remained friends despite having followed sharply divergent career trajectories. "When he learned of my ambition here, he said to me, 'Richard, to become a Swiss maestro is like being the chess champion of Mars.' I didn't appreciate it. I told him that I thanked heaven because at least I didn't have to lick the boots of the Huns the way he did."

It was during one of their twice-a-year boozy get-togethers that the *Tell* was first broached. Grieder was dumbfounded, he said, when Emil showed him the opening section of what he claimed to be his own "dramatic symphony" tracking Schiller's blank-verse drama of Swiss valor. Emil's claimed hope was that his old friend's orchestra would be the first to bring the *Tell* to the world's attention. The opening portion of the score seemed worthy enough, even with the bumps and snags that Grieder told him needed addressing. But he had his doubts from the start. "Nobody becomes an accomplished composer so late in life," he said. "I suspected that something else was going on—which, for his own mysterious reasons, Emil wished not to share."

And suddenly, after Emil's cancer struck, he totally altered his story about the *Tell* manuscript and the true identity of the composer. Grieder claimed that he was "utterly appalled" by his friend's reckless self-indulgence for failing to go public when the manuscript—whatever it was and whoever wrote it—passed into his hands. "I refused to have anything further to do with the project." Not that he doubted Emil's zeal and devotion, Grieder said, or his unique credentials to evaluate the ragged composition and meticulously repair it. But there was a proper way to do it—the painstaking, scholarly way, however long the process took, "and Emil knew the difference better than anyone." His ego and, perhaps, his advancing age had driven him to the wrong choice, Grieder saw—fixated him until he was totally possessed by the idea of singlehandedly restoring what he had convinced himself was Beethoven's Tenth Symphony. In doing so, the conductor lamented, he had suppressed if not eradicated the almost certain truth—that the *Tell* had been composed by some pretender and fobbed off on him as a lost masterpiece.

"Once you saw the situation," Mitch asked, "why didn't you try to talk sense to him?"

"Because he'd moved beyond appeals to reason. Emil had a terminal disease and was fiercely resentful of his mortality. And suddenly here was a means of cheating death—by grabbing the tail of Beethoven's comet, so to speak, and riding it to his own place in the musical firmament. Do you think Emil Reinsdorf would have abandoned his consummate ambition just because I asked him to?"

"Then why not blow the whistle on him?"

"Oh, now that's a different matter." First, he said, Emil was a very old friend, and old friends didn't betray each other. More to the point, it was just possible that Emil was right—the *Tell* might actually have been written by Beethoven—it certainly approximated his sound and passion—and who was the provincial Grieder to say the great Reinsdorf was mistaken? He was satisfied that the academic authorities would ultimately settle the matter. But when Emil sent Felix to explain the devices they had settled on to gain credibility for the suddenly surfacing manuscript, Grieder drew the line. He actually prayed, he said, that their scheme would never come to fruition, and, given Emil's failing health, it seemed a good bet.

His zealotry prevailed, however, and a year or so later, Emil called Grieder again about the details of the imminent *Tell* unveiling, including firm plans for the Swiss Philharmonic to give the premiere performance, once the work had been properly authenticated, and for the establishment of a government-run Tell Fund greatly benefiting the philharmonic. The only quid pro quo that Emil sought from Grieder was silence and a pledge to make Felix his concertmaster and to rehire cellist Ansel Erpf, whose family would be of vital help in the staged discovery of the manuscript. He gave Emil no immediate answer, prompting Felix to pay him a follow-up visit a few days later. If Grieder refused to help or chose instead to give their game away, Felix said they would be obliged to implicate the conductor as an active accomplice in the faked discovery in Zurich. "And for good measure, he hinted none too subtly that my so-called 'moral issue' would be spread all over the media—'defrocking the queen,' as Felix so sweetly put it. I rank him on a par with the less-likable forms of amoebic dysentery." He glanced over at Tonio, who nodded vigorously. "I felt trapped, humiliated—and immobilized."

Jake Hassler's flight with the manuscript thus came as a godsend. After an obligatory lip-service show of patriotic outrage over the American's theft, Grieder lost little time in reneging on his promise, extracted under duress, to promote Felix and reemploy Ansel. "It was an error in judgment—I needn't have reacted so rashly," the conductor conceded. "You see how vindictive Felix is—and for Ansel, I'm afraid, my haste fueled his fatal depression."

"You mean that your decision not to rehire him affected his state of mind," Mitch asked, "as in the straw that broke the camel's—neck, in this case?"

"In a manner of speaking. But you might as well know the truth about Ansel's death since I'll be going to the authorities shortly, as soon as my resignation has taken effect."

Grieder had been spending Christmas/New Year's week at the hotel in Rethymno, a lively resort town on the north coast of Crete, where he and Tonio vacationed free from inhibition several times a year. Toward the end of the week, he related, Ansel telephoned him—everyone connected with the orchestra knew where the maestro went on holiday—to say he was at his ex-wife Lisa's place on Santorini, where he had come to say goodbye because he was about to be institutionalized, perhaps for a long while, and might emerge, if ever, as a lobotomized shell. But Lisa was away, so now he wanted to ferry over to Crete, he said, "to reach closure" with Grieder. The conductor replied that he didn't see the point and assured Ansel that he bore him no ill will. "But he said, 'Humor me, maestro—one last time,' as if admitting that I had been more than indulgent toward him over the years. So, being a compassionate soul, I relented—but asked dear Tonio here to stand sentinel until my unwanted visitor had come and gone."

Ansel showed up the next day looking unrecognizably downcast and haggard, Grieder recalled, his tone darkening. "I asked how he was, and he said, 'As you see me,' and then added that things had never gone right for him since he had walked away from the philharmonic. Now his family was about to put him away as a lunatic, he said, his parents had all but disinherited him, his damnable drug habit had returned, his involvement with the *Tell* discovery had proven fruitless, and I had gone back on my promise to rehire him—so frankly all seemed lost. At which point he produced a suicide letter—to be mailed to you, Mr. Emery—and insisted that I read it. It was full of anguish and self-pity, with a soupçon of the gallows humor he excelled at."

Putting the letter aside, Grieder urged Ansel to reconsider and suggested that an extended course of hospital treatment might well send his demons packing. Instead, Ansel pleaded to be taken back into the philharmonic—"far better therapy than any available to him in hospital," he said and reminded Grieder that his professional skills had never been at issue. Grieder, no longer pressured by the Erpf family to forgive Ansel for his past insubordination, said it was impossible. But Ansel, wild-eyed by now, wouldn't take no for an answer. "He claimed I had constantly provoked and belittled him—and then he was shouting that he had a loaded gun in his pocket—he hadn't bothered to remove his coat when he arrived—and was going to blow my brains out for making his life so miserable. 'I'm taking you with me, you worthless load of shit,' he screamed, 'because what can they do to me after I'm found flat as a pizza at the bottom of a cliff on Santorini?'"

Grieder said he had no choice by then but to assume Ansel was in deadly earnest and gave the prearranged signal—a tug on the right ear—to Tonio, who was standing by in the entry hall, poised to intervene. The conductor told Ansel that killing him would do neither of them much good, which made Ansel laugh. He asked for a drink and wondered if Grieder might now want to reconsider his refusal to rehire him and thereby spare both their lives. "So I said, 'Well, perhaps I might.' But he said that wasn't good enough, I'd have to write out an irrevocable promise to restore his position with the orchestra. I said he was being unfair, which made him explode and appear ready to do what he'd threatened. I nodded at Tonio, who bounded in from the hallway and gave Ansel a great wallop with a poker he had borrowed from the fireplace in our suite. I'm afraid it inflicted fatal damage on the poor, hopeless fellow."

Although the homicide was indisputably an act of self-defense, Grieder was unwilling to risk the scandal from any investigation. They cleaned up Ansel's blood from the floor, where it had pooled neatly, saved the suicide letter that had been left on the coffee table, and made arrangements "through friends in our community" to have Ansel's bundled remains put aboard a fishing vessel that same evening for the voyage to Santorini. "The next night they shoved him off the jagged cliffs below his ex-wife's house—she was notorious on the island, so finding the place was no problem," Grieder wound up, "and his injuries were consistent with a thousand-foot plunge onto a bed of rocks." The local gendarmes were accustomed to suicides by swan dives off the cliffs. Then Grieder's hirelings went into Thera, the main town on the island, and posted the suicide letter Ansel had pre-addressed to Mitch. While the letter had viciously defamed Grieder, it also served to spare him, and anybody else, for that matter, from a homicide charge, notwithstanding a suspicious absence of splattered blood at the site where Ansel's remains were found.

"I see," Mitch said, struck by the cold-bloodedness of the account. "Any regrets?"

"Not really—it was my life or his. As I say, I was getting ready to report all I know to your company about this *Tell* business. And the police were to be my next stop. I'm hopeful they'll be discreet—but not counting on it. Thus, the timing of my resignation."

"And Ansel had nothing whatever to do with dreaming up the *Tell* project?" Mitch asked.

"Not so far as I know. He was a gifted performer, but his creative skills were limited."

Mitch made a final entry in his pocket-sized notebook and, before closing it, looked up. "Oh, what sort of gun did you say Ansel had on him—the one he threatened you with?"

Grieder shrugged. "I didn't say."

"Now would be an opportune time, then."

"He didn't have a gun. It was all just a bluff to scare me out of my wits. His letter might have been part of it—he may never even have intended to take his own life. Poor sad chap."

"Poor, *mon derrière*," said Tonio. "He was a psycho—and *tout le monde* knew it."

ON TUESDAY, THE SWISS AUTHORITIES turned up the heat.

Gordy came by their hotel room at midmorning with his star Zurich legal recruit in tow directly after the two of them had conferred at police headquarters with the team pressing the inquiry into Margot Lenz's murder. Ruedi Lutoff carried himself with self-assurance and spoke English nearly accent-free, having read law at Oxford and won his JD at Georgetown. Before opening his own office, Lutoff had worked seven years in Bern with the Swiss Ministry of Justice and was acquainted to one degree or another with all twenty-six canton prosecutors in the country. "Ruedi knows the ropes," Gordy told the Emerys. "He's running our show with these folks from here on in."

And the show was no comedy, Lutoff made clear to them. "The police think you're obstructing their investigation in order to protect your employer more than yourself," he told Mitch.

"They're right," Mitch said. "What I can tell them about my interaction with Mrs. Lenz is proprietary information—strictly about our efforts to explore all aspects of the *Tell* manuscript. It has nothing whatsoever to do with her death."

"How can you be so sure there's no connection, Mr. Emery," the Swiss lawyer asked, "unless you know more about how and why she was killed than you're letting on?"

"With all due respect, I don't think that's what their detaining me is all about."

"What are you saying, Mr. Emery?"

Mitch began to pace their hotel suite like the caged tiger they had seen at the zoo two days before. "I'm saying it's no secret that your government— and Swiss public opinion, from what I gather—is not kindly disposed to my company's efforts to help our client Mr. Hassler sell the *Tell* manuscript he removed from your country in the belief he had every right to do so. I'm afraid anything I tell the police about my ongoing investigation of the writing and discovery of the manuscript will be leaked to the media and seriously compromise my firm's ability to conduct its business. I think your government is trying to hold me hostage in an effort to sabotage our auction of the *Tell* manuscript, which may attract bids in eight or nine figures. And if we give in and cancel the auction, our client will probably have little choice but to accept a far more modest offer from a Swiss national—perhaps Mrs. Lenz's parents or her husband—or from the government itself, so the property can gain worldwide prominence as a Swiss national treasure."

The Swiss attorney looked at Gordy with disbelief and then back at Mitch. "I admire your loyalty to the Cubbage & Wakeham company," he said, "but frankly you sound obsessive and paranoid—if you'll forgive my saying so. Besides, you give our police and government far too much credit for scheming in tandem. This is a criminal investigation, not a national policy issue. And even if there were a grain or two of truth in what you say, it doesn't mitigate the right of the police to interrogate you thoroughly. Which, by the way, is what Mrs. Lenz's husband—he's now back from the Himalayas—strongly urges. He says his wife was somehow mixed up in something 'rather odd'—his words—but he doesn't know what, having to do with the Beethoven manuscript, if that's what it is. He thinks Mrs. Lenz may have been acting in some sort of connivance with her late brother, whose death he suspects was not really by suicide, and with her lover—yes, he's known all about her affair with Mr. Utley—"

"It sounds," said Mitch, "as if the good doctor knows a lot about a lot of things. Perhaps the police ought to be concentrating on him instead of harassing me."

"They say they're considering everything and everybody, Dr. Lenz included. And as you've heard, the police know Margot was keeping Utley as her well-rewarded lover, so he's still very much on their radar screen even though he volunteered to take the polygraph test. So they need you to tell them everything you know about all of these people, however remote you may think it is from the woman's death—which has become a national sensation, by the way. They're giving you till noon tomorrow to begin talking to them."

"Or what?"

"Hard to say. They can jail you again and hold you as a material witness and a flight risk until they've solved the crime or you've been conclusively absolved from it. The courts will decide how long you can be held."

Gordy phoned Harry Cubbage in New York to report the latest chilling news. At the end of their exchange, Gordy put Mitch on the line. "You didn't sound so hot when we talked Sunday, kiddo—I'm worried about you," Harry said. "Great that you're being ballsy with these Swiss jerks, but we don't want them shoving you in their pokey and tossing the key off the Matterhorn. Will telling them what they want to know really mess us up all that much more than we already are? I'm afraid we're in an endgame mode."

Mitch was grateful for his employer's sudden solicitude. "I don't know, Harry—to be honest, I'm still processing everything. It's even messier than you think—and not really phone talk, if you follow me. If I tell the Swiss cops all I know and word leaks out, it would probably kill the auction. I'll lay it all out for you when I'm back."

"Okay, hang tough, tiger—I'm still working the phone with the State Department. I'm told the Swiss government isn't all that eager to yank Uncle Samuel's beard ever since we've begun leaning on them hard over their bank secrecy laws. Meanwhile, maybe Johnny W.'s people will come up with something." Harry paused to listen to someone talking to him in the background. "Oh, tell Clara that Lolly sends her love—and promises to treat her to the works at Elizabeth Arden—whatever that means—as soon as you're back."

Noon Wednesday came and went.

"I think they're just trying to make you sweat," Clara said as Mitch crumpled the day's issue of the *International New York Times* and sailed it toward the refuse can like a lumpy basketball.

At one thirty, Gordy and Lutoff came by to advise them that the government might at any moment deport Clara as an undesirable alien.

"On what grounds?" Mitch demanded.

"As a possible accessory to a crime who is interfering with their investigation just by being here and comforting you," said Lutoff.

"Can they do that?" Clara asked.

"They think it's their country," Gordy said.

"But Clara's got nothing to do with this—she's just here because—"

"The government can claim whatever it likes—it deports foreign nationals every day," Lutoff said. "They know expelling Mrs. Emery will upset and demoralize you—and may force you to cooperate a lot faster."

Gordy phoned the US ambassador in Bern and left word with an aide that the Swiss Justice Ministry ought to be advised not to use Clara, wholly innocent of suspicious activity, as a pawn and risk negative attention from the global media.

Then he went into the Emerys' bedroom for a private conversation with Harry, at the end of which he reemerged and presented the anxious couple with Plan B. "Harry's about to phone Sedge in London and have him contact Clara's father— they're well acquainted, remember," Gordy laid it out. The chief financial officer of Unilever had a major say about where his huge company parked its international revenues—Swiss banks prominent among the depositories, in all likelihood. Then, besides ringing up the Swiss Embassy in London to protest its government's planned manhandling of his daughter, Piet would be asked to call his opposite number at Nestle's, Switzerland's largest corporate exporter and the world's leading producer of processed foods, and suggest how foolhardy it would be for their government to set off a global boycott of Swiss products by persecuting innocent foreign visitors like Clara Emery.

Clara was momentarily dazed by the sheer cheekiness of the idea. She glanced at Mitch, who nodded at what he knew would follow, and then told Gordy, "I won't hear of it. Daddy's not to be involved in any of this—it's not a family affair, and it would weaken his position at Unilever for indulging in special pleading on his daughter's behalf. He works for a heartless corporation, not a benevolent patron. Please call Harry back and thank him but tell him to forget it."

Gordy fell onto the sofa and shook his head. "Right—Harry and I knew you'd say just what you did. But I'm instructing my friend Ruedi here to advise the police and his pals at the ministry that Plan B is already in the works, and they should expect to be instructed at any time by their superiors to back off the threat to deport Clara."

Ruedi Lutoff gave a quizzical smile. "It's what you people call playing hardball, right?"

Gordy stretched his arms wide. "They called it Poker 301 at my law school— the art of the bluff. Let's give it a try, Ruedi—and blame it all on me."

Lutoff went off to carry out his assignment while Mitch and Clara, fearful of their imminent separation, took a pre-parting walk down the Rennweg, glancing idly at the merchandise crowding the colorful shop windows, followed by an early dinner delivered to their suite by room service. At eight o'clock, Chief Inspector Wydler and a flunky from the Justice Ministry tapped on their door to hand Clara deportation papers and instructed her to be ready at seven thirty in the morning for a nine o'clock flight to New York, her ticket courtesy of the Swiss Confederation. "Unless Mr. Emery advises us by midnight," the inspector said without emotion, "that he's ready to cooperate with us in the morning."

Their lawyers were out, probably at dinner, when Mitch called them with the news but had to leave a message on Gordy's cell phone. Clara was frightened and briefly teary-eyed before she steeled herself for a stringent appraisal of their situation. "Is all this really worth it, Mitch? You're a very upright guy to stand on principle like this. Forget about me for the moment—but is Cubbage & Wakeham worth risking your neck for? You can work at a lot of other places—and for people a lot more endearing than Harry Cubbage."

Mitch reflected a while before answering her. "First, it's not just a principle that's involved here," he finally said. "It's potentially a shitload of money, and C&W's future financial well-being may depend on it. Second, I like my work there—it's different and challenging—almost never routine. Third, as to Harry—let's see just how endearing he is."

It was mid-afternoon in New York, and Harry was at his office desk when Mitch phoned in and described their plight. The conversation was relatively brief. At the end, Mitch handed Clara the phone. "Himself wants to speak with you."

"Tell your beau I heard that," Harry said jauntily when she came on the line. "Now you listen to me, Clara Hoitsma Emery—this will all work out fine—and soon. Mitch will tell Gordy to call me with your flight information, and Lolly and I will pick you up at JFK—unless you come in at Newark, wherever that is. And you'll stay over at our place till this thing blows over—no point in your knocking around alone in your apartment, brooding all day. And I'm not taking no for an answer, you hear? Besides, if you don't accept my gracious offer of hospitality, Lolly will move in with you by brute force, and you'll never get rid of her."

"Okay," Clara said with a smile after Mitch hung up, "so Harry's semi-endearing."

Mitch grew increasingly irritable as time passed without a call back from Gordy. Then, at eleven thirty, he phoned them to say—with subdued ecstasy—that Johnny Winks's people had saved Mitch's bacon. They had picked up the trail earlier in the day of a couple of punk drug dealers operating on Niederhofstrasse near the student quarter who had been overheard bragging about a jewelry heist they scored recently and were looking for a fence. Johnny's agents passed the word along to the police, who picked up the pair at a tattoo parlor, found one of them with a large diamond brooch in his pocket, and hauled them down to headquarters for a considerably less genteel interrogation than Mitch had faced.

The brooch was rushed over to Dr. Lenz, who at once identified it as his late wife's property and, on checking her jewelry cases more thoroughly than he had on his melancholy return from Bhutan, discovered that half a dozen of Margot's prize baubles had been taken. Within an hour, the two captives confessed that they had been friends and drug suppliers of Ansel Erpf, were angered when he told them that his "slutty sister" was about to have him put away in the loony bin, and decided after Ansel's suicide to take vengeance on "the nasty bitch" by robbing her apartment. Semi-zonked as they broke in through the building's fire escape, they lost it when they found Margot there, and she tried to resist. They beat her senseless with a crystal vase and grabbed a few handfuls of the dying woman's valuables before running off.

The tragic intrusion had evidently occurred, according to the Zurich coroner's best estimate, about midway between Mitch's departure from and Felix's arrival at Margot's apartment. What were the odds against that fortuitous timing? Mitch asked himself. Longer perhaps, he mused, than against Beethoven having composed the *William Tell* Symphony.

Mitch joined Clara on her morning flight home, but the Swiss government declined to pick up the airfare for either of them.

"SO HERE'S WHAT WE KNOW—or think we know—but don't, really," Mitch said, hiding his fatigue as he laid it all out at the review session Friday morning in the C&W library for Harry, Gordy, Clara, and, listening in absentia, Sedge at the firm's office in London. "In fact," Mitch concluded, "the supporting forensics aside, we know nothing at all for certain—especially the Reinsdorfs' account of how they came by the *Tell* sketchbooks in the first place. We have only Hilde's word for it—and she gave us two totally different versions, both equally implausible but not entirely impossible. And Felix says he was given both versions by his uncle, but we have only Felix's word for that. As to how the manuscript and the supporting evidence got into Otto Hassler's attic in Zurich— well, we have multiple accounts, including poor, tormented Ansel's London letter—which Felix confesses he wrote, pretending to be Ansel—and some solid forensic studies concluding that all the documents presented to us *appear* to be authentic. As to our panel of experts—well, its key member *seems* to have been the perpetrator of the fraud—if it is a fraud—unless it isn't—"

His custom-made shoes resting on the edge of his oversize desk, Harry seemed to sink deeper into his chair with each nail Mitch had hammered into the *Tell*'s coffin. The emerging evidence that C&W was masterfully manipulated from the first—by somebody or other—had now reached critical mass and left Harry's smart-aleck tongue a badly diminished weapon. "So we're forced to conclude," Harry grumbled, "that the entire Zurich story is just that—a fable from start to finish. Furthermore, the alleged original sketchbooks from which our alleged masterpiece was allegedly derived are likewise kaput—but actually existed until Frau Reinsdorf trashed them at Emil's instruction—right?"

"We don't *know* that, of course," Gordy said. "We just have her word for it. There may never have been any original sketchbooks or a lawyer named Osterweil—only the supposedly restored versions of the alleged originals that are sitting downstairs in our Safe Room vault."

"And when I asked Clara to phone Hilde back from our hotel in Zurich," Mitch added, "to see if by some chance she still had the cancelled check for the purchase of the manuscript from this Osterweil guy, she said Emil thought it would be best to pay him with cash—so no record of the sale would exist and potentially conflict with whatever plan he might eventually hatch for staging the discovery of the restored symphony. Cute, huh?"

"Adorable," said Harry. "Okay, let's get our last joker in here and dispose of this b.s."

Jake Hassler's face was downcast as he trudged into the C&W library the next morning, along with his wife and lawyer. The old cedar box found in his grandfather's attic—was even that part of the story true?—sat in the middle of the conference table, waiting to bear witness to its present owner's veracity. But his sin, if any, was not unmitigated, Jake's solemn features seemed to insist as he listened to Mitch spell out everything the auction house now knew about the *William Tell* Symphony. "Oh, geeezz," Jake winced, dripping anguish.

"The floor's all yours," Gordy told him.

Jake took a couple of deep breaths before launching in.

"First off, there wasn't any damn 'understanding' between us," he said after clearing several frogs from the rear of his throat. "That scumbag Emil made me do it."

The sightseeing bus C&W had hired for its panel of experts' Sunday outing had just left the Princeton Battlefield site, Jake recounted, when Emil slid into the seat beside him. "There were only about a dozen of us on board, mostly spread out, and he spoke real low so as not to be overheard. He asked me how I thought the panel would vote, and I thought, 'Holy shit, he shouldn't be bringing that up with me—of all people.' So I just shrugged and looked dumb—which I'm good at. So then he says he's talked to his expert buddies, and it's his guess that they'll all go along with him if he says he thinks this *Tell* Symphony is for real. But if he votes no, he says, the *Tell* is down the old crapper. So what did I think of that?

I said I guess he's the big knockwurst, all right, and he laughed—he had this real bad kind of horror-movie laugh—and says he's got a problem, a real big one, that maybe I can help him out with. I said, 'Try me'—a big mistake.'"

Emil told him, said Jake, that he had an advanced case of lung cancer, probably wouldn't live all that much longer, and didn't have much to leave his dear wife, who deserved not to suffer a miserable widowhood—"and did I get the picture? Which got me sick to my stomach right off, but I managed to look even dumber and shook my head. And he says, 'Okay, let's cut the shit, Jacob—fifty-fifty, you and me. Come to my hotel on Tuesday night, and we'll sign an agreement letter. If you don't come by, the game's over. If you go to the auction house or the cops, I'll tell them it was *you* who tried to bribe *me* to vote in favor of certifying the symphony as genuine Beethoven, so you can forget any funny stuff.'" Jake threw up his hands and appealed to his listeners. "What the fuck was I supposed to do? This mean old prick had me by the proverbials—so I figured half of something is a lot better than all of zip."

"What you should have done was come straight to us," Harry said.

Jake's head began to bob rapidly. "I was afraid that without him, the game was over."

"Did Reinsdorf say anything to you to indicate that he thought the manuscript might be a fake?" Gordy asked.

"No way!"

"So you thought he was just taking advantage of you?" Gordy gave him the out.

"Damn straight. But I figured the way he was hitting on me wouldn't be hurting anyone except me—and Daisy here—who, by the way, I never said boo to about any of this, or she'd have marched my ass in here pronto."

"The trouble is," Gordy pounced, "nobody was twisting your arm after you learned that Mitch here wasn't ready yet to okay the manuscript because he still felt the Nina story was too thin. So you became actively involved in Emil's put-up job—right?"

Jake lowered his eyes in abject defeat. "I guess," he said morosely and exhaled a great sigh. "I figured this creep was my partner, whether I liked it or not, and he knew everything there was to know on the subject, so what was there for me to lose by calling and asking if he had any bright ideas, maybe, while there was still a little time left? He says to give him a few days and watch the mail but never to phone him again because you could never tell." Soon the Nina #2 batch arrived from Berlin—in German, of course—except for the short note supposedly written by Ansel, explaining how the items had been separated from Nina #1 and its accompanying letters, along with Emil's instruction to Jake to say the material had been mailed to him from London after Ansel's death. "And if you guys asked to see the envelope to check where it really come from, I was supposed to say there was no return address and that, like an idiot, I just put it in the garbage." Jake crossed his arms over his chest. "So then I got right on it and had the new stuff translated fast by my neighbor who knows German pretty good, and then I had Owen here call you to say that I had big news for you guys."

His lawyer gave Jake a stern look.

"Oh, yeah," Jake added hastily, "Mr. Whittaker here had nothing to do with any of this shit—especially my deal with old Emil. It was all my dumb-ass thing—but what could I do?"

"But by then you had figured out that something was fishy?" Gordy pressed.

"I didn't know how it all fit together, but, like you say, I knew it sure smelled to high heaven if he could just pull this document stuff out of a hat. Only, well, Emil wasn't the only one with big needs. Daisy's lost her business over that friggin' chandelier accident—she's out looking for a situation to bring home some bucks—and what I'm pulling down at the lumberyard doesn't get us too far, not with a sick grandchild we're helping and grown kids with needs—"

Harry let Jake's crestfallen apologia hang heavy in the air for a moment.

"But you knew then, when you brought us the second Nina batch, that it was a three-dollar bill?" he asked.

Jake shot a sideways glance at his attorney, who betrayed no emotion. "I guess," he said.

"That means you were scamming us, Jake," Harry said, concluding his examination.

"Basically," Daisy Hassler now spoke up sweetly, "he's a very decent person."

Harry tossed her a stare of blistering contempt. "So decent that he's cost our firm the better part of six million dollars. Will he make it up to us?"

Daisy pursed her lips in thought. "The thing is, most of that money was probably spent before Jake knew the score. And, anyway, how come all your super experts didn't clue you in about this second batch of Nina stuff being a load?"

"That doesn't let Jake off the hook, though," Gordy said.

There was no disclaimer. "Are you going to press charges?" Owen asked.

"Is there some reason we shouldn't?" Gordy asked back.

Whittaker strummed his fingers on the tabletop. "The Hasslers don't have any money to speak of—and sending Jake to jail probably won't do much to help your P&L statement. I think he's genuinely sorry for what he innocently got everybody into and didn't see any easy way out. He'd be more than willing to try to atone for your loss in some fashion or other."

"For example?" Harry asked.

"Jake used to be a master carpenter before he hurt his back, which is okay now. He could spend every weekend doing whatever your company needs to have done around this office—or in your own homes—or wherever."

Harry looked interested. "Lolly and I were talking the other night about reconfiguring the second floor of our place in Southampton. Of course, that's a four-hour drive or better from the far side of Jersey—"

Jake shrugged. "It'd only be once a week—if I stayed over—in the attic or somewhere."

"I think we'd better keep Jake away from attics for the duration," Harry said, and then turned back to Whittaker. "How long would Jake's services be available to us?"

"Whatever it takes," the lawyer said. "Right, Jake?"

"Whatever," Jake said, resigned to his fate. When he and Daisy were shown the door, the cedar box was returned to him with all its discredited contents. The next day, Jake splashed generous amounts of kerosene over the box and tossed a match on top. And then another.

AT HARRY'S SUGGESTION, THE LOADED lords and ladies who had pledged serious money to purchase the *Tell* manuscript at auction and donate it to Lincoln Center were advised confidentially three days ahead of time that the remarkable discovery was about to be publicly disclosed as a dud—or, at any rate, uncertifiable as the genuine work product of Ludwig van Beethoven. At the same time, these public-spirited citizens were urged, as a gesture of exemplary benevolence, to contribute half of their pledged amount to the general fund of the nation's leading center for the performing arts. And some actually did.

As a result, Cubbage & Wakeham was permitted to hold its press conference in Lincoln Center's Alice Tully Hall, where a small army of media representatives heard Harry read aloud his company's mea culpa. It began by stating that "in the wake of findings during the final phase of our firm's authentication process," the *Tell* manuscript could no longer be classified as "probably a composition by Beethoven," as earlier evidence had strongly indicated, so the planned auction of the document had been permanently shelved. Harry read on:

...While not judged a forgery in the conventional sense, the two composition sketchbooks comprising the manuscript were found to be, at best, an artful restoration of what may in fact have been an original Beethoven work that was lost and damaged. Nor is there reliable corroborative evidence—beyond anecdotal reports—about the origin and subsequent history of the documents from which the so-called *William Tell* Symphony is said to have been derived, even though the character of the music and the musical handwriting are highly suggestive of Beethoven's.

It now appears that a scholar who came into possession of the manuscript acted to refine and convert it into a presentable form, yet acted in a reckless and unconscionable manner, notwithstanding his apparently sincere belief that the work is authentic. Indeed, this conviction should have made it all the more imperative for him to have left the problematic manuscript untouched and turned it over to responsible, objective investigators to assess.

Cubbage & Wakeham's investigation has determined, furthermore, that the circumstances of the *Tell*'s discovery in Zurich were likely staged. But our firm does not plan to lodge criminal charges because the apparent principal perpetrators are deceased. Nor will our company seek punishment for several others who abetted the nefarious effort since no money appears actually to have changed hands under false pretenses.

A brief statement, issued by Cubbage & Wakeham's ad hoc panel of experts, chaired by Dr. Macrae Quarles, executive director of the Curtis Institute of Music in Philadelphia, whose group had originally found the *Tell* sketchbooks to be "probably authentic," reads: "Upon reconsideration of the further evidence now presented to us in its totality, we are forced to conclude that this work, however much musical merit it may have on its face, has likely been adulterated by artful tampering—and perhaps even ingeniously counterfeited in its entirety—and thus stands irreparably discredited as the original work of Beethoven's towering genius.

The so-called *William Tell* Symphony must thus be categorized as a highly accomplished curio and consigned to the precincts of illegitimacy."

During the hour-long question period after his announcement, Harry managed to dodge reporters' innuendos that C&W had acted prematurely in scheduling the auction of a document not yet thoroughly vetted. "We had every reason to believe we were acting responsibly and appropriately," said Harry. "Our decision to withdraw the manuscript from public auction is, we believe, testimony to the vigilance and integrity of our staff. Things happen—unscrupulous people are always with us, sad to say—and Cubbage & Wakeham are ever on the alert for them." To repeated pleas that he name the chief villain in the piece, Harry held fast. *"De mortibus,"* he said without elaboration. "To quote the immortal words of the Beatles' farewell, 'Let it be.'" When asked what lesson his company had learned from the unhappy episode, Harry paused briefly, then said, "A thing of beauty is a joy forever—except when it's not. Thanks for coming by."

In an age when celebrity and notoriety had become interchangeable, Cubbage & Wakeham was well rewarded for its painful pursuit of the truth in the *Tell* matter. During the month following the cancellation of the auction, the debunked symphony was headline news around the world, featured on *Sixty Minutes*, *Frontline*, and countless talk shows on TV and radio, parodied on *Saturday Night Live*, and treated as a masterful deception in a *Time* cover spread. Sleuthing on its own, *Time* guessed that the recently deceased Emil Reinsdorf may well have been its perpetrator, but neither C&W nor the surviving (and well-paid) members of its panel of Beethoven experts would let on. Several of Dr. Reinsdorf's colleagues at the Berlin Conservatory, however, said it would not entirely surprise them if he had been implicated. Jake Hassler declined to pose for the media but issued a short statement written by Daisy, indicating that their family had thought it best if the now notorious manuscript never again saw the light of day.

The conscientious manner in which Cubbage & Wakeham conducted its *Tell* investigation helped the firm attract an unprecedented number of new clients. In the first several weeks after the debacle, the auction house was hired to sell the furnishings, fine arts, and jewelry for thirty-seven estates with an average estimated revenue potential of $22.8 million. It also beat out several larger rival firms for the right to handle the sale of a collection of eighteen certified masterpiece paintings, likely to draw bids totaling in excess of $400 million. The gross commissions to C&W for handling these transactions were expected to pay many times over for the expenses Mitchell Emery had incurred in his vain quest to authenticate the *Tell* symphony.

Accordingly, spirits were buoyant at the regular monthly strategy meeting of the C&W staff held on the first business morning in May. Sedge Wakeham, joining the session as usual by conference call from London, reported that his favorite Hyde Park flowers, the blue moon roses, were about to bloom.

"I nipped over there after lunch at the club—just a ten-minute stroll, you know—though the Park Lane traffic is getting worse by the month—" Their eyes rolled upward as the firm's British principal nattered on a few more moments, but suddenly they all converged on the speakerphone as their numbed ears heard Sedge delivering a weighty piece of news.

"My boy Oswald has decided on neurosurgery for a career and the devil with the family business," Sedge advised them. "And neither of my nephews has the gray cells to run the show at this end—one's into horses, the racing sort, and the other sleeps a great deal." And so, given his advancing age, Sedge had decided to seek a London buyer for his half of the business. Under the partnership's long-standing bylaws, either party wishing to sell needed the approval of the other, lest the successor partner prove uncongenial, and if said approval were withheld, the remaining partner was obliged to buy out the selling partner at the same price the latter had been offered. "But I suspect you'll be pleased with the chap I've found for you," he told Harry. "Let me put him on the line to say hello to all you lads and lasses."

"Hello, all you lads and lasses," the crisp voice parroted the muzzy one, "and a specially fond greeting to my son-in-law, who knows nothing of this arrangement but also has the power—after you, of course, Harry—to quash the deal."

Mitch thought at first he was hearing things. A moment later, though, it all made wonderfully nutty sense. "Is that really you, Piet?"

"You've caught me red-handed, son. But before you fire me, be assured that this was Sedge's idea—Gladys and I wouldn't have dreamed of intruding on your turf otherwise. The fact is, my mandatory company retirement is right around the corner, so we'll have time on our hands and a certain familiarity with the arts—and Cubbage & Wakeham's balance sheet appears robust enough." There was a brief pause to allow for a pleased outcry from Piet Hoitsma's listeners. "And Harry, if you're not disenchanted with the idea on the instant, we'll be flying in tomorrow to talk over the details."

No less shocked than Mitch at first, Harry now appeared to welcome the prospect. "Swell," he said. "I suppose I'd better learn how to spell Hoitsma if we're going to add it to the firm name."

"On that score, actually," Sedge put in, "keeping my family name in there would make for rather a mouthful—and, without a Wakeham active in the firm, it wouldn't make much sense. You'll get to make the call, of course, Harry, old boy, but Piet here and I have been thinking that Cubbage & Emery has a nice ring to it—if no one has any serious objection."

Clara, for one, did not. Although pleased, she was reserved about expressing it when Mitch phoned with the news. Her father had in fact called beforehand to test her reaction and to ask whether Mitch would likely embrace or resent the whole idea. "I'd hate him to feel this is being foisted on him or that he'll be in any way beholden to us," Piet told her. His intention, he said, was to divide the Hoitsma half of the company into three equal shares held by Mitch, Clara, and himself—"so I'll be governed by your two votes if there's ever a dispute." When she relayed her father's assurances, Mitch said he was flattered but asked to sleep on it all.

Before the evening was out, Lolly Cubbage phoned Clara and reported breathlessly, "It's a done deal, kiddo—I've let Harry know. He was fussing that he had to be sure there was no downside to it and that Mitch wouldn't become even more uppity. But deep down—he actually has a deep down, though you wouldn't think so to look at him—Harry's really thrilled. And he knows that Mitch saved his bacon in this *Tell* fiasco. Oh, I think it's all fantabulous, darling!"

The prospect of an even more entangling alliance with Lolly Cubbage did not excite Clara. But the woman had her virtues, and her failings could be addressed over time.

"Me, too."

"It'll be a blast—trust me. Oh, now here's a little piece of news that'll amuse you no end, partner. Remember that St. John outfit you brought over to Berlin for Hilde Reinsdorf to cheer her up after Emil's death? Well, she shipped it back to me—just like she did with the one I got her at Bendel's for our dinner party. There was a little note with it, saying that under the circumstances, it seemed wrong for her to keep it. A class act, right?"

"For a world-class forger."

"Oh, don't be so picky—her husband made her do it, the brute. Anyway, I phoned her, and we got to talking. She's anxious to get away from Berlin—and she's been thinking about taking up painting again. So I said what about coming over here, and we'd get her started with a commission to paint a mural in our dining room? I mean she's really gifted, right? A mural would work beautifully in there, and we could even let her stay over in the second maid's room while she's working for us. She said thanks very much and she'd think about it."

"Lovely," said Clara. "But you may want to run the idea past Harry. He may—"

"True," said Lolly. "But it's not as if she and Emil intended to do us injury—exactly."

"I don't think we'll ever know what they really intended," Clara corrected her. "At any rate, if she shows up on your doorstep, I'd keep my checkbook out of sight if I were you and lock up all the silverware."

She and Mitch slept poorly that night.

At 2:37 a.m., Mitch whispered, "I hear you brain whirring—wanna share?"

"I was thinking about Hilde sending us the edelweiss painting. Maybe it was her way of confessing—she must have known we'd turn it over sooner or later and find the staff lines and figure it all out."

"And why would she have done that?"

"Because she knew they had done something very wicked—"

"And what exactly is it they did?" Mitch asked.

"I'm not sure exactly. Either Emil laid hands on something sacred, believing he was rescuing it from oblivion, or he made it up out of whole cloth. Either way, she went along with it—and shouldn't have—any more than he shouldn't have—"

"But maybe she didn't really buy that."

"Unless," he said, rolling over to face her, "Scherzie put them both up to the whole shebang—with three growls and a tail wag?" He leaned in and kissed her. "Now give it a rest, bunny."

At 3:52 a.m., Clara whispered, "I hear you thinking—wanna share?"

"I've been wondering if we really want to own half an auction house, even a swell one."

"It's not an antisocial activity, and it beats hustling hedge fund shares all day—"

"Yes, but it's not really all that ennobling an occupation."

"What's ennobling—shooting an apple off your kid's head to save your country?"

"No, that's just stupid—your kid's more important than your country."

"So what's noble, then?" she asked.

"Healing the sick, lifting the needy, transmitting wisdom, creating beauty…"

She tucked her head beside his. "You're back to wanting to save the world."

Mitch snorted. "Someone should think about it."

They fell quiet for a minute; then Clara asked, "Couldn't we think about it while living in London? Harry may want to move you there to run things—Daddy would probably just be a figurehead. I know my parents would be thrilled if we came over. But you'd have to want it."

"I suppose there are worse places to be. But they sure talk funny."

"Would you want a child of yours to be brought up a Brit—hypothetically?"

"A child of mine—would that be the same as a child of *ours*?"

"For argument's sake."

"What brings that up?"

"Nothing much except, well, I wasn't going to say just yet. You know—about what the White Rabbit ran around shouting in *Alice in Wonderland*—"

Mitch thought for a moment, then smiled hugely enough to light up the dark. "You're late—for a very important date?"

Clara matched his smile and rolled over into his arms.

"Four weeks," she said, "It could be a skip or something—though I never do—" They embraced fiercely, without words, until she said, "A lot could still go wrong—I mean even if I am, nothing's ever certain—"

"So I've heard."

Clara mused for a minute or two. Then she said, "If it's a boy, we would call him Ludwig. He'd probably be the only one in his class—"

"And an endearing memento of our great misadventure—unless we called him Emil—or Ansel—or Nina if it's a girl."

They fell silent for a time. Finally Clara said, "I still feel sorry for Nina—she didn't deserve to be treated like that."

"Sweetie—it was all made up—remember?"

"I wonder—"

"Go to sleep."

"Easy for you to say."

Coda

Emil Reinsdorf had been in his grave for two years, ten months, and thirteen days when Rolfe Riker, thought by many to be his successor as the foremost living authority on Beethoven, arrived late on that Sunday evening in the Moravian town of Olmütz in the Czech Republic. Professor of musicology at the University of Salzburg and lately turned fifty, Riker was blessed with an engaging manner, a questing intellect, and brooding good looks. He had come during a sabbatical semester that he was devoting to research for a book on the relationship of the Hapsburg Imperial Court to the great musicians of the classical and Romantic movements, 1750 to 1850.

Earlier, Riker had devoted several years to examining the archives of the Gesellschaft der Musikfreunde in Vienna, the richest repository of materials for his subject. Expecting far fewer gleanings at the ecclesiastical library for the Archbishopric of Olmütz, he had allotted himself five days to look through the papers of Rudolph, Archduke of Austria, brother of Emperor Franz I, and Cardinal of Olmütz from 1820 until his death in 1831, four years after his revered maestro, the commoner Beethoven, had died. It was their link that had drawn Riker there.

Although Rudolph's papers filled many shelves, most of them, of course, were concerned with religious matters. Only five of the large boxes, according to the archival register, contained personal papers, mostly correspondence; the last box held what the register identified as "Music Manuscripts," which Dr. Riker assumed to be compositions written by Rudolph in his younger days. He began working on a Monday morning in a small, cell-like room just off the diocesan library. In the first box of Rudolph's personal papers he found a matted, cellophane-covered engraving of the archduke in his Cardinal's robes. Riker studied the face intently. Its expression was rather less vacuous than one might have expected to encounter in a prominent member of the Hapsburg court, the professor decided. Instead of folly, arrogance, and condescension, the young Cardinal wore a look of quizzical irony, as if in recognition that his high birth was, as all births, accidental and far from divinely ordained. The brow was high and smooth, the eyes dark and searching, the mouth pouting like a child's, and the light hair oddly parted in the middle and cascading in curls that hid his ears.

But then Riker, who had been a member of the panel of experts assembled to appraise the *William Tell* Symphony briefly attributed to Beethoven, was hardly surprised, for he knew a lot about the unorthodox prince, a silent rebel against the lockstep regimen of the royal court and possessor of an artist's sensitive soul. Beethoven himself had taught Rudolph to play the pianoforte and the rudiments of musical composition. The young, frail pupil was so gifted that, given a brief melodic line by his maestro, he turned it into a work known to musicologists as "Forty Variations on a Theme," which Beethoven called "masterly." Such praise from anyone else in the composer's circumstances—namely, financial dependency on the archduke—might have been suspect; from Beethoven, contemptuous of designing flattery, it was surely honest.

This keen mutual regard continued to flower even in the years after Rudolph attained the spiritual dignity of membership in *Il Collegio di Cardinali*, as their correspondence reflected. Mostly, Cardinal Rudolph's exchanges with Beethoven, held in a separate file of five boxes, were banal, dealing with matters of health, weather, and news of mutual acquaintances. For Dr. Riker, the correspondence was disappointingly dull, and by Wednesday afternoon he had completed looking through all but the last portion of the fourth box and the final box. At his hotel he phoned his wife, hoping to tell her he expected to finish up a day early and would return home the next evening if he could make the right train connections. She failed to answer the phone, however, so Dr. Riker decided that, rather than leaving a voice-mail message, he would surprise her by his early homecoming.

After the archives of the Olmütz archdiocese had been closed to credentialed outsiders that Wednesday, Sister Maria Immaculata of the Holy Order of St. Barthelm attended to her custodial duties. In this case, the chore required only a few moments of sweeping up and replacement on the archive shelves of the five boxes of long-dead Cardinal Rudolph's dealings with Beethoven that the handsome professor from Salzburg had been examining.

It seemed foolish to have to refile the boxes each evening since the scholar would requisition them anew first thing the next morning, but regulations,

Sister Maria told herself, were regulations. And so once again, as she had done the two previous nights, she lugged the heavy boxes, one by one, back to the shelves in the rear and darkest sector of the library. The fifth and final box, marked with the roman numeral "V" next to the identification label, was remarkably light, she had noticed earlier in the week—indeed, it felt almost empty, she thought thankfully, placing it at the end of the row beside the other four boxes. But it alone, she observed, was not labeled with an Arabic numeral.

Curiosity got the better of her this evening, and so she lifted the lid of the fifth box and found inside just a single envelope. The nun glanced about her to be certain that no one else was in the room, then removed the envelope and withdrew the two sheets of vellum inside. At first she found the handwriting hard to decipher by the light of the single bare bulb mounted high on the wall behind her. But soon she saw from its heading that it was a letter, bearing the Cardinal's seal, dated 23 July 1823, and addressed to a "Msgr. A. Wetzel, First Archivist, Ecclesiastical Library, Archdiocese of Ulmütz." Peering intently through her thick eyeglasses, she read:

Father Anton, my esteemed colleague in Christ:

I am recently in receipt of a letter from my devoted Maestro B., who kindly enclosed a copy of his new sonata in C minor with the advice it is dedicated to me—yet another honor from this soul of genius, sent to test my humility—and the further intelligence that he is adding three new movements to the glorious Missa with which he marked my ordination & will be forwarding a copy of that addition as well. We must find a place of safekeeping for these texts, given their historical value. Perhaps you will also be interested to learn that the maestro is but a few weeks shy of completing a new symphony, his ninth & the first in many years—truly splendid news for all lovers of his matchless artistry.

I was less delighted with the rest of B.'s letter and the receipt of the two volumes attached to it, which I am hereby committing into your care. For you to grasp their import, I must relate some personal history before I took the cloth. As archduke of the realm & attendant at the court of my brother, His Imperial Majesty, I studied privately with the maestro and joined with several others to provide an annual sum for his sustenance. My gift to him was a form of compensation for all he taught me about the joys of music. In time I began to compose under his tutelage, & we often discussed his own current work.

In this connection I learned he had once been asked to participate in a production by our state theatre of the dramatist Schiller's play dealing with Wm. Tell & the Swiss uprising against our imperial troops then ruling their land. Removed as I had chosen to become from the court's political currents, I nonetheless counseled B. that his involvement with such an undertaking would likely displease my brother, due to the playwright's notorious republican leanings. "But I share them, as you well know," B. replied, and I was forced to point out that for him to announce as much by composing even the incidental music for the staging would doom all his hopes for official honors in our capital & he had best seek asylum in another land. Given his ardor, I had my minions see to it that the Schiller production was cancelled, never revealing my intervention, of course.

Imagine my distress, then, when I learned from him some years later that he was quietly at work on a full-dress opera based upon Schiller's Tell. At first I took this for a subterranean act of social defiance, a gesture in which he was practiced. Later he advised me that he had set the work to one side—a source of genuine relief to me, not least because opera was not a musical form much suited to his genius. But still later he confided that he had taken up the Tell task anew, this time in an innovative form he called a "dramatic symphony," interweaving instrumental and vocal music but with the stress on the former. I thought the notion foolhardy until he sent me a copy of the first movement. I was enthralled by the charm & sincerity of the work, which he pursued, he assured me, fitfully at best & in privacy lest it be misunderstood as subversive to our court. Perhaps at some future time, if it came to fruition, he said he might try to have it performed abroad, in London or Paris possibly (or even Zurich, he added in mirth), so as not to shame either of us in His Imperial Majesty's eyes.

I heard no further from him on this matter and thought it most prudent not to inquire after it—until yesterday. His letter, which he recommended I destroy as a precaution for all concerned, said that he had progressed as far as his powers would allow on the Tell symphony, which he had dropped some time back in order to concentrate on his new "Chorale" symphony, which suffered from no political overtones and was now happily nearing completion. In the past, he reminded me, I had been kind enough to hold for safekeeping in my vault at Schoenbrun palace other manuscripts of his. But given the peculiar sensitivity of the Tell, which he now feared he would never manage to refine as it needed, his choice was to destroy the sketchbooks, which he had not the heart to do, or to deliver them into my hands for safety inside a cloistered precinct. Perhaps he would someday summon the will & energy to resume the effort, but he thought it doubtful. "Let posterity judge its worth, if any," he added and begged forgiveness for so burdening me with the chore.

Do me the kindness, then, faithful Anton, of placing these two volumes, rather the worse for wear as they are, in a dry, dark place known only to you and me, until further notice. This authorization from me ought, I think, to be placed with the books. Go with God.

The letter was signed, "Rudolph, Prince and Cardinal."

Sister Maria Immaculata, unacquainted with the identity of the individuals discussed in the Cardinal's memorandum, nevertheless found it of interest—but hardly worthy of a box entirely its own. Whatever had happened to the two volumes originally accompanying it, she could not imagine; things just naturally got lost over time or, she heard, stolen. Wishing to be respectful but not wasteful, she inserted Rudolph's directive to the ecclesiastical librarian at the very front of the fourth full box of correspondence on the shelf next to it and brought the now entirely empty box with the "V" on it to the counter presided over by Father Rafael, the chief filing clerk, for disposal the next day.

In the morning, Father Rafael asked the nun where the empty box had come from, and she explained it was the final one of the five that the professor from Salzburg had been examining all week. The priest wondered how she knew it was the fifth box in the series, and Sister Maria pointed to the "V" next to the label identifying the box as part of Cardinal Rudolph's Beethoven correspondence. "But our boxes," the chief clerk explained to her, "all carry Arabic numbers. The 'V' is the abbreviation we have always used for 'Verboten'—such a box is closed for inspection without permission of our archbishop or Cardinal. The professor would have needed to apply for access to go through it. But if, as you say, it was empty, no need for him to—"

"Very good, father," Sister Maria said a bit uneasily, hesitant to reveal that she had opened it, found inside only the single letter from Cardinal Rudolph, and placed it at the front of the fourth box. "Whatever was in it must have been transferred somewhere. You might tell the professor—he's due in shortly. I have other chores just now."

Dr. Riker did not mind learning that there was no longer a fifth box for him to examine. Nor did he wonder, if it was empty, why it had been shelved with the other four and saved until being disposed of overnight. Instead he opened the fourth box, paused while trying to remember precisely where he had left off the day before, then remembered he had covered all but the back quarter or so of its contents. That remnant took him scarcely an hour to complete and yielded nothing of interest. He replaced the cover on the box, advised Father Rafael that he was finished, thanked him and his staff for their courtesy, and walked briskly to the railroad station. It had not been a fruitful visit.

The music professor made excellent train connections and arrived at home one full day ahead of schedule, surprising his wife and their next-door neighbor, a onetime member of the Austrian Olympic ski team, who were in bed together. Speechless, he left them there without rebuke and repaired to the nearest rathskeller for a stein of beer. And then another.

SIX WEEKS LATER IN NEW YORK, Stanley Burke, longtime employee in charge of security and storage services at Cubbage & Wakeham, was clearing out abandoned items from the steel-encased bins in the auction house's vault, known as the Safe Room—a chore he and his assistant Guido undertook every two or three years. Three of the bins, they were aware, held items left over from the cancelled auction of the *William Tell* Symphony. One bin contained the transcript that had been made of the sketchbooks, belonging to Jake Hassler, for inspection by the panel of Beethoven experts during the authentication process and for would-be bidders at the auction; the other two retained photocopies of the transcript and the sketchbook manuscripts—the original of the latter having been returned to its New Jersey owner when the auction was called off.

Burke phoned upstairs to Harry Cubbage and asked the co-proprietor if there was some reason to retain the *Tell* materials. Cubbage told him he couldn't think of any but to wait until he consulted his partner in London. The next morning he reached Mitchell Emery, who professed no emotional attachment to the documents—quite the opposite—and also doubted that his wife, then teaching at the Royal Academy of Music (thanks in large part to her brilliant doctoral dissertation on Franz Schubert), would have any interest in holding onto the *Tell* papers for what he laughingly called "sentimental reasons." Mitch suggested, though, that Harry put in a call to Macrae Quarles down in Philadelphia to see if the noted musicologist, who had presided over the panel of scholars invited to pass judgment on the authenticity of the "dramatic symphony" attributed to Beethoven, cared to store the transcript and photocopies of the sketchbooks in the reference library at the Curtis Institute, over which he presided.

Mac Quarles, as it happened, was just then delivering a series of three guest lectures at the Yale School of Music and did not catch up with Harry's message until two weeks later. "Might just be something worth puttin' in mothballs—you never know," Mac told him. "Send it all down here—and you want to get a trackin' number from the delivery people. My best to all."

Harry, belatedly attending to Stan Burke's inquiry, instructed him to pack up the *Tell* material and ship it off to Mac's office. A moment later, Stan called him back to advise, a bit hesitantly, that his assistant Guido had assumed—having heard no more about the matter—that the abandoned material was no longer of interest to anyone and had fed it to the office shredder.

Author's Note

No composer has been researched and written about as extensively as Ludwig van Beethoven. All aspects of his life touched upon here, including his whereabouts, activities, acquaintances, health, finances, social habits and attitudes, artistry, and writing, are well established historically—except those dealing with the *William Tell* Symphony, which are revealed on the preceding pages for the first time. Readers incapable of suspending their disbelief are reassured that, in particular, the maestro's meeting and exchange with Rossini, his relationship with Archduke (later Cardinal) Rudolph, his 1814 correspondence, and his invitation to compose incidental music for a Viennese production of Friedrich Schiller's play, *Wilhelm Tell*, in 1807 are fully documented.